Cracks in the Rainbow

Cracks in the Rainbow

Mark Bouton

Five Star • Waterville, Maine

First Edition
First Printing: August 2005

Published in 2005 in conjunction with Tekno Books and Ed Gorman.

Set in 11 pt. Plantin by Minnie B. Raven.

Printed in the United States on permanent paper.

Library of Congress Cataloging-in-Publication Data

Bouton, Mark.
    Cracks in the rainbow / by Mark Bouton.—1st ed.
        p. cm.
    ISBN 1-59414-349-8 (hc : alk. paper)
    1. Government investigators—Fiction.
 2. Conspiracies—Fiction.   3. California—Fiction.
 I. Title.
 PS3602.O894C73 2005
    813′.6—dc22   2005007909

This book is dedicated to my mother, Maxine Bouton,
a lovely lady and a teacher
who helped correct my grammar.

Acknowledgments

Many thanks to Ellen Byers Bouton, Ben Bouton, and Daniel Bouton for their patience in allowing me the time to write this novel. Thanks to my writing group who helped form parts of the book: Eleanor Bell, Karen Brown, Kristi Pelton, Karen Barron, Olivia Harris, Bill Burns, Alice Dewdney, George Paris, and Tracy Simmons. I appreciate the support from my writers' groups: The Kansas Author's Club, Kansas Fiction Writers, Inc., the Pike's Peak Writer's Club, Sisters in Crime, and Mystery Writers of America. Thanks to my friends and acquaintances in Topeka, Kansas, and across the country, who have encouraged me in my writing. My appreciation to my many co-workers in the FBI and friends in other law enforcement groups who serve as models, fact checkers, and thought provokers in writing about crime and punishment. I'm grateful to my agent, Nancy Ellis; Pat Estrada, Editor; Mary P. Smith, Sr. Editor, Five Star Publishing; production and marketing folks at Five Star Publishing; John Helfers, Acquisitions Editor at Tekno Books; and my publicist, Milton Kahn, for their help and hard work.

Chapter 1

One morning the Santa Anas ceased, unable to summon another puff, and wind-weary folks in the City of Angels, all of them parched and edgy, sighed with relief and resumed their frantic lives. At day's end, the sun sank into the ocean, and despite the winking of a million lights, darkness slid in like petulant fog. The night crawlers—dopers, thugs, gangstas—slunk from their lairs to seize the streets, while cops strutted with bravado, but watched for lurking predators.

Some hours after sunset, a telephone rang in a musk-scented bedroom in Marina del Rey. The intrusion, sudden and harsh, startled two tangled lovers. April grabbed the phone and said, "This is *not* a recording, so unless someone's dying—"

"Hey, it's Stretch. Put Rick on."

"Can it wait, Stretch? He's all—" She listened, frowned, and put the phone to Rick's ear.

"Yeah, big guy," Rick said, "what's up?"

"Partner, I've gotta see you. Right away."

"Uh . . . I'm really tied up, Stretch, could we—"

"Sorry, man, it's urgent."

"Hold on." He whispered, "Cut me loose, babe, I have to talk."

April untied the nylons binding his wrists, saying, "Stud, you're out to pasture." As she strode toward the bathroom, her taut flanks rippled like music. A glance back said: *Your loss.*

Rick had the urge to choke Stretch. But he knew it was duty calling. "You coming here?"

"I'm rolling now. Be there ASAP."

As he hung up, Rick glanced across the room and heard the shower start. The drive from Topanga Canyon to here was a good half hour. And he could use a friendly cleanup.

Stretch limped across the room to shut off his computer. The message still glared on the screen: *IMPORTANT* NEXT MEETING—DETAILS OF FIRST ACTION.

"Damn!" he said, banging the table. The monitor trembled, and the screen went dark, but it flickered back to life. He wished the words, the idea, the plan would vanish.

Those damned riots in Compton had sparked this trouble. The arson, looting, and violence scared some folks, enraged others. He recalled that someone said, "That's it. This means war." Soon, they began to organize, devise plans, and build up membership. The big dogs kept saying, "Guys, we're just defending our own." And Stretch, for one, thought it made sense.

Then other disasters happened: the Oklahoma City bombing; the bomb at the World Trade Center; the jetliner attacks on the WTC twin towers. More fuel added to the fire.

He shook his head, feeling like a weak pawn with a crucial chess match about to begin. He'd talked with some members of the bunch, trying to feel them out, but no one seemed as scared shitless as he was about the coming actions. Now they'd announced the plan would soon be launched, and he felt it was gaining power, like a tsunami, a giant force that couldn't be stopped.

Still, there might be hope. Rick had always saved his ass when he got in the deep stuff. Maybe, just maybe, the two of them could deuce out how to bust this scheme.

He ran a hand through wiry hair, then touched the floppy disks in his shirt pocket. *There's gotta be someplace . . .* He crossed to a bookcase, took out some volumes, and carried them to the front hallway. Placing the books on a table, he cracked one open, then pulled out his knife.

Two minutes later, he stepped into the hall closet, grabbed his Beretta, and yanked on a jacket. Figuring Terri was asleep, he eased out the front door. The houses across the road were lit up like jack-o-lanterns, and a sweet smell of hibiscus hung in the moist night air. As he neared his Bronco, he scanned the asphalt road, seeing nothing out of place.

Clambering in, he squeezed his legs beneath the wheel, then winced at a knifing pain in his knee. "Man, not now," he said. *Another of life's mistakes. He'd stuffed the winning basket against Duke, but at what cost? When he landed wrong, the ligament popped, ending his chances.*

He backed out, shifted gears, and surged ahead. *Yep, one wrong move—in basketball, chess, or life—and you'd find yourself slap dab in deep shit. Like in chess, you can't take a move back, even if you know it was dumb. And in real life, like in hoops, even a round ball can take screwy bounces.*

At Topanga Canyon Boulevard, he turned south onto the snaky road. *If he pushed it, he could make it in twenty-five. Man, he should've told Rick sooner, but the guy probably would've freaked.*

"Where the hell's he going?" said the driver of a gray Olds, nervously squeezing the wheel, the veins in his arms standing out. He made the turn, following the Bronco.

"Shit if I know," his passenger said, flicking a spent cigarette out the window, "but don't lose him. Tonight, he's ours."

"No chance. I got him." He stomped the pedal, catching up, then kept pace at a distance.

"We'll get a damn good view," the passenger said, slipping another smoke from the pack.

Stretch let the Bronco run, recalling those awful days of the riots. Hellish flames roared skyward, dense smoke choked out the daylight, and firemen dropped, overcome, as they fought the firestorms. Most Angelenos said there'd never be more riots like Watts in '64 or Compton in '92. But some weren't taking a chance—they moved to Oregon or Washington. Others felt jittery, but ignored the danger, the same way they dealt with quakes.

But if the plot took hold, if they pulled it off . . .

Bad luck that his proof was circumstantial—he fingered the disk in his pocket—and that he'd been part of the conspiracy. *Real ace detective he was, just like that rubber-faced actor, Jim Carrey. Damn, now he was thinking like his starstruck pal Rick, with all that movie bullshit.*

Besides, hindsight's always twenty-twenty.

He checked his rearview mirror. Saw a pair of headlights in the distance. *Anything to it?*

"Don't run up on his ass. We can't let him make us."

"I'm hanging back." He pumped the brake, slowing, but keeping the Bronco in sight.

"Don't want him getting hinky," he said, flicking an ash. "He might do something crazy, screw us up."

"Hey, it won't happen. How much longer, anyway?"

The passenger checked his watch. "Any friggin' minute."

Stretch would soon drop down to the PCH and then cruise into Marina del Rey. He'd lay out the program for

Rick, who'd probably think he was zoned, but he'd make his partner listen. The plot was crazy, but simple. He glanced at the mirror, now seeing no trailing car.

Thinking on it, Stretch felt better. *Rick would come up with an answer. He was a smart guy who could always handle trouble with both perps and the brass.*

He punched on the radio. Speakers vibrated as the station played "Mi Vida Loca." He took a curve, singing along, got to the part about destiny when—

"There it goes!" He banged the dash with a fist, sending ashes flying.

"Ho-ly shit." The driver hit the brakes hard. "What a goddamn show. Look at that fireball."

"Just drive on, quick. We don't want to get stopped as witnesses." He flipped his cigarette out the window and leaned back in the seat, smiling.

"No one's gonna stop me. But, man, you did a damn fine job."

Rick took a quickie shower with April. Sometimes you couldn't get all lathered up. Still, they both emerged clean and refreshed.

"Happy now, Detective Dover?" April teased, pulling on a robe.

"As a clam in Newport Harbor." He grabbed some clothes.

She gave him a look, shrugged, then lounged on the bed like a pampered cat and turned on a TV talk show. Dover watched the chatter for a while, then headed for the kitchen to brew some coffee. After downing two cups, he glanced at his watch. What was keeping Stretch?

He opened the mini-blinds and studied the boats bobbing in the marina. The rich sure knew how to stock a golden pond. He watched the street, but no Bronco turned into the complex.

Plopping down at a table in an alcove off the kitchen, Dover took three ibuprofen, rubbed his sore shoulder, then twisted in the chair to pop his back. First aid for his various war wounds from being mauled by linebackers in college and battered by scum on the streets of L.A. as a cop.

Another look at his watch, then he picked up the phone and punched in the number for Stretch's cell phone. No answer. He thought about it, and decided to try him at home.

She sounded half-asleep when she answered.

"Terri, it's Rick. Sorry I woke you."

"No problem." She yawned. "What's going on?"

He hesitated. "Stretch was coming over, but he's late. Has he left?"

"Yes, I heard his truck leave a while ago, but he didn't tell me where he was going."

Funny. "Then I'm sure he'll be here any minute. Thanks."

Ten minutes later, Dover shrugged into a light jacket. April was in a deep sleep. She looked like a child with honeyed curls framing her face. On a pad beside the bed he jotted a note, then bent and kissed her cheek. He pulled a blanket over her, stuck his AMT Backup in his waistband at the small of his back, and punched off the TV.

The '57 Bel Air rumbled to life, and the tires screeched each time he shifted. Stretch might've had a flat tire or some engine problems. In L.A. at this time of night, that could get you in big trouble.

He drove up the PCH, watching the traffic for Stretch's Bronco. He'd probably miss him and look like a fool, but he had a strange feeling that was making him uneasy. He and Stretch had worked homicides together for six years, developing a telepathy that had saved their butts in clashes with the bad guys more than once.

But he was getting no vibe on this 'deal.

As he turned up Topanga Canyon Road, he felt sweat trickle down his cheek. His eye twitched. Nerves felt like frayed wires.

No, it would be all right. He was probably getting anxious about nothing. Stretch always said he'd worry the warts off a frog, whatever that meant.

Around each curve he knew he'd meet him. Stretch would say, Sorry, I had a blowout, but everything's okay. He'd give the big guy hell, saying, Why didn't you call me? The carrot top would say something like, Hey, I forgot my cell phone, and do you see a pay phone out here, Mr. Jumpy? Then they'd laugh and go get a beer.

But around this curve he saw two CHP units pulled to the side of the road, lights flashing. Uniforms milling around. Smoke coming up out of the canyon below them.

No way. Couldn't happen. Not to Stretch, anyway.

So where was the guy? Shit. Better go take a look.

He whipped a U-turn and pulled over. One of the officers started toward him to run him off. He jumped out, holding up his shield.

"What's going on?" Dover asked.

The patrolman probably wondered why a detective was interested in an accident. Two tall, sturdy men stared at each other. "A car drove off into the canyon."

Dover felt cold. No, couldn't be. "What kind of car?"

"Shit if I know, there's a helluva fire."

"You're not looking for survivors?"

"No one's walking away from that one. But we've got an

ambulance, a fire engine, and a rescue truck on the way."

From under his car seat, Dover pulled out binoculars. He paced to the canyon's edge, where tire tracks cut across the dirt shoulder. Peering into the abyss, he saw flames leaping from a dark shape which could be a Bronco, could be a Blazer. He hustled back to his car.

Snatching a coil of rope from his trunk, he ran back to the cliff. He tied a timber hitch to a patrol car bumper. "Don't make any emergency runs," he said. "If I get past that first drop-off, I can hang on to the brush the rest of the way."

The big officer looked stunned. Then a siren in the distance pierced the night air. "There's the rescue truck, Detective. You'd better hold off."

Dover stared at the blaze below. "No, it'd be too late."

Clutching the rope, he crab-walked down the hill, skidding on loose soil. He imagined Stretch arriving at his condo, getting a beer, and watching TV as he waited for his idiot partner to return. He was going to kill the guy.

Dover's foot slipped on the doughy loam, and he smacked his bad shoulder against the hillside. A stabbing pain wracked his arm, but he clung to the rope like a lifeline until, finally, he found a solid foothold. He gazed down at the flaming debris. The patrolman was right about survivors, unless someone had been thrown free.

A hundred feet to go. Fifteen feet of rope. Still a steep drop.

He climbed down to the end where he secured a toehold and a grip on a small tree. Then he yelled up for the CHP guys to untie the line and let it drop. They did, hitting him on the head.

"I've got it," he hollered. They just shook their heads.

Dover tied off to the tree, which looked sturdy. Then he

recalled a lot of well-built, supposedly sturdy houses had gone down hillsides in L.A. in the past year. But he had to see what was burning below.

Ten minutes later, covered with dirt and as scared as he'd ever been, he reached the burning hulk. The vehicle lay upside down and crumpled, still on fire, radiating scalding heat. It was a Bronco.

He glanced upward. Firemen had arrived and were rolling out hoses at the edge of the canyon wall. The rescue truck had extended a mechanical arm with a cable attached. Some of the recent arrivals were gazing down at him.

There were lots of Broncos in L.A. Could be a coincidence. A charred body was strapped into the driver's seat. He steeled himself, then took a look. Barely recognizable as human.

He circled the vehicle, looking for bodies; he now realized the fall would have killed any passenger. No one around. He took a deep breath, then checked the scorched license tag.

"Oh, God," he said, and sank to his knees.

Chapter 2

The firefighters doused the flames, leaving the Bronco life-less and forlorn, like a deer that'd been mauled by a semi. Steam rose from the hot metal. EMTs stared at Stretch's remains and shook their heads. Feeling sick from shock, Dover turned his head as the coroner's techs pulled the corpse from the vehicle to zip it into a body bag.

The rescue truck lowered a cable, hooked up, and hauled the mangled hulk of the Bronco up the side of the hill. As it crested, Dover began to fight his way back up the canyon wall. When he reached the top, the big CHP officer motioned him over.

"I hear he was your partner."

Dover nodded.

"I'm real sorry." A pause, then the officer said, "You know his next-of-kin?"

"His wife lives up the road."

"She a friend of yours?"

"I'll go with you."

The patrol car followed him to Terri's. The drive seemed far too short. He pulled into the driveway and cut the engine; he'd rather be anyplace else.

Lights were on in the house. She must've called his condo and talked with April. She knew something was up, and that it wasn't good.

He and the patrolman approached the front of the house, and he knocked. Terri flung open the door, saw the two of them standing there like statues, then read the look in their eyes. She sagged like a rag doll. Another casualty of the awful accident.

"I'm so sorry, Terri. He went off the road."

She stared at him as though he'd pulled a knife and plunged it into her heart. Tears filled her eyes. She trembled and began to sob.

As he moved to her, she collapsed against him. He hugged her, patted her back, and said, "There, there." It was all he could think of.

The officer offered his condolences and left.

Rick and Terri talked for an hour, maybe two. Afterwards, he trudged back to his car for the drive home. He felt numb all over. As he came to the curve where Stretch went off the road, his scalp began to tingle. He slowed to stare at the tracks as he eased past.

He tried to think of a reason for what had happened. To make some sense of it. To understand the wrenching plot twist in this horror show.

He imagined Stretch's car careening out of control on the curve, hurtling into the canyon, and exploding in flames when it smashed to the ground. That's what everyone figured. But somehow, the explanation didn't sit right with him.

He replayed it in his mind, not knowing why, not wanting to see the accident that had snatched his partner's life. He shook his head and switched on the radio. Some country sounds might block out the nightmare video—the haunting strains of music, another interest he'd shared with Stretch, his partner and best friend.

Soon he caught the PCH, still buzzing with traffic. He'd adapted his driving techniques, blending in with the west coast racers. But he missed those languid times in Kansas where the roads were straight and empty, and a driver could cruise for miles, just thinking or searching his soul.

On duty calls, Stretch always drove. He had quick reflexes and a deft touch on the wheel as he flowed with the hurtling traffic. Dover ragged him, calling him the Freeway Ferret.

And now he realized why the video kept playing.

His subconscious was telling him something. The Freeway Ferret never lost control. He was the best driver Dover had ever seen, handling a car like a kid could play a video game.

The tingle moved down his spine. This story sucked. Stretch didn't sound like he'd been drinking. He wasn't sleepy, but agitated, wanting to talk about something urgent.

Had Stretch been driving too fast? Maybe, but the curve wasn't tight, and, of course, he'd driven that road many times. Something was wrong, and with doubts clamoring in his head like raucous bells, Dover vowed he'd check it out.

The clock wailed like a fire alarm. Dover slapped the button, ran a hand through his unruly hair, then slumped back into his pillow, groaning. April patted him on the arm.

Last night, she'd been devastated about Stretch. They'd talked a long while, then held each other until they finally fell asleep. He didn't think he'd slept at all until he was suddenly roused by the alarm.

April had a casting call this morning, and he decided to go into the office. To check the lay of the land. To see if anyone had noticed anything suspicious and called it in.

Brushing back a wisp of champagne hair, April said, "I'd better get ready. You going to be all right?"

"I'll make it. Sorry I kept you up last night."

"Don't even think about it. You sure you want to go in?"

"I need to be there."

As she went into the bathroom, he lingered in bed. He'd always hated the "rise and shine" routine, even long ago doing chores on his grandpa's ranch in the Flint Hills, where an early start made some sense, following the bio-rhythms of the cattle. Besides, there were rewards: crisp morning air, green rolling hills, and a big rosy sky.

But with smog smothering the L.A. basin, cars cruising the freeways bent on his destruction, and thrusting towers strangling his need for space, he felt no incentive.

Especially since his partner, his buddy, his mentor was gone. Stretch was the one who'd hooked him on working homicides, and now he loved the puzzle of solving who-dunit, how, and why. Mysteries exuded a magical aura, much like the movies he'd always loved, and one he couldn't resist.

He was energized by the challenge of the hunt, just as he'd been thrilled by cinematic adventures. Truth was, Hollywood was the tarnished jewel that'd beckoned him to La La Land. That, and trying to escape his problems, like many transplanted Californians.

As Anthony Perkins said in *Psycho*, "We all go a little mad sometimes." His insanity had been moving to the place he'd dreamed of since boyhood, when he sat in theaters watching heroes smash enemies, something a kid couldn't do.

Now he lived near the production lots where the stars worked their magic. Film legends were born, held sway, and were laid to rest in one of the "parks" of Forest Lawn. John Wayne would surely have said, "The movies beat the tar outta real life."

Sighing, he rolled out and walked into the kitchen. He

slid wheat bread in the toaster, then gazed out the window, studying the flotilla of boats bobbing on the water. Gleaming yellow arrows streaked across the glassy surface, casting a gilt edge on the masts and spars, providing a suitably ritzy setting.

He studied his condo. Costly and comfortable, it was a sparkling diamond set in a Tiffany area. But he felt it was tainted with blood. Glen Campbell had sung it: that song about compromisin'. He'd sure done a ton of that.

The toast popped up. No time to get immersed in that reverie. He poured a cup of coffee, then sat down, blinking gummy eyes against the morning light.

"Got some for me?" April said, cinching a towel around her.

He poured her a cup, then said, "I assumed you meant coffee."

"A good cup of brew is hard to get. Men are everywhere."

He watched her smile as she pushed back frosted bangs and took a sip. Through silicone-injected lips. Over bleached teeth. A semblance of beauty could be bought in California. Plus, April had started with more than her fair share.

He kissed her, then headed for the shower. In a while, he dressed in a suit and pocketed his shield. Shoved his Beretta in the holster, and snugged his AMT Backup into his belt. Strapped a switchblade to his ankle. Straight razor in his shoe.

He was as ready as he'd ever be to meet this day.

For half an hour he whipped his '57 Chevy through surly traffic in marmalade haze. When he wheeled into a parking lot, Chuck sauntered over. He was smiling and smoothing his long, sandy hair.

"Still stokes me to scope your ride, Detective."

"No XK8, but she putts along."

"Sounds like a muscle car to me."

"Not too lame. I'll let you try her sometime."

"For real? Way cool. Thanks, man."

He hiked four blocks to the Glass House, blank staring panes of glass fronted by white vertical cylinders. In day-time the place would waver, giving the impression of ephemeral justice. Which it provided, in spades.

He flashed his shield and took a crowded elevator to the third floor. In the squad room the dicks jawed and slurped coffee, same old, same old. But when he walked in, he sensed a wariness like a herd of antelope scenting a lion. No one said how ya doin'?, or go hump yourself, or did ya sleep in that suit?

He could almost hear eerie music keening in the background.

If this were the movies, it'd be a horror flick, or maybe a film noir. But he wouldn't have the part of a werewolf, vampire, or zombie. He wouldn't play the crafty detective or a hard-boiled private eye. He'd be the invisible man.

Dropping into his chair at the homicide table, he pretended to study a murder case binder, but he was reading the room. He spotted a raised blind in Lieutenant Cardwell's office. Though near-sighted, the Lou seldom wore his glasses, and he peered out of his glass cage with a stare like Hannibal Lecter.

Cardwell opened his door and headed over. He sauntered with one hand in his pocket, the other fiddling with a Bic lighter. Slick black hair reflected the fluorescent lights. His darting coffee eyes never met Dover's until he was beside his chair. "Rick, can we talk?"

"Sure, Lou."

They ambled wordlessly into the office where the Lou plopped his hatchet ass onto his swivel seat and Dover eased onto a rickety chair. Cardwell picked up his black horn-rim glasses, then tapped the single sheet of paper on his desk.

Before speaking again, Cardwell grabbed a ciggie from a pack in his shirt pocket. Then he had a little coughing fit. A wet one.

"Sounds like you're catching a cold," Dover said. Force of habit. He always needled the Lou about smoking.

Frowning, Cardwell thumbed his Bic, sucked the cancer stick into a glow, then blew out a brackish cloud. Dover imagined the guy's lungs must look like a deflated football inside that hollow chest. Pity.

"I'm sorry about Stretch," the Lou said. "A terrible accident."

He didn't want to talk about it. "I can't believe he's gone."

Cardwell nodded. "A tragic thing." More nodding. "I hear you were at the crash scene." He took a heavy drag.

"Yeah, it was . . . awful."

"I'm sure." Cardwell drummed his fingers on the desk, then moved his ashtray an inch to the right. "Kind of a coincidence you were out there at the same time, I guess."

Dover glanced at the Lou's glasses on the desk. Then he looked up. "Sometimes I can't sleep, so I drive along the PCH. I went up Topanga, and I was going to turn around, but I saw flashing lights."

Cardwell lifted his chin, then took a thoughtful puff. "I see."

"I just stopped to help. Never thought it'd be someone I knew."

"Quite a shock, I imagine."

"Horrible." He didn't know why he wasn't being straight with the Lou, but he sensed something strange was going on.

"I just talked with Terri and offered her a department funeral," Cardwell said. "She'll try to get a minister for Wednesday. So, why don't you take a few days off? We'll call it administrative leave. Then, after things are back to normal, come back and we'll line you up with a new partner."

He stood up. "Stretch was burned to a crisp. Right now, I don't want to hear about a new partner. And nothing will ever be back to normal."

Cardwell shrank backward. "No, I realize that. I just meant that we have to go on, do our work. Stretch would want that."

Dover suddenly felt exhausted. "Maybe so. I'll take the days off, as soon as I clean out his cabinet."

"Don't bother. I'll get someone else to do it."

"No one handles his stuff but me."

"I just . . . hey, go right ahead."

"Damn right. Don't touch the fuckin' cabinet."

Dover rolled out of the office like a roaring combine. Crossing the room, he struggled to regain control. He stood by Stretch's cabinet, his nerves buzzing.

Terri's picture smiled at him. He grimaced. This was too hard.

He felt dazed and off-balance, unable to concentrate, as though he'd been zapped into *The Twilight Zone*.

He heard footsteps behind him, then Eddie gripped his shoulder with a hand like a vise. "Hey, Ricochet, I'm sorry, man. We're all gonna miss him." Eddie stood there like a drill sergeant with his thick, dark buzz cut, angular jaw, and his arms bulging in a tight shirt as though he'd just done fifty pushups.

Deadeye sidled up. A stream of smoke wriggled from yellowed fingers. Taller than Eddie, he had a bit of a paunch and narrow shoulders. Blunt features. "Terrible shame, man. Sorry." He never said much, and his voice was as chill as a threat from Jack Palance.

Dover turned toward Deadeye. "He was the best. In a lot of ways."

Eddie glanced at Deadeye, clapped Dover's arm and said, "We gotta split. They found a suspicious dangler in Studio City, and we caught it."

"Sure, see you guys later."

Watching them leave, he felt envious they had a partner, sensing even more what he'd lost.

He picked up Terri's photo, studied it a bit, then set it down. He'd kidded Stretch about getting hitched, what with all the babes in this fantasy land, but if he'd met someone like Terri, he'd have been tempted, too. For a second try.

Anyway, just get it done, then get the hell out of here. He checked the drawers, finding forms, pens, binders on homicide cases, note cards, the usual. Stretch was very orderly. The guy kept few personal items: the framed photo, a fishing knife, and a Raiders ball cap he wore on surveillances.

Dover rotated the cap in his hands, then studied the picture again. Stretch and Terri had a great relationship. And now this.

He slid the bottom drawer closed, but it didn't catch. He slammed it shut, stared at the mute cabinet, and turned to leave. Then he stopped. He'd seen movies where guys taped envelopes full of cash behind drawers.

Nah, no one would really . . . he reached down and pulled the drawer out a few inches, then pushed it back in with his fingertips, feeling a spring-like tension. He jerked the drawer open and groped behind the end. There, a crumpled note card dangled from the back, taped at one end.

Pulling it loose, he smoothed it on the top of the cabinet. There was a series of numbers and letters and a single word hand printed in capital letters. It meant nothing to him. He shrugged and stuck the card in his pocket.

Maybe Terri knew something about BLACKFLASH.

Once he finished his search, Dover stuffed Stretch's property into an accordion folder, then pounded down the back stairs. On his way to the parking lot, he thought about the past week and what he might've said or done if he'd known his partner would soon be gone. Crushed and fried in his car late at night.

He shook his head. Was there a time he could have helped avert this awful destiny? Probably so. Could he please go back to that time? No way in hell.

So why did he feel so guilty?

Nearing his Chevy he pulled a starter from his pocket, which he punched, bringing the throaty engine to life. In his former life in Kansas, the gizmo saved him from freezing stiff on sub-zero days. Now it was more a habit. Chuck came out of the hut looking curious. Dover waved to the kid as he zoomed out of the lot.

Zipping along the Hollywood Freeway, memories flooded in—the times he and Stretch cruised the streets searching for killers, inched out of alleys crawling with gangbangers, slammed down beers celebrating the latest bust.

They'd solved murders other dicks might've shitcanned. Everyone called them the Dauntless Duo, some in admiration, some not, but no one doubted they were an unstoppable team. Until now.

In a while he caught the Ventura, heading west.

Stretch got his nickname growing up in Tennessee. Tall and lanky, he was a natural on the boards, with a promising future in the NBA. But the knee injury never healed right. So he sold insurance, managed a computer store, then drifted into police work. Like Dover, he'd headed for California to start a brand new life.

Dover took the turnoff south on Topanga, and the road climbed into the Santa Monicas. Sunlight broke through the smog and twinkled on his gleaming hood. On this road, on a mild curve, Stretch went off the road and tumbled to his death.

Dover's heart felt like a rock as he turned into the driveway. With wooden legs, he tramped toward the Craftsman house. The front door swung open, and Terri stepped out, her chestnut hair in tangles, nostrils red, eyes sunken.

"I brought Stretch's stuff from the office."

"Don't talk," she said. "Just hold me."

She moved into his arms. They said nothing, but each knew the loss the other felt. Pain sliced through them, sharp and deep.

She sniffed, dabbing at her brimming eyes with tissue. Then she turned and walked inside. He followed, into a vacuum of dead air and futile dreams.

In the living room she sat on the edge of a wooden chair, and he perched like a rigid soldier on the sofa. "This isn't right," she said.

"If there were any way I could change it . . ."

"We can't. It's just that something was bothering him, but he kept it inside. Then last night he snuck out of the house and got himself killed."

"I don't understand. Snuck out?"

"He'd been moody for a few months. He went out in the evenings, trying to pass it off as work, but I knew better. I suspected he was seeing someone."

Dover held up his hands, palms toward her. "No, Terri, no. He'd never fool around. Stretch loved you completely."

Her face relaxed. "Thanks, that means a lot."

He let her savor the moment. But his curiosity was burning. "Did he tell you he had a problem?"

She sighed. "Last week I found him in the den with the lights out, just staring. I asked what was wrong. He said he was worried about a group that was out of control."

"What group?"

"He wouldn't say. Said he had to work it out himself."

"Did he say anything else?"

"Oh . . . all I recall is something about a connection . . ."

He let it float there a minute, then said, "A connection?"

Now she frowned. "Yes, it was some damn . . ."

She was trying too hard. It was better to let it steep in her subconscious. "Forget it. Not important. Let's have a drink and remember the good times."

She smiled, a bittersweet look. "You could always cut through the crap."

"You bet. Scotch and water, please."

She blew her nose. "Coming up."

As she left the room he came to his feet, as restless as a caged bobcat. He noted a computer on a card table in the corner. Then his gaze fell on Stretch's coveted chess set. Stretch had spotted the marble set during a search of a smuggler's warehouse. The confiscated property had been destroyed, on paper, but Stretch had snagged the set when the evidence was loaded.

Dover stepped over to the board. He had to forgive his partner a momentary lapse. Chess was one of Stretch's few ardent passions.

He picked up the white castle. He'd challenged the big guy a few times, but had soon given up. Stretch was a near master.

Terri came in with the drinks. "He'd want you to have that set."

"No, I couldn't." He placed the castle back on the board.

"I insist. Stretch said you were a very good player."

"He was being charitable."

"Please take it away." It was a brittle command, her gaze peering into a future when memories would have a razor's edge.

She handed him a scotch, then sat down clutching a gin and tonic. "This is weird, but I keep expecting him to walk in here, red cowlick sticking up."

"I feel the same way. Like he can't be gone." His thoughts drifted. "Remember when we went deep sea fishing?"

"You and Stretch and Deadeye—"

"Fishing like crazy, and Stretch got revved, had to catch a trophy marlin."

"Always after the prize."

"And he hooked that hammerhead shark. Goofy eyes sticking out. Snuck it into the Captain's office early on Monday morning."

"Plopped it on his desk."

"Then hung a board on the Captain's door, painted in big black letters, ENTER THESE WATERS AT YOUR PERIL."

They laughed, getting red-faced, then slumped back in

their seats, sipping at their drinks. Suddenly, her eyes got wide. She'd remembered.

"He said the group had a 'computer connection.' "

Chapter 3

Dover loaded the chess set and the table into the Chevy's back seat, then shoved the computer and some diskettes into the trunk. The process sent a mixture of pain and curiosity swirling through his insides. He felt like an archeologist who'd found a mummy's tomb with a deadly curse.

The Chevy growled down the winding canyon road, skirting Topanga State Park. As he drove, Dover spotted the curve where rutted tracks headed for the cliff. He angled over to perch on the narrow shoulder.

He still wondered how the wreck had happened. The door swung open. Nothing he did would change the result, but detectives can't help themselves.

A breeze wafted the scent of scorched brush, a familiar aroma. Wildfires often swept through these canyons like tidal waves of flame. He paced the few steps to the edge, then peered downward.

The hillside was gouged as though with a huge shovel, making wounds of bare dirt. He imagined Stretch's Bronco tumbling down the killer cliff, bouncing, exploding in flames below. He'd watched such scenes in a dozen flicks.

Now he studied the ground leading to the cliff's edge. Though other vehicles had driven over the spot, he could still make out crinkled bits of burned grass and some patches of soot in the dirt. He studied the blacktop. Hard to tell, but he thought he saw a scorched area on the road. He rubbed it with his fingertips, which turned black, then sniffed them, detecting a smoky, oily smell.

He gazed back down into the gaping chasm of death. Now in the sunlight he could see the winking of light off several bits of metal that had snagged on the hillside. Perhaps the pieces fell off when the truck was hauled up. Or maybe . . . the hair on his neck bristled. Maybe the Bronco exploded before it pitched downward. But how? Why?

At the edge of the cliff, some scraggly brush had been scorched black. All wrong. The fire hadn't reached the top of the canyon wall.

Back in the Chevy, he whisked along the curving ribbon of pavement, the smell of death in his nostrils and icy suspicion chilling his insides. From the PCH, he exited onto Sunset Boulevard and drove until he spotted a copy center. From there, he called the CHP. A nice lady in Records faxed him the accident report.

In his car he skimmed the pages. Accident reported eleven fifteen p.m., nighttime with no artificial lighting; road conditions dry; no skid marks; no other vehicles involved; no witnesses; no other occupants; vehicle totaled; probable cause of accident: driver intoxicated or asleep and lost control of vehicle.

He threw down the report. Generic crap. The officer took the easy path.

Slamming the Chevy into gear, he sped away, headed for the LAPD impound lot. Maybe he could get an arson team out here. But first he wanted a closer look at Stretch's Bronco.

Carl Kissler ran the impound lot the way Rommel commanded his tank brigades. With total discipline. Faultless order.

"Hey, Commander, *vas ist los?*"

Rheumy green eyes flicked up. *"Nicht.* Same old *sheist."*

"Stretch's car here somewhere?" A rhetorical question.

Carl handed him an envelope, saying, "I'm real sorry about Stretch. He was a good detective. And a great guy."

"You know it, buddy." He blinked to clear his eyes, then read the numbers on the envelope that gave the car's location on the lot.

"Want me to help you find it?" Carl rose from his chair, his heavy shoulders swelling from a massive chest.

"Come on, Commander, it's your battlefield."

A couple of minutes later Carl pointed. "There it is."

The Bronco's top was flattened, hood buckled, tires shapeless blobs. Seared a dull gray, the Bronco looked like an industrial carcass. Dover stared at the bare seat springs, scorched steering wheel, and blackened dash.

"You see a lot of these wrecks, Carl, is this typical?"

His green eyes searched the past. "Worse than most."

The doorframes were bent. Dover yanked on the driver's door, and it screeched open. On the floorboard lay a rubber heel. In the glove box were a melted flashlight and a garage door remote. The rear area held a jack and tools.

Gazing back at the front seat, imagining Stretch sitting there just before he went over the lip of the canyon, Dover said, "Find anything else in it, Carl?"

"Nothing but what you see."

Dover started to slam the door, but something caught his eye. Beneath the front seat springs were two small silver items. One rectangular, one round.

He fished them out, wiped soot off, and looked them over. He was pretty sure they were parts of a computer disk. Was the disk being brought to him?

He stuck them in his pocket, then circled the car, stopping in front. He popped the hood, the hinges squealing. The engine looked burned to shit. On the hood was a raised spot, directly over a dark crater in the engine block. Strange.

"Let's go back," Dover said.

On the way Carl checked the lot and nodded, seeming satisfied that everything was in order. Dover wasn't. He was going to view the autopsy.

At the same moment that Dover moved away from the Bronco, Jarroll shuffled through a razed lot in South Central. Past three winos cussing and shoving over a bottle of Night Train. Two little kids ran by, screaming like crazy.

Jarroll stopped, wiped his sweaty face, then spotted a hammer buried in the ashes. He picked it up and checked out the seared handle and smudged iron head. Then he turned and flung it at a piece of jagged glass in a charred window frame. Smash! Got the muthafucka. Last piece of glass in a Korean grocery.

Next door sat a burned-out pawn shop. Splashes of blue and black glared from the cement walls. He saw an open patch and drew a spray can from his back pocket. With a flourish, he lettered J-83. He nodded, then heard footsteps.

"Wha's up, little brother?" a deep voice said behind him.

He stiffened. Turning, he saw three Rollin' 60s. Rivals of the local gang.

"Looks like we got us a baby Eight-Tray."

He wasn't ganged up, but they'd never believe him. "Yeah, wha's up?"

"We looking for punks that jumped our brother. Guess you be one. You can join him in the hospital."

The 'banger's hand moved, and a blade was out.

Jarroll had seconds to do or die. Crip or cry. Fuck it, he was dead.

Then he remembered the sound of breaking glass. He

threw a forearm into the chest of one kid, knocking him back, then ran toward the spot where he'd trashed the window. He saw a hole in the ashes, dove toward it, and came up clutching the hammer. Turning back, he faced the nigga with the blade.

The dude was rangy and his hand blurred as he jabbed the point of the knife toward Jarroll's face. Jarroll blinked, a mistake. Now the hand whipped the blade across his chest, a painful burning zipping along behind the slicing edge.

Jarroll hurt, but he was mad, and he whipped the hammer back and forth.

"He a down li'l homey," one of the dudes said.

The lean nigga glared, then lunged at Jarroll's thigh.

Jarroll jerked his legs backwards and swung the hammer in an arc, whacking the top of the dude's wrist. The skinny kid yanked the knife back, cussing and rubbing his hand. His face went hard.

Jarroll grabbed a handful of dirt. Come on, nigga. Le's go.

The dude moved side-to-side, and Jarroll backed away. He bumped against the wall that said We Buy Gold and Silver. At once, he threw the fistful of earth and swung the hammer.

The kid dodged the flying dirt, then pressed again, close enough to cut him. Jarroll felt cold. The nigga looked into his eyes. Here it came.

Then the air exploded all around them.

Jarroll froze. Had they shot him? He never felt it.

Now the 'banger backed off, twisted his head, and froze in place.

Behind the dude holding the knife stood three Eight-Tray Gangster Crips. Jarroll had seen them around the 'hood. The one called Freak clutched a smoking Mac-10.

Jarroll glanced upward to see a dozen gouges in the concrete blocks.

He heard the sounds of running. Down the street the other two 60s homeboys rounded the corner. Couple of real busters.

Now a huge Crip called Gorilla moved forward. His arm muscles flexed like chunks of rock, and he pointed a .45 pistol at the skinny dude, holding it solid in his big hand. Jarroll figured they were waiting for orders from Skull.

Skull took a few steps toward them, ran a hand across his gleaming, shaved head, and stopped in front of them, his eyes like marbles made of ice. He scoped the punk up and down. "What you doin' around here?"

The skinny guy seemed to shrink. "Just passin' by. Ain't no thang."

"Check the wall, this our territory. Ain't dope for you to cruise it. Gorilla, learn this fool to stay out our 'hood."

Gorilla reached for the punk. Jarroll saw a spark of fight in the dude's eyes as his hand jittered with the knife. But Freak pointed the Ten at the 'banger's crotch, and he cringed and dropped the blade. Jarroll shook his head. The dude shoulda broke bad. He'd have been aced with less pain.

The punk slouched away, clamped between Freak and Gorilla. He'd never dis' them again. The Eight-Trays were some hard guys.

Skull glanced around, then said to him, "Where you live at?"

Jarroll told him. "J-83, tha's me," he said, pointing at his work.

Skull studied the wall. "Tha's cool. You put in some funky work for the 'hood today. Just might be you gets jumped into the Eight-Trays one day."

Jarroll's heart pounded like a jackhammer. In this 'hood that was the best that could happen. Only way to make yourself worth something.

In the back of Carl's office Dover dialed Larry Brightonfeld at the coroner's office, but he got the recorder, so he hung up, told Carl thanks, and climbed into his Chevy for the evening motor mania. Once back at his condo, he shed his suit and tie and slipped on some jeans. Then he unloaded Stretch's stuff, setting up the chess board beside his recliner and aligning the pieces.

Dumping the computer system on a card table in a corner of his bedroom, he stared at the equipment, aware of his minimal experience with PCs. He'd compare his ability in the field of chips and bytes to the acting wizardry of Cindy Crawford. He hoped initiative counted for something, as he was burning to pick the brains of this electronic enigma.

His stomach rumbled, but he was too upset to eat much now. So he grabbed some of April's homemade chocolate chip cookies and poured a glass of milk. Dropping onto a chair in the dining room, he stared out the window, absently munching.

As he ate, he wondered if April had gotten her acting part. Nah, she'd have left a message. She was probably in the dumps.

He called and found her crying. So much for a thick Hollywood skin. "There'll be other parts, babe. You'll knock 'em dead, no sweat."

In a minute she sniffed, then asked, "How are you feeling, Rick?"

He didn't want to go there. "I need a day or so to get my stuff together."

"Promise me you'll call if you feel like talking."

"Absolutely." He hung up, blew his nose, then grabbed a cold Coors and bolted half of it. Picking up the phone again, he dialed Brightonfeld.

Larry was a no-bullshit guy. He knew better than most that death was inevitable, and that when it came, it might not be pretty. Larry said the autopsy on Stretch was set for tomorrow morning, and he'd be doing the cut.

Dover asked if he could watch. There was a pause, then Larry said, "I don't mind. Be there by nine."

But his curiosity couldn't wait. "Did you see Stretch?"

"No, I missed work today."

"Hmm. Then I'll see you tomorrow." Dover hung up, puzzled. Larry never took days off. The brass complained about his time piling up. And there was something peculiar in his voice.

He stared at the wall calendar by the phone, a present from Stretch. Miss Beach Ball, the bikini beauty of the month, had an earthquake-proof frame. A necessity in L.A.

Then an emotional shock wave went through him.

Of course! How stupid. The date should have caught his attention. Would have, except for Stretch. The day meant everything to Larry.

The guy was about forty. Came to California from Michigan fifteen years ago. Almost a native. Was married for a few years, and they'd had a son with a heart defect. The boy never felt well, was always puny, and died before he reached three. Then the marriage became terminal. They couldn't look at each other without remembering.

But even with the divorce, the memory didn't fade. He'd told Dover about it late one afternoon after doing an autopsy on a little girl who'd been raped and murdered. They'd sought out a nearby bar for some painkiller.

"Next month is Timmy's birthday," he said, guzzling a longneck.

"What day?" Dover asked, not knowing what else to say.

He said the date like it was a very hallowed thing.

As Dover thought about Timmy and the birthday that would never come, Larry said, "He'd be ten years old next month."

"Oh, really? Ten?" Could he counsel friends, or what?

"Yeah, I think this year we'll go to Hermosa Beach. He'll get a kick outta watching the surfers flying across those waves."

"I don't understand."

He opened another beer and took a big gulp. "I don't tell this to many people. It's private, you know?" His eyes glittered.

"Absolutely." Dover drained his bottle.

"Every year I go somewhere different on Timmy's birthday. Somewhere I think he'd want to go if he'd lived. I spend the day with him in my mind. I think about what he'd look like, how he'd sound, what we'd talk about and do together, just the two of us."

"Sounds great." And it did.

"Yeah," he chuckled in a hollow way, "I almost got fired one year. The Sergeant wanted an autopsy done that day. Had pressure from on high to solve a murder. I told him to stuff it, I was taking the day off. Didn't tell him why, either. None of his fucking business."

Dover felt honored his friend thought it his business. Tomorrow he'd ask him what he and his son had done on Timmy's birthday. He hoped it was fun.

Back in his bedroom, he stared at the computer parts scattered on the table. Better try to get it assembled. He studied the cords and hookups, and after a few false starts, he had it humming.

Moment of truth. But was he ready? Unsure, he fumbled through Stretch's diskettes, wondering which one held the mummy's curse.

They didn't sound that sinister. Chess Challenger, tax format, balance sheet, Spymaster Game, and a correspondence file. One had no markings. He slipped the unlabeled diskette into the port.

Hitting the index function, he brought up the menu. There was one file on it: The Untouchables. Whatever. He punched the retrieve key.

Saw the glowing words: TO UNZIP FILE, ENTER 4-DIGIT CODE. He stood up, nervous. Never expected this. What now, Houdini? He picked up the phone.

"Hello," she said, sounding spaced-out.

"Terri, it's me."

"Oh, I'm glad you called. I'm like a zombie, numb from my ankles up. It's good to hear someone's voice."

"Good to hear you." He hated to intrude on her grieving, but he needed help.

She paused, then said, "Were you calling about something specific?"

"I hate to bother you with it, but I set up Stretch's computer, and I had a question about a disk."

"I never used his PC. I've got my own. But what's your question?"

Damn. "There's a file called 'The Untouchables.' Mean anything to you?"

"I know he liked that movie."

Sure, didn't everyone? "When I tried to access the file, it asked for a password. Do you know what it might be?"

"A password? He never mentioned it to me."

"Or maybe a number. Could be letters. Looks like it's four digits."

"Nothing comes to mind."

"I know he was born in September, but I forget the day."

"September seventh, but what—"

"That would be 9/7/71. Or nine-seven-seven-one, a four-digit number."

"Oh, right. Anything else?"

"What's his Social Security number?"

"Just a minute."

As he waited, he tried to think of other combinations. Stretch's shield number was 5134. And his locker number was twenty-eight something, two over from his would be . . . 2868.

"Here it is . . ." She gave him the number. The last four digits were 7049.

"Great. And I've thought of some others to work with."

"If you find out anything, will you let me know?"

"You got it. Can I do anything for you?" It sounded so hollow.

"Just keep in touch. Don't leave me by myself in this." She started to cry. "Oh, if we'd only . . ." But her tears flooded out her words.

He waited a minute, then asked, "Only what?"

She sighed. "Stretch wanted to have children. I put him off, thinking we could wait. No hurry. But now . . ."

"No one can outguess something like that. It's just—"

"I know, but I wish I had part of him here I could hug."

"Terri, I—"

"I'd better go. The funeral's set for Wednesday afternoon. You'll go with me, won't you?"

"Of course."

Her goodbye was in a small, sad voice.

Larry would do the cut tomorrow. The funeral was Wednesday. And facing Terri there would be . . . well, something he couldn't imagine.

He plopped down at the computer and punched in a number. Reminded him of pulling the lever on a slot machine. He hoped his odds were better.

Chapter 4

Dover whipped onto the freeway en route to the autopsy, his mind reeling with visions of gory bodies.

At the same time, firefighter Kirk McLaren exited into South Central with images of a recent warehouse blaze haunting his thoughts. The roof had collapsed, and they'd lost two firemen, both good friends. In L.A., the specter of death was always in the air.

McLaren drove a few more blocks, then pulled into a parking space behind the firehouse. As he reached for the door handle, steeling himself to take on another day, a sharp pain jabbed his chest. God, it hurt.

He froze. Couldn't be his heart, he was too young. Besides, he was in good shape from jogging and pumping iron. Not to mention wrestling hose, bashing in doors, and carrying victims overcome by smoke.

He took a slow, deep breath. Leaned back against the seat, trying to relax. In a minute the pain slid away, like unbuttoning a tight collar.

Maybe it was from stress, he thought, with the deaths of his friends so tough to handle. And there were worries about his career. Going for a promotion. Terrific pressure to earn the extra money the lieutenant's slot would bring.

His daughter, Tasha, with her bright smile and smooth mocha complexion, a beautiful and smart kid, would start school this fall. And L.A.'s public schools were not the best education. Worse, they were often dangerous or even deadly.

But Catholic schools were expensive. He sighed. Should know the results soon.

Erin had toasted him, saying, "Faith and all that, here's to the patron saints of bedraggled parents and exhausted wage earners."

"As in crime and farming and firefighting don't pay?"

"As in you've done an almighty fine job for twenty years now, and here's looking to the Lord and the Department for a little appreciation."

Yes, he'd spent his time in the trenches, battling raging fires in decayed buildings in South Central. If it was meant to be, it would be. He entered the firehouse with memories of leaping flames and roiling smoke playing in his mind.

Dover fought his own memories of torched cars and computer disks. He thought of Terri, her face twisted in pain. And now he had to face the autopsy.

He pushed into a room that was cold, Spartan, and reeked of formaldehyde. His best friend was in there; he felt as if a truck had parked on his chest.

Larry walked in. They took it slow, chatting about the Dodgers, traffic, and movies. Discussed the weather. Hard up.

Then Dover asked about Timmy's birthday, and Larry blinked back a mist in his eyes. He said they'd taken the Universal Studio Tour.

"What'd you guys think of Jurassic Park—The Ride?"

"Real scary when the T-rex started chomping on folks in the boats. But what rattled my cage was the simulated earthquake. The ground lurching, that gasoline truck smashing into a bridge abutment. Eerie as hell."

"Tremors spook me now," Dover said. "Could always be the Big One."

"And no one knows if the city will hold up."

"After seeing Kobe, Japan, I lost my California insouciance."

"Christ, Rick, what's that?"

"Just burst my bubble. Made me get real."

"Hard to do in Xanadu, where dreams are reality."

"Damn, Larry, you do have poetry in your soul."

"No, I lost all that. California's not for me anymore. I'm going back to the Midwest as soon as I put in my twenty."

Might be the thing to do, Dover thought. He imagined a big quake cracking highways like pieces of chalk. Toppling buildings. Why stay for that?

"But after the tour," Larry said, "we drove around Griffith Park. Parked at the observatory to watch the sun set over the city. It was real pretty."

"Sounds like a fun day," Dover said.

"I got the whole trip on video. Sometimes I look at the tapes between birthdays. Keeps my spirits up."

Dover imagined the spirits of Timmy, Natalie Wood, and James Dean drifting over the observatory. Only one rebel. But all of them gone.

"Timmy said the sunset was the best part. Except it ended the day."

Dover got a painful knot in his throat.

"Oh, the camera." Larry retrieved it from a gym bag.

Dover gripped the table's edge. "Hope I know what I'm doing."

"You don't have to be here, Rick. I'll copy the report for you."

"No, I feel there's something I'm supposed to see."

"Whatever you want, you got it." He set about preparing the table and the stainless steel instruments. Then he glanced at Dover, pulled up his mask, and paced to the wall of cabinets. Sliding one open, he tugged Stretch's body onto a mobile cart. Wheeled the wrecked corpse to the table.

Dover stared. Bile rose up in his throat; blood drained from his head. Stretch looked like a slab of fricasseed meat.

Larry positioned the body on the table. He looked it over, shaking his head. Then he started the video camera.

Dover took some deep breaths. Sensing Larry's hesitation, he focused on the scene. Worse than any Hollywood horror show. Stretch was scorched over most of his body, with crisped edges of skin. Multiple lacerations. But one thing was preeminent to all that.

The upper part of Stretch's legs were black, with hunks of flesh torn off or shredded. His pelvic area was a mass of gore. Lower abdomen dark and ripped.

Bottom line, his balls were blown off.

Dover shut his eyes, feeling faint. He was losing it. But he held his breath and fixed on a thought: Stretch would want him to scrutinize, to analyze. So he peered back at the ravaged form, taking it in with detective's eyes.

"This's weird," Larry whispered.

"Can I get a still photo?"

Picking up his Minolta, Larry snapped a couple. Then he took some shots with a Polaroid. He handed several to Dover.

Larry switched on a backup recorder, then he spoke out loud, describing his observations. He shot another look at Dover as he picked up a scalpel. Then he sliced a Y-shaped incision on the chest and abdomen, down to the pubic area.

He described aloud the various organs as he severed them, weighed them, performed chemical tests, and placed them in jars. Body fluids drained through holes in the autopsy table, collecting in a stainless steel tank below. The scene reminded Dover of his step-dad, hunting knife in hand, field dressing a deer.

Dover never liked hunting, causing his step-dad to doubt his manhood. But he and Stretch would kick open doors, barging in behind a shotgun and a handgun, taking down whoever lurked in the dark corners of those rancid rooms.

Try that, tough guy.

In those encounters there was always the nervous high of fear and excitement, adrenaline pumping hard and fast, senses tingling. But he'd never realized how bad those situations could have been. Death had been a tantalizing presence, not a raw, pulpy reality like what he now faced.

Stretch was dead. Something terrible had happened to him. Dover didn't know which he feared more—knowing what it was, or not knowing.

Larry finished the autopsy with brusque efficiency, but he was deliberate in cleaning up the massacre. Even after he'd stowed Stretch's remains, he had a far-off gaze in his eyes.

"So what do you think?"

"Well, I'm sure of some things—massive skull fracture, third degree burns over ninety percent of his body, collapsed lungs—but I guess what puzzles me is his midsection."

"Not from gasoline exploding?"

"Don't think so, but I could be wrong. I'll run some tests."

"But can't you at least—"

"I'm not going to spout off with any harebrained conjectures. My imagination's wilder than *Quincy* on TV."

"That's off the air. Unless you've got three hundred channels with reruns of everything."

"But I taped all the shows."

"Yeah, me too. When will you know?"

"Check with me Thursday."

"Thursday?"

"Funeral's tomorrow. So come by Thursday—make it in the afternoon, just to be sure. Sometimes it gets crazy around here."

Dover took in the jars full of body parts, the skeleton hanging on the coat rack, and the tools of dismemberment strewn willy-nilly. "How can you tell?"

"You know any humor is totally lost on us ghouls. Go home and quit thinking about it. You look beat. Take it easy, get some—"

"Rest, Mommy, dearest?"

He ushered him to the door. "Thursday afternoon. Don't call me before then, just to see if maybe I finished sooner."

Dover trudged down the hall. He felt like a dead man walking. During the autopsy his sensate wiring had flared and burned away. He stopped, slumped against the wall, and dissolved into a hurting human being.

He'd suffered like this only a few times before. The worst was when Jenny's plane had crashed just before their third anniversary. To most folks, it was just another disaster splashed in the headlines, but it crushed his soul.

And it drove him out of Kansas City, far from the memories. At least, that was the intention. But even having the insurance money threw a spotlight on the past, so he'd sunk it all into the condo. He'd tried to live a new life, to make new friends. But now, just as he was getting used to L.A., Stretch had left.

He pulled the photographs of Stretch's ravaged corpse from his shirt pocket. As he studied them in turn, a shell hardened around him, formed by the cold steel of suspicion. Now anger roared within him like flames eating chaparral. Burning rage about Stretch's death. Seething fury.

No way this was on the up. He had to find out exactly what had happened, and why. And no matter what "mother" Larry said about how he looked, he wouldn't rest until he knew.

As Dover left the building, memories of the autopsy roared through his mind like Strelnikoff's Red Troop train in *Doctor Zhivago*. He was pumped. He strode toward his Chevy as though his legs were steam-driven pistons.

Just as Dover slid into his car, Jarroll was waking up with a squeal boring into his head. It was his little sis. She could screech like a bad set of brakes.

Padding down the hall, Jarroll peeked into Momma's room. Sprawled on the bed, hair a mess, some fat nigga lying beside her. Pipes on the table.

She must've found him at a crack house last night. She was too broke to buy any dope herself. If she didn't quit using the shit, she'd be a cluckhead for sure.

Jarroll ambled into the kitchen, all jittery from the bawling. Sink was full of dirty dishes, floor sticky where he'd spilled some juice, box had half a carton of milk, a hunk of cheddar, and three eggs. He poured two glasses of milk.

Holding the cold glasses, he peeked into Alceeda's room. She sat in the middle of her bed, clutching a stuffed doll. She let out another shriek.

He held the milk in front of her face. She kept the howl going until she ran out of breath, then wiped her nose with the back of her hand, sniffed, and leaned toward the glass. Took a big swallow.

He swiped the top of her head. She grinned, then drank

some more. "Le's go into the kitchen, I'll get you sumthin' to eat."

"Where's Momma?"

"She's asleep, you bawl head. Come on."

She skipped through the doorway, her doll clutched by one tiny arm.

They ate toast, eggs, milk. Rest of the folks could find their own stuff.

With his hunger sated and energy boosted, he now felt like doing something—maybe pumping the rock. He liked putting the ball up from the top of the key, watching it drop through the hoop. Any fool tall enough could slam it.

But no way to tell if Momma was going to watch Alceeda or not. She could be nice to her. Or Momma might just pay attention to her pipe.

Big thing was, he needed to clock some presidents or everybody was going to starve. He slapped at a bug that skittered across the table. Missed.

A bump at the doorway, and Jarroll glanced over.

"Hello, boy."

Dumb nigga, never seen him before. The guy saw he wasn't going to answer, so he shrugged and slouched over to the box. Fat gut on him. Ugly, too.

"You got a beer?" His head jerked around, checking the bare shelves.

"You see one?" Jarroll asked.

Red-splotched eyes looked crazy at him. He stared back. No way was he scared of this fool. Had a switchblade in his pocket that'd slice the fat fucker up.

The guy came toward him. Jarroll went to his pocket and pulled out the blade. The guy slowed, but kept advancing.

"Wha's up?" They both froze and stared at the doorway

where Momma sagged against the frame, clutching a wrinkled robe to her chest.

"Just lookin' for a beer, baby. You got any?"

"Chill, George. There's a store down at the corner. Get yo'self over there and buy some. Leave my babies alone."

He glared, then pushed by her. Jarroll heard him fumbling with his shoes in the bedroom. By the time he went out the door, they'd forgotten about him.

Momma rubbed Jarroll's head and pinched his ear. "You're a good boy. But, hey. Fix me something, okay?"

He stuck his head in the box. Damn near empty. He realized how that dumb nigga felt. Momma had slumped in a chair, humming to herself. The pit of his stomach clenched, and he wondered where their next meal was coming from.

Dover cruised the surface streets, trying to put things together. He stared at the buckskin-colored sky. What's going on, Stretch? Any ideas, partner? I'll bet you can hear me, you could always read my mind. Give me a sign or a clue.

He tried to let his mind go blank. Be receptive to the vibes, the emanations, whatever. But his psychic channel seemed to be on the fritz.

Touching the pictures in his jacket pocket, he imagined Stretch spouting one of his maxims. They were a mixture of street savvy, investigative skills, and philosophy of life all jumbled together. This one was: When in doubt, consult an expert. A DNA expert had helped them nail a serial rapist and killer. A forensic dentist identified a victim from a jawbone with four teeth. A photo specialist helped them locate a perp's hideout.

C-r-a-a-k! The figurative lightning struck a synapse in his brain. His big question was: What had exploded in that car and blown Stretch's balls off?

He made a squealing U-turn. Drove to the Harbor Freeway, heading south toward Long Beach. Don Harsha of ATF was a top-notch explosives expert.

Traffic was heavy as usual, and the drive took an hour. Finally, he pulled into the lot, then marched into the building. Luckily, Harsha was there. Seated in his office, permed hair all bouncy, tinted glasses halfway down his hawkish nose.

But maybe not so lucky. Harsha was leaning over his desk, absorbed in the act of thrusting a piece of wire into a hand grenade. Dover noticed the pin was lying on the desk beside those sensitive hands.

"Hey, Ri-co-chet! What gives?" His hands were poised over the grenade.

"I was driving by, and I . . . uh, what the hell are you doing, Don?"

He glanced down as if he had no idea what his hands were up to. "Oh, this. It's a grenade we couldn't get deactivated at the range. The fuse is hung up in there. If I can work it loose and wiggle it out without touching the sides . . ." Then with the wire, he jiggled around, poked, and scraped. He frowned and threw the wire on the desk.

"It's not going to give. Crappy tooling job. American manufacturing." He shook his head, then dropped the grenade into a wastebasket by Dover's feet.

Dover went ballistic. He could've skywalked with the best of 'em. Hang time beyond belief. By the time he landed, that stupid, ornery, no good Harsha was laughing his tubby ass off, his face flushed sunrise red.

"You sorry jerk-off. You set me up. Probably been salivating all over your—"

"Hey," he said, fishing out the grenade, "it's a paperweight. But when Betty told me you were coming back, I couldn't resist."

51

Dover laughed at himself. "If you weren't so good with explosives . . ."

"Ah, hell," he said, running a hand through his springy curls, "if I took all this stuff serious, I'd go wacko in a week."

Dover could relate. Like working in a cancer ward or on a homicide squad, you had to let the crushing sadness roll off you. No one could shoulder it all.

"You look like something's wrong," Harsha said.

"Stretch was killed in a car wreck."

"Jesus! I didn't know. When did it happen?"

"Late Sunday night. He went off the road in Topanga Canyon."

"Shit, I'm really sorry, Rick. He was the best."

"Yes, that's why I'm here. And, Don, I don't know how he died, or why."

"But you said—"

"Car wreck, I know. But there's more to it, I'm sure."

"What makes you think so?"

"Weird stuff at the autopsy. The accident scene was wrong."

"And there's something you want to ask me, Rick?"

"I'm guessing at things you'd know dead bang, pardon the expression."

"I'm used to it. Explosives?"

"Possibly."

Harsha leaned back in his chair, his eyes shining. "When do you need it?"

Two days ago, he thought, but said, "How about now?"

"You buying lunch?"

"Know any way I can avoid it?"

Harsha grabbed a black case. "C'mon, let's beat the crowd at Morton's."

"I was thinking more like Barney's Beanery."

"Methane leaks are awful dangerous around explosives."

Dover smiled. "Okay, I'll bow to the expert."

Chapter 5

Harsha had an errand in Beverly Hills, so they went to Ed Debevic's Diner, a joint where you could relax, which Dover needed. And Harsha was the kind of buoyant guy who could lighten his black mood. Sitting in a green padded booth, they ordered burgers, fries, and shakes. The place shook, rattled, and rolled with the busy lunch crowd and the booming back beat of a Wurlitzer juke box. It evoked memories for both of them.

"Man, Elvis was my favorite back then," Harsha said. "That 'Heartbreak Hotel' really burned the place down."

"I liked 'Hound Dog Boogie' and 'Blue Suede Shirt.' "

"Rick, your ignorance is pathetic."

"Sorry, I was more of a Beach Boys fan."

"Would've figured you for a devotee of Debbie Boone."

"And you a groupie for Chubby Checker."

Harsha took a big bite of his burger and waved away the insult. "So what movies did you like from back then?" He slurped his shake.

Dover dabbed a french fry into ketchup and munched on it. "I liked the ones where the heroes struggled against huge odds and nothing could break them. Like *Rebel Without a Cause* or *Mr. Roberts.*"

"Good flicks," Harsha agreed. "Want another shake?"

Dover patted his stomach. "Nope, I'm full as a tick."

"A-h-h-h, the h-a-y-s-e-e-d," Harsha said in a W. C. Fields impression. "Betcha could buck bales better'n anyone back in K-a-a-n-n-s-a-s. The land so easy to f-o-r-

54

g-e-e-e-t." He signaled a frowzy blonde balancing red plastic baskets full of fries. She popped her gum as Harsha ordered, then flounced away.

A brunette who could create a jet stream with her Marilyn Monroe chest gave Dover an appraising look. He smiled, but then looked away, not wanting to get involved. Another time and place, maybe. As they always said in show biz, everything's in the timing. And, lately, his had been lousy.

Soon the blonde came with Harsha's shake, plus more in a tin shaker. He took a slug, gave it a long "a-h-h-h-h," then said, "You still on our planet, pal?"

"I was thinking about Stretch."

"Mmm. A damn shame." He fiddled with the shaker. "But accidents happen, and the living got to go on living, and all those platitudes that say it all."

"Usually, I'd agree with you. But something's out of sync here. Something's not, as Stretch used to say, in tune with the moon."

Harsha frowned. "So that's where I come in? Like an astrologer brought in to fine tune the firmament for Hollywood celebs?"

"Man, can you wax philosophical."

He drained his glass. "Don't be shy, say I'm a pain in the ass."

"If you can help me on this, you'll be a superstar."

"What've you got?"

Dover pulled the autopsy photos from the pocket of his windbreaker and handed them over. "Stretch's mortal remains."

Harsha took them, looked at a few, said, "Bad fucking burns," flipped through a couple more, then stopped dead. "Jesus H. Christ."

Dover glanced over. A shot of Stretch's groin. The gory hole where his equipment should've been. "The car exploded after it went off the cliff."

"Yeah, but this . . ." Harsha shook his head.

"From the photos, would you say it might be a bomb?"

"I've seen a lot of demolition. Maybe, maybe not."

"What's your gut feeling?"

"Can I look at his car?"

Dover and Harsha slid into the Bel Air. On the freeway Dover spotted an open space in the mechanized herd and stomped it. The Chevy surged ahead.

If Carl was surprised to see him again, the big guy didn't show it. He dropped the keys on the counter. "You remember where it is?"

"Sure, Commander. Everything in its place."

Carl turned back to a computer printout. "Good luck."

They found the skeleton of the Bronco. Harsha set the black case on the ground, paced around the wreckage, then said, "Let's pop the hood."

Harsha stared at the raised place on the hood and the black crater where the starter had been. He turned, hunkered down, and flipped open his case. Flashlight in hand, he shot a spear of light into the Ford's yawning trachea.

"Hmmm," he said, changing the angle of the flashlight.

"You see something?" Dover asked.

Harsha slipped off his sports coat, got down on hands and knees, then slid his upper torso under the vehicle, peering upward.

Dover wrung the sports coat in his hands.

"Son of a bitch."

"What's the matter?"

Harsha eased out from under the frame, and Dover gave

him a hand to stand up. "C'mon, give."

"I think you were right."

"A bomb?"

"I'm gonna try a test," he said, rummaging in the case. Pulling out a couple of vials of liquid, he mixed them, then slipped back under the vehicle.

"What're you looking for?"

"From some indicators I see, I think it's a plastic explosive."

"Jesus." His wild conjecture could be true.

"Maybe C-4, which is mostly RDX in an oil-rubber binder. I'm testing with some thymol in sulfuric acid." He shone the light, "Ah, there's the blue."

"Is that good?"

Harsha reappeared from under the Bronco, set the vial on the ground, then slapped at the dirt stains on his shirt. "Blue is positive for RDX. Probably C-4 or a similar explosive. There's a bit of putty-like substance there that looks like some unconsumed explosive. Also, I saw a couple pieces of electrical tape and a bit of hook-up wire. And this."

Dover looked at the sliver of gray metal. "Yeah. What is it?"

Harsha's eyes rolled upward. "Good thing they usually shoot your clientele. Hard to miss those lumps of lead."

"Don't be more of a smart ass than usual. Spell it out."

He juggled the gray sliver. "Battery fragment. Put it with the electrical tape and the hook-up wire, you got items used in bombs with time devices."

"Damn. A time device?"

Harsha nodded. "Probably hooked into the ignition to start it."

Dover's eyes turned as gray as a tempest. Then the video

in his head kicked in, making sense when Stretch's car approached the curve, blew up, then catapulted into the canyon. "Those rotten bastards," he said.

Harsha asked, "Can I help with the case?"

"I was hoping you would, Don. We don't see many bombs."

"You got it. But, man, I can't believe anyone did this."

"Me either. But they'll be sorry they did."

Dover pulled to a stop in front of Harsha's office. Harsha said he'd do a complete crime scene investigation on the Bronco in the morning. Dover would go to the funeral, then hook up with Harsha. Before getting out, Harsha said, "Can you clear channels with your office about my investigation?"

"Right away. Thanks for your help." So why didn't he feel grateful?

Harsha caught the baleful gaze. "I know this's tough, Rick."

"At least now I know it wasn't an accident I could've prevented."

"No way in hell, buddy."

"Guess I thought I was the only one could keep him out of trouble."

A stream of cars whizzed by. Life went on. For the lucky.

"Let me do my thing," Harsha said. "It'll all work out."

Dover nodded. As he accelerated away from the curb, he realized he'd often told the relatives of homicide victims the same thing. He wondered if they'd thought he was an asshole.

He knew Harsha was just concerned. But it was hard to let anyone else run with this ball. He felt too wired, too upset.

He pulled into the parking lot, slammed the door, and locked it. Chuck strolled over. As he watched Chuck appraise the car's silhouette, he asked, "Hey, you ever cut out of here?"

"I bagged the duty a coupla times. Maybe gone an hour."

"I need a fill up and an oil change, and I'm jammed for time. Think you could . . ." He let it hang there, keys dangling.

Car salesman's smile. "No prob, you're covered."

"Thanks, my ride and I owe you." He handed him two fifties.

Chuck's choppers dazzled in the sunlight. Where were the talent scouts when needed? Probably shitfaced in the Polo Lounge.

As he walked, he decided he'd tell the Lou what Harsha had found, then let him do his twaddle. ATF would run the case; they'd nail the bastards. And then maybe he'd feel a sense of personal revenge.

He mulled over methods of inflicting mayhem. Hurrying past the palm trees, he climbed the stairs to Parker Center. Yanked open the front door and dipped into his pocket for his shield.

What mystified him was who would want to snuff Stretch? It made no sense. The guy never hassled anyone but killers, most of whom were in the joint. And their scumbag friends were busy running their own hustles.

There was one thing certain—Stretch had been wasted, no matter what the motive. A bombing and homicide case. On his turf.

The glass cubicle around Cardwell's office was fogged with secondhand smoke. Dover knocked on the doorjamb, held his breath, and peered inside. Deep in consideration of a blank wall, Cardwell quickly scooped up a report from his desk, glanced at it, then looked back at Dover as if he'd broken a shrewd train of thought.

"I see wheels are turning, Lou, but you got a minute?"

"Dover, what are you . . ." Then he motioned as one would do to a dog. "Come in, come in. Have a seat." He glanced at his watch. "I've got a few minutes before the meeting starts."

Sure. "Long and short of it, Lou, Stretch was murdered. Autopsy showed mutilation of his groin. There was a bomb in his car."

Cardwell stared at him. "You were at the autopsy?"

"Right."

"Why? And besides, you didn't clear it with me."

"I was on my own time. You gave me days off."

He shook his head. "Yeah, to get some rest and get your head straight. Not to go crashing autopsies and conjuring up murder theories."

"Lou, it wasn't an accident."

"The patrolman thought it was."

"It looked like one. But if you study the scene, Stretch's body, and the car, you can see a bomb exploded prior to the crash. That's murder one."

The lieutenant lit up, coughed, then said, "Hold on. How do you know the gas tank didn't just explode?"

"Burn marks on the road and scorched brush at the lip of the canyon. Besides, Stretch drove like a pro—he never lost control. I called him the Freeway Ferret."

Cardwell ignored the metaphor, the illiterate prick. "Did the coroner's deputy call it a homicide?"

"He's suspicious. Still running some tests. But mean-while—"

"So how do you know there was a bomb?"

"ATF examined the car, and they—"

"What?" Cardwell came halfway out of his chair, then plopped back down as though his legs had collapsed. "Let me get this straight," he said, then took a monster drag. "Someone from ATF investigated Stretch's car?"

"Yeah, and they found—"

"I don't give a shit what they found," he said, his wan complexion all blotchy. "What I want to know is why the fuck ATF was examining a car in our impound lot that belonged to a deceased member of our squad."

That's all Stretch is, a deceased member of our squad?

"Can you tell me that, Dover?"

"Fucking right, I asked him to."

Cardwell's eyes bugged. He flicked off an ash. Glared at Dover.

"Lou, I saw a hole blown in his engine, and his balls were—"

"Wait a minute." He held his hands up in front of him. "Okay, okay. No use in us getting upset here."

"Us?"

"Dover, why'd you do this without advising me?"

"I wasn't hiding anything. I just asked a friend at ATF to look at it. Figured my judgment was hazy, I'm too close to the murder."

"Murder? The murder? Man." He took a drag and stubbed out the butt. "Okay, listen, I suppose I understand what you're thinking." He waggled a dismissive hand. "Sorry I got bent out of shape."

Dover shrugged.

"You know us paper pushers. We get caught up in the details of rules and regs. Always worried about some unexpected snafu."

"Gotta watch out for those." He waited, sure there was more.

Cardwell lit a new smoke, inhaled deeply, blew out a heavy cloud.

Dover studied him, recognizing an aspect he'd been trying to place. Put Cardwell in a German uniform, he'd pass as a skinny Erich von Stroheim, the actor who played the arrogant Nazi officer. He was only missing the riding crop.

"Who'd you contact at ATF?" he said. Bit of the SS there. *Achtung.*

Dover debated, but he needed cooperation. "Don Harsha."

Cardwell nodded. "And he thought there was a bomb?"

"Said it could've been C-4."

"Jesus! Was it guesswork, or did he test it?"

"Quick field test. He'll do a full crime scene tomorrow."

Cardwell scratched some notes on a pad. "I'll have Eddie and Deadeye check this out, and I'll bring in our bomb squad."

"Good call."

"And I'll coordinate the matter with ATF."

Cardwell seemed to be getting into it. Maybe he did care that Stretch had been killed. Maybe he wasn't a total dickhead after all.

"We're not gonna let the feds scoop us on this. After all, it was our guy got hit, we have priority. And I'll handle any press release."

Settled that question.

Chapter 6

At the fire station, Kirk McLaren was buffing his shoes when he realized the question about his promotion was about to be answered. The captain's secretary clumped down the hall, halted at the bulletin board, then squashed a thumbtack through the announcement. All official.

Several others who were playing cards, or reading books, or eating sandwiches spotted her as well. They all figured she'd posted the name of the new lieutenant. Someone would be pleased, three others disappointed as hell.

Eventually they'd saunter by the board and glance at the announcement. Nothing was said the first day of such postings. The next day they'd congratulate the person who'd gotten the nod. Friends of the also-rans would say they'd been screwed, but not to lose hope, because they'd get it next time.

McLaren knew he couldn't wait. He needed the money now. Tasha was starting school this fall, and a good education cost primo bucks.

He polished the hell out of his shoes. Went to the john and took a leak. Then he headed for the board, his heart booming.

Skimming the bureaucratic jargon, he got to the bottom line: The L.A. Fire Department had promoted Edgar Jackson to the position of lieutenant.

Damn. Of the three other guys vying for the position, McLaren had been the least concerned about Jackson. McLaren and the others all had more experience and more savvy about planning assaults on killer fires. It made no sense.

McLaren's legs trembled as he walked away. He spotted Ed tossing out a card at a table in the corner. The guy was in his thirties, capable, dependable, but with only eight years experience, three of those in South Central. Divorced, no children. Ed was friendly, but not one of his close pals, and now for the first time McLaren focused on the fact that Ed was African-American.

When he and Erin discussed the promotion, he told her there were other factors involved in the higher ups' decision. He was thinking about office politics, but he hadn't considered race. He never thought that affirmative action, official or unofficial, would play a crucial part in the choice for this position.

Another dumb assumption by an Irish potato head. It happened elsewhere—college admissions and construction contracts—the plums going to those who could fill the corporations' ethnic quotas.

The Supreme Court said this should occur only in necessary situations. He couldn't see why it was important here. What would make color a vital issue in this job? But nothing else could account for it. How could he tell Erin?

Dover sat in his recliner contemplating what'd taken place the past couple of days, planning his next move. Stretch's wreck was no accident—it'd been arranged. But bombings were a bitch to prove.

Even if ATF found who planted the bomb, Dover realized he still wouldn't know why. Might've been a contract job. He'd still have to find the person behind the scenes and his motive for doing Stretch.

Then a chill crept along the back of his neck. If someone

wanted Stretch dead, odds were he might be next. They worked everything together, bringing down L.A.'s scumbags.

So who had they pissed off? Lots of people, but not the types who plotted bombings. They mostly jailed goons who killed their victims face-to-face. Or face-to-back. Using baseball bats, knives, or pistols.

Terri mentioned a group that was out of control. Enough to kill Stretch for what he knew? Maybe, but Stretch hadn't told him about them.

The big guy had been protecting him again. As per usual. So what now, Stretch? Where do we go from here? Give me a clue.

He took a swig of beer, then shut his eyes and waited. But he got no hints on the telepathy channel. Stretch was probably swapping high fives with some Dream Team in the sky, or kicking Oppenheimer's butt in a super game of chess.

That reminded him of another of Stretch's maxims: Answers to life's problems are found in the psychology of chess. He stared at the chessboard and the figures set to do battle, wondering if the saying could help him in this case.

But nothing came to him. He was drawing another blank. Maybe if you were a master player the maxim rang true, but at his level, it clunked.

Things had calmed to a dull roar, so he pulled a notebook from his desk and began to reread the latest entries, cracking his knuckles as his thoughts spun like cyclones. It had been a day to recall, assess, predict. The agenda was unfolding fast, like a boulder gaining speed downhill.

The plan had congealed, the organization taken shape,

the early protests subsided. Years now since the plan was devised. Or kindled.

In perfect irony, the L.A. riots had germinated the project. And when the ragheads blew up the World Trade Center and the Pentagon, all of America realized the country was being destroyed by foreigners and misfits. Hailstorms of fire and destruction, and the awful loss of life during both the L.A. riots and the New York disasters had caused the seeds to take root, sprout, and reach fruition.

Three days of mayhem in South Central and a day of Hell on earth in New York, followed by months of graphic reminders of the violence, had informed rational people they'd seen the eye of the beast. Much like the mythic Hydra, the hateful fury seemed to grow two heads for each lopped off. It would have to be destroyed by a Herculean effort before it rampaged again.

He fiddled with the notebook. L.A. and America had deteriorated for years. Minority groups had exploded in numbers and dwindled in productivity, while spies and terrorists moved freely within the country, working hard to destroy our democratic society. The big problems being that whites had supported the deadbeat minorities and had too-long ignored the swarthy terrorists.

Gangbangers held neighborhoods hostage while they sold dope and sprayed public areas with automatic weapons. The Mexes got sloshed on street corners, blared their raucous music, and tooled the streets in their moronic lowriders. Chinks worked, but they never learned English, crammed families of twelve in small apartments, and added zip to the community. Now the fucking Muslims were outright blowing up America and its institutions.

He worked at a stiff joint in his finger. The blacks pointed to slavery and their mistreatment by the whites as the wellspring of their problems. But slavery was ancient history. And poverty could be overcome by strong moral values, hard work, and education, not by welfare handouts or affirmative action job giveaways.

And the camel jocks had the nerve to call us infidels. They should be wiped out here and blown away and buried in their sand dunes and caves in Afghanistan, Iraq, Iran, Syria, even Saudi Arabia. Give 'em a little napalm solution.

Blacks, Mexes, Chinks, Arabs, whatever—all a tidal wave of humanity as worthless as salt water in the desert. Dregs that would swell until they poured over this great country, pulling the decent folk down to drown in the morass. If they didn't blow us off the map or poison us first.

He banged the desktop with his fist. His jaw muscles clenched. There was no rational way to deal with these savages. They emerged from the jungle, the mountains, the deserts—people with no souls, no morals, no values. All plain violent by nature.

All right, assholes. He tilted his chair back. And he smiled, because he knew their innate streak of violence would be their downfall, leading them like lemmings to their ruin and destruction.

He jotted ideas in the notebook—some matters to discuss at tomorrow night's meeting. When he was satisfied, he closed the notebook, placed it back atop a large scrapbook, and locked the drawer. Then he allowed himself a moment of smug satisfaction.

The plan was so simple as to be brilliant. They live by the sword, and they so perish. Wiped off the face of the earth. He was convinced that he was part of a plan that would solve the country's problems. So his grandchildren could enjoy a brighter future.

* * * * *

Dover stared at the computer; he had to crack the code. It'd be the quickest way to identify The Untouchables and maybe even to solve Stretch's murder, because they could be the out-of-control group Stretch had mentioned to Terri. He inserted the diskette.

Could the access code be a random number? No, that wasn't the way Stretch thought. He'd have used something unforgettable. Like one of his maxims: K.I.S.S. (Keep it simple, Stupid.)

He punched that in, but it didn't work.

Or maybe one of the carrot top's favorites: Fine as W-I-N-E. But no, that one soured, too.

He'd ask Terri for Stretch's SAT score and his graduation date from college. The dates he entered and left the Marines. Go fish.

Just then, April called. She wanted to see how he was doing. He didn't want to tell her the bizarre developments—some weirdo blew Stretch up, and I'm trying to hack into a computer for a clue, so wish me luck.

He asked how things were in show biz. No offers at present, but she had more auditions. Break a leg, he said. They made a date, then he hung up.

After another hour of trying combinations, he flipped off the machine. As the screen went blank, his mind replayed the video of Stretch's car taking the curve, exploding, hurtling down the hillside. Plastic explosive with a time device; someone who knew their stuff. But who wanted Stretch dead? And why?

He shed his clothes. He had no answers, and he wasn't likely to puzzle it out tonight. He was bone-weary and brain dead.

Out of habit he skimmed the movie schedule. Some

good flicks: *Dirty Harry, The French Connection,* and *Bullitt,* with Steve McQueen. But he'd have to pass tonight. Big day tomorrow.

He hated cop funerals with their pomp, formality, and rigid posturings. Too militaristic. Uniforms, rifles, stern-faced men standing straight and stiff.

He'd do it for Stretch and for Terri. But he'd be more comfortable with an Irish wake or a jazz musician's soulful sendoff. Go out with a flourish.

Besides which, while he was at the cemetery, Harsha would be under the Bronco, finding bits of evidence against the son of a bitch who'd blown Stretch's balls off; he hated to miss that show.

Dover awakened early, having slept in fits and starts. This afternoon Stretch would be laid in a box that was too small for him and lowered into a cavity in the ground. He'd never be back, except as a memory.

After pumping some iron and putting in a half hour on the treadmill, Dover battled the computer for a while. Finally, he shook his head in disgust, punched off the machine, and made for the bathroom. Stepping into the stall, he turned on the shower full blast. He needed a good cleansing of his body, mind, and soul. Something akin to baptism in the river, Elmer Gantry style.

The funeral was at Westwood Village Cemetery. It played out for Dover as a swirl of pressed uniforms, deep voices, and set faces. With pain escaping the throats of friends and relatives like the mourning of doves.

Terri asked him to sit beside her. She looked as pale as a crescent moon hung out to dry in a cobalt sky. She cried very little, looking as if her tears and her hope had been wrung out.

Still, she radiated a solemn beauty. Some spirit seemed to illuminate her face. She grasped his hand, squeezing it from time to time, probably when the pain sought to rise up and crush her.

C-r-r-r-a-a-a-c-k-k a-c-c-k-k-k! went the rifles. Terri jumped. The gleaming bolts slid open, then rammed home. Twice more, shots cleaved the smoggy air.

The riderless horse plodded by. No destination. Not a glimmer of prospect.

A swarm of police helicopters buzzed in and hung suspended in midair. Their rotors whirling in a whop-whop fashion, they canted to view the casket. Having paid their respects, the clamorous machines tilted and veered away.

The flag was folded and presented. Terri hesitated, then took it in trembling hands. The casket was lowered and a final prayer intoned. Friends and family passed by to give their condolences. Blue jays rose, took wing, and fanned out in all directions, and mourning doves grew silent and faded.

Soon it was just Terri and him staring at the gaping hole and the oak casket within. Stretch's spirit had flown, and his ruined remains were too tragic to view. All that remained were the dregs of life.

She stared at the shiny box, as though it might speak to her. But it was still and silent. And then her tears came. She shuddered, and Dover put his arm around her. She leaned against him, her head down, her hand to her face.

Looking up at him she said, "The worst thing is not having Stretch to talk to about this. He'd have known exactly how I feel."

Now tears pooled in his eyes. "He was always the one I told my problems to." And in that moment his fury about Stretch's death, the need to know who had killed him, and the craving to exact revenge all loosened their stranglehold long enough for him to face the awful loss of a true friend. And to feel the pain.

"That house has gone so cold without him," Terri said. "It's just a place now, not a home anymore. There's no life in it."

"How can I help?"

"Just don't forget about me for a while, at least until I regain my sanity. Last night I walked around the neighborhood for an hour. I didn't see anything until I noticed I was back in front of my house."

"Walking around asleep is one of my specialties. Next time, call me, and I'll join you. We'll be twin somnambulists."

She smiled and squeezed his arm. "I'll need your company at times. Then sometimes I'll want to sink into a black funk all alone."

Though the sun had claimed the sky, Dover felt a chill snake up his spine. Like the Angel of Death had just passed over them. He looked across the green expanse and said, "You ready to leave?"

She glanced at the coffin, solid and polished but still mute, then clutching the flag to her breast, spun around, and walked away.

He followed, as silent as the casket.

Then she turned to him. "Have you found out anything?"

"You mean on the computer?"

"That's not all you've been checking, is it?"

Had Stretch told her?

"I haven't broken the code. But some things look, well, a bit . . ."

"Suspicious?"

"You could say that."

"I knew it. I want to know everything."

He opened the car door and she slid in.

He got in, but before he fired up the engine, he appraised her. "I thought this might not be a good time to talk about it."

"I don't expect many good times for anything in my life for a while. But I need to know what happened."

As they drove, he told her what he'd found out, and what he'd do next.

She let out a deep breath. "I knew it wasn't an accident." She gripped his arm. "But who could have done it? And why Stretch?"

"Tough questions. But I'll get the answers. You can be sure of that."

Chapter 7

At Terri's house, aromas of fried chicken and hot rolls filled the air, and long tables held a small army's supply of salads, casseroles, and desserts. Throughout the rooms, clusters of people produced a mesmerizing babble of conversation. Dover nibbled some food, chatted a bit, then stood in a corner of the living room feeling drained.

He scanned the various reminders of Stretch all around the room. In the large bookcases were several trophies, team photos, and game balls the big guy had been awarded. Stretch had said that his favorite item among all this memorabilia was the game ball from an NCAA Final Four Tournament playoff.

Tennessee made it to the semi-finals against Louisville. A point behind with two seconds left, Stretch took a pass at the top of the key and put up his patented turn-around jumper. Ripped the cords. Then they lost the final game.

The next season, Stretch hurt his knee, so this game had been his last hurrah. Dover picked up the ball. The score was inked across it, and all the team members and coaches had signed it. His chest got tight as he felt the nubby texture of the ball. Stretch had touched this surface with his talented hands. Dover felt a desperate ache in his throat.

After a while, when he sensed it was proper, he told Terri goodbye.

"Wait a minute," she said, then came back carrying some books. "I found these on the hallway table. Stretch

73

must've put them there not long ago. One of them had this in it."

She handed him a slip of paper on which was written FOR RICOCHET.

"Which one had the note?" he said, glancing at the covers. There was a book on chess, one on quantum mechanics, and another called *Hyperspace*.

"I don't remember. Just take them all."

He laid the books on the seat and fired up the Chevy. It took a minute before he gathered the strength to leave. Would he ever come back here?

As he zipped along the Ventura, he pondered the mysterious group, a bunch who might've wasted his partner. No group was omnipotent—they'd have a weakness, an Achilles' heel. To fight them he'd have to seek them out, locate their soft spot, and go for the underbelly.

It was like any homicide investigation: find who had the motive, means, and opportunity. Examine the victim. Study the crime scene.

Stretch had parked his car outside in a dark driveway. No dog, no outside lights, no alarm system on his car. Probably left it unlocked, as if he still lived in Tennessee.

The house was set back from the road, and the lot was dotted with several trees. Bushes guarded the driveway's edge, blocking the neighbors' view. Not a busy road, no street lights. Guy with a bomb parks his car, walks a block, sneaks alongside the bushes. Then he ducks under the Bronco and does the deed. Mission accomplished.

So anyone who knew where Stretch lived and who knew how to make a bomb and hook it up to a car would've had unrestricted opportunity to carry it off. But that left motive. Who had wanted to whack Stretch? And for what possible reason?

He delved in his mind into the cases of gory slashings, shootings, beatings, stabbings, and stranglings. Two poisonings. Guy tossed out a twelfth story window. Woman run over with a truck.

Admittedly not a nice clientele, but usually a killer's rage was directed toward the victim. Once caught, the murderer felt relieved and repentant. Most murderers killed only once in their lifetime. Despite movies with cannibals and spooky guys prancing about with butterflies, rarely did a person kill repeatedly or commit mass murder.

And he and Stretch had arrested no bombers. Even the mob guys usually didn't resort to that. Too big a fuss, too much publicity—and hey, the ocean so handy. Let the fish clean the carcass.

He swung onto the Hollywood Freeway. That meant no revenge motive. At least, not with any bomber he knew. He saw no jealousy angle. Stretch never chased skirts. He spent his paycheck on food and his home, so no extortion potential. What the hell could it be?

Back to the group that was out of control. What group? He still couldn't believe Stretch was in a group and didn't tell him. And what were they doing they might consider important enough to kill over?

Terri said there was a computer connection. The Untouchables file. If he could decipher the code, maybe the file would give him a handle on this shadowy group.

Four lousy digits. Numbers, letters, or a word. Not that many combinations. He knew hackers used software programs to run possibilities when they were trying to crack data banks. Maybe an expert could tell him the numerical combinations from 0000 to 9999, and any combination of all the letters of the alphabet, or a mixture of both.

So get into the file and find the motive.

Then a glimmer of insight lit up his frantic brain. Stretch was always armed, was a crack shot, and spent most of his time around other armed cops. Small window of opportunity. Not an easy target for your stabbing, shooting, or bashing with a tire tool, ball bat, or whatever. Besides, all that stuff left clues, helping the homicide dicks identify the killer.

Not so dumb after all, setting a bomb to explode when Stretch wound through the mountains. Logical that he'd career off the road, crash into the canyon, then burn up. Just another accident.

Bombings were hard to solve. For one simple reason: The bomb scattered most of the evidence. Going over a cliff would help. And the guy who made it would be shrewd enough to use common parts.

So focus on the means to commit the crime. Surely C-4 couldn't be that easy to obtain. Unless you were in the military, had ever been, or knew someone who had been, or you were in the National Guard or a militant group, or stole it from any of the above or bought it from a crook. Damn.

Which meant that to solve this case he'd have to find the motive as the only way to identify the killer. And he knew of no reason for anyone to blow the balls off one of the greatest guys in L.A. At least, not any one specific person.

If you threw in the X-factor of an anonymous group involved, you might have an unsolvable crime. But he couldn't shitcan this one. No way.

Dover approached the large impound lot filled with cars and trucks of every description, all surrounded by a tall chain link security fence. He found a parking spot, screeched to a halt, then gripped the wheel hard, trying to find an anchor to steady his whirling brain. Like everyone else in this fractured city, he was stretching as far as he could for a golden ring that even if he grabbed it would likely be brass. And it wouldn't be a ticket to heaven, just a token worth a few more turns on the same merry-go-round.

Not like the days of Ferris wheels and baseball and picnics in Kansas. For a boy, those were carefree and happy times, with only a few exceptions. One he recalled was the day he played cowboy in a pasture on his grandpa's ranch.

Summertime, the sun blazing, and a ten-year-old wouldn't stay inside for anything. But by noon, he grew weary of battling bloodthirsty Indians. He headed for a patch of shade trees bordering a small creek.

As he neared the water, he spotted a branch on the ground and scooped it up. He whipped it through the air, back and forth. A perfect sword for fighting evil guardsmen, like the Three Musketeers always did.

He dropped his new weapon, fell to his knees, then lay on his belly at the edge of the creek, where he scooped handfuls of cold water, slurping them down. When he'd had enough, he rolled onto his back, put an arm under his head, and watched the leaves of a cottonwood tremble in the midday breeze. Clouds as big as grain storage elevators floated across the huge blue sky.

Then the rattles of the fury coiled a couple feet to his left buzzed like a chainsaw in his ear. Grandpa, help! he thought. But he knew the big man was haying another pasture with the hired hand. Grandma would be in the house. He'd brought a sandwich in his pack instead of going back for lunch.

It was just him and the snake. No one could help him fight it. He reached behind his head, searching the ground. His gaze held on the snake, whose forked tongue darted out and back, its eyes as hard as chips of flint.

Any moment the rattler might strike. The fangs would sink into his arm or side. He was so far from the house he'd never make it back in time. His fingers felt the stick, then gripped it. This was his only weapon against the monster.

He clenched his teeth, then swung the stick as hard as he could, whipping his wrist and turning his shoulder into it as he came off the ground in the same motion. The snake struck, its mouth as wide as the gates of hell, fangs curved and white. But the stick whacked against its side, deflecting it just enough. Legs scrambling, he jumped up and ran so hard and fast his feet seemed not to touch the ground.

Grandma could tell he was scared, and she hugged him and patted his back, comforting him, but she didn't want to hear about the snake. "You better not be tellin' that tall tale to Grandpa," she said. "He might tan your backside for fibbin'." And so he hadn't. He never told Grandpa, or his mom, or any of his friends. Only he and the snake knew it ever happened.

But it made him realize that when monsters attacked, you had to fight them by yourself the best you could. No one would help you. If you failed, that was too bad. And if you triumphed, no one believed it or wanted to hear about it. The only score for victories or defeats was kept in your head, or on your tombstone.

He opened his eyes, released his hold on the wheel, and climbed out of the car. Another dragon to slay. By himself.

He approached Stretch's Bronco, taking in the scene. Something was off. Three men stood there gawking at it—Eddie, Deadeye, and a guy in an LAPD bomb squad uniform—but Harsha was nowhere in sight.

Eddie spotted him. "Hey, Ricochet, how ya doin'?"

Sensitive question. "What've you found? And where's Harsha?"

"He didn't show. Some other ATF guy filled in. He went to the office to make a call. Oh, here he comes."

Dover turned to see a chipper guy in his forties, shiny pate, steel-rim glasses. Short, but animated. The man extended his hand.

"Duncan, Claude Duncan, ATF. Supervisor for this area."

"Dover, LAPD Homicide. Where's Harsha?"

The eyes shifted. "He had to handle a matter in Riverside."

"Will he be working this case?"

"I'll handle it today. He can take over when he gets back."

"That's good. He knows what's going on. What've you found?"

"Not much." He shrugged and gazed across the lot.

Dover turned to stare at Eddie, his eyes wide.

Eddie said, "The car's so burned out the bomb squad guy can't tell if an explosion happened before the crash or by the gas going off."

The bomb squad officer was stocky, with messy hair and a deadpan face. Name tag read Sgt. Fennimore. He stood wiping his hands on a rag.

"That right?" Dover asked him.

"That's about it. There's flamed-out spots, but gas can collect in pockets and go off like a bomb."

"But did you do any tests? Harsha found traces of C-4."

Fennimore jerked his head toward a machine resting on the ground ten feet from the hood of the ruined Ford. "That's our 'sniffer.' She collects vapors and analyzes them a damn lot better than any field test."

"You're telling me field tests aren't—"

"They only give indications. They can't be used as evidence."

"But the test showed C-4. And Harsha saw traces of it."

"He was wrong. The 'sniffer' got no C-4. There were some particles of clay down there. Looks about like C-4, you might say."

"But he . . ." Dover collected himself. "Did you see any duct tape or bits of electrical wire under there? Maybe battery fragments?"

The bomb guy gave a look that said, Can you believe this mutt? Sighing, he said, "There was a piece of electrical tape. It means nothing. Someone could have been working on anything and stuck some tape there. And I didn't see any wires." He lifted his shoulders.

Stretch's murder was being shrugged off. Dover felt his fists clench. This guy might get a bomb on his chin.

"As to battery fragments," he said, "I saw zero. A car couldn't do cartwheels, be hauled out of a ravine, and there'd be any little fragments left. Besides, that would indicate a sophisticated device."

The bomb squad officer shook his head and walked away, then he stopped and looked back.

"Yeah?" said Dover.

"Just that I saw no indication of a bomb. 'Course I've only been doing this fifteen years. I'll send my report."

"Don't bother."

The guy bristled, but he turned and stalked off.

"Hey, Rick," Deadeye said, "we've been all over this scrap pile, and we ain't seen nothin' wrong. It's just busted up and burned out."

He took a deep breath. "Okay, I'm a little worked up. You know, I just came from the funeral."

They nodded, their faces sympathetic.

"Anyway," he turned to Duncan, "what about your report?"

He coughed. "I'll send it to your lieutenant. Be a few days."

"Fine." He eyed Eddie and Deadeye, then walked away.

He'd see what their reports said and show them to Harsha. Go a few more turns on the merry-go-round. And bring a stick.

Chapter 8

Dover slammed his condo door, snatched up the phone, and punched in the number for ATF. The receptionist said Harsha was out of the office. When pressed, she said he was out-of-town.

Maybe he was being paranoid. Maybe Harsha *had* been called out on a new case. But what about the field test, was it valid or not?

He had to talk with Harsha. But he didn't call back asking for his number. Didn't want to press the issue. For now, let them think he bought their cow flop. He'd be cool and let this farce run its course.

He went straight to the bedroom. He hated to face the computer again, but there wasn't anything else to do until he talked to Harsha. There was an answer to every puzzle, but could he find it?

The four blank spaces glowed on the screen. He rubbed his chin. Okay, he'd try a new tack. Stretch had majored in history. Maybe some important historical date would get him into the file.

He opened the notebook to the numbers he'd tried. Here's one he hadn't used. Columbus sailed the ocean blue—tap, tap, tap, 1492. No luck. Wars were good, numerically speaking. War of American Independence, 1775, ended 1783. Nope. The War of 1812. Nah. Civil War, 1861, ended in 1865. Slavery abolished forever. You bet. No cigar. Try World War I, 1914. Victory in 1918. World War II, began 1939, ended 1945. Nope. Korean War, 1950 to 1953. No dice.

Vietnam conflict started in . . . hell. He pulled a desk encyclopedia from the bookcase in the living room. Back at the computer he typed in 1957. And the South Vietnamese government was overthrown in 1963. The U.S. got involved hot and heavy, we took on the Viet Cong, 1964. Just a police action, though, which only lasted until 1973. Then we pulled out and North Vietnam won the war in 1975. None of the numbers worked. Ain't war hell?

Try other battles, crusades, and treaties. He skimmed the pages. William of Normandy kicks butt in England, 1066. Magna Carta, 1215. Spanish Inquisition starts, 1478. In 1517, the Reformation begins. Pilgrims land in Cape Cod in 1620. Boston Tea Party, 1773.

Assassinations. John F. Kennedy, 1963. Martin Luther King and Bobby Kennedy, 1968. The good, they always die young.

Like Stretch. His dreams of pro basketball wrenched away from him, and then his life of happiness with Terri. So unfair that a man's life can be pummeled and tossed and yanked about until his body is torn to shreds. Fate: cruel and uncertain. By human standards.

But at least Stretch had lived somewhat of a good life. Not like a crack baby who knows only agony, torture, and pain from birth to death. Unforgivable in even the most barbarous of worlds.

Stretch had been given his shot. He'd had the opportunity to dream and to work to see some of those dreams come true. He'd loved basketball. The ebb and flow of a game, he'd once said, was like a force of life itself. He felt as if he were creating a bit of history.

And Dover supposed he had. Stretch had enjoyed some shining moments in the sport. Not many people could claim that much. Not many mere mortals won trophies and game balls for their shelves.

He stared at the four blank spaces. Trophies and game balls. Hmm. An NCAA Final Four Tournament game ball. He ran a hand through his hair. Saw himself in Terri's living room, holding the ball. Forced himself to concentrate. The score. It was . . . one point difference, something like . . . and he smiled.

Okay, 80 to 79, thanks to Stretch's turn-around jumper that ripped the cords—swish! He tapped in 8079, then held his breath.

Hot damn! Unreal. The Untouchables file sprang into view. He jumped up and did a little victory dance around his chair. When he'd expended most of his nervous energy, he sat back down, ready to make some headway.

Now that he thought about it, Stretch was never one to make it easy for him. The big guy used to say that fine wine took the longest to make. Whatever.

He studied the file a bit, then printed it out. Double-spaced, it was a page of names followed by telephone numbers. None of them were familiar to him, and he couldn't imagine why they were untouchable.

But Stretch usually had a method to his madness.

Jarroll kicked broken bricks and other bits of rubble on his way home that afternoon because the school lunch, his main meal of the day, had been fish sticks and macaroni. He'd gagged down a few bites, then bagged the rest of the shit, and his stomach had felt wrung out and jittery ever since.

As he walked past an alley, he was thinking on grabbing a banana off old man Roosevelt's fruit stand. He wasn't scoping where he was going. Never noticed three dark shapes leaned against a wall.

A figure moved toward him quick and quiet. A hand grabbed his shoulder and yanked him into the alley. The specters converged.

He caught a fist in the gut, knocking out his wind and buckling his legs. An elbow smashed into his nose, causing a crunch that made him want to puke. A tire iron smashed his kneecap, sending spikes of pain through his leg.

He swung his fists hard, hitting bodies that absorbed the shock without flinching. Then he smacked the side of someone's head. But as the buster went down, another form moved, and a shoe caught him right in the balls.

He held his crotch and went to his knees. Blows crashed on his head, arms, and shoulders. He collapsed to the ground, and kicks slammed into his ribs, legs, and ass. He raised his knees to his chest and threw his arms up over his head. Blood spurted from his swollen nose. He felt cold all over, and darkness seeped in.

After a while, his mind came back. First it registered that the blows had stopped. Next it told him he'd be feeling the pain of the bruises and cuts and lumps for a long time. He tried moving his arms and hands, then his legs. They were stiff and hurt like hell, but they didn't feel broken. He ran his tongue over his teeth; they were there.

Then he touched his nose, and felt a sharp pain. It was like a fat sausage. Seemed like he was breathing through cotton.

Now he sensed movement, and when he looked up, he made out the three figures still standing there. He crossed his hands over his face and drew himself into a ball. This time they'd kill him for sure. No way he could fight or run. He just hoped it'd be over fast.

But several seconds passed, and he wasn't waled on. He risked taking a peek. One of the guys lit a cigarette. It was

Skull, and he was smiling. One of the other shapes was enormous. Had to be Gorilla. Third one looked like Freak. Jarroll's heart was a chunk of ice.

"You awake now, little brother?" asked Skull, exhaling a stream of smoke real smooth and easy.

"Uh huh." His tongue touched his split lip.

"You put 'em up damn good for a li'l dog," Skull said, rubbing his jaw.

"Uh huh." When were they gonna take him out?

"So you with us now," Skull said with a quick nod.

"Huh?"

"Eight-Tray Gangsters, dog. You got jumped into our unit."

Jarroll struggled to sit up. He hurt in a hundred places, but his mind was clear. "You sayin' . . . ?" He couldn't ask it. Couldn't believe it.

Skull moved toward him, and Jarroll fought against covering up. He struggled to his knees, then to his feet, wobbling on weak legs. But he stared the leader in the eye.

The dude flipped the cigarette away, then smacked him on the shoulder. "Come by on Friday. We be making some plans. You can put in some work for the 'hood."

"Tha's cool," he said.

"Fact," Skull said, appraising him, "you be Hammer now." He glanced at the others. "That's good, huh?"

They nodded and grunted their approval.

"Then we catch up with you, Hammer."

Jarroll watched in awe as the three brothers swaggered down the sidewalk. They was tough, straight up dudes. His homeboys.

Morning came with its usual slings and arrows of outrageous sunshine needling Dover awake. Worse yet, he realized the shadowy group that had stalked him through his nightmares most of the night wouldn't disappear with the dawn. He stumbled to the kitchen where he fixed cereal, toast, and juice, then ate as he browsed the headlines, trying to get the bastards off his mind.

Big producer announces megabucks film starring mammoth action hero and super sexy actress, directed by mythical boy wonder. Wildfires engulf palatial homes of movie stars in the brushy hills of Malibu. Mudslides to follow as the second half of a double bill, with several houses primed to slither down the hillside on the murky gloop.

More controversy about affirmative action. Done all it can do, prejudicial in itself, abolish it. No, bias still alive, keep the plan to maintain equal opportunity, only bigots are against it. Intriguing question, especially in L.A., where whites were in the minority.

And just part of the bigger issue of racial groups continually gnawing at each other's throats. With pressure building like a shaken bottle of champagne ready to blow at any time. Sadly, he didn't see any solutions on the horizon; folks seldom changed their attitudes.

He tossed the paper in the trash, showered and shaved, then slipped into a gray suit and loafers and holstered up his Beretta. Ready for work, physically, but not mentally. He knew it was going to be hard, but he never expected such a wrenching reluctance.

The commute wasn't awful. And at the parking lot, Chuck seemed glad to see him back in his routine. Some folks don't like change. Like in Kansas, where new ideas had to be tempered by resistance and forged in the blast furnace of distrust. Couldn't say that about California. New fads sprang to life with a full head of steam, then dissipated into the air before he even heard of them.

Up the stairs to get the heart pounding. Try to be calm. Don't sink your fangs into Eddie's oversized neck or strangle the Lou for sending such dunderheads to uninvestigate Stretch's crash. Eddie, Deadeye, and . . . oh, yeah, Fennimore. The Three Stooges of sleuthing perform feats of prestidigitation: Thumbs up their asses, their brains frolicking in Disneyland.

He surveyed the squad room. Eddie glanced his way then looked back at Ken Jenkins, a new guy on the squad. The kid was probably asking Eddie's advice on a case. He'd have to straighten out the rookie later.

Cardwell was staked out at the water cooler, trying to be one of the guys. He blathered on about the time he arrested the dope dealers in Inglewood. The body language never changed—the Lou had the story choreographed like a Janet Jackson chorus number.

Included in the audience was a curvaceous brunette from Records, Paulette, who dazzled in her micro-mini-skirt, snuggling a couple of lucky record folders up against her 36D ballast, paralyzing the brain pans of a dozen homicide dicks.

As Dover neared, the Lou told the part where he kicked the feet out from under the doper in the kitchen who was clutching an Uzi. He thereby disabled the baddest muthafucka of them all and defused any attack on the brave cops. All in the line of death-defying duty.

Dover, knowing the not-so-dauntless Lou, had checked out the story with another member of the raid team. Tony Quesada said Cardwell and three others attacked the steel-plated dope den door with a cast-iron battering ram. On the third swing, the door flew off the hinges, sending Cardwell stumbling into the room. Dover imagined Chevy Chase headed for a pratfall.

There was bacon grease on the linoleum, and Cardwell skidded, then went down in a full body slide. Tony swore he could've made the Dodgers. The kamikaze kop clipped the Uzi-toter's ankles, dropping him like a bowling pin.

It'd been Cardwell's only moment of glory on the Job prior to scrambling through the administrative hierarchy toward whatever pinnacle the poor mope envisioned, and he never failed to trot out the threadbare tale whenever a new guy came on the squad, senior brass was around, or a lush female entered the harassment zone.

Cardwell said he grabbed the Uzi and covered the dopers. Tony said the goof's hand happened to land atop it, and when he lurched to his feet, dazed from his crash and slide, everyone, dopers and cops alike, hit the floor. A SWAT guy disarmed him, to everyone's relief.

Listening to the bullshit was worth it, though, just to see Paulette's eyes get as big as Alicia Silverstone's, and to watch her breathe deeply in amazement, bending her folders like dousing rods. The view from the south end must've been spectacular too, as everyone sitting in that area dropped and retrieved pencils several times during the Lou's soliloquy.

Cardwell basked in the glory, bumping against the Magnificent Two as he reached over to fumble a cup from the dispenser. He swigged several gulps as he laser-eyed the departure of the swiveling skirt. Leather always fascinated cops.

As she turned a corner, Cardwell's smile dropped off his face. The Anthony Perkins bit again. "Dover," he jerked his head, "in my office. Now."

Dover trudged into the dead air zone and dropped into a chair. Cardwell sparked a cigarette. His lungs must rival rawhide.

"Smoggy day, huh?" Dover said. "Especially in here."

"Close the door, Dover."

Damn. He stepped to the door and whipped it closed. Cardwell blew smoke at the ceiling. Dover could tell his nerves were twangy.

"We made a decision while you were gone."

The mope made it sound as if he'd been hunkered down in a rubber room for a very long time. "I'll play. What's that, Lou?"

"I feel it was the best way to handle this unfortunate situation."

"Hey! New cars for everyone?"

"Of course not. It concerns the partner thing . . ."

"You mean for me? Don't think I'm ready—"

"The Captain picked someone," he blurted out. "He'll be here soon. Name's Garrett Jones, out of Vice. To be frank, he's not who I would have chosen, but you know how the department's so politically correct."

Dover's brow crinkled. "What the hell are you talking about?"

"He's black." He nodded, as if confirming an incredulous fact.

"I don't care if he's purple. Does he have a good record? Have you talked with him? Can he fit in on the squad and work this stuff without becoming a prima donna? Not puke when he sees a stiff?"

"No, I haven't . . . I mean, the Captain sent him over, so he's ours. There's no way to fight it. We've got to go along—"

"To get along," Dover said, shaking his head. Then someone knocked on the door. Cardwell stared with a look as lost as that of Talia Shire in *Rocky*.

"I got it," Dover said, and opened the door.

The guy studied him. "Garrett Jones. They said to report here."

He gaped at the wiry man with his baggy blue pants, bright ruby shirt, and formless tan sports coat. Black sneaks with red laces on the left one, blue on the right. Eyes as piercing as solar flares.

"Rick Dover," he said, sticking out his hand.

Jones was stronger than he looked. He smiled, revealing a star-shaped indentation in a gold front tooth. He stepped inside, then seemed to appraise Cardwell. "Lieutenant," he said.

Cardwell said, "Jones, good to see you. Sit down. Sit down."

Jones did, crossing his legs, waiting for the patter.

Cardwell speared him with an imperial glare, like Yul Brynner in *The King and I*. "You'll find we do things differently on the Homicide Squad."

After they left Cardwell's sparkling company, Dover asked Jones, "You got a department ride?"

"Old hoopty Dodge. Ain't nothin' hot."

"Better than a Ferrari F50 in the shop."

Jones shrugged.

"So I guess I'd better tell you about Homicide."

Now his eyes shone.

Dover explained the operations in detail. Of course, it was all duck soup until you caught your first dead body. That's when you found out if you were made of the right stuff. Or if you were clueless.

As he talked, Dover imagined what his stepdad's reaction would've been to his new "partner." Something like, "Ain't that shine lookin' fine? For a jungle bunny." Real classy guy, his stepdad. Called 'em as he saw 'em, and saw 'em all the same. A cross between Archie Bunker and David Duke.

Jones told him his history on the Job. He'd worked a few years on Patrol, handled a stint in Burglary, then did some time with Vice. He liked the pizzazz of undercover work. Hated handing out tickets.

All well and good, Dover thought. But now he was dipping his toe into the heavy stuff. Homicide was as dicey as it got.

A good detective had common sense, bravery, and guts. But no one knew the depth of their own character until they'd had a baptism of fire. Homicide cases put you in the crucible; lots of guys couldn't take the heat.

They talked the rest of the morning, then went for lunch. Jones had a good sense of humor, seemed stable, and didn't look like he crawled out of a bottle every morning. And he ate two Delgado's hot dogs without farting in the car or doubling over with cramps. A cast iron stomach was a must.

Back in the squad room they reviewed Dover's cases. Jones made some good suggestions. Never hurt to have a detached mind review a case.

Surprisingly, Dover didn't already hate his new "partner."

The shift ended, and Jones took off. Then Dover steeled himself to call the shop and chat with the mystic mechanic. Fingers crossed.

"Sure, Detective Dover. It'll be ready any day now, no prob."

"Titus, it's been in the shop two weeks. The motor was missing a little. A minor tune-up should've handled it."

"Let's see, that was the Riviera?"

"No, no, the Grand Prix. Dark blue."

"Right, right. With these electronic engines you gotta

check out the whole system. Anything outta sync'll screw up the works."

"Did you check the fuel filters, fuel pump, stuff like that?"

"Prob'bly. We got a bunch of clunkers. I can't recall ev'ry one."

"Right. But could I get another car to drive until it's repaired?"

"Let me check." A few seconds later, Dover heard the distinct thunk of a soft drink can hitting the bottom of the chute. Then a click and a fizz.

"Sorry, nothing's left in the shop." Dover heard him take a gulp.

"But the Pontiac's about ready, right?"

"Any day now," he said, burping. "I'll let you know."

When he got home, Dover felt whipped. Explaining things to a new homicide dick was draining. Not to mention dealing with Titus.

He tossed his jacket on the back of a chair and snatched a frosty paralyzer from the fridge. Better than Tai Chi or yoga. *Salud.*

He dropped into his recliner, sipped the suds, and stared at the TV. He'd told April he'd see her tonight. He felt as horny as Colin Farrell, but his body was trashed. Was he up to a command performance? April could be as demanding as a fledgling director on a tight budget.

Another cool swallow trickled down his throat and into his stomach, bubbling alcohol into his veins. Ah, yes. He heard the call of the wild.

He reached for the phone, and it shrilled at him. His heart went skittish as a colt. He blew out a breath, then lifted the receiver.

"Rick, I'm glad you're there."

"Hi, Terri. Is something the matter?"

"Ohhh," she said, "I wanted to act cool, but I'm pretty shaky."

"Why? What—"

"I had coffee with a friend, just to get out of the house. But when I got back, it was . . ." She was fighting tears.

"Don't be upset. We'll take care of it."

"I'm sorry. Someone broke into the house. It's . . . it's a mess."

"God, Terri, lock your doors. Call the sheriff, turn on the lights, sit in the living room. Better yet, are any of your neighbors home?"

"Wait a minute," she said. Then, "None of my close ones are."

"Okay, make the call. I'll be there as quick as I can."

Chapter 9

When Dover wheeled into the driveway, Terri was staring out the front window, her outline shining like a hologram. Princess Leia waiting to be rescued. As he stepped onto the porch, she flung open the door.

"Oh, Rick," she said, sobbing, "what's going on? First someone kills Stretch, and now they've torn up my home."

"Let me have a look."

The place was a mess, but not chaotic. Stuff had been dumped out of drawers and cushions yanked off furniture. Books were pulled from their shelves and dropped on the carpet. The house had been tossed. By a pro.

"Did you call the Sheriff's Department?"

"Yes, as soon as I hung up from talking with you."

"Then I'll look around. When the deputies arrive, call me. I don't want some trigger-happy rookie thinking I'm the local cat burglar."

"Why don't you wait for them?"

He blinked. Not a bad idea. "Nah, I'm too curious."

He pulled out his Beretta and moved through the house room by room, checking closets, behind doors, and under beds. He peeked into all the traditional spots. The house seemed clear.

"The Sheriff's car is here."

A beefy Hispanic, about thirty, and a muscular blue-eyed Anglo in his late twenties tramped to the door. Their uniforms were crisp and neat. Police work could be civilized outside the city.

It took them ten minutes to glance around and fill out their report. They were professional, except for Blue Eyes checking out Terri's short skirt too often. They didn't offer much hope they'd find any stolen items.

Deputy Garcia turned to Terri. "So you lost no jewelry, cash, TVs, VCRs, or firearms. That right, ma'am?"

"As I said, they just took my Apple computer and some disks."

"Looks like they were searching for something. You got any drugs on the premises?"

"Not a crumb, Deputy. Now if that's all you need . . ."

"That's it. We'll let you know if this computer turns up."

Terri let them out, and Dover sank into an easy chair. Then Terri sat on the front edge of the sofa, crossed her legs, and tugged at her skirt. He could see why Blue Eyes was impressed.

"I think the deputy was right," he said.

"About what?"

"This wasn't a usual burglary. They'd have taken anything they could sell or hock. Unless you'd surprised them, which you didn't."

"Then what was it?"

He glanced around. "It was a methodical operation. Not a kid after cash or TVs, and not a junkie looking for a quick score."

"So you're thinking—"

"They knew what they were doing and what they wanted."

"But they took my computer and disks. That stuff was junk. Personal letters, our budget, addresses of family and friends."

"Maybe they were looking for Stretch's computer."

"And took mine by mistake?"

"Only way it makes sense."

"But my Macintosh was in plain sight in the bedroom. And they searched the whole house."

"Yeah, that's odd. Unless they were looking for Stretch's disks."

"The ones you have."

"Um hmm," he replied. He waited a beat. Now she'd ask—

"Did you find out what's on them?"

Damn. Should he involve her any further? "No, I—"

"You did, didn't you?"

He palmed his face. "There was a list of names and phone numbers."

She thought about that, then her gaze flattened. When she looked up, fear darted behind her eyes like butterflies. "Throw the disk away. The computer, too. They'll only bring us trouble."

"I don't think we can—"

"Stretch is gone, and that can't be changed. But I couldn't stand it if something happened to you because of a crazy group he got mixed up in. Please just drop what you're doing."

"I'm afraid it's not that easy. They have to assume we know what's on the disk they're looking for."

"But we don't, not really." Her eyes were wet and pleading now. She looked exactly like Jessica Lange in the grasp of King Kong.

And he felt like Robocop. Insensitive and intransigent. "They can't take that risk. I think our best defense is to analyze what's on it, determine what we're up against, then decide how to fight it."

She shook her head. "I don't have any fight left in me."

He moved to sit beside her on the sofa. She smelled like peach blossoms. "I know how you feel. Let me work it out."

She turned her face to his. "But how can you—"

"Stretch was coming to see me that night, right?"

"That's what I assume."

"And he said something about a group and a computer connection?"

"Yes, but what—"

"Did he say anything else? Maybe another time?"

She blinked her wet blue eyes. Took a deep breath and stared across the room. Tried to remember.

He waited, aware of her closeness.

"He did say something once when he was fooling with his computer, but I didn't understand it."

"What was it?"

"He said something like . . . I think it was . . ." She dug hard for the memory, her forehead scrunched in wrinkles like a bulldog. And then he could tell she had it. Her expression opened like a sunflower, and the words flowed out like nectar. "He said the link for the group was Nisik."

"Nisik?"

"Yes, that was it." She nodded, pleased and relieved.

He pinched his chin, frustrated and disappointed. "I don't know what that is. You're sure he said Nisik?"

"Yes. Uh, no. It was something else that I sounded out as that."

"Something else?"

"It was, like, the letters."

"What letters?"

She squirmed for a moment, then said, "N-C-I-C," and smiled like Julia Roberts.

He slapped his thigh. "My God," he said.

"You know what it means?"

98

"NCIC is the FBI's National Crime Information Center computer. It's the mainframe that lists fugitives, stolen property, arrest records, you name it. Every police agency in the country is linked into it."

"But why would Stretch be involved with that?"

"I don't know," he admitted. "I'll have to check it out."

"But can you . . . how could you enter it?"

"I think I may have the code."

Dover drove home, scheming how he could pry open the group's secret files. At the same time, Kirk McLaren blew a shrill whistle at a South Central community gym. The squeaks and thumps of hi-tops on the wooden floor stopped as all eyes went to him, no longer a fireman, but the referee.

"Charging foul on number thirty-three, blue team," McLaren yelled.

"No way, muthafucka," the rangy kid protested. Sweat trickled down his face. Stamped on his features was the pain of injustice.

"Red side out," McLaren said.

The tall kid glared, then swore and flung the ball away.

The Soldados moved fast. Trailing by two, twenty seconds to play. They whipped the ball around the perimeter. The air was as moist as summer in New Orleans. The only sounds were the screech of shoes and the slap of the ball. Ten seconds left.

A lanky forward broke toward the basket, and took the pass. Two Warriors converged on him. He flipped the ball to a teammate on the baseline.

Number thirty-three was out of position, but he was quick, and he sprang toward the red player like a cheetah after lunch. The Soldado went up high, twisting, and number thirty-three jumped with him, jostling the boy's outstretched arm. But the momentum of the heavier Hispanic kid carried him to the goal. The ball banked against the backboard and dropped through the hoop.

Tie ball game. Time expired. Going into overtime.

But McLaren blew his whistle like a tiny foghorn in the night against the din of the crowd. He pointed a finger at number thirty-three. Called a foul.

There arose a cacophony of derisive whistles, jeers, and curses, blended with delighted screams, claps, and cheers. Number thirty-three was in McLaren's face, screaming. McLaren put his hand on the boy's chest and pushed him back.

"That's enough, son. Let's finish the game."

The slender youth cursed, made faces, and hung his head.

The Soldado toed the free throw line, bounced the ball, and grinned at number thirty-three, then shot the ball upwards. It soared to the hoop and zipped through the net. Soldados seventy-six, Warriors seventy-five.

McLaren strode out of the gym into the cool night, away from the raucous noise, striving bodies, and conflict of competitive sports. He refereed because he believed in the value of sports as good self-discipline. But after tonight's bitter contest, he had his doubts.

Reaching his Honda, he fumbled the keys from his pocket. As he unlocked the door, he could feel a presence behind him.

"Don't turn around, muthafucka, or I'll cut your white ass."

He'd heard that voice before. Number thirty-three.

"Billfold's in my back pocket. There's about forty bucks."

Fingers scrabbled the wallet out. He heard a thump as

the billfold plopped to the asphalt.

"That watch, too," the boy spit out.

He slid his Seiko off his wrist and handed it behind him. He glanced around the parking lot. A couple of small groups were close by, but they were looking in the other direction.

"Now we gonna even up for yo' sorry muthafuckin' calls."

Menace filled the boy's voice. The social mugging was over; it was blood and guts time. McLaren whirled to his right and whipped his arm across his body. He deflected the blade, but not enough.

The point caught his right side. The sharp blade thrust through the meat and came free. Warm blood spurted from the sliced flesh, and McLaren felt his head go light.

But the kid was off balance, as though he'd lunged for a ball and someone had tipped it out of his grasp, so Mc-Laren reacted before things got worse. He shot a straight left punch into the middle of the kid's face, flattening his nose. Protest that, shit head.

The boy straightened, blood running from his nose, his lip cut. Then he brought up his left hand to protect his face and held the knife out toward McLaren. Good defense, but with an opening.

McLaren lifted his knee and kicked hard, his shoe catching the boy in the groin. The kid's eyes bugged out like a frog's. The knife hit the ground as the boy cupped his genitals.

Number thirty-three was out of this game. His shoulders and head drooped forward. Looked like he might puke.

McLaren kicked the knife, sending it spinning away. He scooped up his wallet, yanked open the car door, and slid inside. With shaking hands, he cranked the ignition. He squealed into the street, then glanced back. A cluster of people had gathered around the sagging boy, patting his back and looking around for assistance.

He kept a tight grip on the wheel. Now pain flared in the ripped flesh, and he winced. At the next light, he turned toward a hospital.

He'd tried to be helpful to folks around here, but this was beyond his patience. He was out of it now. Anyway, when he resigned his referee's job, it would give him another night each week to be with Tasha.

When Dover got to his condo, the light was flashing on his answering machine. Damn, he'd forgotten to call April. He listened to the message. She missed him. And she wondered where he was.

He punched in the numbers, and she picked up right away.

"Rick, what happened? Did you have to work late?"

"No, I got tied up. Someone ransacked Terri's house."

"Oh, no. And on top of all she's been through. But is everything handled? I mean, can we still get together?"

"Ah, it's getting late, maybe we'd better do it tomorrow."

"Uhhhhh," she moaned, making the blood rush to his groin. "I'm all dressed for action now. Can't we have a drink and cuddle on the couch?"

Now he had no doubt where his brains resided. "I suppose one drink would be fine. Give me an hour, then come on over."

"I'll be there in the flesh, big boy."

Now what script was that from?

He took a shower and threw on shorts and a T-shirt. Then he plopped down in front of the computer. Forty-five minutes to work.

He pulled out the note card he'd found in Stretch's desk and read the typed message. HAL: 202-555-7624. Access LAPD: 598734204. F Field: Biograph, 7632493J. And the hand printed notation, BLACKFLASH.

Stretch loved the movie *2001: A Space Odyssey* where HAL 9000, the talking computer that ran the space ship, had gone haywire and taken over, trying to kill everyone aboard.

So HAL should stand for the FBI computer, which runs NCIC info, and the phone number should be the contact number. The next number would be the LAPD terminal identification code. He wasn't sure about the rest.

He booted up, got on the phone modem, dialed the number, and got a short, recorded message to stand by for access. So the number didn't go to the LAPD office where there was always a terminal operator. But how had they bypassed that? It was a closed system, with the NCIC computer sending information directly to that terminal. Maybe they'd—

"You may now access the terminal," came up on his screen.

His fingers trembling, he punched in the code number. And like a dream out of Universal Studios, he got the NCIC main index. Unbelievable.

How could it be? He kicked around a few ideas. Best guess was they'd hard-wired a line from the main terminal to another room, then put in a secondary terminal. Programmed it to be accessed by modem. They could call from outside the building and check NCIC without going through the operator, and with no record of the query.

Why go to all that trouble? Not to mention it'd require collusion between the LAPD and the FBI, which ordinarily kept track of all the NCIC terminals and what information was sent when, where, and to whom. Besides, what would they want to check on the sly in NCIC?

Maybe they were just using the system as a connection among group members. It'd beat the hell out of e-mail. Just as fast, but with super security.

Now if he could only figure out how it worked.

He scanned the index. The banks held information on criminal records, fugitives, and stolen property. Nothing crucial, but the information probably wasn't the key. It was the nationwide system in place, accessible by city, state, and federal groups, that was critical.

Only the most highly trustworthy groups had terminals. Cops, feds, and the military. Who would suspect it was being misused?

Whatever, he had to break into the system. Did he have any other clues? He studied the notes on the card.

The F Field. He wasn't sure what that was or how he could access it. He let his mind relax, be receptive to cosmic emanations.

K.I.S.S. Right, Stretch? As in, pick the only field starting with an F, which was the Fugitive Field.

Bringing it up, he got the normal format to be filled in. He realized that entering "Biograph" as a query would get no response. A name was required.

However, he knew some history that could be pertinent. One of the FBI's most famous fugitives, John Dillinger, was gunned down by agents in front of the Biograph Theater in Chicago. The number after Biograph on the note card had to be an identifier known as an FBI number. So he typed in Dillinger's name and the number. Hit Enter.

His PC whirred. But instead of bringing up warrant information, a request popped onto the screen. TO ACCESS, ENTER PASSWORD.

He drummed his fingertips on the card table, then glanced back at the note card. Underneath the other instructions, with a circle around it, was the word he'd noted before: BLACKFLASH (less 12-6). Terri had said it meant nothing to her.

He typed it in. B-L-A-C-K-F-L-A-S-H.

INCORRECT PASSWORD flashed on.

The notation "less 12-6" meant something. He typed all of it in.

INCORRECT PASSWORD.

Twenty minutes to go. What did "less 12-6" mean? Noon to six? No, black would be midnight. Six a.m. would be when the "flash" of the rising sun peeked over the horizon. So was the code word supposed to be Nighttime? Clack, clack. No, it wasn't. All night? Overnighter? One night stand? Dead of night? Black of night? Clack, clack, clack. Nope, none of the above.

He studied the card for any other clues. He saw nothing. Except . . . the word BLACKFLASH was hand printed in black ink. The note after it was written in cursive in blue ink. Maybe the note was added at a later time. A reminder to Stretch himself about the password. It wasn't BLACKFLASH, it was BLACKFLASH (less 12-6).

So take something away from BLACKFLASH. Twelve minus six? So you take away six letters. But which six? Not enough letters to delete every other one. Taking out the first six or last six made no sense.

Could it mean take away both twelve and six? The numbers for those letters of the alphabet? Letter twelve is L. And six, the letter F. Dropping those letters would leave BACKASH. Doubtful. He tried it. Failed.

Maybe just the first letter L and the letter F should be

cut. That left BACKLASH. At least it was a word. He tapped it in.

The computer hummed, then displayed an index of files. Yes! He raised clenched fists in triumph.

But it was short-lived. There were five files: Meetings, Select Group, Volunteer Group, Special Group, and Contacts. He tried to access one, then another. Big surprise, the FBI version of HAL asked for passwords for each file.

Back to square one. And the doorbell rang.

Okay, he'd made some progress. A little diversion might let his subconscious work on this. Unfortunately, he didn't know how much time he had to puzzle it out before something terrible happened.

He signed out of NCIC and flipped off the computer. When he opened the door, he cheered his libidinous decision. Take a hike, HAL.

Chapter 10

"Hello, mighty Eros," April said.

Dover's eyes glowed like blue neon. "Does your mother know you go out like that?"

"Tonight, I didn't dress for other women."

He took in the wispy see-through top unbuttoned to her navel and the black lace bra, and said, "You get the male vote. Come in."

She swivelled by in hot pink shorts cut well below her navel and slashed off on the south end somewhere near Brazil. White leather boots hugged her calves, and white plastic bracelets dangled on one wrist. Her lipstick matched the shorts, applied in a super pouty look. Her perfume whispered, "Pleasure me, love slave."

She reclined against the back of the sofa. The effect was staggering. Catherine Deneuve in *Belle De Jour*. She could be likened to a great Cabernet Sauvignon: robust, full-bodied, savory. Bring me a magnum, wine steward. And hurry.

He cleared his throat. "Can I get you a drink?"

"If you don't want me to burst into flames. White wine, please."

"Coming right up, I mean, I'll be right back." He stumped to the kitchen and fumbled the cork out of a bottle of Chablis. His hand trembled as he poured two glasses of the bubbly liquid.

"Here, my kitten," he said as he returned and sat down beside her. Her aspect reminiscent of "Le Bebe" Bardot could not be ignored.

She smiled. "A toast?"

"Sure." He raised his glass. *"Vive la difference!"*

"Whatever you say, Frenchie." She took a languorous sip, then twirled the stem of the glass between her thumb and finger.

"Your wine looks better than mine," he noted.

"Want to taste it?" She offered her glass.

"Mom said not to drink after others, but . . ." He leaned in, tasting droplets from her mouth with the tongue of a connoisseur.

The bra took on strong symbolism as it floated to the floor. The hot pink shorts landed atop a reading lamp, casting an ardent glow. The black lace bikini panties vanished into the night, a la filmy noir.

The pressing of flesh, California-style, began on the sofa. The scene developed with flashbacks to old moves, flash forwards to new experiments, and, two bottles of wine later, climaxed with a grand finale on the kitchen table. Ah, life could be better than the movies.

Finally they fell into bed, talked for a bit, then April dropped into her enviable deep sleep. Dover didn't tell her about the bomb, the computer connection, the whatever was going on. He was too drained to explain it all, and he supposed he didn't want her to worry. She tended to be anxious—like everyone in Hollywood who had to wait for the phone to ring—so why rain on her already soggy parade?

As the country song said, if life was like the movies, he'd never be blue. But it wasn't. And he was. Maybe Sinatra could always do things his way, but most mortals he knew got buffeted daily by pompous circumstance. The gods were jealous. Of what, he couldn't hazard a guess, but it seemed to make them testy and vindictive.

On cue, his insomnia reared its sleepless head, so he kissed April on the cheek, caressed her soft blonde hair, then extricated himself from her brown arms and pulled the sheet up over her. He snatched a blue cotton bathrobe from the closet and slipped it on.

In the kitchen he washed down three aspirin with two glasses of water. He hoped to diffuse and defuse the *vino* in his bloodstream. Carrying a Coke back to the bedroom, he sat down and clicked on a small desk lamp beside the computer and turned on the machine.

He opened his notebook and studied names of the files he'd jotted down from the index. Which to try? Meetings, Select or Volunteer or Special Groups, or the one called Contacts? Maybe if he could get the meetings schedule, he could scope out who went there.

But he'd have to come up with more passwords.

He stood and began to pace about. He picked up the printout sheet from The Untouchables file. Tapped it, then walked into the living room, flopped in his recliner, and switched on the lamp.

Chuckling, he pulled the hotpants from the lamp shade. Then he stared at the sheet of paper, hoping a clue would leap out at him. Only about twenty of the fifty or so telephone numbers on the list were preceded by names, none of which were familiar to him.

The prefixes of the numbers were from all over the country. He could make a few pretext calls, see who answered. But sometimes a call and a hangup, or someone floating a phony spiel, would signal the person that someone was checking him out. And he'd have to make any such calls from pay phones, in case his line was tapped.

He put his hand to his mouth. Did he really believe a

sinister plot was unfolding, and that maybe he and Terri were in the way of the perpetrators? Even in the blackness of this midnight scene, he could see the plot was weak. Still, some odd events had happened. And truth could be stranger than a Joe Eszterhas screenplay.

What he needed was facts. So he could determine just what the hell was going on. He glanced back at the sheet. Okay, he'd run out the subscribers to these numbers. Get a program of the players.

Back at his computer, he got on the Net and called up a locator Web site. Tried some numbers, finding—big surprise—they were unlisted. Okay, he could still get them, for a fee, with some waiting time. But would anything else be cheaper and faster? Calling police departments around the U.S. would be unwieldy and time-consuming. And the person he talked to might not want to help. Worse, they might call back to verify his identity or talk to his boss.

No, he'd have to get help. From someone whom he could trust to help him in confidence. The FBI? He had a couple of friends there, but they were so strict about playing by the rules he wondered whether they'd do an unofficial favor. Besides, they might be involved.

Harsha. He couldn't be in cahoots with them or he wouldn't have said there was a bomb in Stretch's car. Harsha could do it, if he was still in operation. Tomorrow he'd call and see.

Back in the living room, he laid the sheet of paper with The Untouchables list on the table next to the hotpants. Tiredly, he leaned his head against the recliner. What else could he do?

Maybe he should consult another expert. A computer expert. Or maybe more specialized knowledge was needed to unravel this riddle.

There was one person that could help. A guy with an unlisted number. He sent a mental request into the stratosphere, hoping to hit the right message machine: Stretch, can you give me another clue?

He waited, but no message from Stretch floated through the ionosphere, stratosphere, or channelsphere into his cogitative hemispheres. But maybe he could still pick Stretch's brain. Dredge up more of his maxims that might help hack through this Gordian knot.

Such as: The most obvious solution is often the best. True, but he failed to see any evident answer to this conundrum. In fact, the entire scenario was clouded in obfuscation, misdirection, and enigma.

Then there was: Learn to think like your adversary. Fine strategy, and one he'd use as soon as he could figure out who that was. This was like trying to solve a jigsaw puzzle without knowing the picture. He had a few pieces in hand, but he couldn't form a concept. His enemy was amorphous. A phantom. A breath on a mirror.

Or: There's a reason for everything, except for coincidence, chance, and randomness. At this point he couldn't tell planned moves from arbitrary incidents. You can't tell the players without a program.

He expelled a breath, then surveyed the room, his thoughts casting about like rebounding pinballs. His gaze paused on the chess set, its marble pieces glowing in the reflected light of the lamp. Except for a few black ones, erotically draped in April's panties.

But now he recalled another maxim: The answers to life's problems can be found in the psychology of chess. Dover was rather vague on the import of that one, but it seemed significant to the big guy. And chess was a huge part of Stretch's dreams and fantasies.

Maybe there was something to that. April had raved about pyramid power, crystals, tarot, whatever—and damned if sometimes the mystical methods didn't seem to work. Could be an instance of mind over matter. Or concentration on a goal. Or human dynamism.

Maybe he wasn't being receptive. God knows, April had begged him to try some of those strange forces often enough. It'd been like trying to drag a hitched mule backwards, plow and all.

He studied the chessboard, its pieces aligned in rank and file, confronting each other like armies poised for battle. He focused on the proud hand-carved pieces, willing them to speak. Insisting they help him solve this riddle.

He picked up the black knight. Both a protector and an avenger. But the piece had never been that versatile for him, playing at his amateur level. Not powerful or far-ranging, though it was treacherous. In the heat of the fray it could sally forth from its square and capture a bishop or a castle. He put the Paladin-like piece back on the board.

So if the answers were there, which piece would have the most revelations? The king? The object of the game was to protect your king and to capture your opponent's. But as far as power and strategic versatility and long-ranging sweeps of destruction, the king was a wimp. Power rested in m'lady beside the royal figurehead.

He reached for the white queen.

Held her in front of his face, waiting. But she didn't speak to him. Majestic in form and figure, she abided silent and impassive. Secretive and mysterious. Like her previous owner, the Colombian drug smuggler from whom Stretch had "borrowed" the set.

Dios mio. The chess pieces had been used to smuggle cocaine. With clandestine cavities to stow the blow.

He studied the old gal. Then he jostled her. Felt a little jiggle? He shook her again, harder. Yes, he thought so. Holding the hapless queen's head, he twisted her hemline, unscrewing the bottom.

A rolled up slip of paper formed a tiny scroll inside the hollow chess piece. He jiggled the paper tube free, then unrolled it and pressed it flat on his knee. Typed on it was the quintessential answer he'd been seeking.

Access F Field files through Liz Taylor and her close associates.

He struggled out of the recliner. Liz Taylor? Maybe Stretch had hung around Hollywood too long. But he headed back to the computer, hoping this was really a clue.

He'd try a password for the Meetings Schedule. Something to do with the beauty with lavender eyes. He typed in E-L-I-Z-A-B-E-T-H. Then T-A-Y-L-O-R. Tried L-I-Z. No dice. Not that simple, naturally.

Movies she was in? N-A-T-I-O-N-A-L V-E-L-V-E-T. No. Maybe *Giant*, or *Butterfield 8*, or *The Father of the Bride*. Nothing doing. Another salvo with *Suddenly, Last Summer*. But, as always happened with Peter Sellers, it was a shot fired in the dark.

Taylor or her close associates. Conrad Hilton? A bust. Mike Todd, Eddie Fisher, Richard Burton? Nah. Face it, the lady had a crowd of close buds. Try M-I-C-H-A-E-L W-I-L-D-I-N-G. No good. Then there was the politician, John Warner. And the big blond guy, Fortensky, a Kato Kaelin type, but without the personality. But the computer was having none of it.

Back to movie titles. *A Place in the Sun*. Or *Who's Afraid of Virginia Woolf?* He was, after seeing the flick. She could play a stone bitch, all right. Go with C-A-T O-N A H-O-T T-I-N R-O-O-F. No good. She'd been a sizzling tart for sure. Try her name in that one: M-A-G-G-I-E T-H-E C-A-T. Nope, neutered again.

What else was she known for? Jewelry, diamonds, necklaces. He held his breath as he typed in T-I-F-F-A-N-Y & C-O-M-P-A-N-Y. But it was fool's gold.

Back to movie titles. Go with *The Comedians*, *Taming of the Shrew* (that role again), or *Reflections in a Golden Eye*. The computer chewed 'em up and spit 'em out like fodder for a movie critic.

A biggie, the one that almost broke the 20th Century-Fox studio: C-L-E-O-P-A-T-R-A.

Then the maddening request for a password, which had glared on the screen like a churlish insult, suddenly blanked out. To be replaced by the reclusive file. Damn.

A schedule came into view, with a heading of "Area Meetings." It showed various Zones, Divisions, and Areas, with the nearest city in parentheses. For Los Angeles, it was "Zone 4, Division 2, Area 3." The schedule showed dates and times for weekly meetings for the next six months, held on varied weekdays.

The next meeting would be next Tuesday at eight p.m. But where? He scrolled down the page. No locations given. Why not tell where the meetings were held? Unless it was always the same place, like the Masons meeting at the Masonic temple.

No, he had a feeling this group was more private than that, more secretive. Privacy to do what, he didn't know. And why would Stretch be involved with such a group? He didn't have a clue. As a precaution, they probably switched meeting places every month or so to avoid notice, announcing the next meeting's location at each session.

But if he could get into the files headed Select Group or Special Group, he could probably identify an officer or member of the group. Then he could watch the man on the night of the meeting and follow him to the rendezvous.

One more time. He started with the Select Group, trying every password he could imagine. Entered all the old ones and a few new ideas. But they all flopped. He felt as played out as silent films.

Liz Taylor or her close associates. He worked until two o'clock, with all the success of a novice actor, then gave up and flipped off the computer. He'd like to work all night, but he was drained, and this job took a fresh mind.

He picked up *TV Guide*, checking late night flicks. But he was as beat as Sly Stallone in *Rocky*. Tonight he'd never go the distance. So he tossed aside the magazine and crawled into bed beside April's sublime curvature. And in that moment, he felt like Jack Lemmon. Because some like it hot.

Morning dawned in the middle of Dover's night. Even the soft domestic thumps and clatters as April prepared breakfast didn't heighten his mood. He stared out a window of his condo at the looming dominoes of high-rise hotels and apartments. Jaybird naked, like Schwarzenegger in *Terminator 2: Judgment Day*, he stood there just as emotionless, not caring about mere mortals gaping in awe.

Traffic rolled by on the street, and yachts wallowed in the water. Life rambled on as usual. But his exhausted body and overtaxed brain disputed the necessity of routine. Showering, dressing, and driving to headquarters seemed Olympian tasks. Never mind actually working.

In that instant, with the sun glinting on the marina, he wished he were rich—California opulent—and could take full advantage of the many splendors the Golden State could bestow on the well-to-do.

He imagined sauntering onto the back deck of his Malibu beach house, cup of coffee and morning paper in hand. Sprawling in his chaise lounge, he'd skim an article or two, drop the paper in his lap, and sip the fine custom blend as he watched emerald waves gliding onto the beach in ruffled rows. Ah, the good—

"—bacon or not?" April called from the kitchen.

He grabbed his robe and padded toward the delectable vapors, his knee joints creaking in syncopation. Legs heavy and sore. "What's that?" Frog in his vocal cords. Body flying apart like the universe.

"I said, I'm preparing an omelet, and do you want some fatty, grease-saturated, nitrite-loaded bacon or not?"

"You bet." He cleared his throat. "Three pieces, extra crisp."

She rolled her large blue eyes then tossed the thick strips into a heated pan. Vibe-o-mation. She'd read his mind, too.

The aroma filled the kitchen like a pleasant memory. April turned down the heat in the electric skillet, studying the omelet. If only he could wean her from California cuisine and convince her of the culinary delights of prime rib, pork chops, and baked ham. Not to mention fried chicken with biscuits and gravy.

Made his mouth water. He'd grown up eating hearty foods, including meat and eggs, and he'd be damned if California was going to rob him of the ingrained dietary habits of three decades. As Zero Mostel insisted, there was nothing so vital as tradition.

"You look tired," April said. "Didn't you sleep well?"

He wouldn't mention his bout with the computer. "You know I'm slow in the morning. My biorhythms are as dead in the water as the Egyptian army."

Of course, April, despite her moodiness, was usually

bouncy and perky and all those annoying traits that slow awakeners consider legal grounds for separation, divorce, or murder.

"Dead as the what?" she said.

"You know, that movie, *The Ten Commandments*. Charlton Heston looking the way Moses wished he did. He parts the Red Sea, well, it's really small waterfalls filmed in reverse action, a process shot. Looks like it drowns Yul Brynner and the Egyptian army as they—"

"Um hmm," she said, turning the strips in the pan. Okay, he was prattling, giddy with the thought of crisp hog meat and fluffy chicken fruit. Not to mention toast and butter.

She poured juice, grabbed a handful of silverware, added a spice to the omelet, adjusted the heat under the pan, and slid four pieces of bread into the toaster. Meanwhile, she skimmed the morning paper. How'd she do that?

"Your horoscope says the moon is in the aspect of your sign. Beware of crowded places and don't sign contracts. Also, cement romantic relationships, especially with Libra and Aries. I'm a Libra, stay away from any Aries."

She laid out place settings, glasses of juice, and a platter-sized green pepper and mushroom omelet. At the stove, she patted the grease off the strips with paper towels, then buttered the toast. She served it all and sat down to eat a bird-sized bit of the omelet while sipping a small glass of juice.

The food was delicious. She curled her lip each time he crunched a crispy strip. He polished off the lion's share of the omelet, slugged back two glasses of tangy juice, then reached for the steaming coffee which April set beside his plate just as he took the last bite of egg.

"That was great, babe."

She waved away the compliment.

His hunger sated and head less fogged, his eyes zoomed into tight focus. The chef's breasts swelled against her thin T-shirt, nipples budding like marbles. Brown legs stretched under the table, as slim and long as Nicole Kidman's.

He felt the nitrites or something hardening his arteries. "Care to slip into the shower with a grump?" No Rob Estes line, but earnest.

She grinned. "I suppose if your blood flows fast enough, the grease will have less chance to clog your arteries."

"A shower can do that?"

"Plus the aerobic exercise that goes with it."

"I don't know any cleansing workouts."

"Me either. But we'll see what comes up and improvise."

Chapter II

Later that morning Dover's four block jaunt to the office felt more like a forced five mile hike with a full pack. He was dragging. Perhaps he'd overdone something.

Meandering into the squad room, he was jolted to see Garrett Jones seated at Stretch's spot at the homicide table. He didn't expect to see Stretch sitting there, but he wasn't prepared to see anyone else. This new partner business would take getting used to.

"What's happening?" Dover said as he dropped into his chair.

Jones had a couple of case binders open in front of him. He looked up and stared quizzically. "You feelin' all right, man?"

Dover peered back. He hoped his eyes weren't too bloodshot. "Just slammin', thanks."

A twinge of doubt crossed Jones's brow. He shifted his wiry frame in the chair. Dover wondered if he'd adjusted the height on it yet.

"Okay, Ricochet," Jones intoned, "if you really, truly say."

Now he was a rapper. Snoop Dogg, Eminem, and all the others weren't enough. Jones made one too damn many. At least. Besides, Dover didn't feel like discussing his nickname this early in the day.

"You got a tag from Vice?" Dover asked, going on the offensive.

"Um hmm, but it don't seem right for Homicide."

"What is it? Give it up."

Dover would swear Jones was blushing. But he hid it. Good poker face.

"No chance of you dropping this, I guess."

"When the Rams come home."

"That's what I figured," Jones sighed, with his eyes averted. "They called me Bemo."

"Bemo? What's that mean?"

"You know that old movie about the white whale?"

"You mean *Moby Dick*? With Gregory Peck?"

"Yeah, that's the one. It's like reversed. A play on words. You know, Be mo' dick? Bemo?"

Dover held back a Brad Pitt grin. "Because you were such a whale of a dickhead?"

" 'Cause I could swamp your little white dinghy, Ahab."

"Listen, Queequeg, call me Ishmael. And in a horse race don't make any bets until you've seen the field. Some nags lay back in the pack then go all out in the stretch."

"And at the wire—"

"Yep, they win by a head."

Jones chuckled. Then he glanced around the squad room at the salty detectives, and a glare came into his eyes. "Just remember ol' Captain lost more than that leg. Stuck his harpoon in the wrong blowhole, y'know what I mean?"

Dover nodded. Not bad. He held out his hands, palms up. "Not to worry, humpback. I won't tell your jaded past to these limp dicks around here. It won't be too hard to come up with something better."

"So why do they call you Ricochet?"

"Long story. I'll tell you about it on a boring stakeout. No big deal."

"That's cool. So, uh, on these cases," he gestured toward two murder binders, "Washington and Randall?"

"What about them?"

"Seems like they could be rival gang killings."

"Could be, but why do you say that?"

He took a breath, "Check it out, they're both young guys. Shot multiple times. Both holding a stash of crack. Probably dealin' the shit. Both flying red rags—Bloods. I figure some Crip did 'em. There was a sawed-off shotgun used both times, probably as cover, and the .45 slugs match in both murders. I say they're turf battles."

Dover smiled. "Y'mean some cuz with a gauge and a four-five splashed on these slobs just to be holding down the corner?"

"That's what I said, and I think the dude's probably dusted."

Dover's eyes narrowed. "A PCP user?"

Jones pointed at a case binder. "At this first murder scene, you've got a glassine envelope found with traces of PCP. The Blood who got aced was a base head, but he had no stash of Angel Dust."

"Fair enough theory."

"I'd say the perp was draped, y'know what I'm sayin', hanging the gold?"

"Why's that?"

"Remember at the second homicide, a uniform found a gold earring that was Turkish? A high dollar item?"

"Right. And we didn't find the mate. Ah, I see where you're going. The dead kid had no expensive jewelry."

"Ya-yo, man, he was a wannabe. Check the crime scene photos. He wore a cheap watch and a nothing silver ring."

Dover was impressed. "Anything else?"

Now Jones leaned forward, really into it. As Jim Carrey would say, smokin'. "At the first crime scene," he said, "there's a witness says he might've seen an Olds Cutlass. At the second, a guy says he's pretty sure the bad guy's ride was a Chevy. Both say an older, but def-looking machine. Red."

"Which would be?" Dover was letting him ride it on home.

"Be about an '89 Monte C. The homeboys are hot for that car."

"That's good, but it leaves us a hundred thousand suspect 'bangers."

"These Bloods got faded on Eight-Tray Crips turf. That makes them our primo suspects."

Dover rubbed his chin. "Bemo, I mean, Jones, I can hang with that. Down to four hundred suspects. You just earned some props."

He unlocked a desk drawer and pulled out the scrapbook, laying it on top of his desk and opening it at random. Then he flipped through the pages, studying various newspaper and magazine articles he'd clipped over the years. Like this one about the Skinheads running rampant through the streets in Europe, beating up immigrants. Nothing like taking a page from the Nazis.

Riffling back and forth in the scrapbook, savoring the tenor of the bold headlines and the raw emotions described in the articles, he rode the crest of a feeling that surged inside him, not that far beneath the surface.

He skimmed an old article where the cops in Detroit shot and killed Malice Green. Riots and looting followed. His heart thrummed with the thought of the dark-skinned anarchists roaming the streets, burning businesses, glomming merchandise. And beating white folks.

At their trial, the cops received stiff sentences. Probably an overreaction because of the light tap that Powell and

Koontz got in the Rodney King mess. Making it only fair to stick it up whitey's ass real good when they got a chance. And King nicks L.A. for three-point-eight million bucks in a lawsuit. Unbelievable.

Then there was the Reginald Denny fiasco. Jesus. Watson and Williams got carried away by the wave of violence and mayhem and rioting, so it was understandable they'd beat the dogshit out of any poor white guy who happened by. Crush his noggin with a brick. Do a little dance. Poor, suffering black folk. Jus' can't he'p it, boss.

So they get off with a slap on the wrist. To keep the rest of the subspecies from going crazy again. Justice of accommodation.

But some of the guys thought that might be a good outcome for the cause. And they could be right. The whites in L.A. weren't stupid. They knew the case would send a message to people of color that there was a different set of rules for them than for whites.

The premise had been restated emphatically in the infamous O.J. solution. With the right jury, you could be home free. And the darkies realized that, especially in a riot situation, all rules were off.

So what were the rich and powerful and light-skinned to do when their laws and cops and judges wouldn't protect them?

Some would arm themselves, indeed many had, then shoot first and ask questions later. They'd add fuel to any racial clash that flared up. Others would twist the arms of politicians and police bigwigs, demanding they do something to restore "law and order." Giving the leaders much more latitude in responding to riotous or disruptive situations.

And this would facilitate their group in realizing certain

crucial stratagems. He smiled, cracked his knuckles, then continued to turn pages. One had to credit the media, too, for fanning the flames.

Ah, Houston, Texas. A cop blasts a greaser with a shotgun, and an angry mob storms the police station. Total rebellion out there.

Here, a rookie cop shoots an "unarmed" sixteen-year-old boy, and riots erupt in Paterson, New Jersey. Seems every town has grown susceptible to the grinding pressure of racial tension. And subject to volcanic upheaval when racial hatred is unleashed.

St. Petersburg, Florida, another eleven dead, fifty wounded. And the warfare between the Hutus and the Tutsis in Africa had wasted half a million blacks. It'd cooled off awhile, but was broiling again.

In Africa rival factions kept massacring each other. Shoot or starve out other tribes. If droughts, crop failures, and AIDS didn't get 'em first.

Then there was Bosnia, with Serbs, Croats, and Muslims all hell-bent to displace, relocate, or exterminate each other. No peace and harmony among peoples of different cultures there. First order of business was to annihilate everyone different from you. The ultimate objective being total ethnic cleansing.

Rather like the Final Solution.

And Palestine, forget it. You think the Palestinians and the Israelis would ever forget the centuries-deep scars in their relationship? Peace treaty? Hah! Any such accord would be merely a temporary solution held together with baling wire and bubble gum. Easily blown sky high by the bad boy bombers of the Hamas.

Much like what the Americans would achieve by sticking their nose into Bosnia, Haiti, or any other loser third world country. Analogous to Vietnam. Face first into a buzz saw.

Yes, the outrageous terrorists and cult leaders and insane political leaders kept various countries at each other's throats. Al Quaeda, Hizbollah, and the Islamic Jihad with their bombs and other inhumane terrorist plots. Shoka Asahara and his sarin nerve gas. And Saddam Hussein was not the only fanatical leader who'd tried to make and stockpile a nuclear and chemical arsenal. All of them vying to produce anthrax, small pox, or whatever else would wipe out thousands of innocent people, spurred by jealousy and hatred of the United States, plus their own dark greed.

The day would come when the world would appreciate the plan their group had devised to save mankind from itself. Even in the Bible, one could see the admonition. The Tower of Babel was God's warning that the mixture of races and languages would lead to total chaos and destruction. It made sense that the mongrelization of superior factions was just as damaging to the human strain.

The president of Rutgers University had come out with the truth and been excoriated. No one is allowed to say, as he did, even if everyone knows it's true, that blacks lack the genetic background to do well on standardized tests. Plus, it was proven in the book, *The Bell Curve.*

The apologists would argue, though it'd been credibly disputed, that we're all descended from one female in Africa. Thus, we're all Brothers under the skin. It was just slavery in America that put the black branch of the family a little behind everyone else. Gets a little drunk and you lands in jail. Shit. Probably more truth in the theory that prehistoric Europeans are a separate and superior ancestry.

He flipped through more articles showing the barefaced truth beneath the hypocritical facade of the racial harmony most Americans felt compelled to display. Their cultural duty and a balm of social conscience. Must watch our tongues, right, Senator D'Amato? No Asian dialects allowed. No diminutive adjectives used, no pejorative comments permitted. An Italian-American should be especially sensitive to the race issue. His forebears were once the wops, guineas, and dagos of America.

Another terrifying problem was the growing militancy of the Muslims. They had twelve hundred mosques in America, for Christ's sake. Effective gathering places for inciting thousands of ardent extremists in our midst who hate us and want to destroy the American way.

Besides, the critical problem looming just over the horizon was that people were reproducing themselves eight times faster than cultivated land area was being developed. So in twenty, thirty years, what would we eat? Our children? The excruciating irony inherent in this situation was that the third world countries were the biggest reproducers of the least worthy humans. Quantity going up, quality down. Dumb and dumber.

So we're all staring at a world population explosion much like a hydrogen bomb that's armed and ready to blow the planet apart. Or sink it under the sheer weight of humanity. Standing room only.

Cold and clear-eyed solutions were called for. No emotional pleas, no compromises, no waffling or watering down of their position. The plan was solid and desperately needed. It would be put into motion very soon.

Dover and Jones barreled along the Harbor Freeway headed for the Eight-Tray's territory to try to shake loose some information. They figured they might even put together a murder case or two. But halfway there, Dover veered across two lanes and made a squealing exit off the freeway.

Jones hung on to the dash. "Wha's up?" he said, looking at Dover as if he belonged in *One Flew Over the Cuckoo's Nest.*

"Got to find a phone. I forgot to call someone."

He dropped some silver in a pay phone and punched ATF's number, shocked when Harsha answered.

"Yeah, they sent me to Bumfuck, Egypt, in the middle of the night on some shitty detail. Guess I pissed someone off with my charming manner. I just got back. Anything new on your case?"

Dover hesitated. "Duncan didn't tell you anything?"

"About what?"

"At the impound lot he stood around while an LAPD bomb guy checked the car with a 'sniffer.' They both said it was negative. Said they'd found no indication of plastic explosive."

"They said . . . you're shitting me! The half pint prick didn't say diddly to me. What the hell was he doing over there, anyway?"

"Claimed to be filling in for you. And he and our bomb tech seemed to think your field test was unreliable."

"What? Listen, the little chrome dome is out of the office right now, but when he gets back I'll brace him, straighten out this snafu, and get back to you."

"That'd be great. But could you do me another favor?"

"Hey, I owe you after that fuckup. What'cha need?"

"I've got some phone numbers from all over the country. Came from a computer disk Stretch had, and I think it's connected to this puzzle. Could you get me the names of the subscribers? On the QT?"

"Sure. Can you fax it over?"

"If you'll take it off the machine yourself."

"No problem."

"I'm on the street, but I'll find a machine. Give me ten minutes."

Dover told Jones nothing about his phone call or about why he next stopped at a computer store. He sent the fax to Harsha, bought a box of floppy disks, then returned to the car. "Ready for gangland?"

Jones rolled his eyes. "Do I look like a fool? Just drive careful, and don't act too white."

As they cruised through Eight-Tray area, they spotted some Crips on the street. They rousted them about the murders, but they hung tough with their code of silence. Late in the afternoon they ran across five or six punks chillin' in a vacant lot behind a slumped wooden fence. Two cases of Colt 45 at the ready. Tongues loose from the booze, they were still badasses, in the mode of Sweet Sweetback, who wouldn't tell Five-O if their squad car was on fire.

They spotted another Crip chilling on his front porch and conned their way inside. Dover studied the slim kid who slouched in the orange easy chair, a grease spot behind his head like a Satanic halo. He wore sagging blue pants, an L.A. Dodgers ball cap with the bill tugged to the right, and an expression that said, You and your fucking shields can kiss my raggedy black ass.

"We heard slobs have been cruising your territory," Dover said.

The kid examined the ceiling.

Jones leaned forward and said, "That so, Hammer?"

The kid regarded Jones with mild surprise, probably because he knew his tag. Then he shrugged. "Whatever, bitch."

Dover said, "Seems like the Eight-Trays would kick their asses."

The kid leveled a stare at him that would mow down a hay field. "More than that."

Dover nodded. "Might light 'em up? Splash on 'em?"

The kid averted his gaze, not interested in murderous small talk. He looked fifteen, but was only thirteen. Going on twenty.

"Two Bloods got hit this last month," Dover said, watching Hammer's deadpan expression. "Both right near here. Four-five did 'em. Gauge sprayed around, too. Looks like a gang thang. Crips."

The boy smirked. "You got a warrant?" Now he's a TV lawyer.

"To talk to you? No, Hammer," Dover said, "talk is still okay. No liberal knee-jerk judge has taken that away from us. Yet."

The kid gave them bored, as if he had better things to do. Hah.

"Two Bloods R.I.P. on your turf," Jones said. "Whassup with that?"

The kid looked at him like he was from Mars. Or Kansas. "Don't know jack about it."

They glanced around the shithole room. Ashtrays jammed with butts dotted Salvation Army tables, the sofa was a spavined horse near collapse, and industrial strength dust clotted every surface. Filthy clothes lay everywhere, providing a dash of color.

"Down little brother like you," Jones ventured, "should be up on wha's happenin' in the 'hood."

"The 'hood watch out for itself. Don't need no Five-O sticking theyselves in here. I ain't saying no more, neither."

Dover glanced at Jones. They both stood up.

"If you were riding on these slobs," Dover said, appraising the kid, "whether you blasted 'em or not, you go up the same as the shooter." He shrugged. "It's your call."

Hammer kept his game face. Randolph Scott asleep. Or dead.

"Last chance to stall it out," Jones said. "You give it up, give us names, you could walk. We bounce, and you done blew it, bro."

A thought scampered behind the kid's dull eyes. But when he blinked, the glimmer went out. Now a defunct soul glowered behind the vacant chestnut marbles. "Crip or cry, Five-O. I don't snitch on my boys."

Back at headquarters, Dover surveyed the scene with new eyes. The squad room, with detectives yakking on phones, pounding out reports on computer keyboards, or browbeating scuzzy clientele, seemed an oasis of fruitful promise compared with the desert of hopeless desolation they'd slogged through in the gang-run 'hood.

As Dover dropped into his chair, Jones said he'd write up the interviews. Dover said that would be great, then his phone rang. "Detective Dover."

"Hey, Ricochet, it's Harsha."

"Oh, yeah, what's—"

"Listen, I can only talk a minute. Someone's expecting me. But I wanted to tell you about those numbers you faxed."

Dover glanced at Jones, who seemed absorbed in transcribing his notes into the computer. "Go ahead."

"I can't give you details now, but there's something strange."

"I'm listening." He cocked a foot atop his desk.

"Since they're all unlisted numbers, it takes some time

to get the subscribers. But I was too curious to wait. I called a few to check them out."

"What'd you find out?"

"Picked up by secretary types. All said 'hello,' except for one."

"And the exception?"

"I think she screwed up. She said, 'SAC Harmond's office.' "

"S-A-C, like that, huh?"

"Exactly."

"What was the number?"

"Area code in Texas. Around Dallas."

"Only the FBI spells out S-A-C for Special-Agent-in-Charge."

"Yep. Other agencies just say SAC, as in a sack of shit. And there's one other goodie."

"So give."

"One of the names on the list looked familiar. A guy who used to work for ATF. He left us, but later I heard he became a spook."

"CIA?"

"No, Casper's Haunting Corps."

"Sorry, go ahead."

"He had this thick Georgia accent. Type you couldn't forget?"

"And you called the number?"

"Yep. Area code was 713, Virginia, so I dialed it, and his 'hello' was enough for me to make him right off."

"Holy cow." Man, he was getting bucolic.

Harsha let it ride. "And there's a couple of numbers in the D.C. area that I suspect . . ." He paused, then said in a louder voice, "Just wanted to check. Yeah, thanks a lot. 'Bye." The line went dead.

"I see," Dover said into the buzz. "Thanks for calling. Talk to you later." He hung up and glanced back at Jones. Dark eyes lingered on the glowing computer screen.

Dover imagined the rattler striking.

Chapter 12

It had been a long day, but as he drove, Dover revved the brawny Bel Air engine to five thousand r.p.m., making him feel relaxed. Then a light glimmered in the frontal lobe of his fatigued brain, like the rapturous red glow when E.T. revived. He pulled over at a convenience store and called Terri to see if he could come over.

When he arrived, she looked puzzled. "What did you want to see?"

"I'd like to look at Stretch's stuff."

"You know I don't want you prying the lid off anything."

"I'm just curious. You know us cops."

She sighed. "Yes, too well. But I suppose it'll be all right."

She began to load the dishwasher, and he wandered through the house, trying to scrutinize it through honorable detective's eyes, watching for anything that might help him unravel this Chinese puzzle. A ball cap reposed on the refrigerator, a photograph of Terri and Stretch at the beach sat on a counter, and a mystery novel peeked from between cookbooks on a shelf.

The bedroom looked as if Terri had tried to eliminate the torment. Stretch's side of the closet was empty, his shoes and clothing given away or boxed and stuck into storage. One photo remained on the bedside table. The two of them at Disneyland, grinning like Anaheim realtors, waving at the camera. Together for always. Wish upon a star.

To keep from dissolving into tears or maniacal laughter, he began to search through the dresser. The first drawer held Terri's underwear. He was surprised at the sexiness of the filmy garments. But this wasn't a perp's house. He dropped the bikini panties like they were on fire and slid the drawer closed, his face burning.

Next he found a few drawers of Stretch's things that Terri hadn't yet gathered up. T-shirts, shorts, socks, handkerchiefs, some jocks and a knee supporter, swim suits and a few sweaters. Couple of electric razors, a dead watch, and a combination lock.

In the last drawer, he lifted a faded basketball jersey in the back, finding a packet of photographs bound with a rubber band. He shuffled through them. Looked like day trips or sightseeing junkets around L.A. On the beach, in the mountains, in the desert.

When someone snapped the two of them, their faces radiated love. Dover felt a wrenching sense of sadness. Guilt, even envy.

There were some shots of Hollywood, including the huge sign on the hill. The Chinese Theater, with names of the princes and princesses of the movie kingdom scrawled in the forecourt. The names, handprints, and footprints (and in Trigger's case, horseshoe prints) of the industry biggies.

There were Alan Ladd, Jimmy Durante, Jane Russell, Gene Tierney. And Will Rogers, Cary Grant, Jack Benny, Al Jolson, Eleanor Powell.

And one that said, "GIANT, '56," with the signature Elizabeth Taylor. He stared at the photo, mouth open. Was it a coincidence? Cleopatra had been the code word to view the Meetings Schedule. Four more clues would unlock the other files. He stared at the shot, looking for the meaning.

Wish upon a star. Makes no difference—

Then he noticed. This photograph was different, the focus was sharper, the composition better. Professional shot, he'd bet.

He studied it closely. The photo showed not only Liz's notice of fame, but also included four adjacent squares. Four other persona of cinematic note. Famous for various aspects of the movie industry.

Ah, yes. Four "close associates" of Liz Taylor. By virtue of being frozen in filmland lore in cement squares next to hers. Jean Harlow, Red Skelton, Edward Arnold, and George Stevens.

He slipped the photograph of the cement legacies of Taylor and her associates into his pocket. Then he smiled. Maybe this was the key to the Magic Kingdom.

Back in the kitchen, he didn't mention the photo. Terri asked if he'd found anything. He concentrated on the pitcher of daiquiris in her hand and said, "As John Wayne so delicately put it, 'Shut up and pour.' "

She did, and they chatted awhile, both keeping it light. But tonight their banter, which usually flowed like well-known dialogue in a favorite movie scene, somehow plodded like a formula western.

During the quiet moments he appraised her. She was as stressed as winter wheat in a hailstorm. But he remembered the good times when she exuded a brilliant aura, flowery bouquet, and a zesty savor for life that made her as delightful as a captivating Chablis.

He wondered if a problem was developing. Maybe Terri felt he'd been hanging around too much. Maybe he reminded her of Stretch, and she needed to get him off her mind, to discard him, to get him out of sight like Stretch's clothes, photographs, and possessions.

Then he realized she was staring at him, and a notion that'd been churning in his head spilled out of his mouth. As per Woody Allen, maybe he could develop it into an idea. But the embryonic treatment came out, "Do you remember when Chief Williams fired Theodore Briseno for his part in the Rodney King beating?"

"Of course."

"It occurred to me that Briseno was the only one there who said they were out of control. Same thing Stretch talked about."

"It was probably just a coincidence. Anyway, the whole thing," she gestured in a half circle, "first King getting beat, then Reginald Denny. And the trials becoming such circuses, the sentences so trivial . . . it all seems so pointless and bizarre."

His take was that a lot of citizens in the City of Angels were keeping score—Whites vs. Blacks. Trying to balance the scales of prejudice. "Maybe it'll all be forgotten," he said, but didn't believe it.

Pain showed on her brow. "I'm not sure our lives will ever be normal again. Polly Klaas kidnapped and killed, and JonBenet Ramsey savagely murdered. Militia jerks bombing the federal building in Oklahoma City, then terrorists destroying the World Trade Center."

He shook his head. "So many killed . . . innocent folks blown apart or crushed or burned."

"Good people killed in car crashes, and who knows why."

The despair in her expression hit him like a kick from a stallion, and he knew he had to expose that shrouded rationale. The motive for Stretch's murder was vitally important. To them and to all Americans who didn't deserve the fury that erupted so often in these crazy times, making life tenuous and dangerous and terrifying.

★ ★ ★ ★ ★

As Dover and Terri talked, Jarroll and a group of 'bangers hung in the back room of a closed furniture store. Jarroll studied weak shafts of sunlight filtering through smeared windowpanes, wondering what was up. The big dogs of the unit were kickin' it in some big stuffed chairs.

"So tha's how we gonna be puttin' in work tonight," Skull said. "The place will be poppin', so we'll move a lot of rock." When Skull said something, it was solid, like that was what time it was. He leaned forward and said, "Go on, you niggas get rollin' that dope."

Hi-top basketball shoes ground out cigarettes, sing song voices murmured, and feet shuffled against the worn hardwood floor of the building as the 'bangers ambled out into the fading twilight, almost nighttime, when they were the unquestioned rulers of the 'hood.

Hangin' in doorways, on benches, and at corners under broken street lights, they watched cars ease by, looking for signals—black, brown, white dudes—wanting to score. They had it all, drugs to dull, speed up, or crazify the head. Folks couldn't take too much real life.

Jarroll wasn't up on what he should do, so he trailed the others. He'd hang around, watch, and learn. Do it on his own soon.

"Yo, Hammer," Skull bellowed.

Jarroll turned his head, pointing a finger at his chest.

"Over here," Skull motioned, then said something in a low voice to Gorilla who hulked behind his shoulder.

Jarroll gangsta-limped back to Skull, who launched himself out of the chair and stood tall, his chest in Jarroll's face.

"We been puzzlin' about some business for you."

Jarroll nodded. "What it be?"

"You a down little homey. You can put in good work for the 'hood."

"Tha's cool."

Skull jerked his head at Freak, who was slouched against the wall. Freak pushed himself away, wavered as though he could barely stand, then slogged the four steps over to them.

Now Freak stared at Jarroll with eyes that every so often seemed to rotate like pinwheels. His tag came not from physical defects, but from too many LSD trips. At times, hallucinations would seize his brain, making him more sprung than any cluckhead.

Freak rolled his eyeballs in Skull's direction, and Skull gave him a nod. Freak reached behind his back and fumbled under the tail of his shirt. His brown hand came out gripping a squarish pistol that was as dark as a rat.

Jarroll's heart surged in fear, and he gathered himself to bounce, but then Freak held the butt end of the gun out toward him.

"Tha's for you, Hammer," Skull said. "Go on, nigga, take it."

Jarroll reached a trembling hand toward Freak and separated the gun from his fist. It was heavier than he'd expected. He wasn't sure where to put it, so he let it drop down beside his leg.

"Hammer, I want you to do some business tonight. You go on with Freak, and he'll lay it down for you."

Gorilla mumbled something in Skull's ear.

"And Gorilla be goin' along, too. Be in charge. He scoped out the place y'all gonna jack."

Jarroll stuck the gun in his waistband and pulled his shirt out to cover the thick handle. His heart boomed. This was his test. What he did tonight, he'd carry with him as part of his rep with the Eight-Trays. He had to be down for the 'hood, not be no buster. Crip or cry. Do or die.

Back home, Dover knew he wouldn't unwind for hours, so he accessed the NCIC computer. Against the monitor he leaned the photograph of the entryway to the Chinese Theater. He had to get into the other secret files in the Fugitive Field. Then he'd run this out like any homicide case.

Except in this instance his best friend and partner had been blown apart. He stared at the computer, and for an instant he imagined seizing the monitor and hurling it against the wall, smashing the glass and twisting the plastic case, then stomping every electronic part inside.

His arms felt rigid, his hands clenched into hard fists. He looked at them, then forced himself to relax. Made himself focus his energies. He was no Michael Douglas in *Letting Go*.

He had better ways to vent his rage.

As Dover sat before the computer, assessing the possibilities of various passwords for breaking into the secret files, Jarroll rode in the back seat of a red Monte Carlo, studying the pistol in his sweaty hand. He pointed it at the floor. "Pow," he said softly.

Gorilla turned. "Yo, Hammer, don't be poppin' no caps back there."

He could tell Gorilla was just goofin' on him.

"Just makin' sure it full up," Jarroll offered.

"Tha's cool," Gorilla said, then told Freak to bend the corner.

At the end of the block Gorilla said, "There it lay," tilting his head.

Jarroll and Freak both knew where the store was, but

they grunted in agreement so as not to dis' Gorilla.

Freak stopped down the street and killed the engine. Two bitches were squabbling over some crumbs of coke. A low-rider rumbled by, boom box screeching some jumpy spic sounds. The air felt hot and wet.

Gorilla pulled a gauge from under the front seat. He fed four shells into the tube and racked one into the sawed-off gun. Jarroll fiddled with his pistol, his nerves jerking crazy on him.

Gorilla turned to Freak. "You stay in the ride, powered up, ready to move out soon's we get back. If you see the Man, bop the horn twice."

Freak just slid down in the seat. Then Gorilla stared at Jarroll, who swallowed hard and pushed open the door. They strolled down the sidewalk. Several niggas saw them coming and bailed, never looking back.

Stopping outside the store they checked the Turkish and the ice in the chink's window—stuff they could hustle on the street—make lots of snaps for the Eight-Trays, maybe stack a little for themselves.

"Check it out," Gorilla said.

Jarroll nodded, sucked in a breath, then pushed through the door. He felt a rush like he'd smoked some rock. Couldn't feel his feet hitting the floor. His eyes never blinked as his head swiveled, scoping the scene.

He spotted a chink behind a counter, fumbling with a tray of rings. The old guy glanced up, and Jarroll looked away. The man bent back to his work. Stringy white hair, skinny, and alone. No problem.

Jarroll peered out the front window and jerked his head. Gorilla gave an icy smile and moved toward the door. Jarroll's hands were so clammy he wondered if he could hold the piece.

The chink half raised up when the bell over the door jangled. The old man started to say something to Gorilla, then he froze, his mouth half open. His eyes went dull and flat.

Gorilla headed straight toward the dazed gook. The gauge hung down behind his leg, but his grip was loose. Real relaxed.

A pillowcase flew toward the yellow man. His curled hand jerked up to stop it from smacking him in the face. Then he stood up, stared at Gorilla, and raised his chin.

"Fill it up, old man. Just the good shit. And no alarms."

The chink squeezed the pillowcase as he studied Gorilla with his muddy brown eyes. His head was working on something.

Gorilla saw it. He squinted and looked crazy at the old chink. "I see a Five-O cruise by, this be the night you meet Confucius." He lifted the gauge.

The guy's face collapsed, and his shoulders drooped. He reached inside the glass case, grabbed some gold rings and shiny chains, looked them over, then dropped them into the pillowcase.

Jarroll said, "Put in some of them diamond ones, too."

The white-haired man moved to another case and picked up some ice and dropped it in the bag. His eyes flicked toward the front door. Splotched hands trembled.

Gorilla told the guy what to do. Old chink did it, moving slow.

Then Jarroll got an idea. "Let's go in back. Open up the can and check out the big chunks of ice and shit."

The chink hated that.

Gorilla jabbed the shotgun into the guy's bony ribs. Marched him back into a little room, all dusty, papers stacked way high on a couple of tables. Roaches scrabbling at pieces of chink food on paper plates.

An old wall safe hung halfway open. Muthafucka. They done won a monsta lottery. The chink near cried as he started pulling out the goods.

Pillowcase getting fat with candy.

Passing time getting heavy on their nerves.

Gorilla stared at the chink and lifted his big chin. "What's that?"

Bony head turned. Gorilla swung the gauge hard, the barrel cracked the thin skull and the guy dropped in a heap.

"Let's bounce," Gorilla said, and they charged out of the room and hustled toward the front door. Then they heard a metallic click.

Jarroll recognized the sound and froze. He turned his head back toward the chink lying on the floor pointing a rusty revolver at them, the hammer pulled back, the barrel shaking all around.

Jarroll went for his pistol.

Gorilla ducked, swung around, and yanked the trigger. The blast from the gaping barrels splattered the old man, spraying blood and flesh all over the safe. Bits of brain flew like confetti.

Jarroll stared at the wasted carcass. Happened so fast. The chink lay there like he'd dropped off a roof, leaking red gunk from his mouth and nose.

Then Jarroll's instincts kicked in, and he ran like a muthafucka.

Dover slaved at the computer like Charlton Heston rowing in the Roman galleys. He punched in the names of Liz's close associates (those etched in stone), as well as any connections that came to mind. For Jean Harlow he tried blonde, platinum, goldie, M-G-M, China doll, Gable, Beery, and Hughes. All with no luck.

And not knowing which person was the clue for which file, he had to try each guess four times. Four unbroken files: Select Group, Special Group, Volunteer Group, and Contacts.

There were a lot of possibilities with both Harlow and Skelton. He didn't know much about Arnold and Stevens. He did know Stevens was a director and had won an Oscar or two. And he presumed from the photograph at the Chinese Theater that Stevens had directed Liz Taylor, Rock Hudson, and James Dean in *Giant*.

Keying on the Select Group, he tried O-S-C-A-R, R-A-N-C-H, and D-I-R-E-C-T-O-R. He'd already entered Hudson, Dean, and *Giant*. But he felt it must be a connection to that movie.

Plot being: Big Texas cattle rancher Rock Hudson marries Virginia beauty Liz Taylor. Marital problems fester on the lone prairie, then Big Complication raises its ugly head in the form of James Dean as a penniless drifter kicked off the ranch by Hudson, but who hangs on to a worthless patch of ground at the edge of the huge ranch, on which he finds bubbling crude. So he gets R-I-C-H because of O-I-L. No. Try C-R-U-D-E, G-U-S-H-E-R, S-T-R-I-K-E. Nothing doing. Okay, derrick, rig, pump, cap, blowout. Nope, dang it. Drill, mud, bit. Hunh-uh. How about R-O-U-G-H-N-E-C-K?

The request for the password faded again, and his heart jumped as the file came on the screen. It consisted of a list of names. Must be five hundred of them. He skimmed some pages. What made them select?

He thought he knew.

He recognized a couple of the names when he first scanned the list. Common names, to be sure—Harold Johnson and Joe Washington—but he had a feeling.

Scrolled back to page one. Studied the list more carefully.

All alphabetized. Yep, he knew that one, too. And that one. Unusual names, no mistaking they were part of the group he suspected.

Then panic rose up inside him. He scrolled furiously through the names. No, no. It wasn't there. His heart pounded like an aging racehorse. But Stretch's name was absent from the list.

As an afterthought, he checked his own. Nope, not there.

And then it struck him. He didn't know if that was good or bad. Why were these particular men (and now he noticed some women's names), all officers of the LAPD, put on the Select Group list?

His breath caught as he recognized another name. Garrett Jones. His new partner.

What the hell was going on here? He studied the list some more, trying to find a message. Jackson, Marquez, Wong. He searched wildly, jumping from place to place, trying to find—what? Hisquierdo, Sanchez, Choi, Perez, Foo, Patel, al-Bayder, Jimenez, Danson. And now he saw it.

He checked for names of other guys on his squad. White bread types. None of them appeared. Only minority members of the force had apparently been so honored. The Select Group.

He wondered how Stretch got The Untouchables disk and gained access to these hidden NCIC files. Maybe he attended meetings of a local faction of one of the other groups. Maybe the Select Group was the one Stretch feared was getting out of control and tried to warn him about.

But Stretch never gave the alert. He got blown apart on the way. And some of the blue jays at his funeral had been these very people—the black, yellow, and brown faces of the Select Group.

The question was, selected to do what?

Maybe they were the core of a conspiracy. The elite band at the center of a coalition of minority groups joining together to take over L.A. Plotting to wrest control from whitey by force, the way Charlie Manson had predicted would happen.

But such a plan seemed ludicrous. And whoever these people were, they didn't seem crazy. Not to the point of losing control.

They'd been very efficient in silencing one threat to them, blowing Stretch apart before he could open his mouth about their plan or identity. Perceiving a danger of exposure, they neutralized it. Problem solved.

No, this was no mob mentality in operation. They were a crafty bunch. Shrewd. Calculating. Their plan would be more complex and longer term.

So now he had to figure out how to think like them. Learn all about their operation. And not get caught doing it.

Chapter 13

Dover lay in bed assessing the Select Group, trying to figure out their mission. Then the phone rang. Call to duty? He wasn't in the mood. He answered like a morose Charlie Chaplin who'd lost the girl again.

"Hey, Ricochet, this is Sergeant Halyard on the night desk."

"Since it's the night shift."

"Right. Sorry to disturb you, but we've got a situation."

"Shit happens."

"But all the night dicks are tied up or M.I.A., and some uniforms called in a robbery/homicide. Korean guy. Ryong's Jewelry in South Central, you know it?"

"I know it. You call Jones?"

"He's on his way."

"SID available?"

"Should be there soon."

"Have you notified the—"

"Coroner will be there in an hour. EMTs checked the guy. Unless they can sew on the top half of his head, no use for an ER."

"Shotgun?"

"I'm just riding this desk, but that'd be my guess."

Smartass. "Any problems with the local gentry?"

"Got four patrol cars there. Store's locked down, and the scene's sealed off. Shouldn't be any looting, and no one gives a shit if some chink got wasted. Besides, a cop didn't do it."

"Point well taken."

146

"Nothing left to do but go solve it."

"I always get the no-brainer stuff."

" 'Cause you're so qualified."

"Thanks, Sergeant. How're the hemorrhoids tonight?"

"You always knew how to go for the jugular, Ricochet."

"Sorry. I'm rolling out now."

"About fucking time."

When Dover rolled into the shitheel neighborhood, it looked like the circus had come to town. Red lights, blue lights, and yellow lights sprayed in every direction, rotating, bouncing off shiny surfaces. A few drunks and curious types hung at the fringes of the center ring, but the brawny cops looked formidable, and Dover didn't sense any hassles on the horizon.

Jones was waiting for him, his face taut, shifting from foot to foot. As Dover approached the crime scene tape, he nodded to his new partner, considering him anew as a member of the Select Group.

"No more theory classes," Jones said.

Ah, his first homicide. "You got it. Welcome to the real world."

He'd puzzle out the mystery of the group later. No time for speculation now. He had to concentrate on the job at hand.

Some SID guys were dusting the front glass doors and a couple of the display cases inside the store. The uniformed officer at the door glanced at their shields and unlocked the door to let them pass. They stepped over the guy dusting the glass.

Dover hesitated and said, "Any footprints or other evidence we'll fuck up if we mosey back and take a look at the deceased?"

He shrugged. "Probably, but I didn't spot anything. Go on back. He's lying in front of an old safe." He brushed a couple of deft strokes across the glass, dark powder drifting downward.

"You get the photos?" Dover asked.

"Yep, but there's not much you can do with gray brain matter."

"There was some blood, I assume. Nice and crimson?"

"Not bad. Got some real good splatters, too. But not to worry, for the close-ups I used the red eye reduction, so he wouldn't look like a demon."

"Nice touch, maestro." He went to meet the corpse.

Mr. Ryong's eyes were glassy, but they showed none of the terror sometimes evident in the stark expression of corpses. If anything, there was almost an aspect of purpose. Beside him on the floor, speckled with drops of blood and tiny clumps of gray matter, was a cocked revolver.

This told Dover a few things. The guy who robbed him hadn't intended to kill Mr. Ryong. If so, he would've dropped him in the front part of the store or after he'd opened the safe. Then there would have been footprints or smears in the gore splattered around the inside of the safe where the bags and trays had been emptied.

No, the robber had grabbed the goods, turned to leave, then Ryong had whipped out the six-shooter. But he hadn't pulled the trigger. Not a natural born killer, like Woody Harrelson and his dad.

Ryong wasn't tied up or knocked out or locked in the safe. Just left there beside the cleaned-out box. Which meant whoever pulled the heist didn't fear the little Korean. Never suspected he'd pull a piece. Only realized it when he heard him cock the hammer.

Someone who knew Ryong. Someone from the neighborhood. Who believed Ryong would be too intimidated to squeal. Someone feared in the 'hood. Who carried a gauge. Okay, Vanna, I'll try a G. For gangbanger.

Which meant that no one else in the neighborhood, who had also been bullied for years by the street scum, would tell them jack shit about anything. No 'bangers would cop. There was no ballistics evidence, since a shotgun was used.

He'd bet there were no prints, no fibers, no hairs, nothing of a physical nature at the crime scene to help them solve the case. So with no witnesses, this one was a shitcan. Color it unsolvable.

Except the SID guy did find some latents on a display case. The only three prints on the pane. Could Mr. Ryong have wiped the glass top before the robbery? A peek behind the counter revealed a squirt bottle of glass cleaner and a piece of cloth. And the delightful, heady smell of ammonia.

Searching on his hands and knees, Jones spotted a glittering 9mm cartridge on the floor behind the counter where the cash register sat. If it had been ejected from a pistol rather than just dropped, the lab could match ejection scratches on the cartridge.

"That's supposing," Jones said, "we find the gun to test against."

Dover nodded, puzzling it out. Maybe someone nervously racked the action when there was already a cartridge in the chamber. Ejecting that little beauty. Indicating at least two robbers, since the first guy was busy blowing Ryong's brains out with a gauge.

"I like it," Dover said. "Much harder for two scumbags to keep a secret than one."

Dover thought of his own secret concerning the Select Group. He wondered whether a hard-working detective like Jones could be part of a conspiracy to take over L.A. Or maybe his theory was garbage.

Anyway, his new partner's persistence in the investigation reminded him of Bogey in *The Maltese Falcon*, so he anointed him "Falcon." Jones didn't seem to mind. Better than Bemo.

After leaving the store, they talked with people at neighboring businesses. That included Desmond's Econo Liquor Store, J J's Shoot-Em-Up Pool Hall and Bar, and Wings, Ribs & Hogfat BBQ. The street was a monument to racial stereotyping.

No one had seen anyone go into Ryong's Jewelry Store late that evening. No one had seen anyone come out, in a hurry, carrying a bag, with a weapon, wearing gang colors, or anyone or anything out-of-the-ordinary, unusual, suspicious, odd, or mysterious, or any vehicles stopping in front of or near Ryong's, or with two guys or more in them, or leaving in a rush, or anything. Hadn't heard a shot. A shotgun blast, for George Burn's sake.

"Noisy as hell around here all the time, man," Desmond said. "Dudes yelling, mufflers roaring, radios boomin' rap. Gunshots crackin' every night, anyway. Gets where you don't pay no mind. Long's they not coming at you."

"How do you know," Dover asked, "when your number's up?"

Desmond rubbed his chin. "Hell, you jackin' with me?"

"If you let the 'bangers run the place—shoot anyone they want, never say anything—someday they'll be the only ones left."

The proprietor looked sullen. "They ain't shooting me, man."

Dover squinted. "Maybe you got a contract with them?"

He waved the thought away. "I gots to close the books now."

Falcon stared him down, pointing at a red neon sign. "Says 'Open All Night.' "

"Tha's right, but I've got to make the night deposit."

"You know where to reach us," Dover said.

"Um hmm, sure do."

Dover wasn't holding his breath.

Arriving home at two, Dover was exhausted, but as wide-eyed as Mr. Ryong. He thumbed the late movie schedule, opting for the super shootout in *The Magnificent Seven*. The lead really flew. And damn, those guys were good.

His head hit the pillow at three-thirty. But his brain pinwheeled in several directions. Problems assaulted him like a flurry of bullets from a Mac-10. To cope with them without getting mowed down, he'd have to be as fast and deadly as Yul Brynner.

He finally dropped off to sleep about four. The tremor hit at six-thirty. Now he was really awake.

About four-point-six on the old Richter. The newscaster described how stress built up along faultlines in the earth until there was a slippage and a shifting of portions of the earth's crust. He reminded viewers about L.A.'s famous San Andreas fault. As though everyone from Kansas and the rest of the sane world didn't know the whole shaky state was one big maze of faultlines.

Dover made some coffee, then sat down with a cup and flipped through the morning paper. He spotted an article about a black teenager who'd been killed in Huntington Park the night before. Two white cops surprised him during the burglary of a hardware store. He came at them with a knife. High on crack. One of the cops shot him in the throat.

By the time the ambulance arrived the kid was dead and the officers had called for backup. The citizens had judged them guilty of racism and had overturned the patrol car, set it on fire, and backed the officers into an alley. They barely escaped with their skins.

He poured another cup, mulling it over. L.A. was fertile soil for quakes, tremors, and aftershocks. And not only the seismological kind. The fabric of society in the city was as fragile and brittle as the shifting ground. The riots in '92 had shown that cultures could fracture and heave up just like the earth. People could take only so much pressure, then they'd crack, too.

Acts of terror in 2001 had put Americans on edge about Muslims. And Saudis, Iranians, Pakistanis, Afghanistanis, Iraquis, Syrians, Libyans—hell, anyone of the Islam religion was suspect. Increased social tensions were destroying racial harmony and negating tolerant social interaction among various races, creeds, and religions. Large cities were tinderboxes waiting to be ignited.

Police actions could obviously escalate the strain beyond the breaking point. Cops and minorities were like tectonic plates, vying for supremacy. When one overrode the other, it'd produce a whole new structure.

He dropped the paper on the table. The Select Group. He had an inkling what their plan might be.

Back at the computer, he logged onto the Net to research race riots, demonstrations, and police brutality. There was a lot of material. He brought up newspaper and magazine articles.

When a Jew ran his car into a group of black children on a sidewalk in Brooklyn, the entire black community reacted with outrage and rioting. And more cases where police shot minority criminals who were caught committing serious crimes. The automatic response would be mob force—rioting, looting, burning—and attacking law enforcement authorities.

A police station in Houston was assaulted by a hoard of blacks. Snipers shot cops in high-rise housing projects in Chicago. Miami was a battleground between cops and Hispanic drug dealers. There were riots and looting and demonstrations in Cincinnati when a black teenager was shot, repeated in Cleveland, with the white cop eventually found not guilty, a result not liked by the black community.

As he sifted through the articles, skimming portions of them, he saw a pulsing theme. His head felt light. His theory seemed sound.

The Select Group was readying for the next big incident. Maybe they'd even start it. The resulting riots could expand into a violent takeover of L.A., perhaps all of California, maybe even America.

Dover sat stunned, pondering the plausibility of his theory about the Select Group's treachery. Could this be a serious threat? A viable plan? It seemed outrageous, but then, most plans by guerrilla factions did, and some of them occasionally succeeded. Especially when the government in charge was not liked by large masses of people, which might be said for the U.S.

The phone rang, and he jumped. It was Falcon, asking, "You ready to canvass the neighborhood?"

Last night they'd decided to talk with more people around the area of Ryong's Jewelry before the grisly shooting became just another bad memory of what could happen these days in L.A. This morning, since loss of sleep had drained him like a day of bucking bales, he almost reneged. But Falcon sounded so eager to rope a suspect, Dover couldn't nix the roundup.

Yet when he saw Falcon striding up the outside stairs, his stomach clenched. Falcon was tinged with membership in the Select Group. Stained with insidious treason.

They drove in silence to the murder scene.

What was going on with this wild bunch, the Select Group? Whatever it was, Dover felt he had to decipher it fast. Before they turned him and a good part of the country into a pile of cinders.

Dover stared at the graffiti-covered overpasses. Garish symbols of pride and hate. And most of all, he thought, a stony despair.

"—creep up on some 'bangers?" Falcon said as they entered the blitzkrieg area, where the '92 riots had exploded.

"We'll save that pleasure for later. Let's see if any civilians around here have a conscience. Or maybe find someone who's fed up with the 'bangers running the place."

"Who would that be?"

"How's your Korean?"

After an hour of banging on doors, they found that the Koreans who lived scattered throughout the area were aware of the brutal murder of one of their own. But the immigrants from the Pacific Rim were also briefed on the rules of South Central. Which being, in order to keep their shops intact, not boycotted or burned out or trashed, they paid homage and financial tribute to the lords of the realm. Dominion by modern day Samurai, with all the ferocity and none of the nobility, to wit: 'bangers.

However, in spite of the law of the 'hood, Dover felt they might have a chance with Mrs. Sam, an elderly widow and a distant relative of the deceased. Her face radiated a reflective wisdom not often seen in the Western world. Frail as a fallen leaf, she was in her eightieth summer. Her fragility only emphasized the steel of her soul.

Perhaps more importantly, she was hurting. Affected by the misfortune of another human being. A sensibility displayed so rarely in the low-lifes around here, that Dover could've hugged her.

"No need for killing him," she said, staring at her lap.

"Poor Mr. Ryong," Dover said softly. "Cut down in the prime of his life. So senseless." He shook his head. "People must fight the evil spirits that do such acts."

He caught her nodding just a trace.

"Help us, Mrs. Sam. Just point us toward them. We'll take them out of action for a long time."

She seemed to think it over, but said nothing.

"We know about the group," he added, "but we need the individual. His description. A name. Please."

She wrangled the ideas through her philosophical framework. So long that Dover gave up hope. He glanced at Falcon, silently asking if he thought they should leave.

"I was going to the market."

Dover stared at her. "You mean last night?"

She nodded again, then said she'd been across the street from Ryong's store, walking to a grocer's to buy some tea. Should've bought it during the day, but she'd forgotten; some days her memory slipped. Anyway, she happened to glance over and see two black boys going into Ryong's.

She bought the tea and walked back past the store. She saw nothing else. Heard no shot. But after she was home a few minutes, she heard the police sirens, then the helicopter's roar. She looked out, wincing at the machine's blinding searchlights. And it struck her that those two had no business going into Ryong's.

"Do you know who they are?" Dover asked.

She shook her head.

Falcon said, "Have you seen them in the neighborhood?"

She appraised the consequences. Took a deep breath. Centered herself with the universe. "The big one, he is with the gang boys."

His eyes as bright blue as a boy's best marble, Dover jotted down the description she gave. Sounded like the black version of *The Incredible Hulk*.

Back in the car, Dover and Falcon figured they'd contact C.R.A.S.H. From the description of the buffed perp, the gang experts could probably ID him. Or at least pull up some candidates from their 'banger database.

Then Dover glanced at Falcon, noting he resembled The Scarecrow in *The Wizard of Oz*. With the stuffing knocked out.

And Dover felt like The Tin Woodsman with his joints rusted tight. They'd had a tough couple of days in Southern California's rendition of Oz.

"Let's do it Monday," Dover said, "when the full unit's there. That'll give us more brainpower to tap."

"I hear that. Catch up with you then." So he took wing.

Dover slid into his Bel Air, started the engine and let it idle, the low rumbling snaking along his legs and up his spine, relaxing him. But before he cruised back to his condo, he had other business.

He took the Harbor Freeway north, the Hollywood east, then exited for Union Station. He paced toward the edifice, gawking at the high arched windows with burnt orange scallops, and the lofty clock tower, emblematic of a more ordered era.

He strolled past soaring Maurita palms and entered a lavish world of gleaming black marble, inlaid tiles, and polished mahogany trim. You could play football in here, if the city had a team. His legs felt sapped. He yearned to drop into one of the huge leather seats, nestle in good, then day-dream until his troubles disappeared like the next bus to anywhere.

Instead, he crossed to a bank of lockers. Slipping a key from his pocket, he opened one and extracted a bulging clasp envelope. His time was up on this locker, so he walked along the bank until he found an empty one. Stuck the en-velope inside, inserted some quarters, then twisted the key.

Back at his condo complex, he ambled to the pool. A gaggle of young women lazed in plastic chaise lounges under a glaring sun guaranteed to burnish even the most bronzed body. He eased into a deck chair where he drew brief glances from the goddesses del sol.

He stared at the poolside fringe of palms, their fans heaving and settling with each warm breeze. When he thought no one was looking, he reached over to a plant that'd been potted in a wooden half barrel. With the locker key he dug a two inch deep hole in the dirt and dropped it in.

Stretching, he took another gander at the poolside ex-pose. He nodded at the tawny-maned lass in the green neon thong who peeked his way. Then he rose to his feet and am-bled to his lonely abode. No bare feet padded behind him on the walkway. Sometimes life was not as floral and fleshy as a good Pinot Noir. *Tres malchance.*

Once inside, he felt weary and at loose ends. Con-sidering his aroused libidinous state, he was thankful he had a date with Mademoiselle April tonight. But he'd better conserve *le peu de energie* he had left.

Then he spotted Stretch's books stacked at the front of his bookcase. He studied the spines. Stretch wanted him to have these. One of them, anyway. But why? Something to do with the group?

Hefting the tomes about chess, quantum mechanics, and parallel universes, he weighed the choices. He needed to understand not just the mechanics of those subjects, but how Stretch's mind functioned. How he'd have reasoned things out. What moves he'd have made if he'd discovered a conspiracy to take over America.

Dover didn't fully understand how Stretch thought, because he would've expected the wacky redhead to tell him all he'd discovered. To ask for some help. After all, they were goddamn partners.

But Stretch had investigated the dilemma alone. Had only tried to contact Dover when he must have suspected he was in danger. A last ditch effort to explain what was going on.

That made no sense. So he had to learn Stretch's inner thoughts. Maybe these books would give him the insight.

He chose the one on quantum mechanics. By John Gribbin, it was strangely titled, *Schrodinger's Kittens and the Search for Reality*. He grabbed a cold bottle of Gatorade from the refrigerator and plopped down in his recliner. Steeled his mind. Opened to page one.

He read for hours, trying to grasp the ideas of the geniuses who'd developed theories as to why and how the world turned. He wondered if Stretch got this stuff. And if it would have affected his thinking about human affairs, such as a planned *coup d'etat*.

Quantum theory explained how stars were born. It defined the workings of lasers, semiconductors, and transistors. It was used to address the workings of genetics and in carbon dating of materials.

Some of the men who developed quantum theory included Max Planck, Albert Einstein, and Niels Bohr. And what had that august group determined? Something so bizarre it took his breath away.

Dover interpreted quantum theory, which was used to explain many modern scientific phenomena, as a hocus pocus, sleight-of-hand, now-you-see-it, now-you-don't sideshow.

It was an approximation of what happened in the world of physics. Meaning there was no certainty to the results of applying it. Bottom line, it was guesswork.

It was hard to say where a particle was located in space while also trying to measure its momentum. Erwin Schrodinger cleared this up with his theory of wave mechanics, postulating that you can't say where a bit of matter is located and how fast it's traveling at the same time, so you make a rough estimate as to both. You call this a wave function showing probability distribution. Yep, you're guessing.

Paul Dirac said almost the same thing, calling it quantum mechanics. Werner Heisenberg noted that since scientists were using probability distributions of coordinates then the momentum calculations would have wide variables. So he gave it the appellation "the uncertainty principle."

All of which left Dover feeling very uncertain.

He put down the book and headed for the shower. The cascade of warm water felt fantastic as Dover scrubbed stress and fatigue out of his pores. He tried to cleanse his mind as well, wanting to solve this enigma. Stretch was gone, but he could carry the big guy's torch a little farther until he lit up the shadows where these slimeballs hid.

April would be there soon. He'd offered to take her to Campanile, Spago, or L'Orangerie, but she was into her special diet, and she was sure she'd found the menu to give her the slim serenity she sought. The ingredients would have to be mixed in his kitchen.

Ironically, she was gorgeous. He thought of Billy Crystal doing Ricardo Montalban's line, "You look mahvelous!" And she did, dahling.

Two things puzzled him: One, why she hadn't been more successful in movies, TV, or theater. Of course, L.A. being the land of angels, there were a lot of bodacious babes traipsing the sidewalks and beaches, showing up at every audition, gracing casting couches.

Fame was hard to come by. Fleeting and fickle. Go figure.

Number two was why she stayed hooked up with him. She wasn't a police groupie, and he wasn't rich or famous or Hollywood handsome. They had little in common, except for that wild thing. He was conservative, rational, and a bit cynical. She was flighty, trendy, and in search of herself or someone she would like to be.

He'd moved to California in a funk, but with the lofty idea of being his own person and letting everyone else do the same without criticism or complaint. But it grated on his sensibilities whenever April leaped full bore into any self-discovery method or New Age philosophy sweeping the collective consciousness at the moment. The California bandwagon was always rolling and always full.

He called it the psy-fi flavor of the month. April flushed to a lobster tone when he said that. But her memory was short when he tried to remind her of the other flights of fantasy she'd already tried.

He dried with a fluffy towel that soothed his skin. And he recalled what was on tonight's menu besides food. Ah, yes.

Sensual Psychic Massage Therapy.

April's latest and best fad. He zoned out when she launched into a lengthy explanation on her recent gimmick, but when she'd treated him to a demonstration week before last, she'd gotten his full attention. Ah-uuuu-gah. All hands on deck. Man the torpedoes.

It combined yoga, tantrism, and acupressure into a process for massaging erogenous zones, relieving stress and removing negativity through pleasurable arousal combined with muscle and thought relaxation. In other words, you got horny and loose, and when your spirits got high enough, you gave vent to your natural desires, thus achieving fulfillment and satisfaction. And damn! It worked for him.

He slipped on some briefs, refreshed and rigid with anticipation.

Chapter 14

April made her appearance as an Indian priestess, her hair weaved into braids and held with a fuchsia headband. A beauty mark accented her luscious ruby mouth. Her blouse was a gauzy affair like a Hindu lady might wear over a sari. But April wore no sari. No bra, tank top, or camisole.

She wore flesh-colored shorts over which she'd hiked a red thong bikini. Hoop earrings, a jade necklace, and two gold ankle bracelets completed the ensemble. Almost.

"Nice nose ring, babe. Really sets off the outfit."

"Sarcastic prick." She swept past, lugging a plastic grocery sack stuffed like an overfed guppy. "I'm famished. Let's go with this right away, because there's stuff we've got to do to be in mindfulness with our food."

"Be in . . ." But she was already in the kitchen. He turned and followed her like a faithful dog. He wondered if Lassie ever had bitchy days and wanted to bite a hunk out of her master's ass. "This 'mindfulness' thing . . . ?"

"It's resurfacing. This Vietnamese Buddhist monk says we need to have a relationship with our food, you know?"

"No, I'm not so sure I—"

"Food comes from the earth, so when we eat, we're re-establishing our link with the earth. The sun, too, of course."

"So we try to be mindful of this connection?" This had echoes of the idea about not eating anything dead.

"Exactamundo, big guy." She made a playful grab for his crotch.

He sidestepped, then wished he hadn't. "So what's on the menu?"

She dumped out greenery identified as herbs, roots, bamboo shoots, bean sprouts, leeks, and watercress, and began to slice, dice, and mince in earnest.

"Could I help with something?" he asked.

"Bowls, silverware, glasses, water, wine."

"Two turtle doves?"

"No meat tonight, Great White Hunter."

He grabbed a Coors Lite from the fridge and set about doing his chores. Laid out the bowls and silverware, then took a swig of the golden brew. Now there was a beverage to get philosophical about.

When she'd finished her preparations, the bowls brimmed with fixings chopped up and mixed. He shot a look into the kitchen, searching for other morsels of food. But this roughage was it.

He picked up his fork, and she gave him a wilting look, so he put it back down with a sheepish smile.

She gathered her concentration; he gathered a peek at her chest.

"First we breathe in," she said. That was good to see. "Then we breathe out and smile. We look at each other. We see each other."

He smiled, getting really hungry now.

"Then we look at the food."

"That works for me, let's dig in."

She frowned, then said, "Let the food be real for you."

"Oh, it is. It is."

"Be grateful to have food to eat and sorry for those who don't."

Now *that* he could relate to. The misery of people starving to death in large numbers around the globe. Of course, he'd rather think about it when he wasn't eating, so he wouldn't choke with guilt.

They acknowledged their food and each other and promised to help others and to be aware of each moment and live in the present.

That completed, he forked in a mouthful. Surprise. The verdant mixture was tasty, and he devoured the entire bowl.

But despite his pleasant acquaintanceship with the food, the showstopper for the evening was the Sensual Psychic Massage. Especially the part where she envisioned his phallus to be a popsicle.

Sunday morning arrived, and Dover heeded the call with reservations. He and Falcon drove back to Ryong's, looked over the area to see what was shaking and to speculate what might have happened there late Friday night, then talked with some passersby and several more residents of the area. But there was still no one who knew or suspected anything, which was not a huge surprise.

Both of them were beat from the late hours and early mornings, and they decided nothing was about to break on the case, so in mid-afternoon, they called it a day. Besides, Dover wanted to get back to his computer. There were other crimes to be solved.

Back in his condo, he spent several hours tapping away at the keyboard. Entering various key words, he was hopeful each time, but he got no results. Then as evening set in, the card table wobbled.

Dover clutched the computer to keep it from shimmying off the table. It reminded him of the thousands of aftershocks after the Northridge quake, which had made Angelenos very nervous. Many had moved out. Others still carried the stress inside them, making their minds as unstable as the shaky ground. Dover wondered if he should get the hell out while he could.

Maybe there were too many threats here.

But he saw another sunrise, so he fired up the Bel Air and motored to the office through the brown L.A. haze and his usual morning brain fog. He and Falcon mapped out their moves for the day. They'd check with the C.R.A.S.H. Unit about a suspect in the Ryong homicide, then follow up with the Korean woman who'd seen the 'bangers enter the store.

Falcon went to the john, and Dover called Harsha at ATF.

"Just busting my ass," Harsha said. "Same old, same old."

"Never changes. Same here. But I wanted to get the names of the rest of those subscribers."

"We already discussed what I found."

"Oh, if you can't talk now, I'll spring for lunch."

"Sorry, Rick, I'm tied up three ways from Sunday." He cleared his throat. "I'm going to Palm Springs. It's a permanent assignment. Should be great—golf and spotting celebs and all—only trouble is, I got to get there yesterday, so I'm up to my ass in movers and realtors."

"I'm surprised, Don. Were you expecting this?"

"Nope, it was a bolt out of the yellow. But I really gotta go."

"Was it something I asked you to—"

"Nah, but no matter what, you got nothing from me, okay?"

"I understand. So I'll call you later."

"When I get settled, I'll give you a jingle."

The dial tone hummed in his ear.

Another aftershock.

Falcon walked up. "You okay, man?"

"Yeah, fine. Let's go see the C.R.A.S.H. guys."

There were a dozen dicks roosting in the Gang Unit, feet up, phones stuck to their ears, or gabbing in small groups. Desks and tops of filing cabinets overflowed with gang rags, jackets, jewelry, a couple of Uzis in plastic evidence bags, photos of punks throwing gang signs, gripping AK-47s or Mac-10s. Wall charts showed the hierarchy of the city's principal gangs.

The detectives were young and husky. The show-no-fear type. A couple of them would've looked natural with jailhouse tattoos on their bulky arms, smoking reefer and guzzling beer.

A guy who went by the nickname Ninja, owing to his long training in kick-boxing, glanced up at them. "Ricochet!" he howled. "What're you doin', slumming?" He motioned them in. "Sit down. Wha's up, cuz?" Then he looked at Falcon. "No offense, podner."

"No problem. Everything is everything."

"That's cool. So R, my man, you lookin' for a 'banger?"

"A witness thinks so. No name, but she gave us a description. The mutt's supposed to be a Crip."

Dover ran the info past Ninja, who had a couple of ideas. The warrior also called over several other detectives to get their take. Consensus was the muscled-up dude could be Hammus R. Jackson, alias Hamburger, Maynard F. Meadow, nicknamed Tractor, or maybe Cletus P. Thornton, tag of Gorilla.

"So these dudes are really buffed?" Falcon asked.

Ninja shrugged. "More like dieseled."

They found some photos of the Three Evil Stooges, all regular customers of the LAPD who came in often for updated mug shots. Dover flipped through other photos to find three goofs who looked similar to their suspects, compiling a photo lineup to show Mrs. Sam.

"Here, you gotta have this one," Ninja said, tossing them a glossy head-and-shoulders mug shot. "He's a Blood, but big."

"Jesus Christ," Dover and Falcon blurted out in unison.

Ninja leered, like Dennis Hopper in *Speed.* "Meet Dr. Doom."

"No thanks," Dover said.

Ninja also called the Identification Division, asking them to pull the jackets on the three muscle-bound mopes, so Dover would have some background material in case the lady should pick one.

They thanked Ninja and the other detectives and left the Gang Unit, both glad they didn't have that job.

They drove to South Central where they pulled into Mrs. Sam's small driveway, crossed her small lawn, and knocked on the door of her small house. Anywhere but L.A. the place would've cost ten grand. Here, you were talking six figures. She unhooked five locks and peeked out.

Trembling, she invited them in. Refastened three of the locks. They all sat and looked at each other. Private thoughts flew about like bats. Each wondered why the others lived as they did.

Then Dover cleared his throat and delivered the pitch. The "identify them and get them off the streets" speech which so often fell flat with street people. They knew the true world of crime and punishment, including probation, parole, and "let's make a deal."

Mrs. Sam listened in silence, occasionally nodding her head. It'd been a long time since Dover had talked to anyone like her. These days, being attentive and respectful was not much in vogue.

"We have some photographs, Mrs. Sam. They may or may not show the boy you described. But please see if you recognize anyone."

He handed her the folder.

She handled it as though it had photos of mass murderers, which it no doubt did. But she considered the faces carefully. Which was brave in itself, since the dudes glared at the camera as though they'd like to bust out and maim anyone caught gawking.

A couple of minutes ticked into eternity. They weighed heavily on the detectives. Mrs. Sam seemed not to notice.

"Do any of them look familiar?" Dover asked.

She shook her head, possibly meaning "negatory on your request there, Five-O," or perhaps just being an assessment of the panorama of losers scowling at her from the folder.

Dover waited. Then he said, "Sa-i-gu, Mrs. Sam."

She looked up, startled. Mentioning the date of the riots brought the horror flooding back. But her alarm diminished, then disappeared as she absorbed the thought, a raindrop falling into a sea of wisdom.

She studied the folder, then looked up. Dover knew she'd make the sacrifice. With a shaking hand, she fingered dope number five. "This boy is the one I see. Big one going into store with the other boy. Belong to that gang—Crip."

Dover checked the photo. The man of the hour was Gorilla. "You're sure?"

"I'm sure, Detective."

Dover regarded the small woman who had outgrown her house, the neighborhood, and the sprawling city with her brave action. "I don't know how to thank you, Mrs. Sam."

"No need. America is my home."

168

★ ★ ★ ★ ★

In the car, Falcon clenched his fist. "We got an eyewitness!"

Dover steered the hurtling Dodge. "Only that Gorilla went into Ryong's about the time of the homicide," he warned. "Our witness saw no weapon, heard no shots, saw no one leaving the scene or jumping into a car. None of the cherry stuff that would sway a jury."

"So we're not going with it?"

"Hell, yes, we are. Now we got a perp to work on. Makes it a whole lot easier. Dig up some corroborating evidence, who knows, we might pull this case out of the shitcan."

"Yo, we got the cartridge."

"Could help," Dover agreed. "Say Gorilla carried the gauge and blasted Ryong. The other kid had the pistol. ID him, and maybe we turn it up."

"And we got those latents on the jewelry case."

"So if Gorilla was the main man on the robbery, he could've leaned on the case while he pointed out the goodies."

Falcon said, "The lab tries a match on his prints. What else?"

"Let's drive by his place. Look it over. See if his car's there."

"The Nissan Pathfinder?" Falcon said.

"Yeah, might as well have a door sign that says, 'I serve dope.'"

"And after we check the layout for making the grab on Gorilla?"

"Come back later, bag him, find the jewelry and both guns."

"That's def, partner."

Dover glanced at Falcon, feeling both a connection with

him as a fellow detective and an icy suspicion toward him because he probably belonged to an organization of violent rebels.

They turned a corner, both watching house numbers.

"There," Dover said. "White house on the right with the Monte Carlo at the curb and the black Nissan in the drive."

"Got it."

"Grab the tag on that Monte C."

Falcon scribbled down the plate number. Just then a mammoth kid, a quart of Colt 45 in his giant paw, stumbled out of the house.

"Shit," said Falcon, looking to the front. "Think he made us?"

"If he didn't, he's drunker than I think."

"So what now?"

"Let's go start the paper." He wheeled toward Parker Center.

Halfway to headquarters, Dover's brain replayed macabre scenes. Stretch's burned out car, the autopsy, Harsha swearing he detected C-4. LAPD bomb squad denies it, Harsha does a fade to black, as in Palm Springs. Don't call me, I'll call you.

And then he made himself face what he'd realized during that conversation with Harsha, but hadn't wanted to believe. What he'd pushed to the back of his consciousness. But now it crashed in like Nicholson's axe splitting the door in *The Shining*.

The reedy tone of Harsha's voice. Dover had heard the pinched vocal cords during hundreds of suspect interviews. No matter how cool or how tough they tried to act, it always seized their throats, caused by that old demon, fear.

Luckily, Harsha had already told him a couple of the

numbers on The Untouchables list were for an FBI boss in Dallas, Texas, and a CIA official in McLean, Virginia. Great information, but he suspected Harsha wouldn't be giving up any more. He'd had a change of heart.

But even if he could unveil this puzzle palace, how could he bring it down? Would his input be like one vote for a presidential candidate, worthless in the scheme of things? Would the machines continue to whir, fueled and oiled and tuned by the rich, the influential, and the powerful?

"Don't miss the turnoff," Falcon said.

"Huh?"

"You a day late. Right there."

Dover flicked his eyes to the sign, then swerved, tires squealing, trying to hold the ramp.

Falcon grabbed the dashboard, hung on through the Space Mountain thrill ride, then sat back, saying, "Man, you've been zoned out for ten minutes. What's on your brain, anyway? As Mr. Potato Head said, 'It's an awful thing to waste your mind, if you have one.' "

Dover said, "Just thinking how we're going to snare Gorilla."

As they entered the squad room, Dover grabbed a message, read it, then picked up the phone.

"I wondered if you could come by the house for a while. I've got some beer on ice, and I'll make us sandwiches if you're hungry."

"You make it hard to refuse, Terri."

"Then don't. See you later."

Falcon called in the tag on the Monte C. "Comes back registered to a Rafael Santos," he said. "Home address in East L.A. No stolen report."

"Check the tag for a report," Dover said.

Falcon ran it. Negative. Not reported stolen or missing. Falcon shrugged. "Maybe Santos loaned them the ride."

"I can't figure the connection."

"Anyway," said Falcon, "we can still get a warrant on Gorilla, if his prints match."

"Fill out the lab request," said Dover.

Dover and Terri sat in cushioned red-and-orange deck chairs on the patio that he and Stretch had built. A breeze huffed through the hills, and the sun lowered inch by inch. Life seemed as gentle and honeyed as a good Sauterne.

"Are you still working with Stretch's disks?" she asked.

He considered the silver can in his hand. A drop of condensation chased down the side. "I fiddle with them some."

"You're getting somewhere, aren't you?"

"I've probably raised more questions than anything. Haven't really found any answers." Riveting as Roy Rogers. Yep.

She nodded, twisting her hands together in her lap. Her beer glass sat on the low table between them; she'd taken only a couple of sips. By now, the suds should be as warm as Trigger's piss.

"I've thought about this a lot." She paused and took a deep breath. "Stretch is gone, and I've accepted that. It's not going to change. Whatever he stumbled across was very dangerous."

"That's true, but—"

"Rick, I know I'm being selfish, but I'm being practical, too. I want you to forget the whole thing. Even if you identify this group, you'll never be able to fight them." Her lip trembled. "I can't lose anyone else close to me. I'd go to pieces." Tears pooled in her luminous eyes.

He placed his hand on her arm. "I've had doubts about

going through with it, too. Who knows, maybe it's hopeless."

"Rick, let's just get on with our lives. Can you forget about right and wrong, just this once?"

He stared at the green lawn. "The bright shining truths I learned as a kid in Kansas have become pretty shadowy. Sometimes I have no idea what to do."

"Then will you drop it?" Her eyes pleaded with him.

"I'll think about it. I'm not sure what's at stake."

"Maybe your life." And the tears began to roll.

He assured her he'd been careful, and that no one knew he was involved. Told her he doubted he could even solve the riddle. Said for her not to worry.

But as he stared into her wet eyes, a phrase drifted into mind. Sent by Stretch or by Spike Lee? he wondered. It said, loud and clear: Do the right thing.

Chapter 15

Dover roared up to his condo, raring to break the rest of the balky computer codes. He threw on shorts and a T-shirt, slapped on a Raiders ball cap, and flipped on the machine. The match was on.

He accessed NCIC and called up the file index under the clandestine Fugitive Field. Had to get a make on the Special Group, the Volunteer Group, and the Contacts. But he was back to deciphering codes through names scrawled in concrete.

That weekend he'd swung by the library and checked out several books on the history of cinema. Jean Harlow was notably featured in all. He tried some titles: *Moran of the Marines*, *The Saturday Night Kid*, and *Hell's Angels*. No go. He entered *Reckless*.

He thought that one might cop the Oscar, but it flopped. Tried *Red Dust* and *New York Nights*. They bombed in a New York minute.

Speaking of which, he tossed in B-O-M-B-S-H-E-L-L.

Direct hit. Brought up the Special Group. Getting the hang of this game. He printed out another long list of names, some he recognized as officers of the LAPD, all flour white.

But not all the white cops on the force were listed. One prime example: His name was missing from the roster. Good, he thought.

He checked for some other guys' names that were in the Robbery/Homicide Department. Yep, there was Eddie. And

Deadeye. Stretch wasn't there, but he could've been deleted.

But now he was confused. Maybe the Special Group was made up of those who'd uncovered what the Select Group was trying to do. They'd organized in order to stop a plot to overthrow the government. That is, if he was right about the Select Group's plans.

Stretch told Terri there was an out-of-control group. The big guy had been on his way to tell him about it, but got his balls blown off. If Stretch had told him sooner, maybe they could've worked out a solution, and Stretch wouldn't have been—

But there was no point in hitching a ride on that freight train of missed opportunities, should haves, and if onlys. It strung out so far it was endless. Clear into hyperspace.

Still, he could assume one of these groups was running rampant. So pick one. Go fish. The minority group or the whites? Select or Special?

There was a meeting scheduled for tomorrow night. He had to see what was going on. He'd tail someone. But who? His new partner, who was on the Select Group list, or Eddie or Deadeye, both members of the Special Group?

It would likely be the whites who were meeting. Stretch probably belonged to the group and had gone to some of their gatherings. But why such an elaborate scheme to protect the identities of the groups? If there was evidence of a plot to overthrow the U.S. government, they should expose it.

But as a detective, he realized the key word in that thought was evidence. Cop theories as to who had committed a crime were cheaper than Kansas dirt. But then came the problem of proving your theory in a courtroom.

Many times the pieces of the puzzle never quite came together "beyond a reasonable doubt."

Especially if the defendant could afford a crafty attorney. Or a gang of them. The O.J. Doctrine.

So maybe the "good" group was still gathering evidence as to what the "bad" group was planning, how they thought they'd pull it off, what their timetable was, and who was involved. This left him like the spy out in the cold who didn't know squat. He had to see what went on at those meetings, and he couldn't go uninvited.

No matter, a bit of reconnaissance might answer some questions. A surveillance on Eddie or Deadeye should lead him to the location. Then maybe he could gather a few facts as to what the Special Group was doing.

But he had the feeling he was crossing a line, and that once he did, there would be no turning back. Once the first piece was moved, and the timer started, the game would be underway for keeps. No let ups, no time outs. He'd be in it until check and checkmate. As Buck Owens warbled, maybe he hadn't seen the worst part yet.

A few hours later, with a game plan brewing in his brain, Dover flopped into bed. He hit the remote, settled back on his pillow, and watched Bruce Willis in a lighthearted romp with dusky terrorists.

The credits rolled, he killed the lights, faded to black.

Slept like a shark cruising gloomy waters, never quite unconscious. In his murky dreams a Select submarine armed its torpedoes; a Special destroyer readied its mines. He manned a foundering rowboat between them.

And the answers were in the game of chess. But they hadn't been for Stretch. Or maybe he'd made a careless move.

★ ★ ★ ★ ★

When the alarm blared, he swatted it into silence and headed for the shower. An hour later, he stumbled into the squad room and spotted Falcon studying some notes. The guy looked fresh and clean; must've slept like a saint. Dover wanted to smack him.

"Morning, Rick. I was looking at . . . hey, man, you feeling okay?"

Dover dropped into a chair and palmed his face. He looked up with Beaujolais-veined eyes. "Didn't sleep well. But I'm listening."

"Check it out, I've got some aspirin in my—"

Dover waved it away. "Let's hear it."

Falcon shrugged then said, "I passed by the lab. They made Gorilla's prints on the jewelry case. Got the fool cold."

"Great!" Dover banged his tabletop, then wished he hadn't.

Falcon smothered a smile. "With Mrs. Sam's ID and the latent prints we should be able to snag some warrants. Then we'll go snatch up the dude."

"Sounds good. You're in charge of thinking today." He gave a groan. "Oh, hell, give me those aspirin and let me drink some coffee."

Dover slugged down two cups of java and three aspirin, then struggled to his feet. "Let's hit it before I succumb to the blue flu."

The Assistant D.A. was in a good mood. He took them to see the judge, who signed off on the arrest warrant and on search warrants for the house, Gorilla's Pathfinder, and the red Monte Carlo.

They left headquarters with a folder full of warrants and hearts as strong as lions. Going for it. Gorilla was about to be caged.

Dover wheeled off the Harbor Freeway, cruising South Central, driving west on Florence. They both cast wary looks as they slid past Tom's Liquor Market at the intersection with Normandie. Ground zero in '92. Making a left on La Salle, he turned onto 76th and rolled into the 'hood with high hopes.

Two patrol cars sat at either end of the block, ready to cut off any getaways. A SWAT team was in a van a block away, prepared to bag Gorilla. The snare was set.

But there was no Monte Carlo parked at the curb, and no Nissan Pathfinder in the driveway. No homeboys kickin' it on the porch. Place looked as barren as the Mojave on a Monday night.

Falcon said, "You think he spooked?"

"Sure as Disneyland sells mouse ears. We're burned."

"We got a Plan B?"

Dover cranked the wheel, made a left on Brighton, and drove to Florence. He radioed the units to meet by Inglewood Park Cemetery.

He hung up the mike. "Your day to think, you make the call."

Falcon pinched his lower lip, his eyes crackling clear. "Gorilla's in the wind, so I say we got two choices: Watch his crib around the clock, hope he drifts back for some stash or somethin'—"

"Can't pull it off in this 'hood. We'd be made in ten minutes."

"I hear that funky music, white boy."

"What else you got?"

"We find a snitch who tells us when Gorilla lights back here, or maybe where he's holed up now."

"Better, I like it so far."

"You want more?"

"The cars?"

"Okay, we put out BOLOs for the Monte Carlo and Pathfinder. We give Gorilla's description at roll call. Lots of eyes on the street."

When the other units rolled up, Dover told them the house looked deserted, and their fugitive had done a ghost. He thanked them for the backup and gave regrets it hadn't gone down. But after the cataclysmic bank robbery shootout in '97, LAPD officers were glad when a situation ended peacefully.

The patrol cars screeched off. The SWAT team's van lurched away. Dover didn't have as much to prove, and he knew the Dodge wouldn't lay rubber, so he pulled away nice and easy like Morgan Freeman in *Driving Miss Daisy*.

On the way to Parker Center, Falcon said, "You want to do a drive-by on Gorilla after dark, see if he crawls back to his crib?"

"I'm busy tonight. Let's see if any of the patrol guys spot the Monte C or the Pathfinder. In the morning we'll check with the Gang Unit about any snitches who could run him down."

"Now I think on it, I'm hangin' with my lady tonight. Fuck the dude, we'll step to him hard tomorrow. Break on his ass big and bad."

"Don't get wound too tight."

"You saw Mr. Ryong. Brains scattered like kibbles and bits."

"You know, staring at too many stiffs can grind you down."

"I dig it, but that gangsta shit is so lame." Falcon shook his head. "They go for bad just for props. No need for it."

"Hey, there's a gazillion sociopaths out there. You can't catch them all, and you won't change any of them. If you make it a private vendetta, you'll end up a bottle baby or a wacko."

"But you don't seem whupped."

"Not yet, but I've seen it happen to lots of guys. And some days are worse than others. I've lost some amps this past week."

Falcon nodded. "That's a hard tune you been blowin'."

Now the Glass House, scene of transparent justice, loomed ahead. Dover pulled over and stopped. "I've got an errand to run. Take the steed into the stable, and I'll see you there later."

In thirty minutes Dover was at the homicide table. He made a few calls and puttered with some papers, pretending to be working. Falcon finally gave a wave and left. Now Dover only had to keep an eye on Eddie.

While he waited, Dover called Titus, who said he'd found the problem, ordered a part, and he'd fix the Pontiac right away. Dover figured he had better odds of Ed McMahon appearing with a big check.

A few minutes later, the iron pumper shrugged his shoulders, pushed himself up from his desk, and lumbered toward the elevator.

Dover hustled to the exit and hurried down the stairway, then stood by a palm tree, waiting. In a minute, Eddie came out and headed for his Thunderbird. Dover legged it along the sidewalk and jumped into his Bel Air, parked at a meter. He watched Eddie fire up his chariot. Then the muscle-bound chump wheeled out and screeched down the street.

Dover waited for some cars to get between them, then he pulled out and kept a casual tail on the T-bird. No reason to stay tight. He was quite sure Eddie was going home. The meeting likely wouldn't start until this evening.

But he didn't want to take any chances with his mystical

detection system. He'd been wrong with hunches before. And this was one meeting he didn't want to miss.

After three hours of staring at the T-bird in a parking lot, Dover realized he'd made a tactical error. He should've laid in groceries. His stomach registered empty and was churning like a washing machine.

Just as Dover decided to head for a Quik Shop, Eddie ambled to his car, burped, and slid behind the wheel. Dover wished the guy a dose of E. coli, then cinched his seat belt tight across his hollow gut.

He followed Eddie back to the Ventura Freeway, heading southeast. Traffic was thick, but it moved along okay. Dover felt a trickle of adrenaline in his blood as the orchestra started warming up in the pit.

They caught the Hollywood going south. Eddie drove past the Hollywood Bowl and the exits for Santa Monica Boulevard and Dodgers Stadium, on through the stack, continuing along the Santa Ana Freeway. Was the guy going back to Parker Center?

Nah, Eddie wasn't big on overtime. Besides, Dover didn't think the meeting would be at police headquarters. At least, he hoped not.

He breathed easier when Eddie rolled south on the Santa Ana, past the logical turnoffs to Parker Center. But where was he headed?

It was twelve after eight. Eddie should be getting close, assuming the meeting was at eight-thirty. And assuming he was going to a meeting. Then Dover had a thought that made his scalp ice over. He rolled up the car window, blocking the cool breeze. A shudder wriggled through him.

What if the Special Group had changed their schedule? When they searched for Stretch's disks and didn't find them, maybe they took precautions. If so, all his work on this puzzle would be for zip.

Still on the Santa Ana. They'd passed the interchanges with the Pomona and the Long Beach freeways. Basically touring East L.A.

Now Eddie angled to the far right lane and took an exit that slanted in a southwesterly direction. Dover eased back, staying loose.

They bumped over some railroad tracks, made a few more turns, and cruised through an industrial area. Warehouses squatted here and there like huge frogs in an amorphous pond. Probably busy around here during the day, but it was still and spooky at night.

Eddie turned onto one of the side streets.

Dover hesitated, not wanting to run up on the T-bird if Eddie had stopped, since he'd make the Chevy in a heartbeat. Now Dover realized he should've rented some wheels for this gig, but he'd missed that angle. Lately, there'd been too many to cover.

So he slowed, watched Eddie drive down the block, then continued for two blocks and turned to parallel the T-bird. He drove a couple of blocks and parked. Then he waited until darkness could cover a figure sneaking down side streets and empty sidewalks.

It was time. He slipped a small pair of binoculars into his jacket pocket. Then he left the Chevy, wondering if he'd ever see it again.

He stopped at the corner, peeked around it, saw nothing. Then he sauntered down the sidewalk toward where he'd last seen Eddie. If he was spotted, no cover story would work.

At the next corner, to his left, there were at least a dozen cars parked along the street. And none of the businesses or warehouses on either side were open. He continued down the sidewalk.

When he reached the next corner, his suspicions were confirmed. Cars lined both sides of the street, stretching for two blocks. A warehouse loomed at the end. It was lit up like the UFO in *Close Encounters of the Third Kind*.

This was it. The meeting place for the Special Group. They hadn't changed their plans. Maybe they didn't know he had Stretch's disk, or figured he couldn't access it, or assumed the information would mean nothing to him. All reasonable assumptions.

They probably decided there was no way he'd know about the NCIC connection, or the code to get into the Fugitive Field, or that he could ever figure out the codes to access the files about their group.

The odds were in their favor, and without Stretch's help, or at least understanding the way Stretch thought, and without the few statements Stretch had made to Terri, the codes would have remained unbroken, probably undiscovered in the first place.

He was halfway there, and if he didn't get careless and tip his hand, he might resolve what was going on in the LAPD and the other agencies—local, state, and federal—across the country. Then he'd—

A noise. Behind him. The scuff of a shoe on cement? Flattening against the building, he turned his head to look down the sidewalk.

The light was dim along the stretch of concrete. He saw nothing. Listened for half a minute, but heard nothing else.

He was slicked over with perspiration. And the night air was cool, giving him a little shiver. Probably just a cat or a rat.

Should he go on? He'd learned there was a meeting as

scheduled, and that Eddie had attended. Along with a bunch of other people who were probably on the Special Group list.

And maybe when he cracked the other codes, the meetings and the attendees would fall into place. He wouldn't have to stick his neck out any farther, risking discovery. That was the percentage play.

He turned to retrace the route to his car. He'd feel a lot better when he dropped that baby into gear and got the hell out of Dodge. He marched five steps and stopped.

Turned back. Walked to the corner, turned left, and crept down the sidewalk. He'd check out a few cars, was all.

No one would arrive at the meeting this late. He doubted there'd be any guards posted, at least not two blocks from the place.

He pulled out his pen flashlight and a notepad and sidled down the street, stopping at each car long enough to run the beam over the back end and jot down the make and tag. Saw a personalized plate he recognized. DED I. The guy was on the list, no surprise there.

Next came an official car. No markings on it, but he recognized the light blue Buick Riviera with the four antennae. Knew who drove it: a DEA agent who'd once been a Vice detective in the LAPD.

Surely these were the good guys. No way so many law enforcement types could be linked with something illegal. Was there?

And speaking of laws, he noticed a car he felt certain he'd seen parked in one of the county attorneys' spots when they'd gotten the warrant for Gorilla. He'd run the tag later to make sure.

End of the block. He could cross the street and check the

string of cars up to the front of the warehouse. Nah, too chancy. Like risking your queen to set up some fancy ploy that might fall through.

He strained his eyes to recognize other vehicles. Only possible was a Lincoln Continental he thought belonged to a district judge. He put the binocs on the tag, but the light was too weak.

He scanned the sidewalks and the warehouse, spotting no one. Probably all inside by now. He hustled across the street, then sneaked along that side, copying numbers. Another one stopped him cold. Personalized tag on a Mercedes. REP 1. A state legislator.

One other vehicle read cop car. Federal, he thought. The good old fucking body inspectors? FBI? If so, the tag would be sanitized.

At the corner now, he crossed the street and boogied down the sidewalk toward his bomber, only two blocks away. Chuck was right: the car was as hot as a Saturday night special at a turkey shoot. He could outrun anything on this street, regardless of their price tags.

Almost to the end of the block he heard a rustling sound in a dark doorway. He hoofed on, now and then hesitating before setting his foot down in his regular rhythm, listening hard in the milliseconds. Once he thought he heard a soft step in the darkness behind him.

Reaching the next corner, he turned left. Saw his baby still hunkered at the curb, its ragtop intact, tires on the rims. Hopefully with its plug wires and distributor cap still connected.

He could make it there. He dug out the starting device. The Chevy fired up, its carbs rumbling like a lion devouring its kill.

Then he ducked into a recessed storefront and waited.

Just to see. In a few seconds, a head poked around the corner, jerked back.

Dover crept like a panther to the corner. The guy peeked again. Dover grabbed his shirt and dragged him into the open, then set his feet and swung a killer right hook at the guy's jaw.

Chapter 16

Dover missed the place on the edge of the jaw boxers swing at when they go for a knockout. But he landed a solid punch on the guy's cheekbone. The man grunted and raised his hands.

Dover still had a handful of shirt, and he yanked the guy toward him and buried a fist into his solar plexus, doubling him over. A black guy. After his wallet? The Chevy?

"You blackass bastard, thought you'd jump me? Jack me up?"

"Wait," the guy wheezed.

But Dover had hitched his knee fast and hard, catching the guy under the chin. The man stumbled backward and landed on his butt. Wait? Funny thing to say in a fistfight.

But this could be more than that. Dover reached to the small of his back and drew his .45 auto. He aimed at the man's chest. "Don't move, asshole. Just stick up your hands. Now."

The guy threw his arms up, saying, "Squash it, Ricochet."

Now Dover had the wind knocked out of him. He fumbled out his flashlight and shone it into the guy's face. The gun felt heavy in his hand, fingers trembling from the rush of adrenaline, the hot pulse of angry blood, and now the shock of realization.

Falcon.

"Son of a bitch," Dover said. "You got a piece?"

Falcon nodded, then with two fingers slowly pulled his

Beretta from his waist and slid it toward Dover.

He picked it up, stuck it in his pocket, then stuffed the backup into his waistband. "What are you doing here? And why were you creeping up on me?"

"Stall it out, man. I was just checking where you were going."

He heard the clarion ring of a lie. "There's more to it."

Falcon blew out a breath. "Damn. You on it."

Dover stared at him, still feeling shaky all over. "So give."

Rubbing his jaw, Falcon sighed, then said, "I guess you got to trust somebody, sometime."

Dover wasn't sure how much trust they could muster, but said, "Why not? Let's hear it."

"Right. Okay, it's like this." He blew out a breath. "The story goes back a few months. A brother at Parker Center overheard some crazy shit in the locker room."

Dover leaned against the wall, staring into Falcon's eyes. "Like what?"

Falcon laid it down. A black cop overheard a paleface sergeant roo-rah about a group that was going to run the off-brands out of L.A. "Black cop told another brother, who thought he was trippin', but word spread, and we figured we best get up on it. So we put a tail on Kojak and eyeballed him going to a party like the one tonight."

Sounded righteous so far. "So what's going on in there?"

"We ain't up on the whole nine, but we dig it's nothin' dope for any dude with off-white skin. 'Specially ones with black asses."

Dover winced. "You spotted me as you eyeballed the meeting?"

Now Falcon rolled his eyes. "No, you peckerwood. Check it out. Stretch, your road dog, was in the group.

Seemed you should also be tight with them."

"Stretch was in it? He was never a racist." But . . . wait. Maybe the redhead got into it, then learned this bunch was out for blood.

Falcon tilted his head in disbelief. "Whatever, I hung on your ass for the ride here."

"You what?"

"We knew these yo-yos were meeting, but they switched spots. So we did a change-up on who we tailed. Your turn tonight."

"My turn?"

"You never made the shadow. Doing your thang on Eddie. Gaffled me up until you started peepin' things out, scribbling tags on the sneak. Same shit we been doing. I'm thinkin', maybe this dude's together."

Dover felt dazed. But he stepped forward and held out his hand. Falcon hesitated, then took it, and Dover pulled him to his feet. Falcon dusted off the seat of his pants.

"Are you all right?" Dover asked.

"How the hell do I look? And don't go thinkin' you're no fuckin' badass, either. If you hadn't caught me blind, I'd have wiped this sidewalk with your lily white ass."

"I'm sorry for what I said. It was a startled reaction."

"Didn't realize I was a special nigger, huh? One you had to watch what you said around."

"That's not it, either."

Falcon stared off into the night. "I'll give you this," he said. "I crept up on you. This is a scandalous 'hood. You didn't want to get jacked, and you had to go for yours."

"Yeah, that's how it—"

"Not sayin' I'm punking out. Just rapping, that's all."

Dover nodded.

"This is the way it lay. I can hang with what you *did*. But what you screamed on me, now that's—"

"Bullshit, I know." And he wondered why his anger had flared up and the hate flowed out. He'd never seen himself as prejudiced.

"Shit," Falcon said. He worked his jaw. "Let's play it off. You ready to chill?"

"That works for me," Dover agreed. "I'm sorry, partner."

They stood there for a moment, then Dover said, "You hungry?"

"Enough to eat a Kansas cow."

Falcon's Mercury sat a block over from Dover's Bel Air.

They took the Santa Ana Freeway to the north, then jumped onto the Santa Monica headed west. At the edge of Culver City, they found a diner where they dropped into a back booth. They ordered hamburgers and apple pie. The waitress poured two steaming cups of coffee which turned out not to be awful.

Dover stared at Falcon, who gingerly bit into his burger, and he hoped he'd found out which side was straight in this imbroglio. And which group was out to take over America. No way to know for sure, so he decided to take a shot.

"Are you up on the NCIC connection?"

Falcon's jaw slackened. "No way. What's up with that?"

"We've got some jaw jackin' to do . . . partner."

They were both beat, and they agreed to hash out the details in the next couple of days. Having worked through the weekend, they'd get Wednesday and Thursday off.

He hoped Falcon could fill him in on the Special Group. And maybe think of codes for the files he hadn't yet cracked. Stretch always said two heads were better than one. Dover always added, "Yeah, as long as they're not dumb and dumber."

Falcon pulled away. Dover had only a short drive to his condo, but he had a lot to mull over. His thoughts roamed to Kansas. To the early years with his mom and stepdad.

Dover's real dad was killed in a car wreck when Dover was two. So his stepdad, Ralph, was the only father he'd known. He was a laborer who did carpentry work, and he was proud of his craft.

But when minority members started taking over jobs Ralph had always seen held by whites, it made him uncomfortable, then uncertain, then mad as hell. Ralph never appreciated cultural differences. And he spotted flaws in the new crew members that he'd have overlooked in his white buddies.

"Some dumb nigger overpoured a batch of concrete today, and we spent half the day cleaning up the mess." Or, "Yeah, we could've finished that framing today with four good white guys. Them niggers got to have their smokes and tell their funny stories. They're flat out lazy—the work just ain't in 'em."

And even as a boy, Dover knew it wasn't right to lump everyone together. A lot of white cops were racist, so he'd heard all the jokes and stories. But he didn't think any of it had rubbed off on him.

Truth was, Falcon had suspected he was in a white supremacy group. And Dover had to admit he'd felt doubt and mistrust when he learned a black man was following him. And, yes, fear and anger bombarded him during the fight.

He'd come to this land of dreams to escape tradition. But he'd brought along bias learned at a stepfather's knee. What a shocking crack in the rainbow.

He focused on the feelings he'd been experiencing about Muslims. Since the World Trade Center and the Pentagon disasters, he'd suspected every Arab he'd come in contact with. He'd secretly wished they could be kicked out of the country.

Three shakers had destroyed his illusions. First, the World Trade Center was attacked and destroyed. Then his best friend and partner was blown apart. Finally, overreacting, he'd almost killed his new one.

The next morning a Mod Squad reject materialized at Dover's condo door. Sporting dark sunglasses, below the knee baggy shorts, and a T-shirt with Charlie Manson's goofy visage on the front. Hi-top Nikes, no socks. Raiders ball cap snugged on backwards.

Dover waved his hand in front of the sunglasses as though Falcon were Stevie Wonder. "Hey, behind those locs. That your ghetto garb?"

"I'm looking mobile as it gets. You can't hang with Charlie?"

"I'm a big fan of Manson, Bundy, Gacy, all the hackers and whackers." He looked Falcon up and down. "It's having no socks that bothers me. Those hi-tops will get gamy before long."

Dover put on a pot of coffee, and they sat at the dining table. Falcon explained that his "Charlie" shirt and ones with reefer or Harley hogs had helped him slip past bouncers when he worked Vice.

The brew bubbled, and Dover poured them each a mugfull, which they carried to the living room. With the blinds up, windows open, and ceiling fans set whirring, they relished the sunny, airy feel.

Life was as fine as chateau-bottled wine. But with cloudy

dregs. Dover told Falcon his suspicions. Explained about the C-4, the computer disks, the files in NCIC. Mentioned the out-of-control group.

Falcon's face pinched into hard angles. "We knew some bad shit was going down, but we never suspected a big country hustle like this."

Dover stared at him with cop's eyes and said, "I still don't know that the Special Group is the bad guys and the Select Group is cool."

"Hey, dog, I didn't volunteer for no Select Group. They put me on the list like all the other people of color. And there ain't no minority plan to take over the fucking U.S. government."

"It's just with all the riots—"

"We've seen the government, and we don't want it!"

Dover laughed from the gut. "Stellar point, partner."

"And you think riots are organized, you ain't never seen one."

Grotesque orange glow against the black sky, with smoke billowing tornado-like. Firemen spewing water into a roaring inferno. Shrill sirens, angry shouts, cracks of gunfire. He'd seen one. "The riots did erupt in minority neighborhoods, not rich white ones."

"You up on it. Most all that torching and jacking is by 'bangers."

"Directed at the Koreans?"

"The homeboys figure they're holding down their turf."

"That plays for me."

"Anyway, most riots start by the man whuppin' on a brother. Dig it, cops treat citizens in Watts different from ones in the Hills of Beverly."

Dover feigned shock. "Get outta here. You got a sheet?"

"I jumped bad a couple of times. Cops broke it up.

Never got bagged, though. An uncle put a close eye on me, kept me straight. Tough 'hood to do that in, but he was a togethah dude."

"You were lucky. But how come you still live in Watts?"

Falcon sipped his brew. "Got relatives and friends there. So I figure maybe I can give back a little of the help I got."

"And why do you rap ghetto gab? You have a good education."

"Who say I gots learnin'?"

"Your former partner on Vice told me you graduated cum laude from U.S.C., bachelor of arts degree in sociology."

"Willie always did run his mouth. You checked me out, dude?"

"Tell me you didn't do the same."

"I'll just answer your linguistics question. I got one strike against me by being a Five-O. If I'm talking white, no brother's gonna listen to my rap. So I talk the talk. Maybe I can help a kid sometime."

Dover appraised him. "You really are a race man, huh?"

"I figure we been down a long time. What go 'round come 'round." Falcon let out a sigh. Then he lifted his chin in the direction of some papers on the table. "What you doing?"

Dover gathered up his notes. "Trying to break into the files on the Volunteer Group and the Contacts. I've done research on Red Skelton and Edward Arnold, but I haven't entered any passwords."

"You lost me there, Ace Kool."

He showed Falcon the photograph of the signatures at Mann's Chinese Theater. Explained about Liz and her associates. And how passwords came from connections with them.

"These bigots make it tough. So what can I do?"

"Jump on those other passwords. I've got to skim a book on *Hyperspace* and maybe one on chess. And we need to re-search some stuff on the Net. Something you said gave me an idea."

"Always out for you, brother Ricochet." He winced. "Don't start trippin' on me, it just slipped out like a wet woody."

"Whatever you just said, forget it."

"You're not gonna come at me for using your tag?"

"I got worse worries than that."

"You ready to give it up about that funky name?"

Dover rolled his eyes. "Okay, kick back, it's a kinky tale of woe. But you know the story's bound to be a letdown."

"Then keep it short," Falcon said.

"Don't be prolix?"

"Summarize."

"Condense?"

"Abridge."

"Ready?" Dover said.

"Sure," Falcon said.

Check and checkma—no, wait. "Okay."

Stalemate.

Falcon rubbed his eyes as though he were weary.

Dover grinned. "Stretch and I were after a guy who'd iced a car salesman with a pool cue in a squab at some shithole bar. We found his crib and hit the place early. He was eating breakfast with his wife.

"We tell the guy he's busted, and he stands up to be fitted with the bracelets. But all of a sudden the wife goes nuts and attacks us."

"She had a gun? And the bullet—"

"No gun."

"A knife? It glanced off—"

"Nope."

"It's your story, take it to the hoop."

"Biscuits."

"Come on?"

"She grabbed a pan of biscuits and started winging 'em. We were making moves like the Power Rangers."

"Two big old gumbies like you? Probably falling all over yourselves. Anyway, what could a biscuit do?"

"Believe me, the guy's eating better in the joint. Those biscuits were harder than hockey pucks."

"And she conked you?"

"One bounced off the wall and smacked me on the temple. I saw stars. Not the Hollywood kind. When the other dicks heard about it, they busted a gut. Then one of them remembered an old song about ricochet biscuits."

"And you're gonna lay it on me?"

"Guy in the song says it's a biscuit you throw against the wall, and it ricochets back into your mouth. Then he asks if you know what happens if it doesn't. And the answer is, you go hungry."

"Funky to the max."

"True as rain."

Falcon shook his head, his eyes rolling up in his head, and Dover laughed again at the old joke. Then he took Falcon to the computer, brought up NCIC's Fugitive Field, and briefed him on what was happening.

"Here's the background on Edward Arnold and Red Skelton. Use any passwords you can think of for the Volunteers and the Contacts. If we can break into those files, we'll crack on these mutts."

"O-kay, Ri-co-chet," he said in rap rhythm.

"Big mistake telling you that story. Anyway, any questions?"

"About a ton. But when I ain't up on it, I'll work some vibe."

"That's how I did it. So chill and enjoy."

As Falcon began pecking at the computer, Dover grabbed the *Hyperspace* tome and headed for the recliner. He soon found it wasn't an easy read. The book dealt with relationships among altered time, our spiral galaxy, and the earth. Time warps and parallel universes were discussed.

Hyperspace meant higher dimensional space. The author, Professor Kaku, expounded on superstring theory, the tenth dimension, and multiple universes. But *Barbarella* was more Dover's level. And he didn't know if any of this concerned the Secret Group.

"Ricochet! Roll your doughboy ass in here."

Dover hustled into the bedroom. "What happened?"

"The Volunteers. I got it, right here on the screen."

"You cracked the code?"

"Did I stutter, muthafucka?"

Dover stared at the list. "Falcon, you're a ghetto star."

He'd used a code derived through Edward Arnold, who'd played a lot of tycoons, fascists, and gangsters. Several movie titles could've been passwords: *Diamond Jim*, *Sutter's Gold*, and *The Hucksters*. But Falcon had struck a vein with the one word movie title, *Kismet*.

The list had over three hundred names with departments, cities, and telephone numbers. They knew a few: High-ranking LAPD officers.

The Volunteers were spread among members of other police and sheriff's departments across the country. Plus an alphabet soup of federal agencies. With the Virginia area codes, Dover counted in the Pentagon.

"Maybe this is too heavy for us soldiers," Falcon said. "Even if we deuce out what's happening, who the fuck we gonna tell?"

Dover had no answer for that one.

As the afternoon wore on, their minds whirled at speeds only achieved in one of Professor Kaku's other dimensions, both feeling overwhelmed by the galactic powers aligned against them. Dover thought homicide investigations were of dire importance, but this conspiracy had incredible magnitude. At least for folks on the third rock from the sun. They were edging into universal proportions.

And even though they had some answers about the who, where, and maybe even why of the conspiracy, they were nowhere near determining what the group had in mind and how they planned to accomplish it.

Late in the afternoon Falcon said, "Sorry, I gotta go. I asked Hammer to come by the court and run. You know, play some ball."

"The baby 'banger?"

"He's still young, maybe I can get his head straight."

"Call me tomorrow, and we'll kick this around some more."

"If it don't jump up and kick our ass first."

"I see great minds spin in the same dimension."

Dover watched him clamber into his old Mercury. Falcon had given him an idea, but he didn't want to give the guy credit for everything. He might get more of a swelled head than he'd gotten from the right hook.

Falcon said police started the conflicts that developed into riots. On the surface, that seemed true. Dover meant to find out. He accessed the Net, requesting info dealing with police brutality. Many items came up. He scanned them, picked a few, and downloaded them. Then he returned to his recliner, a yellow highlighter in hand.

Hordes of people shoving, screaming, and throwing rocks. Looting, lobbing firebombs, pushing over cars—an insurgence against the forces of law and order—the squads of uniformed people forcing them back, yelling commands, throwing smoke grenades. Beating heads with riot batons. He highlighted some words.

Sometimes the tornadoes of rage would spin themselves out, exhausted. And sometimes the violence would escalate until no one knew if it could be controlled. Dover marked the other constant in these riots. They'd call in the National Guard. A military response.

So the gleaming yellow words were police, minorities, military. The tripod legs supporting violent civil riots. A catalytic combination.

Could there be a pattern here? Phrases floated in his thoughts: police brutality, minority neighborhoods, gangs, civil disobedience, riots. Police and firefighters battling the lawlessness and the conflagration, the National Guard on standby in case of a crisis.

He tried to put it together with what he knew about the groups listed in the NCIC files. Police, military, and federal agencies. But why would these groups secretly band together? What connection would they have with riots, other than an interest in law and order? All of them pitted against looting, civil disturbances, and urban violence.

But they kept their association secret. Why hide their co-operation to eliminate crime? Unless the targets of their mission and the methods to accomplish their goals couldn't be made public.

Maybe they'd given up on old methods. Grown sick of politicians promising security and peace they couldn't deliver. Become scared to the bone the lawless were gaining the upper hand, and that America could only be saved by drastic means.

Could a powerful covert group have been formed whose goals were to achieve law and order, restore peace, and eliminate violence? To strike down the criminal, the wanton, and the dregs that wished to sink the rest of the nation in their mire? At first, it seemed incredible.

But Dover reviewed the elements: The overheard comment about eliminating off-brands, Stretch's remark about the wanton group, and the indication that cops, feds, and the military were in cahoots. Combine that with the racially-stimulated riots across the country, and a viable theory emerged. A white elitist group could use the law to batter minority groups into submission, or even out of existence.

The historical precedent was clear. Police brutality often resulted in angry crowd response, acts of civil disobedience, and resistance to police actions. Sometimes escalating to lawless gangs running in the streets, looting and arson, and full-blown riots.

If enough uprisings were incited, a "backlash" of lawful authority would be logical, rational, necessary. When you'd raised the specter of fear in every white person's mind, drastic action would be demanded. Bold police response called for to protect the law-abiding citizenry. Military preparedness urged as a back up measure. Besides, they'd probably be eliminating terrorists, to boot.

They'd have to use any means to control the deadly urban violence the press would scream about in banner headlines daily:

STREETS RULED BY THUGS
GANG VIOLENCE RAMPANT

RACE RIOTS EXPLODE ACROSS AMERICA

Causing a national sense of despair. What to do? A politician would speak out, his message clear and simple: We won't let "them" control our country by civil disobedience or violent acts. Send in the military to fend them off, control them, and kick their butts.

The police and military would take over, using restrictive and/or destructive containment of various sectors of the cities. Violent, rebellious sectors. Ones populated with minorities.

Backing the forces would be the politically powerful white segments of society. They'd finally achieve what they'd tried through many stratagems for hundreds of years: white separation and supremacy. They were plotting to launch ethnic cleansing in America.

Chapter 17

Dover stared at the books Stretch had wanted him to have. Books that had been set apart from the mysteries and thrillers the big guy usually read. They had to mean something. Some clue was hidden in one of them. But which one, he had no idea, so he supposed he'd struggle on through the rest of *Hyperspace*. Assuming there was an end to it.

Kaku began a discussion of wormholes. They could connect us to other places in our own universe, thus providing for interstellar travel or travel to other eras. Intriguing, but Dover figured he'd stick with the Bel Air on the freeway.

The book also explained superstring theory as a method of unifying the electromagnetic, strong nuclear, weak nuclear, and gravitational forces by postulating that all matter in the universe consists of tiny vibrating strings. But the harmonies of all the particles playing their tunes are only melodic in ten and twenty-six dimensions. Go figure.

He walked to the window and stared at the sky. Watched for UFOs, scanned for comets, squinted to see wormholes. Nothing.

But by analogy from information in the book, if he could understand the interaction of the weak and strong players in this conspiracy, discover the force binding them together, and determine who was pulling the strings of this covert group, maybe he could reverse the process. Fiddle his own song in a dimension they could never find. Whistle a happy tune.

Actually, he felt he knew the identity of the puppetmasters twirling and whirling the dummies, which included himself. No real uncertainty principle there. It had to be the Contacts.

So as the country song espoused, it was time to kick a little.

At ten o'clock in the morning Falcon arrived wearing baggy red shorts and a Shaq-sized Planet Hollywood T-shirt that hung on him like a bed sheet.

"Come in, coffee's in the kitchen." They sat down at the table.

"You break on the Contacts file?"

"No, I stayed with the book." He told Falcon what he'd learned from his reading. Or at least postulated.

Falcon shrugged. "Maybe Stretch was just interested in space."

"He did have his quirks. Or in this instance, quarks."

"And your old road dog would be a top quark."

Dover stared in awe. "As you'd be a strange quark."

"Charmed."

Falcon bandied theoretical physics like it was so much rap. He was weirder than Schrodinger's cat. Or the Cheshire Cat. Curiouser and curiouser.

"I relent," Dover said. "No more *Star Trek* shit."

"So we work on the computer?"

"From your chicken scratch notes, I couldn't tell what you'd done."

"Check it out, Leonardo da Vinci wrote right to left and backwards. So I got my style, too."

"Your penmanship smacks of the Forrest Gump school."

"I cover my tracks," Falcon said with a wicked grin. "Want me to lay it out for you?"

Dover poured them both another cup of coffee, then headed for the bedroom, saying, "So show me."

At the card table, Falcon studied his own cryptic notes. "Here's my play."

Trying words from Skelton's movies, *Du Barry Was a Lady, Ziegfield Follies,* and *The Fuller Brush Man,* he'd had no luck. And he used names of other actors in those films, such as his co-stars in *Du Barry,* Lucille Ball and Gene Kelly, and in *Follies,* Judy Garland, Fred Astaire, Keenan Wynn, Kathryn Grayson, and Fannie Brice. Also tried the director of *Follies,* Vincente Minnelli, getting zip.

"So that leaves us with a few more movies," Dover said, his fingers poised over the keyboard. "*Three Little Words,*" which he typed in with no luck. "And the words, I recall from the song, were 'I love you.' " But the computer didn't accept the affection. Cruel.

"Skelton was in vaudeville," Falcon said.

"I played past that one." He tried it, but it flopped. "We're overlooking the essence of this man. Tell me who or what he is."

Falcon thought it over. "The dude's father was a clown, but he died before Red was born."

"Talk about a father's influence on a son."

Falcon studied some scribbles. "This is poignant," he said.

Dover stared at Falcon's pained face. Out of character in both speech and demeanor. Never make it in show biz. "What?"

"Red worked as a comic on Mississippi showboats when he was fourteen. Just a kid. Not much older than Hammer, I mean Jarroll."

"Oh, and how was your roundball session?"

"He never hooked up with us. Just as good, I threwed up

bricks all day. Couldn't hit a shot to save Aunt Jemima."

"Thought all you guys had the gift."

"You mean like white guys can't jump?"

Dover squinted one eye. "Stereotyping, huh?"

"Big and bad. But you admit it, that's a start. You gonna enter it?"

"Here goes," Dover said, and typed the word C-O-M-I-C. Then he entered the rambling M-I-S-S-I-S-S-I-P-P-I. Neither worked.

"And then," Falcon said, "he joined the circus as a clown."

The hair on the back of Dover's neck rose. He skimmed his notes. "One of the movies we haven't entered was *The Clown*. And before he died, Red said that's what he wanted to be remembered as."

"Mamma jamma. There be your 'essence.' "

Dover nodded and typed in the word with assurance.

And the Contacts file popped on the monitor. Contacts one through ninety-five. No names, just telephone numbers.

Dover stared at the screen. The puppetmasters of the universe. Deluxe string section. Creme-de-la-creme.

Or the slag that gathers at the top of a casting of pig iron.

Friday morning, and the plot simmered, but Dover had to go to work. At his usual spot at the homicide table, sipping a cup of brew, Dover reviewed the murder book on Mr. Ryong. Nasty killing, but he'd seen worse.

Victims like Stretch burned to death, their flesh crisped. Bodies found underwater, with pasty faces like rubber ghost masks. Corpses not found for weeks, in wretched states of putrefaction.

Other times he'd seen or smelled or felt something that brought back distant memories of death. In his only semester of law school, he'd learned that a medieval land conveyance was memorialized by whipping the children, then treating them to a feast and games. Pain and pleasure, the memories that last. Often so similar they're hard to distinguish.

Then from the corner of his eye he glimpsed Lt. Cardwell leaning out the door of his glass box. Gaping like a garfish. "Dover, get in here."

He trudged toward the torture chamber.

Cardwell gave him a smug look that officious assholes always got when they reminded you who gave the orders. Only consolation was the bosses knew which troops saw the big picture, no bullshit accepted. The ones they feared, hated, and stuck it to whenever possible.

And Dover was one of THEM. The questioners, the ignorers, the independent thinkers. One who'd have the gall to think: You're so full of shit.

Cardwell was nervous. He fiddled with his hands, cracking his knuckles. Reached for his smoldering ciggie.

Dover watched benignly, exuding malignant wishes. Enjoy your nicotine jolt, Tobacco Breath. Cardwell was no Marlboro Man, for sure.

"Rick, I want to ask you something." Squashing the stub.

"Let's have it."

"I'm curious how you're getting along with your new partner. I know he's inexperienced working Homicide. Do you think he can hack it?"

"He's doing fine. Why?"

"Because I was thinking of replacing him."

A wildfire flared along the sides of Dover's neck, the

burn creeping upward to redden his ears. "Why would you do that?"

The Lou shook another ciggie from the pack, tamped it, then held it loosely in his fingers. Giving him Bogart in *Casablanca*. What restraint, what resolve, what a moron.

"I've been watching him," the Lou forged on, "and I don't see Jones as a team player. Maybe he had to act like a maverick in Vice, you know, but in Homicide . . ." With his palm raised, he let the implication hang.

"What're you saying, Lou?"

"The fellow's reserved. He seems secretive, even aloof."

"He assesses situations before he jumps. Like any good detective."

"But we're all on the same team, so we have to back each other." He lit up and arched an eyebrow like he must have seen some hack actor do in a B gangster movie.

"You got a point?"

"I won't make a decision yet. I'll look around and see who else is available. Then we'll discuss it further."

"Nothing to discuss. Falcon's smart, reliable, and a hard worker. I want him as my partner. End of story."

Dover gave Cardwell a flinty look, then headed for fresh air, thinking that this meathead, whose name he'd found on the list of the Volunteers, could be a leader in this covert bunch of racists.

Dover dropped into his chair, steaming. He stared at Ryong's binder, but he couldn't concentrate. Too many questions blazed in his mind.

What could be done to stop this group? Who could he tell about them? And what solid proof did he have?

The last being the toughest. He had no concrete evidence. Stretch's death was ruled accidental, though the deputy coroner disagreed. Neither ATF nor the LAPD

Bomb Squad verified Stretch was killed by explosives.

All he had were the computer disks.

Disks and NCIC files that asked you to play mind games before revealing lists of people by ethnic breakdown.

So what? The Constitution lets people associate and hold meetings. The framers called it "lawful assembly." But was it? Not when they were planning what he thought they had in mind.

But you still got back to proof. He had only conjecture about the goals of the organization. They could claim to be anything. Probably had fallback proof to substantiate it. Plausible stories cooked up in case they were discovered and exposed to the public.

If anyone lived long enough to blow the whistle on them.

Now Falcon stormed in, tossed his jacket on the back of his chair, and plopped down. His tie was tugged loose, his shirt wrinkled, his brow sweaty.

"Damn," he said. "My sister's car blew, and I had to roll over to take her to class. Traffic was a MF. And I thought I'd never claim a spot in the lot."

"And good morning to you." Dover smiled.

"Yo mamma." He scoped the murder book. "So wha's up?"

"Thought we'd try to round up Gorilla."

"Chill out with that rodeo shit. Let's go bust the muthafucka."

Dover blinked. Maybe the Lou was right about his wiseass partner.

From the C.R.A.S.H. Unit, Dover collected some solid intelligence on the Eight-Tray Crips. The dicks knew Gorilla and who he hung with. Gorilla was an enforcer for the set, so he was tight with the leaders.

Dover could work two angles: Twist the homeys Gorilla kicked it with, and tweak the high rollers running the show. Let 'em know it'd be bad for business if Gorilla stayed in the wind. 'Bangers hated pings in their capital-enhancing machine. And getting a hard stare from Five-O was like tossing a bucket of sand in a hot-running Ferrari.

"Delbert Leroy Manning," Falcon read from Dover's notes, "alias Bullet, a tight homey of Gorilla's, crashpad on 92nd Street."

Dover took the Manchester exit, heading west. Left on Harvard. Falcon told him the number on 92nd. The house was a stained pastel cube with dead bushes in front, a postage stamp yard with grass as high as winter wheat, and a driveway packed with shiny cars.

"Gorilla's ride is MIA," Falcon said. "No Pathfinder on the scope."

"Hard dog to keep under the porch. Let's call in the blue Beemer."

Falcon radioed dispatch. Owner for the BMW was Mr. Bullet.

"Figure he's up yet?" Dover asked.

Falcon wrinkled his brow in disbelief. "Mickey say it ain't nowhere near five o'clock. Bullet's just in the middle of his first wet dream."

Dover shook his head. "It's no wonder the Kluckers claim you guys of color got your brains in your dick. Everything you say's about sex."

Falcon got out and said over the top of the Dodge, "When you white boys start gettin' half the pussy we African-American gentlemen do, you might have more to say on the subject."

They shut the doors. "I practice restraint. Never kiss and tell."

"That's your trip, it's cool. Just don't dis' studs knocking balls in the pocket while you standin' around chalking your cue."

They walked toward Bullet's house, checking the windows for gun barrels, and eyeing the street for G-rides creeping up in a shooter's coast. No sense going down in this morning's random drive-by shooting.

They eased up to the house, ten feet apart, and stepped onto the porch. Dover banged on the door. Loud and long.

Silence.

Dover jerked his head and Falcon stepped off the porch and slipped down the side of the house, skirting the cars in the driveway.

Dover pounded again. "Police. Open up."

Then a little boy, maybe five years old, opened the door a couple of inches and peered out with huge eyes.

"Hi, kid. Bullet around?"

"He not here." And the kid withdrew into his clamshell.

Dover stuck out his hand, stopping the door. "There's no trouble, really. He up yet?"

"No, not . . ." and the kid realized he'd messed up.

Dover stuck his business card inside. "Tell him I just want to talk."

The boy hesitated, then snatched the card, turned, and ran toward a hallway. Dover pushed open the front door. The kid disappeared around a corner, and Dover followed, listening hard as he moved.

He paused by the hallway door. Heard two voices, but couldn't make out what they said. Checked behind him, seeing no one around.

The kid reappeared, glanced at Dover, then headed for the kitchen.

"Hey, Rick. Come on back," Falcon yelled.

He drew his pistol and eased down the hallway, careful not to trip over the pants, shirts, socks, bras, and panties littered along its length.

"Where are you?" Dover yelled.

"Back here. Bedroom window."

Dover took the second doorway to his right.

Bullet stood by an open back window, wearing tattered gray briefs and a "get fucked" expression. His arms were loaded with clothes.

"Going somewhere?" Dover asked.

"Maybe he want to go jogging 'round the 'hood," Falcon said, covering the 'banger with his Beretta, "and suck in some L.A. smog. You a jogger, bro?"

Bullet's face was a rock. "What you muthafuckas want?"

Dover jerked the barrel of his piece. "Let's go deuce it out."

The guy was pissed, but he came along.

The living room carpet, slime green with multiple stains, felt slippery as they trod on it. Beer and wine bottles littered every tabletop. Huge ash trays sat heaped with butts, battleship gray ashes, and eraser-shaped filters. Cardwell would love this dump.

Dover and Falcon reluctantly lowered themselves onto defeated armchairs as Bullet flopped on a deceased sofa.

"Bullet," Dover began, "we're not interested in you. Not now, anyway. But we need to find Gorilla."

"I don't know no—"

"We'll play it this way. You find him, you call us, we pick him up. Then you're out of it. No testifying, and we never tell him you dimed him."

"I don't know what you—"

"Or we'll carry your ass down to Seven Thousand for a visit. The county lockup can always handle another customer." He looked at Falcon. "What were Bullet's warrants for?"

"Agg robbery, resisting arrest, DUI that he skipped on."

"Maybe we're making a mistake here. Maybe we should be cuffing this dickhead instead of Gorilla. In fact, I think—"

"I did see some dude last night I heard called that."

"So give it up," Falcon said.

"He be hangin' at some homey's place. Say Five-O lookin' to jam him up, then he break. Tha's all."

Falcon got in Bullet's face. "What's his ride?"

"He got a Pathfinder."

"What color?" Dover asked.

"Be black."

Dover rubbed his chin. "Ever see him in a red Monte C?"

"Nah, I never." His eyes flicked away, and he touched the corner of his mouth with his finger. Fidgeted with a large gold ring. Lying like a rug.

"We'll let that slide. But where's Gorilla? Right now."

Bullet's eyes spun like the rotors on a Las Vegas slot machine. Figuring the odds on several plans of action. Trying to save his ass.

Falcon stood up and yanked the cuffs from his belt. "Let's go, Bullet. You a lie. I'm tired of fuckin' around."

"Chill out, man, I'll come right with you."

"Righteous. Now where he be?"

Dover slapped a pen and notepad on the table. "Draw us a picture."

Bullet stared at the paper lying there among the beer bottles. He picked up the pen, stuck his tongue out the side of his mouth, and drew double lines for streets and small squares for houses.

Chapter 18

Dover and Falcon glided by the address Bullet had coughed up. Home of one Martin King Roosevelt, known as Freak. Muggy air pressed against their faces like warm molasses. Question was if Bullet had been straight, or if he'd set them up. The latter could spell disaster.

Falcon spotted Gorilla's Pathfinder in an alley behind the house. He grinned like Jack Palance about to do pushups. Or ice someone.

Dover called Parker Center. He talked with Eddie, asking him to put together the paper for a search warrant. Meanwhile, they eyeballed the place to make sure Gorilla didn't take off.

After a while Eddie radioed that a patrol unit would deliver them the warrant. As Dover gave Falcon a thumbs-up sign, a dark cloud drifted across the sun. Dover asked for a SWAT team.

As they waited, Falcon suggested a pretext move. He reasoned that it was better to trick their fugitive out than to hit the place. 'Bangers tended to answer violence with violence, so they'd be inclined to shoot.

Dover agreed. Falcon pulled one of his funky outfits from a gym bag in the trunk. Black jeans, a T-shirt with Ice-T on the front, and Nike hi-tops.

A uniformed officer drove up in the undercover car Falcon had radioed a request for, a dark blue Chevy with shiny laces.

Dover found a spot at the corner where he could watch

the front of Freak's place. A SWAT guy with a sniper rifle perched atop an apartment building down the block, covering Falcon's ass. The rest of the SWAT team waited in a van two blocks away, ready to move in on signal. Patrol units covered either end of the alley in case Gorilla did a ghost.

They were set. Dover radioed Falcon to do his number.

"Be cool and remember to call out the code word if you get jammed." If Falcon sensed the 'bangers had made him or he was in danger, he was to say "Hollywood." Then all units would move in, balls to the wall.

Falcon drove down the street. He pumped the clutch on the standard shift, making the vehicle slow, then buck, like the engine was stalling. Then he flipped off the ignition and coasted to the curb in front of the house.

He struggled out of the car and stood there weaving. Slammed the top of the car with an open palm. "No good sorry muthafucka." Stumbling to the front of the car, he searched for the latch. He finally wrested it open and stood staring at the engine as if it had leprosy.

After fiddling with a couple of things, he shrugged. Lurched back inside the car and made several attempts to start it. No luck.

The front door of the house swung open, and a black shape moved onto the porch, looked up and down the street, then stared at Falcon as if he'd like to stuff him into the tailpipe.

Falcon made a few more awkward adjustments, then got back in and ground the engine until it flooded and died. He smacked the wheel, flung open the car door, and climbed out, filling the air with a string of curses.

The shape moved to the steps at the front of the porch. Not a five hundred pound Gorilla. Had to be Freak. "Hey, nigga," he yelled, "wha's up? What the fuck you doin' out there?"

Falcon peered at him. "Fuckin' bucket boned out on me. Muthafuckin' hoopty won't start."

Freak stood there, shifting his stance, his jaw working, deciding his position on the issue. Finally he yelled, "Get that shitwagon outta here."

Falcon held his hands out, palms up. "What the fuck'm I gonna do? Muthafucka won't fuckin' start. Hey, tell you what, you got a phone?"

Freak stepped off the porch and walked a couple of steps toward Falcon. He stared at him as if he could beam both him and the Chevy into orbit. When they didn't disappear, he said, "You goin' to get that bucket outta here, or do I got to light up your dumb nigga ass?"

Falcon acted scared. "Chill out, dude. You the man. But check it out, I gives you fifty to use the phone. Call a truck. Then I'm gone."

Freak looked uncertain. He gave Falcon the red eye. Looked like two cauldrons of boiling Beaujolais.

Falcon stepped into the yard. "Man, I'll book as soon as the truck hooks up. Throw in an extra fifty when I scoot."

Dover radioed the sniper, "Boone One, you got the guy?"

"Ten-four. Got the mutt right in the cross hairs."

"If he twitches," Dover said, "blast his ass. I know he's packing."

Freak looked up and down the street. He stared hard at Falcon, then shook his head. "Shit, nigga. Get in here. Bring them presidents."

Falcon headed for the porch. Once inside, he scoped out the scene. Two teens sagged into a limp sofa. One with a sawed-off gauge across his lap, the other with a nine next to his leg. In a lumpy recliner sat Gorilla, loading cartridges into a magazine for an Uzi that rested on the table.

Falcon gave Freak a questioning look, and the 'banger jerked his head toward a doorway. Falcon headed into the kitchen with Freak just behind. French fries dribbled across one countertop, and the smell of pizza hung in the air. Falcon grabbed a phone book with curled up pages and called a towing service.

Dover and the SWAT guys could hear everything from a small transmitter snugged inside Falcon's hi-top.

While he went through the patter with the towing company, Falcon decided he'd grab Freak, shove his pistol in the dude's ear, and use him as a shield. Then he'd call Dover and the SWAT team to move in on Gorilla. He hung up the phone and turned toward Freak.

Then Jarroll walked into the kitchen. The recognition shocked them both. Just like in *High Noon*, there was no place to hide.

Jarroll blurted out, "That muthafucka's Five-O!"

At the same time Falcon lunged toward Freak, swinging an elbow, catching Freak in the forehead. Then he slipped his arm under the dazed 'banger's chin and pulled the sagging body up close. Falcon yanked out his pistol and got the drop on Jarroll. The kid froze.

"What the fuck?" someone said in the other room.

"Hooray for Hollywood," Falcon screeched.

Falcon heard Gorilla grab the Uzi off the table. Do not forsake me, he thought. You out there, good SWAT buddies?

Falcon dragged Freak behind the side of the refrigerator. He motioned at Jarroll with his pistol. The kid's eyes bugged.

"Stall it out, homeys," the kid hollered. "He got Freak

jammed in here. More Five-O muthafuckas be bustin' in soon."

The kid was smart. Which was good. Now for the others.

"What Hammer said is dope, Gorilla," Falcon yelled. "Five-O is crawlin' all over the place. Be cool. Don't be poppin' no caps or you gets faded real fast."

Gorilla must've been thinking it over when the front door flew open and one SWAT guy burst into the room pointing a shotgun, while another followed with an MP-5. Then a body crashed through a kitchen window, shattering glass, knocking pans off the counter, and scaring the shit out of everyone. Falcon almost popped a cap in Freak's ear.

More cops poured in, kicked away weapons, slammed Gorilla and the others to the floor, and cuffed them. Dover and a uniform burst into the kitchen, grabbed Freak and Jarroll, and clapped on the bracelets.

Everything was under control. It was cool. Dope.

Falcon wished he could get that idea across to his jangled nerves.

Dover and Falcon started booking the bevy of 'bangers a little after two o'clock. The cloud moved on, and the sun shone bright as a spotlight. But the locked-down Crips weren't basking in the glorious rays.

Gorilla would be stuck in the high power block on the tenth floor, based on the murder warrant. The others, booked for aiding and abetting a fugitive felon, would kick it on the seventh floor like kids caught in a scampish prank. Boys will be boys. Disregarding the principle, Dover thought, that they'd go from Boyz II Men. And as the twig is bent . . .

But Dover couldn't solve all the social ills of mankind. He could only do his job and put away some of the worst of the worst. On the way to the lockup, he'd talked with Gorilla, searching for what made him tick. Trying to help the kid see the light. Or make an incriminating statement.

He gave the overgrown teen some spiel about the stickup going bad and Mr. Ryong trying to shoot the robbers, so maybe it was self-defense, or maybe Gorilla wasn't even there—a case of mistaken identity.

He asked casually, "Remember where you were that night?"

Gorilla grunted as he adjusted his massive shoulders and flexed his powerful arms. Falcon's eyes widened, as though he thought the big goon might break the cuffs apart and go berserk. Not a pretty picture.

Dover considered the odds. When he'd first spotted Gorilla, he experienced a flashback to the movie with King Kong on a feral rampage. He'd been glad the SWAT team was there when they made the arrest. Although they busted up a lot of stuff making their grand entrance.

"That would've been a week ago today," Dover said, filling the silence. "A Friday night. About ten o'clock or so." He waited. Nothing.

"Maybe you were out-of-town. Took a bus to Pasadena or something." A lie they could disprove would be helpful.

"I wanna see my lawyer. Burton Jamison. Card's in my pocket."

Ah, yes, one of the priciest and wiliest mouthpieces in the city. Beloved by the criminal element. So much for getting a confession.

"Sure, Cletus, you can phone him later."

Gorilla's eyes bugged, and he strained against the cuffs for real. Apparently he didn't cotton to his given name. But thanks to modern steel alloys, the bracelets held until they turned him over to the jailers.

In fact, Gorilla didn't even have to let his fingers do the walking. His attorney arrived, prepared to post any necessary bail money for the poor lad and the other 'bangers before the county finished booking them. Do these mopes have telepathic communication? Dover wondered. No, that would presuppose the existence of a functional brain.

But there were procedures to be followed: strip searches, property inventory, paperwork, mug shots, fingerprints, the issuing of county jumpsuits. And the shark in Armani clothing was forced to wait for the inconvenience of his clients' hearings before a judge. But the polished performer wasn't too strained, as he and the judge chatted more about golf than the charges against the kids.

Everyone there, including Dover and Falcon, knew that the charges on the 'bangers other than Gorilla would get kicked. The D.A.'s office simply didn't have time to mess with such insignificant offenses. The weapons possession charges weren't even filed. Who cared?

A large bond was set on Gorilla. The county had to pretend it was going to be stern about brutal killings during armed robberies. But Dover was sure the lawyer would do his lawyerly duty and get the bond reduced or come up with the princely sum, no sweat. L.A. justice in action.

Having done their detectively duty, Dover and Falcon trudged out of the smelly, cacophonous joint and drove away. As they fell in with the flow of traffic, Dover said, "What were you saying to Hammer?"

Falcon hesitated. "Just rapping. I dunno, I just think the boy still has something inside him. A shine, maybe."

Like the kid in *The Shining*? Dover wondered.

Back at the squad room, Dover got another call from Terri. "We'll have seafood, if that sounds good," she said.

He glanced at Falcon, saying, "I'm so hungry I could eat a saddle."

Falcon rolled his eyes and walked to the water cooler.

"Me, too. And thirsty," she added.

"Don't wait for me," he said. "I catch up fast."

"I'm not into drinking alone. I'm not the merry widow."

"I know, it's awful."

"God, yes." They mulled it over. She said, "But you see a lot of people get their hearts ripped out. When you tell them about a murder."

"Worst part of the job."

"Stretch felt the same way."

He stopped at a liquor store and bought a bottle of good Chardonnay. Like in the song, it was dusty. The best kind.

He climbed into the Bel Air, surged onto the Hollywood, and coasted in sync with the swirling traffic. Would he and Terri spend the rest of their lives afraid something terrible might happen to someone they cared about?

Sure, life could be as fine as mellow wine, in spurts. But most of the time he just tried to stay afloat in a vat of sour grape vino, hoping no one made too big a wave.

In the family room, they sat making small talk. "Been to any baseball games this summer?" she asked.

He took a gulp of beer. "A couple. I haven't had much enthusiasm. When the players had their strike, then a couple of years later threatened another, it took the fun out of the game."

"And all of them making millions. It's crazy." She folded her legs under her and sipped her wine.

"Plain greed. Seems Americans don't understand what's important in life. They're totally clueless."

"To quote a great movie theme," she said, smiling.

"What I do best, I suppose. That, and buck the system."

★ ★ ★ ★ ★

In South Central, Skull paced about the back room of the former furniture store. "Them muthafuckas knew where Gorilla was hidin'. Any of you niggas give up where Gorilla was at?"

Hammer and Freak and two other 'bangers shook their heads.

" 'Cause you best be tellin' me now. If I finds out later about any of you tryin' that nickel slick shit, you goin' to get jumped outta the 'hood, and prob'ly lit up, too."

Freak finally spoke into the heavy silence. "You know, them Five-O muthafuckas are always tapping everyone's phone, and they follow you all around. They prob'ly heard where he was at or saw some dude slip into the pad and Gorilla was by the door, or some shit like that."

Everyone nodded.

"Anyhow," Jarroll said, "they got nothing on Gorilla. Don't even know I was with him. Didn't ask me shit about jackin' that candy store."

Now Skull beamed on Jarroll so hard his heart revved up like a Porsche. "Tha's def. Now if they ask, you gonna tell 'em . . ." And he gestured for Jarroll to finish.

"Not gonna tell 'em jack."

Skull gave him an approving look. "Tha's slammin'. Don't tell the man shit, Hammer. They got zero on Gorilla as long as you stays cool."

Jarroll said, "Crip or cry." But he saw something moving behind Skull's dark eyes.

Skull dropped onto a recliner and hung a leg over the arm. "I been thinkin' about some work for the 'hood. You down for it, Hammer?"

"Tha's cool," he said.

"Tomorrow night," Skull said, "be here about eight.

Could be you gets initiated. We gonna have us a bonfire."

Jarroll knew nothing about bonfires. But long as he was going to be a real 'banger, he didn't give a care. He and his momma and li'l sis were never going to be hungry no more.

Chapter 19

Saturday night the station got a call on a fire in a claptrap hotel in Morningside Park, so Kirk McLaren hugged the metal pole, hit the floor, and kicked off his shoes. He stepped into his boots, yanked up his rubberized pants, and snapped on the suspenders. After he crawled into the growling fire engine, he shrugged into his turnout coat and slapped on his hat.

The big machine took corners like a tank charging at full battle stride. McLaren thought of those hellish days when he'd been in country, and he shivered. Then the tower ladder engine screeched to a halt in front of the inferno. The old building glowed with dancing flames, and smoke rolled skyward like a dense fog bank. He knew they had to get people out fast.

He spotted a man on the fourth floor, waving his arms and screaming. Smoke poured out the window. McLaren clambered into the bucket, fastened his mask, and rose skyward on the aerial ladder.

Heat pulsed from the incandescent wooden frame. As he ascended, vibrations from the lift engine shuddered through his body. The fire gave an angry roar as it devoured decaying timber in its crimson maw. The building was a goner. All he could do was try to save some people from certain death.

Blasts from hoses sprayed around him, spinning currents of smoke in every direction. Now the bucket bumped against the building next to the window. But the man was gone.

McLaren's heart thrashed. Had the guy run for it? If he'd tried to go down the stairs, he'd never make it.

Scrambling over the side, McLaren hurtled through the window into the enveloping black cloud. He groped along the floor, scalding heat pressing him from all sides. This room would blow any second.

He strained to peer through the roiling smoke, seeing no tall rectangle of flame. The man hadn't opened the door; he was still inside. On hands and knees, scrabbling left, right, then forward, McLaren searched as panic constricted his chest. His throat tightened. He couldn't do it; he had to back out.

Then his hand hit something. A limp form on the floor. The man had passed out.

The door blew open, and a surge of flame shot across the room. McLaren knew they had only seconds to escape. Yanking the man to a sitting position, he realized how huge he was. Might as well heft a walrus.

Pulling the man's beefy arm over his shoulder, he squatted, grabbed onto a bear-sized thigh, and heaved with all his strength. He halfway straightened up, with the man sprawled across his back. Legs aching from the strain, he staggered toward the window. The man slipped downward, and soon McLaren was dragging him across the room. Spears of pain stabbed his arms and legs. His back locked up solid. But he was almost there.

Then an explosion slammed them against the wall.

He felt lightheaded. He had to twist himself free from the enormous man lying atop him. Struggling to his knees, he took a deep breath, straining every fiber as he shoved against the guy's upper torso, just able to keep it moving, until the man's head and chest poked out the window.

McLaren gulped for air. But there was no time to rest.

He braced his shoulder under the man's bulky haunch and heaved, his legs trembling like a fawn's, moving the stubborn mass an inch at a time until the man at last tumbled out and fell inside the bucket.

Then he flung himself out, landing atop the still figure.

An enormous tongue of flame leapt out the window just above them. McLaren tucked his head. The fiery blast scorched the back of his coat.

The bucket swung away from the inferno and lowered toward the ground. They moved out of the smoke's suffocating snare. McLaren tore off his mask and sucked in fresh air, coughing, his lungs aching.

He pressed a finger against the man's carotid artery and found a pulse. Placed his hand on the wine cask chest and felt it rise and fall. Then he dropped his forehead on the man's shoulder, saying a prayer of thanks.

Skull and Freak and Hammer hunkered down beside a building across the street from the fire. Other 'bangers were also there to catch the action. They had perfect seats. And they saw it all from the git-go, since Freak had started the "bonfire" with a flaming quart of gasoline.

All eyes bugged wide open as the building went up fast. Stoned winos and hypes and dusters staggered out from the rickety hotel. Scrawny drunks and cluckheads fell down, screaming, some with their raggedy clothes on fire.

There was a whine in the distance, then a wail getting closer, then a shrill yowl about to bust their ears as the trucks screeched to a stop in front of the blaze. Go for it, muthafuckas. Fat fuckin' chance. They thought the best part was when the guy went up in the bucket, tossed in the blubber belly nigga, and rode on down to the ground.

Then Skull recalled the reason for the gig.

He watched as the fireman whipped off his mask and tanks, pulled the fat dude out of the bucket, and put an arm around him. The brotha sat there hacking away. The fireman patted the dude on the back.

He was a honky muthafucka. Skull turned and stared at Hammer. "Showtime, homey. He be's the one."

"You're okay, buddy," McLaren said. "You're going to be fine."

The man coughed hard. "I hopes I is."

But then he looked past McLaren, and his eyes got big. "What's the—"

Something thudded like a pickaxe into McLaren's back. He heard a loud crack. Felt a searing pain that ripped its way through his shoulder blade, skewered his lung, then bored out through the muscles of his chest.

The flabby man's mouth opened and closed, and his eyes glazed over. He was going into shock. But then he tried to scramble to his feet.

"No!" McLaren yelled, grabbing the man by the shirt. "Get down!" He wrestled the man off balance and flung him to the ground.

The wrenching pain kept McLaren from blacking out. Now he struggled to stand up. Another shot exploded, but missed.

He lurched toward the truck, his shirt and coat soaked with blood, his chest warm, but his hands and feet going cold.

Another crack. Caught him in the left arm. Like being shot with a flaming arrow. Hurt bad, but not so much as the first one.

Make it to the truck, he thought. Make it there. Have to—

Crack! Crack! Crack!

★ ★ ★ ★ ★

"Fade him!" Skull screamed.

"C'mon, Hammer," Freak said. "Splash on that honky."

Blood cries buffeted Jarroll. His ears ached from the explosions, and he wanted to stop, but the others shouted curses and shrieked, raging for a kill. Do whitey. Do him!

Jarroll pulled the trigger. The gun kicked against his hand. He pulled the trigger. The white dude crumpled like a beer can. Pulled the trigger again. Guy went down flat.

Straight up, the dude was R.I.P. Gone to honky heaven. And for an instant, Jarroll wondered if it was better than black heaven.

The homeboys started to bail, but Freak said, "What's that bear doin'?" They all froze and stared as the fat brother crawled over to the honky's body and shook his shoulder. Dude didn't move. Bear looked close at his eyes.

What the fuck? Jarroll thought.

"Naw, bro, chill," said Skull. "He a honky muthafucka."

Then the bear dipped down the dude's pants and came out with a wallet. He wobbled up to his feet, glancing around. Then he boogied down the street, never looking back.

The phone's shrill, late in the evening, meant only trouble, especially since Dover was on call. Bad timing, as he was heavily involved with an arching, supple, thrusting torso. April could really get into a scene. She deserved an Academy Award for—

Damn phone wailed again. He strove to ignore it. Speculated whether he could finish his present commitment before taking on a new project.

But the rings were spaced by an expert Pacific Bell sadist, quiet just long enough for him to refocus on his carnal endeavor, then screeching to yank away his attention. Sixth ring he compromised his position and withdrew from his implied contract. Failed to deliver. Warranty expired.

The Watch Commander said he was sorry to disturb him, but that a firefighter had got aced while battling a suspicious blaze at a blighted hotel in South Central. He wondered if Dover would be so kind as to grace the crime scene with his invaluable presence.

"Sorry, babe," he said to April. "Caught a case. Saturday night fun in South Central. Kill a cop or a fireman and earn some props."

"Go on," she said, having danced this routine before. "See you later."

He donned casual pants and an old sports coat. The drive there was plagued with regrets. Missed opportunities, he thought, shine the brightest.

But another challenge awaited him.

The scene was pure chaos. The hotel's carcass burned like a huge Olympic torch against the black city sky, while firemen sprayed water from behind the truck, mostly missing the flames. Ambulances, police cars, an SID truck, the Coroner's van, and TV news vans were chockablock in the street. Nervous cops stood with their backs to the flames, their eyes fastened on dark buildings that rose up like monsters across the street.

Dover sensed the show was over; the curtain had fallen.

Falcon drove up. They discussed the potential danger of investigating the murder right away, deciding it was minimal. It was a shoot-and-run hit.

They checked the body, told the crime scene tech what photos they wanted, and interviewed people in the area. They all must've been struck deaf and blind at the exact same moment. And the water level in the reservoir must've dropped six feet when all the people who claimed they were in the john at the time of the shooting flushed their toilets.

Grand total for the evening: one dead fireman, no eyewitness to the shooting, no one who heard anything, no suspicious persons seen in the area, no one observed leaving the scene of the shooting, and a nasty job ahead of them— notifying the next-of-kin about the capricious murder.

But there was one climactic moment. Across the street from the ravaged hotel, next to one of the brooding buildings, they found cartridge casings scattered on the ground. Seven of them. All 9mm.

Not a random, accidental shooting by any stretch.

Late Sunday morning Jarroll sprawled facedown on his bed where he'd passed out with his clothes on. He opened his eyes and blinked. Muthafucka. A killer pain stabbed behind his eyeballs. His skull felt swollen up, maybe cracked. He lay there not moving a bone.

Memories spun in broken bits, flying through blasts of rock and rap. Ho! Ho! The par-tay was live and long after the "bonfire." He'd done Bud and Liquid Juice and Sherm. Hit that dope big-time.

He'd been the man at the party. He'd claimed and got taken in as a 'banger. A righteous Eight-Tray Gangster Crip.

He should be feeling super cool this morning. But his brain kept spitting out shit, even with the spike in it. Flames raged in his dreams all night. Sirens, shouts, screams. People twitchy and gaffled up.

Skull, Freak, and some others were hangin', waiting for him to . . . He ran his hand under the pillow, searching. Felt the hardness of steel.

Pulling out the pistol, he rolled onto his back. He held

the dark gun up and stared at it. Jagged pain sliced through his head, but he didn't pay no mind, studying the nine with his finger on the trigger.

The roar outta that gun was so muthafuckin' loud, he almost dropped it. First time he shot it for real. He wasn't up for the blast, the kick against his hand. Slugs of lead tearing through meat. He near broke out.

But he couldn't. His homeys were scopin' him.

The door whipped open and crashed against the wall.

He swung the pistol toward the noise.

"Wha's that?" Alceeda said. Eyes big. Staring.

He stuffed the nine back under the pillow. "Ain't nothin'. You never mind."

She ran over and scrabbled at the edge of his bed until he pulled her up. Then she lurched forward, her fingers digging under the pillow.

"No, Alceeda. Stop dippin'."

Had to stash the nine somewhere.

He wrestled with Alceeda and tickled her stomach. She laughed like crazy. Kicked her legs, jerking the bed and making his head pound. He tried to get her to settle.

"Listen, baby, is Momma here?"

Then he heard footsteps coming down the hall.

"I gonna tell," Alceeda said.

"Don't be no gap mouth." He gave her a stare.

Momma stuck her head in the door. "About time you decides to come alive, boy." Her eyes were clear. She was talkin' plain. Made him feel better, even with his busted head.

"I been awake some," he said. "Just thinkin' on things."

"Like what?"

"About how we gonna change some stuff around here."

She glanced around his room, then back down the hall.

"Why we wanna change anything?"

"Let's talk about it later. My head hurts."

She gave him a look. "That how you livin'?"

He stared back. "Things gonna change. There it is."

She nodded, and her gaze dropped away.

Alceeda jumped from the bed and skipped over to her.

Momma scooped her up and kissed her on the cheek, fiddling with her tight corn rows. "Come on," she said, turning to leave his room, "I fix you some eggs. Bacon, too. You feel better if you eat."

Alceeda squealed in the hallway, and Jarroll's head almost busted open like a watermelon dropped on the sidewalk.

"Hush that noise, girl. Your brother needs to get his stuff together." She looked at him over her shoulder; her eyes said she knew about his pain.

After she left, he groped under the pillow for the pistol. Looked at it again. Maybe she knew about his head, but there was more.

The gun heavy in his hand. Flames, heat, and smoke. Dudes yelling, engines roaring, sirens shrieking. Aiming the nine at some honky he never saw before. No big thang.

Until the gun blasted and the man jerked when the slug struck his back. The homeboys yelling, slapping his shoulders. A chill seeping through his body.

"Do 'im, bro!" Skull screeched over the roar of the fire.

So he yanked the trigger again. Over and over. But he couldn't hear the shots no more. Everything got quiet. And slowed way down.

And what the guy did then, so weird, pushing the brother down, like he was trying to save the dude. The fool couldn't even save himself; he was near to bein' R.I.P. Finally, the dumb honky slumped to the ground. And they all lit out, with everyone running like cornerbacks.

No one knew what'd hit the guy, except Jarroll and his homeys. Then the party started. And he got made a true Crip.

He sucked the juice and the reefer and whatever else there was to do. To par-tay. And to kill. His senses, his memory, his pain.

Which he couldn't figure. He didn't even know the muthafucka. Just some whitey.

He pushed the button on the side of the pistol, dropping the clip onto the bed. Racked the action. A bullet popped out. Six left in the clip.

Musta shot seven or eight times. Not that many. No big thang. Lots of 'bangers had splashed dudes way more.

But this time he'd pulled the trigger.

Dover lay in bed, nearly comatose. When he'd returned to his condo, he'd found a note on a pillow. April was sorry to leave, but when he'd gone out, she'd felt lonely and depressed. Lately, she'd been unsure about their relationship. Perhaps they should spend some time apart while she sorted out her feelings.

He'd been in enough relationships to know what that meant, but he couldn't believe theirs had come to that point without the ebb tide that usually preceded a breakup. No golden parachute for him on this one. Just here's your notice, don't expect any references.

He tried to make some sense of it. But like an overloaded computer, his brain refused to process the information. He sighed, rolled out of bed, and headed for the kitchen. Maybe with a clearer head he'd know what moves to make. Or he'd simply wander as bereft in romance as Chaplin.

As he brewed coffee, his thoughts returned to the senseless murder of the fireman. Most killings involved passion. Love, anger, or hatred. He had the gut feeling this one was done for callous reasons beyond belief.

There seemed no limits to men's bizarre actions. Gunmen spraying strangers with assault rifles, mass murders of children in schoolyards, drive-by shootings. Gangbangers dying because of vaguely perceived insults. Terrorists blowing up innocent civilians. And themselves.

He sipped his brew. In this area, revenge killings, turf battles, and pure wanton shootings were relief from boredom. Murder a mere rite of passage.

The fireman shooting fit the crazyquilt pattern. He figured it was gang-related. Had that feeling to it.

He topped off his cup and wandered into the living room, rethinking last night's murder. Flames, smoke, and noise. Total confusion.

He retraced each investigative step. Culminating in finding the cartridge casings. Across the street from the blazing building, its skeleton melting like sticks of licorice.

Casings lying right where the shooter would have a perfect view of the fire. As if the guy knew everyone would be looking the other way, watching the conflagration. Because he'd set the fire to get those results.

Dover took a slug of coffee, getting excited now. The shooter had done exactly that. All premeditated.

He'd check with the arson investigator, but he already knew what the outcome would be. An intentionally set fire. Validating his premise.

Ideas pinged about in his head. A passionless killing in South Central. Had to be a gang thang.

Gorilla and an unknown partner, a smaller kid, robbing a jewelry store, gunning down the owner. Then a senseless shooting at the scene of an arson. With a 9mm pistol at both locations. Of course, such firearms sprouted like dandelions all over South Central. Still, it was the same type of pistol.

Who hung with Gorilla—someone younger and smaller? Dover thought about the morning they'd nabbed Gorilla at Freak's pad. Freak, Skull, Hammer, and a couple of others around.

The physical description didn't match Freak or Skull or any of the others, as he recalled, with one exception. With Hammer, young master Jarroll, it fit like a spandex leotard. Young, smaller than the others, and the kid was a wannabe all the way.

Now Dover gulped the rest of the coffee and stood up and paced. The jewelry store robbery would have been a test for Hammer, putting in work for the 'hood. But offing the fireman . . .

Hammer's initiation into the gang! Just what the Eight-Trays would come up with. Brutal and senseless, but testing the kid's loyalty to the max.

It all fit so well he was sure he was full of shit. Jigsaw puzzles in South Central had a way of turning into shapeless, ugly pictures. As a theory, it wasn't bad, but in fact could be way off.

But there were tests that'd tell him if he was tracking right. He'd ask the lab to check Hammer's prints against any stray latents lifted in Ryong's jewelry store. And have them compare extraction marks on the cartridge found there with marks on the casings turned up at the fire. If anything matched, he'd be back in the game.

Later, Dover called Falcon to tell him his incipient theory about Jarroll.

"Lit up a fireman? On a dead bang set-up?"

"It's just an—"

"Ricochet, the kid's only thirteen. I know that's ancient in South Central, but I've seen him in action—"

"I know."

"—and he's got some stuff working. He's not burned-out dead like most of 'em. He's smart, and he cares about his family and himself."

"I hear that." And Falcon had a point, the kid might not be a stone killer. He might not have the requisite vicious streak.

"This is fucked," Falcon said.

"That's a fact, partner."

"Shit!" Falcon said. "Even if he was with Gorilla on that jewelry store job, he didn't do no shooting."

"Our reports show that."

"First offense, just along for jackin' a candy store, the shot caller goes off and pops a cap, Jarroll stands there, don't do a thing. At his age, Juvie Hall would send him to Miller or Kilpatrick for two or three, tops."

"Sounds right."

"But if he's a straight killer on top of that . . ."

"They'd come down on him a lot harder."

"Even if they don't go after him as an adult, he'd go to Youth Authority until he's grown. By then he'd be a no good nigga mess."

"No doubt."

"Damn. We'd better go for those ballistics tests, am I right?"

"Just to cover the bases. Might help us out later when we get a good suspect. Or eliminate some people, any-way."

"Like Jarroll?"

"Of course."

"That's cool, then."

"Sorry to bother you, I just wanted to see how it played."

"No, it's gotta be done." He sighed. "You and April kickin' it today?"

"Actually, April's entered a new phase of her consciousness."

"Like what?" Probably expecting him to say psychometry, holistic health modality, or nude rock-climbing.

"Like she'd be more in harmony without my discordant ass around."

"Unnhhh. I'm sorry, man."

"I'll get by. Been there, done that."

"So don't let it sweat you."

"Hell, no. See you tomorrow." And they hung up.

He realized he was sweating.

He glanced at the computer, then stepped into the living room and cranked up the air. The blank computer screen had brought the faceless group back to mind, and he wondered how well organized they were. And whether they were too powerful for him to fight.

Then he recalled a play April was in. By the Bard, which had not proved her forte. The only line he remembered was: "Our doubts are traitors and make us lose the good we oft might win by fearing to attempt."

And he thought about John Wayne as Rooster Cogburn throwing down the gauntlet. Whirling his horse around and hollering the challenge, "Fill your hand, you son of a bitch!"

Time to take the reins in his teeth and charge.

Chapter 20

Dover's mind whirled with questions. Was he right about Jarroll killing the fireman? If so, could they prove it? Was someone really out to take over America? If so, who and when and how?

Often, when he needed to puzzle out complex problems, he took a stroll around the Marina. Frothy green water lapped against the docks, and gleaming craft perched regally on the water, emitting splashy siren songs. Studying the liquid shimmer of the watery wonderland helped him relax.

So now, he pulled off his shoes and sauntered barefoot along the beach. Sunbathers had abdicated the narrow stretch of sand, but vapors of their lotions hung in the air. The setting sun spread a glow on the waters, soft sand scrunched beneath his feet, and he felt tense muscles loosen.

L.A. made him claustrophobic, enclosing him with its soaring buildings and pressing throngs of people, the sky shuttered in haze. He longed for the open spaces of Kansas, especially the Flint Hills, with rolling grass prairies and a huge blue sky. But now he had to settle for this strip of sand and slice of the Pacific.

Within half an hour he had his head straight, and his mind felt renewed, ready to do battle with the demons. Back at his condo, his heart pumping strong, he popped a cold beer, then glanced at the books on the table. He'd made no headway with quantum theory or the one about parallel universes.

He picked up the one on chess and for the first time regarded it closely. Entitled *The Psychology of Chess Skill.* Written by Dennis H. Holding. Hmmm. Didn't really mean any—

But of course it did.

Stretch's favorite maxim: The answers to life's problems can be found in the psychology of chess. Maybe he'd ignored the most important clue.

He cracked the book, skimming the chapters. The author noted the game was believed to have developed in India. A war game: infantry (pawns), cavalry (knights), elephants (bishops), and chariots (rooks).

One chess champion, Philidor, was so enamored of pawn play that he coined the epigram: "Pawns are the soul of chess."

An interesting statistic: The white pieces have a definite advantage over the black pieces in games won. An edge of about fifty-nine percent wins to forty-one percent, favoring the white. Stretch was right again, chess is a whole lot like life.

Top players stated that to improve chess skill, one needed to develop "position sense," which they defined as being able to determine the strengths and weaknesses of their situation during the game. He took a gulp of his brew, mulling that over. At this point, he felt in a pretty helpless position.

But he wasn't going to forfeit the game. Not until his last pawn was captured. Because, after all, pawns were the soul of chess. Only problem was, they were weak. Which was how he felt in this match.

He continued browsing until he came to page 107. Son of a bitch. Stretch had taken a lesson from the smuggler. He'd cut a hole in some pages of the chess book big enough to hold a computer disk. Which it did.

Dover pried out the disk and headed for the computer.

There was one file: Contact Identification. A four-digit code name or number was called for. But beneath the request to ENTER CODE NAME was a notation. It said, "This one should be easy for a dauntless guy."

Dauntless? As in Dauntless Duo? Had to be.

Which consisted of Stretch (too long) and R-I-C-K.

And the file popped onto the screen.

It was identical to the Contacts File on the other disk, except that to half the list of Contacts previously identified only by telephone number, Stretch had added the name, title, and agency to which the person belonged. The carrot-top had conducted an investigation. Then they'd found out about it and killed him.

But they'd never found this disk and weren't aware of who he'd identified. Or that he'd noted the goals of the group. And the dates and target locations for each stage of their plan to achieve ethnic cleansing in the United States. Oh, my God. The first stage was a police provocation in South Central.

He bounded out of his chair, picked up his beer, and paced about the condo, his thoughts spinning. Sucking the can dry, he crumpled it and flung the disfigured remnant across the room, as if to smash his foes with one blow. It glanced off a wall and clattered across the floor. It looked like Stretch's Bronco.

He turned and tramped into the bedroom where he stared at the list of Contacts—some identified by Stretch, some hidden behind a number. Like a game of chess: Plan your strategy, go for the jugular, but protect your ass. And anticipate your opponent's moves.

He stared at the telephone numbers printed after the unidentified Contacts. Some of the area codes were familiar. He grabbed the phone book and looked up others. Then he picked up the receiver and called the operator, checking what towns had the listed prefixes.

Back on the Internet, he checked a reverse directory for several of the numbers, finding they were unlisted. And he wanted information now. If he placed calls to the numbers, he'd have to conjure up plausible stories. Hope to hell he'd pick the right one at the right time so it'd fool whoever answered the call. Or concoct another one on the wing.

Of course, when someone answered, he could always hang up. But that might be the wrong thing to do. Might make them suspicious. It'd be better if he could trick them into thinking the calls were legit.

He walked into the living room and dropped into his recliner. Sat there thinking about what lies to tell. Tried to decide which numbers to call.

Exhaling, he picked up the phone and punched in a number in D.C. Like everything in this sinister script, it was a shocker.

"Secret Service."

"I'm sorry, who did you say?"

"This is the U.S. Secret Service. Treasury Department. Our regular offices are closed, but I'm the night supervisor. If you have an emergency complaint or want to furnish some information, I'll pass it on."

"I'm afraid I got the wrong number. Sorry to bother you."

So much for clever stories. After the blood seeped back into his head, he checked with the telephone information operator. The telephone for the main switchboard of the Secret Service in Washington was the same as the number he'd dialed, except for the last two digits.

The number listed for Contact thirty-five was for a certain person at Secret Service. Since it was Sunday, and the guy wasn't in his office, the call had rolled over to the main switchboard. The night man fielding calls had picked it up.

He'd learned just enough to freeze his balls. Someone at Treasury was involved in the conspiracy. He hoped Secret Service got a lot of weird calls, just like any police agency, and the guy who answered wouldn't think anything of it.

And it made him even more curious.

He dialed a number in St. Louis. It was a National Guard Armory. He asked to speak to the commander and was told he was on weekend maneuvers, but that he was due back in a couple of hours. He said he'd call back.

Instead, he tried a number in San Francisco.

"U.S. Customs." Not a surprise. Another rollover number.

"I was wanting to get some information about job openings."

"Sure, I'll send you a packet. What's your name and address?"

He furnished them, for a Wilbur Bagley in Oakland.

He tried a number in Chicago. A recording said it was the Drug Enforcement Agency. He could leave a message or punch zero and an operator would answer. He hung up.

In Albuquerque a guy answered, "Sheriff's office."

"Is the Sheriff in?"

"He'll be in tomorrow. Is there a message?"

"Nah, I tried him at home and he was out, so I called here."

"Probably took the wife to the country club for dinner."

"Yeah, I'll catch him later, thanks."

He'd been lucky so far. He didn't think he'd aroused any suspicion. And as lucky streaks go, he'd taken enough charter hops to Vegas, testing his fortune on the Strip, to know he should quit while he was ahead.

But a number in Arlington, Virginia, intrigued him. If his high school geography was etched correctly in his brain folds, Arlington was just across the Potomac from D.C. The site of some very strategic action.

He'd try it. This would be the last one. Absolutely.

It rang three times. No answer. Just as well.

Rang again. He started to hang up. He wouldn't even wait to see if it rolled over. Wouldn't tempt fate.

"Hello, General Fanning here." White male, forty to fifty. Deep voice, authoritative ring to it, slight east coast accent. Type that wants you to tell him what you've got or what you want in twenty words or less. Bottom line guy.

"Telephone repair service. You called in a complaint Friday? Noise on the line? We'll come by tomorrow and take a look, if that's okay."

"There's nothing wrong with this phone." Pause. "What's your name?"

"Jenkins, C & P Repair Service. This 555-3698?" He'd called 3689.

"It's . . ." The guy thought it over. "That's right, but I'll have to call you in the morning to see about scheduling. Give me your number."

"I'll be out on other repairs then, but . . . oh, I've got another call. Listen, I'll call you back after lunch tomorrow and we'll work it out then. 'Bye, sir."

"Just a—"

Dover killed the connection.

Later that night, a phone rang in a bedroom in Westwood.

A man fumbled for it, sleep clouding his brain. He

grasped the receiver. "Hello?" he said in a gravelly voice.

A brash foghorn came through the line, saying, "Lieutenant?" More a challenge than a query.

"Yes?"

"This is Contact Forty-three, D.C. area. Do you understand?"

"Of course." He sat up, rubbing his eyes. "What is it, sir?"

"I received a call from one of your men tonight. I've done some checking, and he's not one of us. He was being very clever on the line."

"I don't under—"

"You don't need all the details, just the name."

"Who was it?" He flipped on the bedside lamp. His wife grunted in protest and turned her back to the glare.

"Your Detective Dover."

He cursed softly. "How do you know he made the call, General?"

A small, weary sigh. "I have call tracing, of course. Take care of this situation at once. As you know, we have a crucial operation about to begin."

Cardwell said, "Of course, sir. There'll be no more problems."

"I expect not." And the line went dead.

He replaced the receiver, snapped off the light, and cracked a couple of stiff joints in his fingers. His wife groaned, and he stopped.

Then he settled back on his pillow, thinking, and he smiled. This wasn't a bad assignment at all. In fact, he'd enjoy it.

The next morning Dover zipped into the parking lot. Chuck ambled over with his usual cheerful smile. "Have a live weekend, Detective Dover?"

A tough question. "It was as bizarre as that flick *Ishtar*, Chuck."

He seemed puzzled, but his attention swung to the Chevy.

Dover jiggled the car keys in his palm. "Do me a favor?"

"Sure, what's the gig?"

Dover held out the keys. "Could you get her a wax job?"

"Hittin'. I know a death detailer. They'll buff her to a creampuff. No scratchy bras on these nectar ladies, they skin it while they shine."

"Whatever you say. Have a good time."

In the squad room, he plopped into his chair and a chill slid through him. He got the sinking feeling that the best part of his day was over. He glanced toward Cardwell's cubicle, and the skinny slimeball leaned out the door, motioning to him.

He'd as soon eat the glass cubicle as go inside it with Cardwell the first shot out of the gate on Monday morning.

"Sit down, Rick. Sit down."

He was repeating things. The Lou had something on his mind other than what he was saying. That happened a lot with Cardwell. A lot.

"I wanted to apprise you of some personnel changes."

Jesus Christ. The hair on the back of his neck felt like a bristle brush. Had someone else been killed? No, Cardwell had on his business face, not his mask that exuded sincere condolences. Dover's heart resumed beating.

He sat down, saying, "What changes?"

"I had to transfer Jones back to Vice."

Jones, Jones. "You mean Falcon?" He felt a lump of dismay in his throat. But it quickly dissolved as hot blood surged into his face.

"Yes, yes. Falcon. I'd forgotten you call him that."

"Who cares what I call him? Why'd you do it? What's going on here?"

"Just a judgment call. I can see he's not cut out for the squad." Cardwell shrugged. "As you know, not many are."

"He did great. He works hard, and he notices the details a good homicide dick needs to spot. Hell, he solved several of our cases already."

"As I said, it was my judgment as an administrator. He was a hotdog, not a team player. That can get a fellow detective killed."

What? Dover felt as flustered as Bruce Lee surrounded by mirrors in *Enter the Dragon*. Nothing made any sense. Nothing was as it seemed. "We're working some hot cases, Lou. I can't handle those without a partner."

"Right, right. So I'd like you to spearhead a special project. And I'll get Deadeye and Eddie to work your caseload."

He stood up. "We were just going to make a bust."

"Sorry, Rick. Some decisions are tough to make. I know they won't be popular, but I'm not in a congeniality contest."

Good thing. "But what project—"

"There's some information we need fed to the computer."

"What're you talking about? I'm no programmer."

"I'll explain it later. Discuss your cases with Eddie, and he can work them when he gets a chance. No use letting them slip."

Something was haywire here. He'd been thrown off balance, and he'd failed to assess the situation. But Cardwell's jaw was set.

Last night's phone calls. Somehow . . .

"This sucks, Lou. Keep Falcon on."

There it was. The vengeful look. "As I said, we're all a team. If you can't play with the others, you're out of the game."

Teamwork, cooperation, play along. A message for him.

"This is a crock. I'm going to the Captain."

The Lou's face turned to granite. "Maybe you shouldn't rock the boat, Dover. Especially in a sea full of man-eating sharks."

Dover stomped out of there before he told Cardwell what he could eat. Loosening his tie, he plopped down at the homicide table, stewing about Cardwell, the Contacts, and The Untouchables. A full house of jerks.

Time to implement some strategies. This match was getting into the endgame. He needed to protect himself, but also strike.

He stacked several binders on his desk. Zipped open his leather attaché case. Inside were three manila envelopes, sealed and addressed. And a piece of paper with names and phone numbers. He placed some calls, reaching two of the people on the list. Left a message for the third.

Then he called Terri. He told her he'd left something in the potted palm by the pool. To be dug up in case of an emergency.

"What's going on?" she asked. "Are you in trouble?"

"It's just a precaution. Pretty stupid idea, really. Stretch always said I watched too many late night flicks."

"Don't try to take them on. Go along with what-ever—"

"Yes, Mrs. Kim, we have the man in jail, and we're proceeding with the case. In fact, Detective Eddie Bradley, one of our best men, will be contacting you about this. And thanks for your help."

He hung up and turned to the hulking form by his shoulder.

"What was that crap all about?" Eddie sat down in Stretch's chair. The sight made Dover want to garrote him with piano wire.

"Falcon's going back to Vice. Until I get a new partner, the Lou wants you and Deadeye to work my cases. I'll go over them with you if you want."

He frowned. Flexed his arm muscles. Cracked his neck. "Maybe later. I got other things going."

"At your disposal," Dover said to Eddie's broad back.

He picked up two blue binders and his attaché case. As he passed by Cardwell's office, murky eyes peered at him. He held up the binders and said, "Going to the lab for tests."

At the lab, he turned in requests for the extraction marks tests that could link Hammer to two murders. Then he left the building and struck out for the post office. Swinging the attaché case as he moved along.

The haze was a gauzy ivory cloud. Sun harsh and burning through. Skid row types out in force, contrasted with zombies in dark suits and mini-skirted femmes with muscular legs.

He stood in line, pressed by the hollow sounds and stale air of this typical federal building. The bureaucratic sword might be double-edged, but both were blunt. Finally, he watched in satisfaction as the clerk tossed his envelopes onto a moving belt.

Emerging from the lifeless atmosphere, with warm sun-rays on his face and his attaché case lighter in his hand, he felt five years younger.

Back in the office several phone messages awaited him. Terri had called back. And George had returned his earlier call.

George was wired on computers, but was still a normal person. They'd met through Stretch. They all played basketball at the YMCA.

George was short with a protruding belly. But he hustled his ass off, could dribble like a Globetrotter, and was a dead shot. Besides, he was enthusiastic. About roundball and about his computer. Go figure.

George reminded Dover of folks in Kansas who didn't need to be rock idols or movie stars or celebrities. Not even rich. Life meant working, taking the wife to dinner, and getting away for fishing or golf. They weren't always searching for new thrills, previous lives, or afterlives. They simply lived life each day. And didn't overanalyze the crap out of it.

He told George a package was on its way, and he made an unusual request. George was happy to do him a favor. He was that kind of guy.

Later in the day a clerk with thick glasses and short hair in tight ringlets rolled a cartful of old case binders up beside Dover's chair, gave him a disdainful look, and clumped away on high heels with taps. She reminded him of Dr. Frank N. Furter in *The Rocky Horror Picture Show*.

Cardwell must've been watching, because he immediately appeared beside Dover to explain how he wanted information entered into the computer. Dover could also picture him in black undies, leather, and garter belts. Ugh.

"It should help us identify any serial killers," the Lou concluded.

"The FBI already has this stuff in their computers."

"Sure, so they can take credit when they get a hit."

"Doesn't matter, as long as we nail the killer."

"It matters to the Chief."

As in, mediocre careers are schemed, not developed.

The Lou schlepped away. Dover stared at the moldy files. Then he called the repair shop.

"Just tell me straight out, Titus. No gobbledygook about engine parts or emergency repairs to an Assistant Chief's turn signals. When's the Grand Prix going to be ready? You know, finished. Keys in my hand."

"Just about got her ready. We're over the hump now. Probably Thursday for sure, maybe Wednesday."

"You wouldn't jerk me around now? Play with my mind?"

"No way. Almost got it licked. Just gotta put her on the computer one more time. Got a minor snafu. Sometimes she bucks a little and conks out."

"The engine dies?"

"Just sometimes. Probably a timing problem."

"Titus, I'm coming to the shop first thing Thursday morning. I'm leaving with the Grand Prix in perfect running condition or I'll take you with me at gunpoint to Hertz and rent a Caddy under shop authority."

"Now Detective, no reason to—"

"You get what I'm saying?"

"Right, I got it. No problem. It's just a minor—"

"Goodbye, Titus." He dropped the receiver in the cradle.

He sighed and cracked open the first binder. His mind whirled with thoughts of the conspiracy, as he read the file's grisly details. The perp chopped off a woman's head with an axe and kept it in the deep freeze between the chops and the steaks. But he wasn't going to eat it. Not without ketchup.

Chapter 21

The clock read 2:52 p.m. The squad room was as barren as the Mojave Desert. The night watch would take over soon, but they were no blazing stars in the LAPD galaxy. They'd drift in late, then go get coffee and donuts. Dover was itching to leave, he had urgent work to handle.

The phone rang, and he hesitated.

Eddie had just risen from his chair, ready to leave. Dover speared him with an expectant stare. So Eddie lifted the receiver and held it to his ear, his face resembling a mistreated basset hound.

The stout detective closed his eyes, frowned, and rubbed his forehead with his hand. Picked up a pen. "When did it happen?"

Dover rested his attaché case on the table.

Eddie talked and scribbled, then said, "We'll be right over." When he hung up, he looked at Dover. "A guy caught two slugs in the chest. Street cop says he's stone dead. Killer got away clean."

"You need a hand?"

He nodded, then added by way of explanation, "Deadeye's water heater croaked. Guy's coming over to put in a new one."

"Let's take your car. Titus is still messing with mine."

"They should fire that fuckin' idiot. He couldn't fix a busted wiper."

"He got booted by the computer revolution. Like the rest of us over twenty. So where was the hit?"

"Some parking lot near here. Attendant got smoked."

Dover felt cold all over. "Not the Cascade Parking Lot?"

Eddie glanced at his notes. "Yeah, that's it, why?"

His mind roared. Chuck left at three, some days a little before. But was this one of them?

When they pulled into the lot, the SID van and a couple of black and white units sat in one corner, and some uniforms and techs in jumpsuits gathered in a cluster inside the crime scene tape circling the area around his Chevy. None of them were checking out the candy apple finish. They peered at the ground like vultures on low limbs eyeing a fresh carcass.

Dover followed their gaze and saw the kid's blond hair and muscular shoulders. Damn it to hell. Chuck lay facedown in a wine-colored puddle.

Dover's head felt light. Like he'd been sucker punched by a strong middleweight. He looked away from the body and stared at the sky.

In a few moments he got out and headed toward the corpse, numb all over, mind a blank. Eddie stood beside the body talking to a uniform.

"Guy in the ticket hut came on duty and found the DB."

Dead body. He was more than that. "His name's Chuck."

The cop looked at him, then checked his notes. "Yeah, Chuck Appleby. So he feels his neck like they do on TV and gets no—"

"You know this guy?" Eddie asked.

"—pulse, you know. So he—"

"From parking here. He was a nice kid."

"—calls 911. I respond, see no one running or gunning away. Guy's a goner, so I tell dispatch to notify you guys,

251

1,2

then I checked a couple businesses real quick, came up with zip, and I figure—"

"Know any reason someone would do him?" Eddie said.

"—he got aced by The Shadow using a silencer, because—"

"Can't figure it, Eddie."

"—no one saw or heard a thing. No car, no one leaving the scene—"

Eddie shook his head. "In L.A., you never know, huh?"

"—no suspicious creeps hanging around. So there you are."

An SID officer with a rigid face rifled Chuck's pockets.

The uniform shut his notebook and stuck it away.

Eddie stared at him. "That's it? That's all you've got?"

The coroner's tech waltzed up and started his practiced routine on another in an endless stream of corpses.

"That's my preliminary investigation," said the uniform. "I ain't been here long."

"You must've left something out." Eddie removed his notepad and a pen from his jacket. "Run it by me again."

Dover saw how unfeeling they were in dealing with someone who minutes earlier had been an active participant in the dance of life. The only chance we'd get on this planet, unless you were Shirley MacLaine. Being callous helped handle the pain and horror. Kept it at arm's length. Made you believe it might not slip by and grab you or someone you loved.

As the uniformed cop's monologue reran, Dover cleared his throat and said to the SID officer kneeling beside Chuck, "Find any keys to a Chevy? Key ring has a pair of miniature handcuffs on it." He felt like a grave robber.

The cop looked up at Dover and then at the Bel Air. "Yours?" he asked, deadpan. A twin for Buster Keaton.

Dover glanced at his car. Gleaming candy apple red. Same as the blood still oozing from Chuck's chest.

"Yeah, he got it washed and waxed for me."

The finish on the Chevy was smooth as a silver dollar. Buffed, no scratches. He hoped Chuck's last ride was fresh.

The officer nodded. "Nice set of wheels."

Dover nodded, feeling like a ghoul.

Standing up and brushing off his knees, the officer said, "Nope, I didn't find 'em." The resignation in the man's aspect reminded Dover even more of "The Great Stone Face," whose movies depicted what everyone knows but chooses not to think about: that catastrophe lurks around the next corner.

In one film, Keaton's house was being moved but got stuck on a train track. A train whistled in the distance and Buster shoved the house in vain. He jumped away, and the train rolled past on an adjacent track. Keaton composed himself, then another locomotive roared into the scene from the other direction and smashed through the doomed house.

Things are never as they seem.

Dover heard Eddie interrupt the uniform's delivery again. "Jesus, I didn't notice. That your car, Ricochet?"

"Maybe he left 'em in the ticket hut," said the SID guy.

"Yeah, I've been parking here the past couple of weeks," Dover said to Eddie, then turned back to the SID cop. "What'd you say?"

"Your keys," the impassive man intoned as though spelling it out for a mental defective. "Might be in the ticket hut."

"Does it mean anything that he's lyin' by your car?" Eddie asked.

"I don't know. He got it washed for me." He gave a wave

to the SID cop who was drifting away, holding plastic bags filled with Chuck's personal stuff. "You're right," Dover called after him, "I'll check there."

Eddie studied Chuck's body. "This is one crazy fucking city."

"Absolutely. Excuse me." He plodded to the ticket hut.

A uniform was inside, checking the list of customers who had assigned parking spots. Dover stepped in and reviewed the board, with numbers painted in fuchsia over small hooks. He spotted his keys and grabbed them.

"I need these to get home with," he explained to the uniform who shrugged and went back to perusing the names.

Dover stumbled out of the hut and headed toward his Chevy. The initial shock had dissolved, but he felt half-dead himself. He couldn't believe Chuck was gone.

The coroner's tech stood up beside Chuck's ruined body and nodded, Eddie gave a hand signal, and two guys in green jumpsuits moved in with a heavy plastic body bag, ready to zip the remains into the cocoon.

And from deep within Dover rage erupted. He wanted to bomb the whole damn city. Wipe out the fucks who killed Chuck and everyone else, too. Maybe a few good people would get nuked, but damn few. Like Babylon, this place could use a fresh start.

Then he froze, staring at the scene as though seeing it for the first time. The anger cleared away his blinding sorrow. Leaving him undistracted by the horror of this needless loss.

"Hold it!" he said. The guys with the body bag hesitated beside the fallen corpse. They looked like surprised mannequins.

Dover needed to assess the details: The Chevy was clean. The keys were on the board. But Chuck was killed behind the car.

Something was wrong with this scenario.

What was Chuck doing at the moment the bullets with his name on them ripped into his torso? Dover stood back from Chuck's body and went over the sequence. Chuck had taken the Chevy to the car wash, returned to the lot, then hung up the keys. Next thing you know, it's almost quitting time.

So why had he gone back to the car? Admiring the shine and giving that approving nod of his? Might have been the way he'd have wanted to go.

But Chuck's body was lying behind the Chevy. He always studied it from the front or side, delighting in the sweeping design, the sculpted chrome work on the front. His corpse was face down, his head close to the rear bumper. He'd been walking toward the car when he was blasted.

A drive-by shooting? Random? Or maybe on purpose, with Chuck involved in drug dealing? He didn't think so. An accident, with the whizzing lead intended for someone else? Improbable, even in L.A. Maybe a jealous boyfriend had it in for the strapping blond kid.

Then Dover noticed another detail. Chuck's right arm was stretched out in the direction of the shiny cocoon. Waving to someone? Signaling? Making a threatening gesture, trying to run someone off the lot?

Or just away from the Bel Air. Some kid with a screwdriver? A crazy fucking kid who'd pull a gun and shoot before he'd turn and run away?

He lifted his chin, and the men resumed encasing Chuck in the bag, hefting the body into the Coroner's van, and slamming the rear doors. Dover's thoughts were a confused jumble. He closed his eyes, searching for vibes.

An idea hit him with the sudden jolt of a killer quake.

He approached Eddie, who was scribbling a note. "Any theories?"

"I think it was done for revenge, love, or money."

"They all are."

"But there's always a new twist."

"So what now?"

"I'll talk to some people in the area. Try and find a witness." He shrugged. "We'll see what the autopsy shows. Have the slugs checked."

"And you'll run down his KAs?" Dover asked.

"Acquaintances? Sure, time permitting. Hey, you look like shit. I'm going to check that loan office. Why don't you go home?"

"I couldn't leave you alo—"

"Bullshit. Nothing's moving on this. I'm just doing the routine."

That was true, but he felt he owed Chuck. Except that he might not be much help in his condition. The shock of Stretch, and now Chuck, being murdered had consumed him. He felt like a scorched California hillside.

"Okay, but page me if anything breaks. And I'll help tomorrow."

"Sure, see you then." Eddie seemed to stare at him a moment too long. Was it pity? Disgust? Curiosity?

Something in those dark eyes set small blades whirring in Dover's chest. Leaving a hollow space where suspicion rushed in to fill his heart. He watched Eddie cross the busy street in mid-block.

He stood alone in the blacktop lot. A hundred thoughts flashed through his mind, but none became formed. Except for one inkling that swam through his consciousness: Things are never as they seem.

Turning, he hiked back to the ticket hut. The other attendant stood there like a stiff heron, pale as skim milk. Dover told the guy to go home, and if the owner complained, to tell the son of a bitch it was police orders.

Dover stared at his Chevy. He strode over to it, unlocked the door, then hesitated. Getting down on one knee, he swung his head beneath the undercarriage, but saw nothing.

He stepped to the front of the vehicle, released the latch and raised the hood. Then he searched the space with his eyes, not moving his hands, not bumping against the front of the car. Various parts of interlocking machinery.

Everything looked normal.

He returned to the hut and studied his shiny car, wishing he and Stretch were in it whizzing along Mulholland Drive, the top down, sun warm on their faces, not a care in the world. No catastrophes waiting around the corner.

He reached in his coat pocket. Taking a quick look around to make sure he was still alone, he pointed the starting device toward the Chevy. Held his breath and punched the button.

It started up. A throaty roar. The car gleamed in the afternoon sun, a resplendent reminder of more carefree times.

No disaster had happened. Keaton's philosophy was off on this one. The movies aren't always right.

Maybe he was being too cynical. Maybe he was full of crap about his racist conspiracy theory. Stretch could've taken a premise based on assumptions and expanded it into a fantasy. And as everyone said about Dover himself, perhaps he had watched too many late, late shows. The loss of sleep combined with immersion into the dreamy cinematic world may have impaired his brain.

He sighed, then started toward his car. Perhaps a drive, even among the throng of freeway lemmings, would clear his fatigued mind. He'd been pushing himself hard. Time to

Mark Bouton

kick back, not fight the system, take things—

Then a deafening whump and a rush of heat erupted, blowing him backwards as his car exploded in a burgeoning fireball.

Dover figured he'd been out for a minute or so. He lay on the asphalt with his ears ringing. He started to sit up, then felt the pain. A piece of whizzing shrapnel had gouged his left shoulder. Another had sliced his forehead at the scalp line. His jacket was ripped, his elbow scraped and bloody. A dagger-like piece of chrome impaled the ticket hut above his head.

He rose up on his good elbow, taking in the surrealistic scene. His Chevy ablaze, fire licking upward, black smoke swirling into the pale sky. The odor of gas fumes and burning rubber filled his nose. This was incredible. He felt trapped in a film noir, like Humphrey Bogart in *Dark Passage*, wrongly accused and hunted by authorities.

Eddie came jogging back across the street. Within minutes, several black and white units, an evidence van, and detectives' cars swarmed the parking lot. Eddie helped Dover into the duty car and hopped in to wheel him to the emergency room. The others snapped photos or watched the flames roar. A fire truck squealed up to the lot. As Eddie pulled away, Dover took a last look at the mutilated chassis of his beloved Bel Air.

The bastards.

After an hour in the emergency room getting his wounds sterilized, stitched, and bandaged, he asked Eddie to drive him to a Rent-a-Wreck agency. He leased a dented Ford Tempo, something to get around in until he bought another car he loved half as much as the Chevy.

Of course, that wasn't the main concern.

The drive home seemed perilous. Once there, he hesitated to open his door. Would it explode?

He got inside safely, then kept the lights on and the TV playing. He wanted company, but feared it. He felt hollow and fragile, and when he finally went to bed, he slept fitfully, dreaming of fire and explosions.

Chapter 22

When Dover awakened early, he recalled no details of what had happened. But as he clattered along in the beat-up Ford, they came back to him in graphic and startling bits and pieces. Arriving early at Parker Center, he found a parking spot on the south lot. As he walked to the door, he skirted the marble statue, a memorial to fallen officers. How close he'd come to joining them.

Deadeye stood at the elevators. His dark eyes took in the bandage on Dover's forehead, then he said, "Eddie called me last night about your car gettin' blown up. That was weird. You got any idea who did it?"

Dover stared at him. "Not exactly."

Deadeye looked away. "Yeah, that was weird." He studied the colored lines painted on the floor. Then he said, "You doin' okay?"

"Guess I'll live."

A door slid open, and they stepped inside. Deadeye punched the third floor button. Dover asked, "Get your water heater installed?"

"Huh?" Deadeye looked perplexed.

"You know, Eddie said you were getting one yesterday."

"Oh, yeah." Now he got it. "I picked it up on the way home. Hooked it up last night. It's fine."

So Eddie had forgotten to clue him in on the water heater sham. Including the part about the repairman who was to deliver and install it.

The door opened. Now the comment about hooking up

the water heater reminded Dover that Deadeye was good with his hands. Handy in a way that Dover had never been. Skillful with tools. Wrenches or guns.

Dover sat at his desk considering Deadeye in a new light. They had always been on different wavelengths. Deadeye had the short haircut, Dover's hair was longish. Deadeye always had a few too many drinks at social occasions. Dover had done the same, but not every outing. He liked to save a few brain cells.

And even in their approach to work they were opposites. Dover liked to analyze a crime, dissect it bit-by-bit, inspect the motive, means, and opportunity, then interview the suspect and finesse him into admitting his guilt or entangling himself in a web of lies. Deadeye went for the obvious suspect, trying to bully him into submission, guilty or not.

Deadeye had capped three guys in the line of duty. One from about fifty yards away as the young man was scaling a fence during a chase. Got the kid in the back of the head, earning Deadeye his nickname.

Dover had killed one man. After the man had shot his own wife and put a hole in Dover's thigh. Dover still woke up sweating after dreaming about the man's waxen face and wet hair and the rose blooms on his chest gushing lipstick red fluids as he lay crumpled in the street.

So many differences between them. Maybe a lot of it explained by the fact that Deadeye had been in the military and Dover hadn't. Neatness hadn't stuck with the man, but other facets of the training lingered beneath the surface. He seemed aloof from human suffering, showing a cold dispassion for others.

To Deadeye, a certain cachet was lent to matters of violence and killing and destruction. Dover now recalled that Deadeye had been a Navy SEAL. A damn tough group.

Witness *G.I. Jane*. Plus they were trained in almost every form of combat and means of . . . demolition.

SEALs were trained with explosives! So that they could slither undetected beneath dark waters to blow up ships or bridges or whatever target was thought appropriate by the high command. They were disciplined. They were determined. They were deadly.

And such a man could easily blow up a car or two. Just give the order and stand back. Fire in the hole. Another trophy of whatever war the man was fighting this time.

Deadeye answered the phone. "For you, Ricochet."

"Rick, I heard on the radio. I'm still shaking. Are you all right?"

"I'm fine, Terri. I was exhausted when I got home, and I didn't want to call and have you be upset all night."

"But to hear it on the news. My heart almost stopped. I was sure they'd say you were dead."

"I was going to call you this morning before you found out about it."

"I get up early. Dreams about the other bombing still interrupt my sleep."

For a moment, that left him speechless. "I don't want—"

"I don't want to find out you've been killed, too." She started to cry. "We've got to do something. Do it now."

"I've been going over every angle, Terri. I'm not on any crusade here. I just want to stay alive."

"Then run, hide, go to Rio. Just do it before they try again."

"I'm working on it. And I'm protecting my backside. But there are a few more questions I need to answer before I run."

As soon as it was out of his mouth, he knew he'd said it wrong.

"If you're set on digging into whatever deadly bullshit is going on, I'm not going to sit around and wonder from minute-to-minute whether you're still alive. I have to get away from it."

"I won't do anything obvious. I'll be careful—"

"We've had this discussion before, and that's all I can take. I'm going to clean the whole house. Top to bottom. Maybe I can think about something besides your safety and keep myself from going insane."

"But Terri—" The line went dead. He sat there, numb, hating that he had to worry Terri, but knowing he had to somehow derail the group in the next few days. More than his safety was at stake.

The phone rang. Eddie picked up. "For you, Ricochet."

Maybe Terri realized she was being hasty. "Detective Dover."

"Oh, Rick," April said, "I was so shocked to hear."

"Yeah, I was pretty surprised, too."

"It really scared me. My feelings came out so strong."

"Your feelings?"

"The thought of losing you. It just crushed me."

"Any reports of my death are greatly exaggerated."

"You know, that's one thing I love about you. You're so fearless, so—"

"Stupid?"

"I was going to say macho. I've missed that about you."

There was a pause. Not pregnant, he hoped.

"Could we maybe get together later in the week?" she said. "Dinner at Emilio's, dessert at my place?"

He realized he'd been missing something, too, but he had only three days to stop a monstrous machine. He felt like the Chinese student standing in front of a huge rolling tank. Only he didn't think this group would be so good-hearted as to stop.

"That's more inviting than you know. But I've got a lot to do on a big case right now. Sort of a night-and-day thing. Maybe a raincheck?"

"Oh, sure, I understand. Anyway, I'm really glad you're okay. So give me a call when you get free."

He promised he would. He hung up, and his mind reeled as he imagined sipping a delicious Cabernet Sauvignon. Touching warm, perfumed flesh. Life could be—

Cardwell darted into his glassed-in office like an eel slipping into a fissure in a rock.

And Dover's strange world came slamming back into focus. In that instant he realized his only hope was to attack the enemy he knew. If he could neutralize Cardwell, Eddie, and Deadeye, maybe he could stop the upcoming riot in South Central.

Dover spent the rest of the morning plotting against the group. He allowed himself several volcanic bursts of rage, blowing away part of the hatred bubbling inside him. Then he forced himself to plan his moves.

He thought about the endgame, trying to establish a sense of his position and developing his strategy. The problem was, he was at a huge strength disadvantage. The other side had all the big guns. The bishops, queen, rooks, and knights all aligned against his one knight and a few pawns.

Maybe he'd pull a Houdini. Now you see it, now you don't. A bit of misdirection. Or a Keaton. Things are never as they seem.

Perhaps he could maneuver them into a draw. Proving that pawns are the soul of chess. Or at least that they can kick the big guys where it hurts.

He opened his pad and wrote down some items he'd need.

At noon he headed for the elevators. Outside, the sun had superheated the smog. He walked south on Los Angeles Street to Winston. A couple of blocks down he stopped at a sandwich shop which served a great Reuben sandwich. Hard to find in this land of dill weed, bean sprouts, and parsley.

Full as a gorged tick, he sauntered back north on San Pedro to Third, then turned east. Stopped at Cuffs 'N' Stuff, a police supply store that offered discounts to members of the LAPD. He stepped inside. Not recognizing anyone, he headed for the display cases.

In fifteen minutes he selected the equipment he needed, passed the plastic one more time without setting off overcharge alarms, and left the store toting the items he hoped might give him an edge the next time his pawns were pushed into a corner or his nuts were squeezed in a vise.

He sensed either might not be long in coming.

He glanced at the sky above the buildings. Not as blue as he liked. Still, it felt good being outdoors, even though he had to breathe the smog. And now he was being approached by the third street person in an hour.

"Hiyadoin'?" the man said. Slurred delivery, but a genuine smile. His rumpled clothes reeked of the grape, and he looked between thirty and fifty, tough to tell with a wino. Leathery skin and a week-old stubble.

"Fine, thanks. You?" Dover didn't have the heart to ignore him, which was the only way to escape without getting touched.

"Not bad." He wiped his forehead with his sleeve. Hair

265

thinning, liver spots on his pate. "Hot one, huh?" More loquacious than most.

"Torrid. Thought I'd go back to the office."

"Parker Center?" They could always tell.

"That's it. Justice for all."

"I used to be a deputy myself."

"That right?"

"Yep. Shot a guy. Couldn't face the Job no more."

"Makes it tough."

" 'Course it's tough on these streets with no paycheck, too. Think you could spare some change for a fellow lawman?"

Dover groped in his pocket. "I think I got a buck left over from lunch. Yeah, here. Maybe you could grab coffee and a donut."

The man brightened, then his expression slipped back to morose. "Used to be you could," he said. "But this damn inflation eats you alive. Nearly a dollar now just for a lousy donut, much less a real sandwich."

Dover stifled a smile. What a pro. He fished out his wallet. "Here's a ten spot. Get yourself a meal. And you tell any of the other guys about this, I'll kneecap you with my blackjack."

He took it smiling. "Detective, it's just between you and me."

"Good. See you around."

"Sure, and if I can ever help you with anything, let me know. I still got cop's eyes. Don't miss much."

"You bet. Take care." But he wasn't buying the guy's assistance. Sometimes he just liked to feel more human than the usual cop.

He hoofed back to Parker Center where he tossed the sack into the trunk of his Tempo, then tromped into the building. Couldn't say he'd missed it. Still, the Job bought him lunch.

Most of the detectives milled about the squad room. Too damn hot to be out on the bricks. Eddie and Deadeye were the only exceptions. He couldn't imagine them busting their asses on the streets, maybe they'd found a cool movie theater or a dark bar.

He slipped off his jacket and pulled out the instructions for the items he'd bought at Cuffs 'N' Stuff. He studied the various pamphlets, making sure he knew how everything worked.

After he'd memorized it all, he shoved the papers into his back pocket. Then, in deference to the faux project that Cardwell had stuck him with, he entered the info from a couple of murder books into the computer database. He stretched, got an icy Coke, and chatted with some of the other detectives.

Then he punched in Terri's number. The line was busy, so he hung up and put his stuff away. He tried her number again. Still busy.

He headed out into the steamy afternoon, steeling himself for the commute in his rickety ride. On the freeway he tuned the radio to a C&W station. They sang of lost love, divorce, and loneliness. Let you know everyone was in the same leaky boat together.

When he got home he found Terri's phone continued to drone on as busy.

He flipped on the radio and drank a beer as he listened to Reba McIntyre, Travis Tritt, and Faith Hill. Then Alan Jackson's mellow voice murmuring the poignant, "Who Says You Can't Have It All?"

He hit the redial button. Busy signal. Hung up.

Was she angry with him? Had she taken her phone off the hook? No, that made no sense. She'd turn on the recorder to screen her calls. She'd once said the message machine was the best protection against salesmen and sex perverts. Not that he thought he fit either category.

Could she be talking with someone that long? Not likely. She wasn't the type. But she could have made or gotten several calls.

He dialed the operator. Told her he'd been trying to reach Terri's number for some time and asked if she'd check whether someone was on the line or the receiver was off the hook.

She said she would, then she went off the line for close to a minute.

"Sir? There's no conversation on the line, so I imagine the instrument's off the receiver. The signal's been activated."

He thanked her and hung up. Terri might've been so upset after their earlier conversation that she'd slammed the phone down, and it hadn't seated right. Then she'd gone to another part of the house, maybe running the vacuum, and hadn't heard the squealing signal on the phone.

It'd be better to leave her alone for a while. Let her cool off. Let them both think about things and consider their relationship.

Wait a minute. What relationship? What made him think of that?

Clint Black and Wynona gave forth with an oldie, "A Bad Goodbye." Harmony so beautiful it made your soul ache.

Then he bolted out the door and climbed into the tin heap. Broiling hot in there. He squealed out of the parking space, headed for Terri's.

Nearly an hour later he rolled by Terri's driveway, his Tempo wheezing from the climb up the canyon road. Her

Buick was in the driveway. Maybe he'd called when she was out.

The front curtains were open, he saw no movement inside, and the house projected an aura of emptiness. He parked down the street at a house with a For Sale sign adrift in an overgrown yard. Standing outside his car, he gave the house the once-over, as if he were a prospective buyer. Just in case any suspicious neighbors were watching.

Then he walked down to Terri's as though he might be questioning a neighbor about the house or the neighborhood. The hinged cover on her mailbox by the street was ajar, with a magazine and some other mail inside. As he passed by her car, he touched his palm to the hood. Cool, no clicking sounds. No water dripping from the Buick's air conditioner. He looked in the front and back seats. No packages, cleaning, *nada*.

As he approached the front door, he scanned every inch of window glass that afforded a view inside. Still no movement. Terri didn't open the door or come out onto the porch to tell him to come in or to get the hell out of there. He would have welcomed either of those extremes.

She had no pets. No barking, meowing, or chirping. No frantic animals to signal that their owner was in trouble.

He rang the doorbell. It echoed throughout the house. He looked through a glass inset in the front door. No one was coming to answer the bell. He saw a chair in the living room lying on its side. Magazines were scattered on the floor.

He glanced around. No neighbors were out in their yards. He stepped to the other side of the house. She wasn't in the kitchen. He heard something and ducked. Then he recognized the electronic, high-pitched sound: the phone.

He checked the back patio and yard, finding nothing.

Back at the front of the house, he looked under a potted plant by the front door. He checked around the porch. There had to be a spare key somewhere.

He paced back alongside the house, checking shrubs and trees for hiding places. On the back patio, he studied the layout, then checked a few spots, with no results. He had no lock picks with him. Never had been too good with them, anyway. Stretch had been the master.

The basketball goal. Stretch had put one alongside the driveway. Dover hiked back to the front of the house. The goalpost was steel, with no indentations. The backboard itself was solid Plexiglas. There was nothing at the base that would work as a hiding spot. And Terri couldn't reach very high, but a wooden stepladder leaned against the outside of the garage.

At the base of the goalpost, he opened the ladder and climbed. On top of the flat piece of metal that held the rim out from the backboard, a key was taped. Dover pulled it loose and hurried to the door.

He unlocked the deadbolt. The doorknob lock wasn't engaged, and he turned the knob. Drawing his Beretta, he pushed the door open and slipped inside. Step by step, quietly. Still heard nothing except the screeching phone.

He stuck his head around the corner, peeked into the living room, then pulled back. No one was around. But there'd been a struggle in there.

In the kitchen two glasses of lemonade sat on a tray on the counter near the telephone. Ice bucket beside it. Most of the ice had melted in the glasses.

Putting it together, he figured someone had come to the door. Someone she knew. She let him in, relocked the deadbolt by habit, then offered to fix lemonade. But before she took it into the living room, the telephone rang. Whoever was with her couldn't let her answer it.

The guy grabbed her, the receiver fell to the floor, and he dragged her into the living room. They bumped into furniture and dumped over magazines. The guy hadn't wanted to risk dragging her outside in the daytime, so he went out the back door. But there was no alley back there, no road but the one in front.

Then he got it. Same concealment the bomber used to sabotage Stretch's Bronco. Tall shrubs skirted the driveway behind the basketball goal, blocking the neighbors' view. Guy made his way from the back to the front, hidden by the garage and the shrubs. Then he tumbled Terri inside a car waiting at the edge of the street.

Dover slipped into the family room. Nothing disturbed in there. But if Terri had been struggling, wouldn't she have banged into something else? He stepped to the sliding glass doors that led onto the back patio. They were closed, but not locked. Some burglar he'd make.

But why had she suddenly quit fighting? Oh, God. His chest turned to ice, and his heart boomed like thunder. Was she dead?

No, wait. There was no blood and no sign of violence. She must've begun cooperating. Maybe the intruder had pulled a gun or a knife.

Damn! If he'd gotten Terri into this mess he'd never forgive himself. He couldn't just drop it, just step back and leave it alone the way Cardwell had threatened him to do, the way Terri had pleaded with him to do, the way his better judgment had screamed for him to do.

His subconscious niggled at him, wanting him to replay the trip through the living room. But why? He'd scoped out the scenario good. He could see himself walking by the chair that lay on its side, by the table where the magazines had been dumped. Into the family room. Everything in place there.

But his replay system kept rewinding to the living room, like a pervert might review his favorite scene in a porno flick. Past the table into the family room. Now again. What was there to see?

He strode back across the room. Stood in the doorway, staring into the living room. Saw nothing new. The head tape played again. He was missing something. He stepped into the room a few feet, stopped, let out all his antennae. Tried to assimilate and process the vibes.

Then it came to him. Olfactory sense. Many times a homicide dick switched it off because of the awful stench at a murder site.

Chloroform. He could smell pungent traces in the air, especially in this area. The guy had put her under and carried her out to the car.

He checked the bedrooms, laundry room, small study. As expected, he saw nothing more. But then, he wasn't that sharp these days.

Back to the kitchen, he hung up the shrieking phone. Checked the message machine—nothing. Then he dialed 911 and reported a kidnapping.

Chapter 23

The deputies poked around the house with little enthusiasm. "We'll put out a bulletin on her, Detective," said the one who had Burt Lancaster's build from the days when he lit up the screen with passionate kisses on the beach. But the kid lacked the energetic charm and the twinkle in his eye.

"And you'll check with the neighbors, of course," Dover said with grit in his voice, "to see if they saw a person or a vehicle in the area."

Lancaster Jr. stared back silently, but the other deputy, who looked like an overweight shoe salesman, spoke up like a plucky Mickey Rooney. He wouldn't want to see this guy's backside, either. "Sure thing, Detective. Never know, huh? Maybe someone saw her."

"Could be some footprints out back or tire track marks in the dirt next to the driveway," Dover added. "Not to mention all kinds of latent fingerprints in the house."

Baby Lancaster said, "I'm sure there are thousands of prints in the house. But I guess the question would be what you'd dust and who we'd compare the prints with."

"Might try the telephone receiver, the knocked over chair, the front and back doors and the door jamb in the family room. The glass patio doors would be good, too."

"Didn't you say you hung up the phone, then called 911?"

"I used my handkerchief to pick it up." He rubbed his hand across his mouth. "Look, I don't mean to be a hardass. I have a strong feeling the lady was kidnapped and could be in real danger."

"There's no reason for us to clash on this," young Burt said, lowering his strong chin. "I'm sure you realize we get a lot of calls on mysterious disappearances that are pure bullshit. People get drunk, go on trips, get laid. Just examples, nothing personal."

"I think this one's for real," he said.

"She a friend of yours?"

"Her husband was my partner. He was killed two weeks ago."

"Jeez," said the other deputy as if he'd lost a big sale.

"We'll hit it hard," said young Burt. "But do something for us?"

"What's that?"

"First, call as soon as she turns up, so we don't keep looking for someone who's not lost." He paused, thinking of how to phrase it. "And if you have some ideas on who may be involved here, I'd appreciate it if you'd pass them on. It's a lot easier than starting from square one."

Young Burt wasn't so dumb after all. Dover glanced at his nametag. "Deputy Rinehart, you got a card?"

Dover studied the embossed badge on the card, fingering it as he made a decision. He looked up and said, "I'm going to check on a couple of hunches. If I come up with anything, I'll let you know."

Rinehart gave a nod. "Joe, go grab the fingerprint kit."

"Sure thing." And he did a heavy man's half-shuffle, really hustling to the storeroom to find the next larger size in a pump.

Dover said, "I better get out of your way." He turned for the door, then looked back over his shoulder. "Thanks, Deputy."

He shrugged. "No problem. Hope it works out okay."
That's what he'd been hoping for days now.

Back in the Tempo, Dover coasted down the canyon road, headed north, his mind in turmoil. The sunset was vin rose glorious. Smog could do that for you. But he wasn't in the mood for glorious, and besides, thinking of the sunset had crystallized his thoughts.

Deadeye lived on Sunset Boulevard. And Dover hadn't cruised that area for quite a while. No time like sundown for a showdown.

As he drove, his nerves sizzled and the back of his shirt got clammy. Terri was at the mercy of a sinister group. They could do anything with her.

No clue where she was. But if he found the guys holding her, he'd have the strength of Frankenstein's monster. He'd rip their heads off.

He took the Ventura eastbound. Deadeye didn't live in West Hollywood, or even in Hollywood, and he didn't really reside on Sunset. He lived on the fringes of Los Feliz, several blocks off the Boulevard.

Then as Dover approached Studio City, it struck him that Eddie's place wasn't far away. Might as well check there. It was a good side bet.

Minutes later he cruised by the lavender and pink complex with its abject aura. Eddie lived on the second floor in a corner apartment. Dover had been inside a couple of times. Good view of the trashy street.

He parked and peered into the mirror, scoping the building, which emitted a gaudy glow like a luminous whale. Lights shone in Eddie's living room and bedroom. Dover slipped out of the car to retrieve a briefcase from the trunk. He set the case on the front seat, then flipped open the clasps and surveyed his hardware from Cuffs 'N' Stuff.

Removing one of the devices, he slipped it into his jacket pocket. Pulled his Beretta out of its holster and checked the magazine. Ditto with his AMT Backup. Switchblade and razor were set to go.

He moseyed down the sidewalk on the perimeter of the complex. Paint on the weathered buildings had peeled off in cereal-sized flakes. Checking the vehicles in the carports, he spotted Eddie's old Thunderbird.

He edged up close to the building, straining to see inside the apartment, but the blinds in the living room were closed, and he couldn't discern any action. In the bedroom he noticed a shadow against the blinds. Someone was moving around. The hair on his arms rose; Terri could be in there.

Maybe he'd go for it. Kick in the door and charge. There probably wouldn't be more than two or three of them, and surprise would be on his side. Not to mention adrenaline and rage.

But if he were wrong, and she wasn't there, then what? He'd have blown it. They'd know for certain he knew about them, and they'd still have Terri. Check and mate, all because he made one impetuous move.

This game required strong nerves. And unearthly concentration. He'd have to play it a lot smarter than he'd done so far.

He crept closer to the building. Then someone whisked out of a downstairs apartment, and he froze. A blonde, about thirty, who was poured into a cotton crop top and a snug pair of shorts, crossed the lot.

She didn't spot him. Opening her car trunk, she pulled out some in-line skates, displaying class-A haunches. Reminded him of the skater he'd met on the boardwalk. She slammed the trunk lid and lugged the skates back inside.

He glanced to the second floor, remembering how Eddie, Deadeye, and Stretch used to accompany him on scouting missions to Venice Beach. An area rife with romantic potential for singles, at least back when things were simpler. Before AIDS and violent crime and racial hatred made everyone into scared stiff neurotics.

Now he spotted something. A slat in another mini-blind in the bedroom was hitched up, allowing a peek inside. The shadow was close by. He sidled over a bit to get a better angle, staying near the carport for cover.

Now he could see bare skin and dark hair. On Eddie's chest. Then he saw a bulging bicep. The guy was lifting dumbbells. Which he likely wouldn't be doing if Terri were in there being pumped for information.

So was he totally wrong here?

Not necessarily. He still had to go by Deadeye's place. And if that was a bust, he had one more idea.

He slipped over to Eddie's car and knelt down by the rear quarter panel. But just then the blonde barged back out of her apartment, carrying the skates. He stiffened like a bunny in the brush, hoping to stay invisible.

She unlocked the trunk and laid the skates inside. The bicep muscles in the back of her upper legs curved like a Chippendale chair. She slammed the trunk lid and turned. "Oh," she said, jumping enough to set her crop top in wavelike motion. "I didn't see you there."

"Sorry, I thought my tire looked low."

"Not your fault. Living around here makes a girl jumpy. At least cautious, you know?"

Now she wanted to talk. He stood up and brushed at the knee of his pants. He looked toward her, but not at her. "Yeah, that's what my wife says. Which reminds me,

I'd better go after that ice cream. No, sherbet. She said it's got to be that lime sherbet." He shook his head and shrugged. "Eight months along. She gets a little crazy sometimes."

The blonde's face hardened with disappointment. She gave a half-hearted smile, saying, "I'm sure she does."

He watched her move across the lot.

Now he reached into the pocket of his jacket, pulled out the device, and stuck it under the T-bird. The magnet clamped on, and he straightened up, taking a final peek at the window. Eddie had finished the set and put down the dumbbells. He was flexing his pumped right bicep—no Claude Van Damme, but impressive—someone to be careful with in a confrontation.

Dover flogged his mixmaster into action and forged on to Deadeye's. He felt a growing sense of desperation, but he had to stay cool and use his head if he was going to stay in the match. This one was for all the marbles.

The apartment lights were on, and the guy's blue Olds 88 was parked in the lot. There were no open slits in the curtains. So now what?

Just then Deadeye traipsed outside, headed for his car. Dover skulked down in the seat. Deadeye opened the door and pulled out two sacks full of groceries. Then he locked the door and plodded back inside. He didn't seem to be terrorizing women this evening, either.

Dover slid out and sidled over to the Olds where he knelt down by the rear fender. As he stuck the device under the car, his hand brushed against the tire. Something crusty fell off.

He felt around on the asphalt until he touched the stuff. Then he stared at his fingers, and at the grains of California's finest beach sand. Had he missed it on the T-bird?

He considered going back to Eddie's, then decided to ride on. He already had the clue. Time to forge ahead.

Approaching the Hollywood Freeway, Dover glanced up at the Metromedia TV studio with its illuminated steel bracket sculpture, Starsteps. In Tinseltown, the right part could make a career. Such as Sandra Bullock playing herself/cute bus passenger. Leading to parts as herself/cute computer expert, herself/cute attorney, and herself/cute witch. Talent will out.

On the Sunset Strip he was assaulted by gaudy vanity boards soaring above the street, all lights and bursting colors and hoopla about the latest movies and recordings coming at you, baby. So many vacuous distractions in La La Land. Most of them with a value of less than zero.

Now past the St. James' Club, an art deco masterpiece. Rising twelve stories, with the upper floors receding, it looked like a chess rook. Topped by a penthouse where they played the game on a different plane.

Reminding him to focus on the sinister match in which he was embroiled. Primary goal: Find and rescue the queen. Preliminary move was to assess the enemy's deployment. Specifically, he wanted to see if Cardwell was at home in Westwood, and if Terri was hidden there.

As Eddie's complex was no comparison to the grandeur of the St. James' Club, neither was Cardwell's place up to the usual ritzy standard for homes in that area. He'd bought it as an orphan of a nasty divorce in the seventies. A rock star had trashed it before leaving for Europe. Still, it was worth a bundle now. Dumb luck can win a match or two. Or maybe he underestimated the Lou.

Dover rattled past the place, a four bedroom with the driveway curving into a side entrance double garage. Lights were on. He parked, waited with his window open, listening to the night sounds, then opened the car door and slid out into the darkness.

He approached Cardwell's house without alerting any dogs or neighbors. Sneaking alongside the driveway, he tried to peek inside the front windows, but some drapes blurred the view. He moved closer. The door to the attached garage was still up, and the Lou's Crown Vic was hunkered down inside.

But he didn't see Cardwell anywhere.

Until he snuck up almost to the car, homing device in hand, and Cardwell banged out the back door, squinting in the darkness, yelling, waving his pistol.

Dover took off, his hips swiveling on a broken field pattern. Cardwell shouted curses but didn't crank off any rounds. Dover reached his car, piled in, and chugged away. He didn't think Cardwell was close enough to recognize him. But he'd failed in his mission.

And just like Pauline, he'd escaped peril by inches. Except this was real life, not the movies. He could get killed bona fide dead.

Terri was still missing, and Dover was running out of ideas.

He steered the clunker past the UCLA campus. Hitting Wilshire, he drove east, then pulled onto Santa Monica Boulevard. Sweaty, dejected, and spent, he steered by rote through Beverly Hills, then into West Hollywood. He knew he was overlooking something.

He replayed events in his head. Taking it all apart, looking at it from different angles. But nothing took root.

Into Hollywood now, he turned north on Highland Avenue. The old movie capital was a wilted rose, but cinematic spirits lingered. Maybe being in the presence of creative angels would inspire an inventive idea.

He turned back west on Hollywood Boulevard and pulled into a parking spot. Hustlers, pros, derelicts, addicts, and banjy boys cavorted along the concrete path of bygone glory like ants on a tattered trail. But the pathetic parade failed to fire his imagination.

He bailed out of his heap to walk and think. Pacing along the Hollywood Walk of Fame, he stopped in front of Mann's Chinese Theater with its green-roofed Oriental pagoda. He studied cement squares with scripted names, impressions of the stars' hands and feet, as well as Jimmy Durante's nose, Sonja Henie's skates, and Donald Duck's webbed feet. Even the hoof prints of Trigger, Roy Rogers' horse, forever galloping off into the sunset.

Famous names jumped up at him. Clark Gable, Lana Turner, Rock Hudson, Bette Davis, Jimmy Stewart, and Elizabeth Taylor. "Giant '56" printed in capital letters above her signature. Just like in the photo.

Leading him full circle to this spot, but still far outside the universe inhabited by The Untouchables. He felt like Sisyphus, condemned to eternally roll a huge stone uphill, only to watch it roll downhill again. Never to say, "Cut, print, that's a wrap."

The pricks were beating him like the stepchild he was. Like Cagney pushing a grapefruit into Mae Clark's face, then strutting away like a banty rooster. Anger smoldered in his gut like the glowing embers of a campfire.

He felt volcanic, as if he could spew hot lava. He was ready to spit in his palms, like John Wayne in *The Quiet Man*, and go at it bare knuckles with these assholes. No holds barred.

But first he had to find Terri.

281

He glanced across the street at the El Capitan theater, thronged with moviegoers since its renovation. Made him wonder who the capitans, the jefes, the bosses were in the sinister group.

He paced down the sidewalk, trying to stimulate his brain. Past the Hollywood Galaxy cinema, a circular dream palace glowing ethereally in swirls of white, blue, and red neon. If only he could light up that way.

He crossed the intersection, stopping at C. C. Brown's malt shop, realizing he was famished. Inside, he flopped into a high-backed wooden booth, blinking at the bright lights from the crystal chandeliers. Ordered a hot fudge sundae.

He spooned in the chocolate smoothness, warm on the roof of his mouth. Took a swig of water. Replayed the videos.

He'd missed something at Terri's house. As sure as Durante had the biggest nose impression in Grauman's sidewalk. So replay the scenario. First he tried to call Terri. Line busy. Again. Busy. Then he'd gotten an inkling.

At her house he'd seen signs of a struggle. Knocked over furniture. Chloroform scent in the air. Cordless telephone lying on the floor.

He'd placed the handset back into the receiver of the answering machine. Next to the caller ID box. Damn, caller ID. Philip Marlowe, he wasn't.

Chapter 24

Dover dropped a ten on the table, headed out the door and hustled along the sidewalk, trodding irreverently on the brass memorabilia of the stars, until he reached his humble wheels. His geargrinder wheezed up the canyon road. Terri's house was as dark as a bat cave. The key was in his pocket.

He opened the front door, looked and listened in the dark, seeing and hearing nothing but the sigh of an empty house, then closed the door behind him and flipped the light switch, illuminating a small entryway. He walked straight into the kitchen. When he'd checked earlier, there'd been no messages on the machine. Punching the buttons again, he still found nothing recorded, but there were two hangup calls.

So he checked the caller ID. Looking for the latest number in the system. The last person who'd called.

It was not a number he recognized, except that it had the same prefix as Terri's number, so it was from somewhere in this area. He picked up the phone, dialed Parker Center, and talked to the lieutenant on duty, identifying himself and asking for the subscriber.

After a couple of minutes, he came back on the line. "Sorry, Dover, I can't do you much good. Unlisted number. We can get it through the phone company, but it'll take a little time, y'know?"

Something he didn't have. "Maybe you could push it. That'd be a big help. Give me a call when you get it."

He stared at the telephone, thinking. Then he slid open the kitchen drawer. There was a pad of paper, some cellophane tape, some rubber bands. And the address book he sought.

Plopping into a chair at the dinette table, he leafed through the pages. He could eliminate most of the entries from the area code and/or prefix. Finally, he found it. Listed under Phyllis Margollat.

She lived on the same street as Terri. He remembered her from the group that gathered here after Stretch's funeral. Attractive, pleasant, maybe the type to check on a bereaved neighbor, even after her husband was planted and the rituals done.

He picked up the handset. Blew off fingerprint powder. Dialed the number.

"Hello?" Amazing, someone still answered their telephone in person, without an electronic go-between. He recognized her warm voice.

"Phyllis, this is Rick Dover, a friend of Terri Ridgeway's? I don't know if you remem—"

"Oh, of course," she said. "We met after . . . I mean, at the reception at Terri's a couple of weeks ago."

"Yes, right." Uh-oh. Terri had told him she was divorced.

"In fact, I'd asked Terri a couple of questions about you. Not then, of course. A couple of days ago. She's a good friend and a wonderful person, so I wanted to keep in touch."

"That's very nice of you."

"It's such a tragic loss. She's been brave, but I know she's hurting."

"Yes, she is."

"I hope you don't think I was being too nosy about you."

"No, I mean she hadn't mentioned anything to me."

"Oh . . . then why—"

"I recalled you were a friend of hers, and I needed to tell her something, but she's not home. Have you talked with her today?"

"No, I haven't spoken with her." She sounded perplexed.

"I just thought she might've told you she was going somewhere. Sorry to interrupt you."

"Minding two kids after working all day is no treat. Interrupt anytime."

He smiled. Good sense of humor. In this crazy society, sometimes that was the finest virtue to possess. "Maybe I will."

"I hope it's not bad news. She's had more than her share."

"No, just something she should know."

"Actually, I did try to call her this afternoon when I got home from the university. The first time I got the machine and hung up. But I tried again later, and she might have been there then."

"*Might* have been? I don't—"

"It was strange. I dialed her number, it rang a couple of times, and it sounded as though she'd picked up. Then there was a terrible clatter. I thought she'd dropped the phone. I held the phone away from my ear for a moment, then I said 'hello,' but she still wasn't on the line, so I hung up."

She thought about it a bit. "I tried one other time, and the phone was busy. Then the kids came in and overwhelmed me."

"Do you remember what time you called her?"

"I don't teach classes on Tuesdays, so I left my office

early. The first time was about two o'clock."

"She probably went shopping and then out to dinner," he said. "I'm sure she'll be home soon. Thanks for your help."

"Sure. And don't forget to 'interrupt' me again."

"You got it. 'Bye."

Now he hit the button on the caller ID box to see the previous caller's number. The prefix was from downtown, and he didn't need to call the lieutenant. The number was for Parker Center, Special Homicide Squad.

He could visualize the scenario. After he left for lunch, Eddie and Deadeye pulled the oldest trick around: Call to see if your target is home.

But they'd been caught by technology. Terri answered the call, they hung up, but too late. After two rings, the caller ID box captured their number. Thankfully, she hadn't erased it.

Got you by the balls, you punks.

So he had it figured out. Somewhat. He knew the means and the opportunity. Eddie and Deadeye involved. Cardwell masterminding it, if such a term could be applied to the Lou's usual piss poor planning. But what still had him puzzled was the motive. Why didn't they just come after him? He was the thorn in the paw in this La La Land fable, not Terri. They could blow him up, force him off the road, shoot him from a rooftop with a sniper rifle. Duck soup.

Unless they'd been called off by higher-ups. People who could see that a bungled bomb attempt was a high profile event, and that further violence toward him could raise eyebrows even in a city that'd seen it all. They didn't want to look like the Keystone Kops.

But why kidnap Terri? He drummed his fingertips on the

countertop. Stared at the caller ID box. Then at the message machine.

They were sending him a message. Not by letter, phone, or e-mail. But he'd received it loud and clear. It was: Fuck with us, and we'll kill you and destroy everyone and everything you care about.

He banged the countertop with his fist. Then he took a deep breath. Sipped his drink and found himself again staring at the message machine.

Another missed clue. He half-expected to hear Stretch saying from above: Finally, you dumbass.

He picked up the phone, punched in his home number, then tapped out the code to rewind the tape and listen to the messages. There was one from April saying she'd called, no biggie. Then the one he'd expected.

An unfamiliar man's voice. "She's okay, Dover. But tomorrow bring all the computer disks, notes, whatever you have about our venture. In a plain manila envelope. We'll tell you more later."

A pause, then, "Don't waste your time trying to find her."

The caller hung up, and so did Dover. The prick was probably right. Except as Stretch used to say: In every position there's a good move.

Unless it was already checkmate.

But he didn't think it'd come to that. He knew a couple of things they didn't suspect. He had a move or two left.

He followed their advice, to a degree. He drove home, gathered up copies of the disks and stuck them in an envelope, then in the bedroom rummaged around in the walk-in closet. He tossed three baseball caps into a backpack. Then stuffed in his skates. Next, he rooted around in his chest of drawers. Tomorrow he'd pick up some other items at the store.

He washed his face, threw his clothes on a chair, slipped on some boxer shorts and a baggy T-shirt, then hit the sack. Didn't even reach for the remote. But at two-thirty his eyes flew open, and he spotted the briefcase on the dresser. No way he'd sleep unless he checked. So he dressed, slipped into the Tempo, and growled off into the night.

He flipped on the receiver. No movement by Eddie or Deadeye. He rolled by and eyeballed their rides to make sure. Checked at the Lou's house, too. Garage buttoned up, lights out. All sleeping as peacefully as babies. Like in *The Bad Seed*.

Dawn came as a yellow threat. Dover grunted and dropped the slat of the mini-blind back into place. This would be a day he'd rather not face, a day he needed to be razor sharp, but he felt more like a blunt axe.

Clunking to work in his low dollar rental, his mind churned, covering every angle. There was zero tolerance for mistakes on this one. His plan was risky, but it was the only one he had.

In the squad room, Eddie and Deadeye showed up late. They never spoke or met his eyes. The Lou ignored him, too.

About eleven, he told the rookie detective he was going to Records and would be back in a while. He took the stairs to the first floor and went out through the glass doors. For about fifteen minutes, he leaned against the building staring at the statue, the palm trees, and the passing parade of winos and lawyers and citizens with complaints. Giving the dodos on the third floor time.

When he got back to the homicide table he saw a folded square of white paper shoved under the edge of one of the case binders he'd been working on. Eddie and Deadeye were gone. The rookie was on the phone.

He unfolded the note. Screw fingerprints at this point. The message was typed, with only two strikeovers, saying: Go to Gorky's cafe downtown at four p.m. Give the envelope to whoever asks if it's a screenplay.

Always the damn dramatic element.

Dover revisited the car rental place. The girl who'd rented him the bush league wheels was tall and tan, but Dover was sure she didn't hail from Ipanima. More like Encino.

"Yes, sir? Can I help you?"

"I'd like to rent that white Volvo on your lot."

Wrinkling of her pretty brow. She had the vacant eyes indigenous to a region where students hit the beaches instead of their books. "But didn't you . . . I mean, is the other vehicle—"

"No problem." He held up a hand. "I just needed to pick up some people, and it has more leg room. I'll only need it for one day."

She seemed relieved. Her chest rose and fell in much the way Marilyn Monroe's did when she emoted wistfulness, sadness, or satisfaction. Marilyn could really project those emotions.

"That's fine, sir. I've got your information on file here." She tapped the keys on the computer keyboard. "Name?"

"I thought you had my information on file."

"We do, but it's under your name, which I don't recall. We get a lot of customers here."

Sure, all desperate. He gave her his name. And verified his address. And driver's license number. And swore or affirmed that his insurance was still valid and in force. And that he was still employed with the LAPD. He wondered if he'd have to pledge his firstborn.

But she finally seemed satisfied. She handed him the keys and asked how long he wanted the Volvo. They never got it all the first time.

"That will be due back tomorrow before six o'clock p.m. With the gas tank refilled. You have unlimited mileage. Did you want to use your VISA card again?"

No, but he had no choice, so he handed it over. Clicking fingernails queried the machine that flagged deadbeats who were over their limit. It grudgingly approved the charge.

He drove the boxy car to a you-want-it, we-rent-it store. The Volvo drove better than the other turd on wheels. He picked out some items and for once paid cash. The clerk had trouble counting out change.

Outside, the sun fried his head as he slid the goods into the trunk. He dropped the lid, jumped in the car, and cranked her up. Off into the great unknown.

Stopping next at a California Mart, he bought some kids' stuff that might come in handy. If it proved appropriate. He was still acting on a daft, but semi-informed hunch.

He parked the Volvo near Gorky's and took a cab back to Parker Center. An hour until shift change. Time to solidify a few notions.

When the little hand hit the three, he stored away the case binders and left the squad room. Then he walked the five blocks to where he'd parked the Tempo. Climbed in and started the beast.

He drove by Gorky's to see if he could spot a setup, anyone waiting around to jump him or drill him through the bean. Negatory. A little farther down the street he parked and reviewed his strategy. It seemed as good as he could devise. For a pawn.

Ten of four. He drove back to Gorky's, parked in front, and shuffled inside. Manila envelope slung under one arm. He sat at a battered table, ordered coffee, and waited. Watched the liturgy of relaxed posturings of the artistic and grunge types gathered there. The specially brewed beer looked tempting, but he decided to keep a clear head.

At four-fifteen, after he was halfway through his second cup, a man sidled up and plopped down at an adjoining table. Ordered a soda. He was about thirty, five-feet-eleven, weighed maybe two hundred ten, short dark hair, intense brown eyes. Sallow complexion, especially for Southern California. Maybe he'd read a magazine and knew exposure to the sun caused cancer. Health conscious or not, the majority of Angelenos could never accept that one.

Dover hadn't seen him before. But the guy oozed cop. Judging by his god-awful sports coat, had to be Vice.

The dick took a sip of his fizzy cola and set it on the table, stared at the wall a couple of beats, then glanced over at Dover. He never quite locked eyes with him. His gaze went to the envelope at Dover's elbow. "You writing a novel . . . or a script or something?"

Good grief. Whatever became of attention to detail? Dover nodded, patting the envelope. "It's a screenplay about how a tsunami, you know, a hundred-foot-high wave hits L.A. during evening rush hour. The only survivors are the superrich who live on Mulholland Drive."

The guy grunted. "My brother's a producer. Maybe he'd be interested. Like me to show it to him?"

"Sure, help yourself."

The man hitched his shoulders. The awful maroon and beige houndstooth rose and fell. He took a gulp of his drink, tossed some bills on the table, then glommed onto the envelope and headed for the front door.

Dover sipped his coffee. Watched in his peripheral vision to see which way the guy went. Then in one motion he tossed a five on the table and bolted toward the kitchen.

He flew out the back door and circled the building. Then he spotted the gaudy sports coat inside a dark green Mazda that careened into traffic. He jogged to the Volvo as he watched the Mazda hurtle down the street. Jumping in, he screeched away from the curb.

The driver of a UPS van stood on his brakes, cursing in fluent and vivid Spanish. *Lo siento, amigo.* But good driving manners aside, he was on the hunt. And no way would he lose this homing pigeon.

Dover figured he had one edge. The guy wouldn't be watching for a Volvo. Still, he'd have to be cagey. At a pause in the traffic, he pulled the white bandage off his forehead. Every little bit helped.

The Mazda made several turns to clear his tail. Dover stayed back, with two or three vehicles between them. Now the line of traffic slowed as the Mazda came to a yellow light.

Then as the light changed to red, the guy floored the Mazda, shooting across the intersection. Dover gaped like Stretch's hammerhead shark. Two cars between him and the stoplight. The Mazda sped down the street.

Dover jumped out of the Volvo and ran to the first car stopped at the light. A lady with silver hair crouched low behind the wheel. Not from Pasadena. Judging by her spotless vintage Rolls and the hunk of ice gleaming on her bony finger, she probably resided in Brentwood.

He ruffled his hair and screwed his face into a frantic look. Knocked on her window, giving her puppy dog eyes. With doubt stamped on her face, she fingered a button and the window slid down a stingy inch.

"I'm sorry to bother you, but my wife's about to have a baby. I've got to get her to the hospital right away." He peered back toward the Volvo, then gazed pleadingly into the woman's milky eyes. "Could you pull over and let me by?" He shot a glance up the street. The taillights of the Mazda flared red in the distance. Caught by a light.

"Oh, goodness. Yes, of course." As he hustled back to the next car she angled over to the curb and yelled, "Good luck, young man."

A twenty-something yahoo in a faded orange VW van scowled as Dover approached. His arm hung out the window, showing a tattoo that read LUV MACHINE beneath a crude banana. At least he hoped it was fruit.

"What the fuck's up? Whadduyah want?"

Dover pushed his hair back and pulled his shield from his sports coat. "LAPD Homicide. Got an emergency. Pull over to the side, please."

The kid gave him a sneer and squinted back at the Volvo. Then he eyeballed the scraggly, stoned-as-they-get redhead beside him and said out of the side of his mouth, "Don't look like no cop car I ever saw. And what emergency does Homicide have? Like the stiff ain't gonna wait?"

Red giggled harder with each sentence, but she was an easy audience. Dover glanced at the signal. Still the same color as the girl's hair.

"Let me put it this way," he said, and the guy turned back. Then Dover shot a right hook to the neo-hippie's jaw, wilting him like a wind-flattened wheat field. He yanked open the door, pulled the gear shift to neutral, and shoved against the frame as he twisted the steering wheel to the right.

He expected trouble from carrot-top. But she erupted in gales of laughter. Could hardly get her breath.

As the van rolled into the curb, Dover ran panting toward his waiting coach. He roared past the two vehicles, waved at the grinning lady in the Rolls, and sped across the intersection. Blaring horns and screeching tires assaulted his ears. But there was no crunch of metal against metal.

The Mazda was in motion, but Dover was only two blocks behind. With a couple of surveillance moves, he made up some distance. Saw the fashion-challenged dude whip into an alley.

As he passed the turnoff, Dover kept rolling. The Mazda stopped halfway down the alley. Mr. GQ was still checking for a tail.

Dover turned right at the corner, paralleling the Mazda. Approaching the intersection, he veered to the curb and stopped. He shrugged off his sports coat, stripped off his tie, and bailed from the car to scurry to the front of the liquor store at the corner. He peeked around the side of the building to spot the Mazda coming fast out of the alley, turning in his direction.

He leaned against the glass window front as though he felt woozy, hoping he wouldn't set off any alarms. Turning his face from the passing Mazda, he crouched to look shorter. A guy inside the store headed toward him. He pivoted and wobbled down the sidewalk, paused to spit toward the curb, and glanced over as the Mazda zipped through the intersection and zoomed down the street.

Now he ran for the Volvo and jumped in, shedding his shirt. Underneath was an orange T-shirt with a design of a rock star hunching his guitar. He clamped a red ball cap on his head and took off after the Mazda.

He hung a squealing left in front of a guy wearing a pinstripe suit and steering a seventy-five thousand dollar Benzo. In keeping with excellent odds, the stiff stood on the power brakes. The Volvo lumbered on, not a scratch on her.

Now a block-and-a-half behind, he glimpsed the Mazda entering an on-ramp to the Santa Monica Freeway, heading west. Dover's heart pounded hard and fast. His hunch could be right. On the freeway he lagged back, not wanting the guy to sense he had company.

They drove toward the coastline. The sand caked on Deadeye's tire had told him they'd taken Terri somewhere near the shore. Problem being, with seventy-five miles of beach along the Southern California coast, that didn't pinpoint it. Still, the route the guy was taking gave Dover an idea of their destination.

Could be Santa Monica or Venice, but no matter which, like in *The Sands of Iwo Jima,* they'd soon hit the beach.

Chapter 25

The guy in the bad sports coat wheeled the Mazda off on the exit to Lincoln, heading south, buzzing along with the traffic. Then he turned on Venice Boulevard. Bingo. Venice Beach was in their sights. The hunt would soon begin.

They glided through the haven for artists, beach bums, and muscle builders. Bright murals sprang up in abundance, speaking of whales, beach scenes, and Venus on roller-skates. Straights from the Midwest sauntered along staring at the crazier-than-most in L.A.

The Mazda turned right on Strongs Drive. They were close to the beach, the air freighted with salt and moisture and lingering smells of shellfish, sweat, and suntan oil. Dover's throat tightened.

About a block down the street, the Mazda pulled to the curb. Dover did the same, stopping behind a Plymouth ragtop. He slid down in the seat and raised a copy of *Los Angeles* magazine in front of his face. The guy slid out and slammed the door. Took a look around, then steamed down the street toting the package under his arm. Delivery time.

Dover eased out of the Volvo. Then he popped the trunk and tossed in his cap, T-shirt, and slacks, plus his shoes and socks. Which left him clad in a tank top and a pair of running shorts. He pulled on some Nike jogging shoes and stuck on a blue ball cap.

At the corner the guy turned and strode toward the beach.

Dover shouldered on a backpack, then yanked out the

rented bike. He slammed the lid, climbed on the two-wheeler, and cruised down the street like a shark after its prey. Even at the beach, the Vice dick still sported his ugly jacket. Which made him a supergeek. But which also meant he was packing.

At Ocean Front Walk he turned right and paced along the boardwalk through clusters of muscular behemoths pumping iron, leggy girls striding on in-line skates, and joggers pounding the hard surface or struggling through soft sand. Accompanied by bikers and walkers, and various clowns, jugglers, sidewalk vendors, musicians, and panhandlers.

Ugly Sports Coat marched on, and Dover coasted along behind, keeping him in sight and watching for whomever he might meet. Two blocks, three. Almost to the Pavilion. Now the guy twisted his head and peeked over his shoulder. Shades of *The Exorcist*. Dover felt the stare aimed at him. He looked away, angling the bike toward the edge of the boardwalk.

And plowed into a juggler. Didn't hurt the guy, just clipped the back of his leg and knocked him down. No big deal, except that the chainsaws that'd been growling up into the air and back down into his sure hands now rained down indiscriminately on whatever was below.

Which at the moment was Dover and his prostrate bike.

The first one landed on the front tire, sawing it in half. So much for his deposit. The second hit about three inches in front of Dover's nose. At that, he rolled away so fast he only heard the third one plopping into the sand.

He sat up, checked to see that his limbs were still attached, then spotted Ugly Sports Coat leaving the boardwalk. He kicked off his shoes and scrabbled in the backpack, pulling out his in-line skates. A crowd of gawkers gathered as the chainsaw juggler stumbled around in the sand, juggling his attention between trying to stop the roar of the saws and yelling curses at Dover.

Dover mumbled an apology to the distraught juggler and rolled out of the knot of humanity, chasing the tasteless dresser. At the corner, he coasted and took a peek. In front of the second house down, the guy leaned in the window of a blue Crown Vic, the one Dover had seen in Cardwell's garage.

A short ways down the boardwalk Dover did a turn-around and skated back to the corner. Cardwell drove away. Ugly Sports Coat strutted toward the house with empty hands.

The Crown Vic turned left on Pacific Avenue and disappeared from sight. The moron wearing the gross sports coat slipped inside the house. Dover skated back and forth, noting the lime green trim, the buzz cut lawn, and the size-able bushes skirting the one-story.

And plotting what to do now that he'd found the hideout. He was about four moves into his mental battle plan when the Vice dick in the tacky jacket sauntered out the front door and turned toward the boardwalk. The guy was only a delivery man. Probably had the night shift on Vice, so he was free to eat dinner, whatever, then go on duty at eleven.

Dover skated back down the boardwalk before the goon could spot him. Toed to a quick stop behind a palm tree. Then watched and waited.

The guy was at ease now. He'd done his assignment by making the pickup and drop-off of the disks. Gotten his attaboy. Now he strolled along ogling the girls and enjoying the ocean breeze; life could be as fine as a fruity Zinfandel.

In spurts, my man.

Ugly Sports Coat frowned at the juggler grousing *en voce alto* to whomever would listen about the tragic condition of his chainsaws. But he ambled on. Didn't concern him.

Dover skated slowly behind him, waiting until the guy neared the weight pen in the heart of muscle beach. Some bulldozer bods putting up serious poundage in there, sweating, groaning, and yelling primally to pump up their adrenaline to lock out that final rep. Awesome. Matter over mind.

Now Dover sprinted hard, wheels spinning, dodging any obstacle to his forward momentum. He built up speed like a bobsled hurtling down an icy tunnel. His focus locked in on the hideous sports coat like Luke Skywalker's targeting gizmo in *Star Wars*.

Spirit and rage and raw emotion propelled him and guided him straight and true at his target. The Force was with him. Darth Vader was nowhere in sight.

Ugly Sports Coat heard him coming at collision minus one second and counting. Too late. The guy half turned toward the ratcheting of the wheels on the boardwalk. Just perfect for Dover to lower his shoulder and catch the mope in the rib cage at full throttle.

The guy was stocky, but Dover was a human cannonball. As unstoppable as the bus in *Speed*. Fueled by white hot anger as pure and powerful as a volcanic belch.

The impact generated a crunch like the tectonic plates vying for supremacy. Dover's shoulder crumpled. A couple of stitches pulled out.

They both went down, but Dover was on top. He shrugged off his backpack. A few muscled mesomorphs waddled out of the weight cage to see the show. Dover crouched astride the guy, twisted his arm behind his back, and scrabbled in the backpack. As the Bicep Blasters encircled him, Dover pulled his shield from the backpack and swung it around.

"Police! Detective Bates, Undercover Tactical Unit. This man is under arrest for terrorism. Everyone stand back."

Every muscle froze.

Then one of the hulks said, "You don't look like no cop. What's goin' on here?" The slabs of abs and pecs and triceps tensed, the beefy chunks staring at each other as they waited for someone in the herd to make the call. Ugly Sports Coat mumbled to himself, probably dazed.

Dover's mental wheels spun without taking hold.

"Hell, yeah, he's a cop," said a deep voice at the fringe of the gathering. Everyone stared at him. "He busted me on drunk and disorderly a couple of weeks ago. I remember him real good."

Dirty, disheveled, down-and-out, the guy stood there in his stained clothes with a frown on his face but a glint in his eyes. Cop's eyes, Dover recalled. Didn't miss a thing.

"That's right, now stand back." Everyone stepped away while Dover grabbed his handcuffs from the backpack and snapped the steel bracelets onto the hairy wrists. He pulled the man to his feet.

The guy wobbled, and he canted over to one side, but now he came alive. "No, wait! I'm LAPD. Check my—"

Using the guy's bent arm as leverage, Dover swung the Vice cop around and slammed his face into the weight pen.

"Careful! He may have a gun. Sometimes they carry explosives. Everyone move back. Now!" A Hollywood murmur erupted, which had a guttural tone coming from this group of steroidal mutants, but they moved away, giving Dover room to operate.

He reached inside the guy's jacket and pulled out his

shield, which he palmed, then patted him down. Extracted a single house key from the side pocket of the awful sports coat. Pulled the cop's 9mm from his shoulder holster and held it up, causing the crowd to retreat another couple of steps.

He leaned down and said, "Is she in that house?"

"You crazy asshole. You almost killed—"

Dover reached under the jacket and probed the damaged rib cage. Hard. A loud moan escaped from the man's twisted mouth. "Just answer my questions."

"You're dead meat, they'll—"

Another impolite gouge.

"Ahhhhhh . . . uhhh, okay, okay. Stop it, you fucker. What do you want?" And he let out an agonized groan like a possum hit by a pickup. But he listened to the questions.

And when Dover had the answers, he turned to the gaggle of glabrous hunks and announced in a commanding voice right out of training school, "Clear the area! He has a bomb!"

Oiled, pumped up, rippling bodies scattered like so many quail. A huge guy in the weight pen who'd just finished a set of bench presses sat up and tried to lumber off. Too slow.

Dover grabbed him by the wrist, pointing at the barbell. "How much is that?"

The hulk stared at him with Harrison Ford's amazement. "What?"

Dover spoke distinctly. "How much weight on the bar?"

"Oh. It's four-oh-five."

"Thanks. Take off."

As the guy stumbled away, Dover unlocked one of the cuffs, tugged the Vice dick over to the bench, then clamped the cuff over the bar holding the heavy iron plates.

"Don't anyone come near this man," Dover yelled. "I'm going to call the bomb squad. They'll have to clear him."

He snatched up his backpack, winked at the homeless ex-cop who'd returned a favor, and skated back to the Volvo.

Dover yanked open the trunk and threw in the skates and the Vice dick's Beretta. He pulled on some pants and a T-shirt, then plucked his .45 auto from the backpack and stuck it in his belt at the back. Slipped the switchblade in his pocket and tucked the razor in his shoe. As the song says, he was revved up, rockin', and ready to roll.

He drove to the end of the street, turned left on Mildred Avenue, then took a right onto Pacific. Another right onto Venice Way, where he parked. Now he paced back to the street where Terri was being held.

Ugly Sports Coat said she was tied up in a back bedroom. Only one guard in the house. Dover had the door key, his gun and blades, and the element of surprise. Strong position. Unless they killed her.

As he neared the house, he decided not to use a direct approach. Just as in chess, it wouldn't be good to telegraph your strategy. Deception, distraction, and deceit were the keys. Devious moves led to winning play. Keep your opponent guessing, and he can't devise a strategy to defeat you. Can even confuse Deep Blue or the new White IBM computer whiz.

He checked the layout of the board. Now what would Bobby Fischer do? Garry Kasparov? Or Stretch? A Honda Civic sat in the driveway. Front blinds of the house were shut as tight as clamshells. No one was outside the other homes.

He ducked down and hustled over to crouch beside the

Honda. Raised up his head and peeked inside it. Spotted a small flashing red light.

Car alarm. He pondered that a moment. Good.

He pulled out his switchblade and pushed the button. Here went nothing. Or more like everything.

He stuck the point of the knife into the door lock and wiggled the blade. The alarm shrieked. And shrieked. He trotted to the side of the house and crouched behind a looming bougainvillea bush. When he heard the front door open, he zipped around to the back and let himself in. Saw and heard no one else inside. In the second bedroom he checked, he found Terri.

She was tied to a wooden chair. Her eyes looked bigger than the Hope diamond. If she hadn't been gagged, she might've outshrieked the alarm.

Clothesline bound her hands and feet. No problem. The switchblade sliced through the cord around her ankles as if it were spaghetti. The car alarm still wailed. Now her hands. She tugged the gag from her mouth. "Rick, how did—"

"Hold it." The alarm had gone silent. Time to boogie.

But some smartass had put a bicycle lock, the kind with the long plastic-covered wire that fed into a combination lock, around Terri's waist and through the back of the chair. Problem. The knife wouldn't cut that, and he hadn't brought any pliers. No one can prepare for everything.

He hadn't heard the guy step back onto the porch. Must be fiddling with the alarm. Maybe figured it malfunctioned.

"Come on, let's go," he said.

"But this stupid chair—"

A car door slammed out front; the guy was through fiddling.

Dover held the chair from behind as Terri hobbled toward the back door. Now they heard footsteps on the front porch. They opened the door.

"Wait," Dover said, and Terri froze in the doorway.

He pushed the chair against the door jamb. "Don't move," he said. Then he backed off a step and shot a hard kick into the chair frame. It shuddered, maybe even cracked. But it held tight.

The front door opened and footsteps plodded into the entryway.

Dover backed off, took two quick steps to build momentum, then jammed his foot into the side of the chair back. Wood splintered and broke into pieces. His leg felt like it might follow suit.

Thudding footfalls came from the front of the house. The guy was either pudgy or a real moose. And he sounded too fast to be fat.

Dover slid the wire down over Terri's hips. The lock and wire fell to the floor with a thunk. Then he pushed her ahead of him out across the back patio, slamming the door.

As they skirted the side of the house, Dover heard the moose pounding through it. He knew they'd never outrun him. Especially if the guy decided to cut the distance with a bullet.

The back door flew open with a crash. They were almost to the front corner of the house. Footsteps scrunched across the patio.

"Keep running, and don't look back," he told Terri. "When you reach the street, turn left." He gave her a shove to overcome her inertia, then crouched down in the midst of the prickly bougainvillea.

The man hoofed it around the corner, and Dover could see his massive form through the leaves and blossoms. Guy could play on USC's offensive line. The giant spotted Terri and churned his thick oak legs.

Dover gritted his teeth. As the buffalo thundered by, Dover lunged out of the bush with his head lowered and crashed into the side of his knee. Hit him with the same shoulder that'd nailed Ugly Sports Coat. Same crunch, but now Dover's shoulder crunched the most. Another stitch popped. The guy's leg bent inward, but he stayed on his feet. Uh-oh.

But Dover had chosen his point of attack well. The guy took two more steps and collapsed, howling in pain, grabbing his knee. He *had* been a player. Thank God for the defensive monsters of the Pac Ten.

The guy's pistol tumbled into a patch of yellow daisies.

Dover reached to his back for his cuffs. Gone. Of course, they were restraining Ugly Sports Coat.

So he whipped off his belt. That'd do. But Man Mountain set his jaw against the pain and lunged for his pistol. Dover's right hand was sore from tagging the punk in the VW van, so he put everything he had into a left hook, smashing the ex-Bruin on the edge of the jaw, stunning him. Barely.

Aw, hell. Dover doubled his aching right fist and punched hard into the man's temple. The guy's eyes rolled up and he pitched forward to sprawl on his mug in the grass.

Dover made a loop of leather through the belt buckle, then fit it over the man's wrists and cinched it tight. As he leaned over to pick up the pistol, he winced. Pain sliced inside his upper chest, beneath his sore shoulder.

He needed an ice pack and some Darvocet. Large glass of Tawny port wouldn't be bad. If he ever got out of here.

He jogged to the sidewalk, then to the corner where he found Terri. She stood like a rigid stork, but she relaxed when she spotted him lurching toward her. He held his left arm against his body with his right, looking like one of the hunch-backed assistants to the cinema's string of mad scientists.

They hustled to the Volvo and clambered in. Dover slipped the guy's pistol under the front seat, fired up the engine, and roared off. And even in L.A., with the dense traffic, looming buildings, and deadly exhaust fumes, they felt as free as a pair of meadowlarks in a sprawling Kansas pasture.

Terri said Deadeye had come to her house, which she thought odd, but she let him in. He chatted about nothing, then she offered to fix lemonade. She was about to serve it when the phone rang, and he jumped her from behind.

She struggled at first, kicked him a good lick in the shin and scratched his cheek, but he clamped a cold cloth on her nose and she blacked out. When she woke up, she was in this house where she could hear the ocean. Tied to a chair. Her eyes misted. She was never so glad to see anyone in her—

"I know," Dover said, placing his hand on her arm. "I felt the same way." Then he smirked. "Even if you were trussed up like a turkey."

She pulled her arm loose, frowning. But it soon transformed into a smile. She giggled. "And when we tried to run away . . ." She burst out laughing. "Wait . . ." she said, catching her breath.

Now he laughed. "And you ran in front of me carrying that—"

"That ugly chair," she said. "What terrible taste."

But now her face went serious. "Rick, they're killers. It doesn't take a genius to pull a trigger or set off a bomb."

"You're right. But still . . ." And he told her about his

boardwalk encounter with Ugly Sports Coat.

After they'd laughed themselves to exhaustion, they talked about what they could do now. He told her part of his plan. Some of it was too foolhardy to mention, and some of it he didn't yet know himself.

Chapter 26

Dover wanted Terri safe until this disaster was over. So he insisted on driving her to her sister's house in the Valley. They stopped at a 7-Eleven so Terri could call ahead. Dover watched for surveillance, saw none, then deliberated on his plan.

His strategy involved desperate moves, but sometimes an unexpected attack against stronger pieces could rattle your opponent and throw his game plan into disarray. Maybe even stampede him into stunning defeat. One could always hope.

Terri pulled open the car door and slid inside. Tears rushed down her cheeks. She held her forehead, her shoulders shaking.

In a couple of minutes, he handed her a handkerchief. "I'm sorry about this, Terri."

She dabbed at her eyes. "No, no," she said, sniffing, "it's not your fault, it's . . . oh, hell, I suppose it's not even Stretch's fault, even though I've been furious with him for getting killed."

"You've been—"

"Yes, of course." She stared at him. "Didn't you know I expected him to stay with me always and have kids and grandkids and clomp around a nursing home together with our walkers?"

Dover nodded. And as he felt his eyes moisten, he realized how pissed he'd been at his best friend and partner who'd gotten himself blown up, deep fried, and killed dead without his permission. Stupid, but there you had it.

Sudden, unexpected death shrieked with injustice. And sadness wasn't enough compensation. What was needed was the force of rage to smash the shock, the unfairness, and the loss.

"But now you're not so mad at him?" he asked, looking into her eyes.

She bit her lip. "No, I've been able to forgive him. Or at least, now that I've seen how easy it is to be victimized, I've transferred my anger to those bastards in that group."

"That's what we'll both do."

Her eyes flashed. "Go after them, Rick. Like you did when you came for me. They depend on behind-the-scenes moves and secrecy. They're racist pigs, grabbing political power to crush minorities."

"As amiable, harmless, and high-minded as the Klan."

"Hiding the way those fools do under their sheets. Rip off their masks and expose who and what they are: a bunch of narrow-minded Nazis."

"Self-important slugs who slime the world."

He revved up the Volvo. Cruised the PCH to the Santa Monica Freeway and caught the 405 north to Van Nuys. When he finally stopped to let Terri off, he felt lightheaded with relief. He'd rescued his queen from peril. While she was in trouble, his concentration had been consumed.

But now he felt like Rocky Balboa, fit and ready to rumble. No side of beef too tough. Bring up the music, maestro. He'd run to the summit against all odds and mow down any champion around. Daaa-ta-ta-ta ta-ta-daa ta-ta.

Before she got out, Terri leaned toward him, her eyes glowing. "Good luck," she said, then kissed him lightly on the mouth. She slid away and ran toward the lit-up house.

Now alone in the car, he felt his power and commitment

insinuated with sorrow and searching. He stared into the distance. His chest and throat ached. For some reason, he remembered the scene in *Pretty Woman* where Richard Gere prances up a ladder to Julia Roberts and says, "So what happens after he climbs up the tower and rescues her?"

Julia smiles her pretty smile and says, "She rescues him right back."

But, of course, that was just a movie.

He gripped the steering wheel hard. Had to get his brain back in sync. Chess masters know that a distraction to your opponent's train of thought is worth two clever moves. He couldn't let any outside ideas, no matter how beguiling, keep him from playing his keenest game.

So he narrowed his scope. Hewed it down to a single sharp emotion: vengeance. As wreaked by Randolph Scott, Alan Ladd, and Charles Bronson. Persistent, unflagging, and wrathful. And, oh, so satisfying.

He rolled away from the homey scene. Minutes later, he spotted a pay phone and stopped to make a call. Thank God, Falcon answered. He told his former partner what had happened, and what he planned to do. "And I was hoping you could—"

"No way you could keep me away, my white-bread friend. You're coming down on the right side on this one."

He thought about that a minute. "Maybe we don't have to be on sides. Just two guys doing the right thing."

"Now you're California dreamin'."

"Jeez, that's straight up. Sounded like a sappy Jimmy Stewart, didn't I?" He shook his head, then told Falcon where they could meet. "Can you be there in thirty minutes?"

"Make it forty, and I'll come dressed."

"Sorry. Didn't mean to interrupt anything."

"No worry. The lady has seen the routine. She's down for it."

"Then I'll see you on campus."

"My first chance to matriculate at UCLA." Then he said something with the mouthpiece covered.

"What's that?" Dover asked.

"Oh, nothing. I just had to enlarge my lady's vocabulary. She thought I might be doing something stupid."

"You probably are."

After he hung up, Dover placed another call and asked for a favor. Something he'd been doing a lot lately. The friend said it was no problem.

Stopping at a Quik Trip, he bought a couple of items. Back outside, he grabbed the briefcase from the trunk and tossed it on the front seat beside him. He started the engine and rambled on to Westwood.

Sitting in the Volvo at the south edge of the campus, he spotted Falcon driving up in his hoopty Mercury Marquis.

"Your right headlight's aimed high. Almost blinded me."

"Must be why dudes keep flashing their brights at me."

"Why don't you get it fixed?"

"There's a time for everything. Headlights not on the list yet."

"Then check out the stuff in that briefcase."

Falcon riffled through the items. "What's this?"

"It's called Tracker. I put transmitters on Eddie's and Deadeye's cars when I was looking for Terri."

"You're throwing down to the max on this gig."

"Can't go after sharks with a minnow bucket."

"So let's put some shit on these necks. God don't like ugly."

"No sweat, we'll slam-dunk these rebs." Then he explained his plan.

Falcon eyed the walkie-talkies. "These blue light specials work?"

"If they don't, I blew twenty bucks. Besides, we won't be far apart."

"I'll go set up and test it. Hope your other gear's more jazzy."

"Best available. This's a one-shot deal. No room for screwups."

"And you asked me along?" He sounded like Alfalfa of *Spanky and Our Gang*. Even did the huge eyes.

"When the shit hits the fan, I want you there every time."

That stopped Falcon's patter. For a moment. "Keep talking smack like that, and you'll be finding another brother to do your dirty work."

Dover held up his hands. "Sorry, I won't do it again." Then he slapped Falcon on the leg. "You ready?"

"My people been waitin' over three hundred years for this. What d'you thinks, boss man?"

"Then let's do it. But keep your nappy head down. Don't want these Westsiders getting nervous and calling Five-O."

"Maybe a few whirlybirds shining spotlights down on their 'hood might make 'em more culturally aware."

"Now you're expecting miracles."

"So let's get to shining on whitey." He slid out.

Dover stuck his head out of the window. "Hey, you cotton chopper, you forgot your walkie-talkie."

He shuffled back, head down. "Now I gone and done it."

Dover tossed it to him. "That's okay, Toby. Anyway, if these don't work, and I get in trouble, I may just yell."

"That works for me. The brothers do it real frequent."

"And you hear any shots, don't be half-stepping."

"I'll jet there in two seconds flat."

Dover knew he would. "See you, partner."

Falcon climbed into his vehicle and pulled into traffic. Dover sat there waiting. Two minutes, three, a lifetime.

A squelch broke on his walkie-talkie, he grabbed it up, then Falcon's voice came over the air. It was as clear as a night in Aspen. "Bird One to Biscuit Man."

"I read you, Bird."

"I'm layin' in a spot where I won't get hassled."

"Good, I don't have time to bail you out. Besides, it's showtime."

Dover figured he'd play it audacious. He opened a beer from the six-pack he'd bought, took a swig, splashed some on his shirt, then tossed the can out the window. Some Mexican gardener or Guatemalan maid or San Salvadoran cook would pick it up tomorrow. Litter was unacceptable in this neighborhood.

A block from Cardwell's house he saw a car he recognized. Good. The favor he'd asked was being handled. Seconds later, he turned into the driveway, drove to the front, and scrunched to a stop, headlights blazing. He hit the walkie-talkie button. "Biscuit to Bird. I'm in place, start it running."

"Okay, I make it nine-oh-two p.m." He gave the date and location, then said, "Break a leg, Detective Dover."

"Thanks, Detective Jones." And with that he tossed the walkie-talkie on the car seat and laid on the horn.

Cardwell came outside, his pistol held behind his leg. He approached the Volvo step by step. Irritation and confusion showed on his face.

Dover cracked open another beer then killed the lights

and the motor, threw open the door, and clambered out. At that moment the line played in his head, "I'm ready for my close-up, Mr. DeMille."

And ready or not, this was it.

As he stood in the driveway, he wavered, caught hold of the top of the Volvo to steady himself, then said in a loud voice, "Evening, Lou. How ya doin'?" He raised the can in salute to the Nazi prick.

"Dover?" He moved closer, his eyes straining in the faint glow of the outside lights, gun gripped tight. "Dover! What the hell are you doing?"

"Just came to find out what you're up to, Lou." He still spoke in a loud and labored voice. "You and your group of thugs." He took a large gulp.

Cardwell inched closer, caught the smell of booze. "Dover, you're drunk. I don't know what you're talking about. You'd better go home and sleep it off."

"Oh, I think you know, all right." Then he giggled and said in a singsong patter, "He knows, he knows, he really, really knows."

"Dover, can it!" He moved close to assert his authority.

Dover straightened up and faced Cardwell. "Now I'm sure the guys holding Terri at Venice Beach, the oversized moron and the Vice cop, have told you about their little slip-up."

Cardwell grimaced. "Okay, Dover, let's pretend I know what you're talking about. So what?"

"So why are you doing this? You guys have a plan. What's up?"

"Why would I tell you?"

"If you don't, I'll blow the whistle about the kidnapping."

Cardwell smiled, looking like a frozen codfish. "Come

on, Rick, there's nothing linking me to anything like that."

"Just that Deadeye grabbed her. Eddie probably drove."

"Impossible, both on special assignment in Hollywood."

And it would be Terri's word against Deadeye's. "Even if you could phony that up, what about the deputies' report?"

Cardwell chuckled and rubbed an itch on the side of his face with the barrel of his 9mm. Dover willed it to fire, but his telekinetic forces must've been undercharged. The Lou let the weapon drop back beside his leg.

"Don't waste your time looking. No report was filed. Small matters like that are easily handled."

Dover considered this. He felt the Lou was telling it straight. "And how about the fact I found her tied up?"

Cardwell's eyes turned darker. "You've been under a strain. Partner's death, homicides rolling in all the time, not to mention a close call yourself."

"Are matters like placing a bomb in my car easy, too?"

Cardwell stared off across the hood of the Volvo, his eyes stormy. "More complicated, but not that difficult."

"But then," Dover slurred, "the problem's not solved."

"Yes, it's too bad you didn't go out with a bang."

"Guess your boys aren't so good after all."

Searing anger melted Cardwell's icy expression. "They were good enough to whack your old partner." Now smug satisfaction slid across his slimeball face. It was all Dover could do not to kick him in the balls. He leaned against the Volvo, feigning drunkenness, but stunned from the staggering realization that these jerks had planned and carried out Stretch's execution. As a theory, it infuriated him. As stark reality, it stomped the wind out of him. They'd killed Stretch. And for what?

"Since we're being honest, why did you do it?"

Now Cardwell's stare struck him like sharpened steel bolts zinging from a crossbow. There was conviction there, a mindless and heartless dedication to a mission, not unlike a Hamas terrorist. "For the same reason we'll have to silence you." He licked his lips. His gun hand twitched.

Dover pushed off the car and faced Cardwell. He might kick him in the balls after all. Or tell him what was going on, before the maniac blew him away.

But he didn't have enough evidence. So he decided to push it. "Tell me like I'm really stupid, Lou. Explain it to me simple."

"I usually do, Rick." Then, when he didn't get a rise, Cardwell sighed and said, "Stretch knew too much. He'd gotten weak-kneed about our plan, and we felt he might hand us up. We couldn't let him foul up our operation."

Dover hoped the transmitter was getting this. "What did he know? What could he say that was worth whacking him for?" He let out a belch, blinking as if to focus on Cardwell's smarmy face.

"In your condition, I don't think you'd understand what prefaced the need for our plan. But keeping it simple, you must realize minority groups and immigrants are overwhelming L.A. with their sheer numbers. City budgets and facilities are strained to the max. With those cretins' incessant fucking and incredible fertility, they produce a tide of bodies as unrelenting as the Pacific."

"I've heard the complaint, Lou, but never put so poetically."

"Just look at the support for Proposition 187. People are fed up with being pushed out and having to pay for the privilege. Do you think our tax money should be squandered pampering a horde of filthy illegal aliens? Hell, no, it's preposterous. Same with affirmative action programs. They make no sense. They're just reverse discrimination."

"And you're speaking for all Angelenos?"

"For the ones who count. The ones who earn their own way. You know, Prop 187 and the legislation against affirmative action are only symbols of the undertone of fear, disgust, and dismay wracking the white population of our state and country. Conditions have been worsening. Something had to be done, Rick, and I mean something more than enforcing immigration laws and allowing greater latitude in allowing wiretaps."

Dover shrugged and leaned against the Volvo. He wanted Cardwell to feel in control, free to talk. "So you'd handle any renegades the way they did in that flick *New Crime City*?"

"Huh?" The Lou crinkled his eyebrows.

An earthquake split the city in this 2020 version of L.A., leaving criminals and anarchists controlling a ruined area. Still, the powers in charge schemed to destroy the rebellious factions. "Never mind, just thinking out loud. Besides, nothing's going to change. What can you do?"

Cardwell clenched the handle of his pistol, smiling beneath his scraggly mustachio, and said, "For lack of a better term, you could call it racial purification. Or ethnic cleansing. Call it genocide, if you want." His eyes darted back and forth as he assembled his whirling thoughts.

Dover kept quiet, both to let him ramble on and because he was speechless. Without thinking, he took another swig of beer.

"We want to save America, Rick. We're trying to prevent the inevitable takeover of California and eventually the whole country by the overpopulated scumbag minorities and the enormous influx of illegal aliens. And that's not to mention Islamic terrorist infiltrations and direct acts of sabotage.

Mark Bouton

"Even discounting outright attacks, at the least, immigrants suck our state dry through welfare, food stamps, and subsidized housing and medicine. And our public education system only serves to teach them English and get them jobs, ignoring the needs of our native Californians."

Now Dover managed a weak smile. "I assume you don't mean Native Americans, the actual settlers here. Say, the Shoshones?"

"I'm talking reality, Dover. Not some rosy history about noble redskins who were little more than savages."

"That makes me a sixteenth savage myself. My ancestors mixed in a little Sac & Fox blood. Debased my racial purity in your eyes, no doubt."

"Hell, I don't mean that makes you—"

"And speaking of immigrants, didn't your great-grandaddy come over from Germany or Romania? Somewhere overseas, I believe."

"Son of a bitch, Dover, the European influence is what made this country great. Anyway, I just—"

"But the African influence just corrupts the bloodline? Like the Supreme Court judges, federal judges, congressmen, cabinet members, and mayors of large cities? And haven't the descendants of Mexican lineage risen to high positions of power and prestige in our dear land?"

"We're way off the point. I was going to say that California was never developed under the Indians. L.A. would still be a parched desert if they controlled it."

"Yeah, they were never clever enough to build freeways, steal water, and make megabucks from oil, movies, and silicon chips. Not to mention fortunes made and comfort afforded the genteel white folks through their cheap labor."

"That's social progress. Development of resources. Survival of the fittest."

318

"It's an illusion of fertility and plenty created in a desert basin that should be populated by coyotes and chipmunks, not rich people with cantilever houses and Rolls Royces."

Cardwell gave him a narrow look. Suspicious? He'd better back off this argument before the mope got wise and started making self-serving statements.

But the Lou went on, "Rick, what's here is here. Nothing will change that. Besides, California leads the way for every reform in our country. Even New Yorkers know that."

Cardwell took a deep breath. He had more to say, so Dover let him. Like playing a big-mouth bass.

"The truth is the minorities will take over unless they're stopped. We've seen what they do in their own countries— Bolivia, Haiti, Guatemala, Zimbabwe, Afghanistan, hell, even Mexico—God save us all. Should we let them turn us into a third world country in the name of justice and equality? We're fighting for our nation's welfare and for the survival of the white race."

"I see," Dover said. "So what do you do? Barricade them like in St. Petersburg? Whip them into submission like in Riverside? Use our military might as we did in Afghanistan? How can more force stop this 'takeover'?"

Cardwell looked wary. Dover was afraid he'd blown it. But as the windbag glanced at his pistol, he seemed to gain confidence.

"We've got a plan, and we're ready to set it in motion. Then we wait until the minorities expose themselves for what they are—no better than the primitives we mentioned before. When they exhibit their basic violence, we'll have to use lawful authority to neutralize their actions."

Neutralize. The savages, primitives, uncultured, un-washed, impure. The tired, poor, and helpless. Dover sighed. "So you'll start race riots, help escalate them, then call in the cops and the National Guard to nuke the rioters?"

Cardwell's grin was cold and stingy. "Oversimplified, but that's a workable description. Many keen minds have analyzed the situation. It came down to the fact we could either act to insure the safety and prosperity of our country by capable whites, or . . ." He lifted a palm.

"Or what, Lou?"

Chapter 27

In a weary tone, Cardwell said, "Or we could watch our fine country fall on its face as the lazy, incompetent minorities take over by sheer numbers, both at the ballot box and in the battle for control of the streets. Even worse, we could be brought to our knees by more terrorist acts."

Dover nodded as though he acquiesced in the Lou's reasoning. But the guy couldn't run a homicide squad of a few disparate personalities. So he'd be qualified to solve the nation's social and internal security problems about when Delta Burke sprouted wings and raced the Spruce Goose.

"Sort of an extension of our crackerjack law and order campaign? Lock 'em up or kick their asses out of the country and ask questions later?"

Cardwell missed the sarcasm. "In a way, but the new system will be more forceful and direct. There'll be no liberal judges handing out lenient sentences, no overfilled prisons releasing felons, no more inept immigration policies. The bastards will all be penned up like the animals they are."

Dover wasn't sure he understood. "You mean you'd intern them in camps the way we did the Japanese-Americans in World War II?"

"Sort of. The hard cases would be sent to prisons and camps. The rest would be restricted to their neighborhoods, just like house arrest. You don't need barbed wire when the threat of retribution is real. They'll have seen their own slaughtered in the streets trying to defy the Establishment.

321

We'll be speaking their language—force and violence. Then they'll catch on to the new rules."

Dover's mouth hung open. Harrison Ford doing shock. He shook his head. "Do the same rules apply to minority cops and military . . . and who makes them?"

Cardwell shrugged. "Some cops of color could be exempted by various boards across the country, others not. And the rule-makers are higher up than you could imagine. Or it wouldn't be workable."

"Are we talking about congressmen, members of federal agencies, even people in the Pentagon?"

Cardwell's face went slack, as though somehow Dover had read his muddled mind. Then he set his jaw the way he always did before issuing some idiotic pronouncement. "That's all I've got to say about it." And he nodded the way Oliver Hardy made famous.

Dover figured he could play Stan Laurel. Bland, innocent look. "Oh, why?"

"Because fortunately," Cardwell said, looking smug, "I asked Deadeye and Eddie to come by to discuss how to deal with you. They're here now, so if you'd thought of jumping me or pulling a gun, you've missed your cue."

Even this ditz talked the industry jargon. "Sure, Lou, so I look around and you whack me with your pistol. Drop me like a stage weight, just like you did the Colombian holding the Uzi."

"Nope," said a voice behind him, "he won't have to resort to such hackneyed tactics."

"Eddie, what a surprise. Especially that you know the word hackneyed."

"Real funny. But if you're so smart, why do I have the drop on you?"

Dover didn't have an immediate answer.

"Just lift your pistol with two fingers," Eddie continued, warming to his melodramatic part, "and hold it out away from you."

Dover did it. No room for ad-libbing or padding his part. Eddie snatched away the Beretta. But there was still a chance.

Now Dover could smell Deadeye's cigarette breath and hear him wheezing. His voice rasped close to Dover's ear saying, "We'd better have this one, too." Pulling the .45-caliber Backup out of his belt.

And there went his chance. Except for the—

"Get the damn frog sticker out of that ankle rig," said Cardwell.

The prick.

Eddie fumbled around down there until he had it.

"Don't have too good a time, Sweetie."

"Always the smartass, huh, Ricochet?" Eddie said as he stood up. "You and that fucking Stretch, always thought you were better than everybody else. Solving the most cases, thinking you were really hot shit."

"Yeah," agreed Deadeye, "the Dangerous Duo. What crap."

"That's 'Dauntless,' Deadeye. Better stick to shooting and blowing up innocent people."

"That's enough," Cardwell sputtered. "We're not here to trade insults."

Dover shrugged. "What, then?"

Eddie held up a finger. "Let me do the honors, Lou." Then he speared Dover with a dark look. "You're going for a drive up the canyon with us. And don't bother to pack a bag."

Dover barely kept from laughing out loud at that cliché. But Eddie played it serious, waggling his pistol from one side to the other, motioning toward their car parked across the street. "Let's go, shithead."

Dover stiffened as Deadeye grabbed his arm. He stared at the two dicks as if they were sacks of horseshit. "Don't think so, fellas."

"Don't get cute," said Cardwell.

Did he watch every Cagney flick that came down the late show pike?

"You don't have a choice," Eddie said.

Dialogue to die for. But not tonight. "No, I still have options." Okay, it could stand a rewrite.

"He's bluffing," Deadeye exhaled again. Stagnant nicotine breath.

Cardwell said, "What are you yakking about, Dover?"

"Just this," Dover said as he reached under his shirt and pulled out a transmitter. "That's a wrap," he said into the mike. "Take off. Catch you later."

"Jesus," Deadeye said.

"Christ," Eddie said.

"Jesus Christ," Cardwell said.

"So I'll see you guys," Dover said, turning toward the Volvo.

"Not so fast," Deadeye said.

More gangsta rap. He paused. "What now?"

Deadeye clutched Dover's arm and gazed at Eddie and then Cardwell for an idea. He looked like a novice director begging for someone to come up with a good line of dialogue.

Cardwell thought of a novel one. "Deadeye, I'd say if Dover's accomplice hears his buddy being tortured, he might decide to bring us the tape. Then we can forget the whole thing and no one gets hurt."

Not too stupid. Every dog gets lucky some day. "Good

try, Lou, but oops!" Dover ripped the transmitter loose, dropped it, and ground it into the driveway with his shoe.

"Now I don't know who you might tell about torturing me. It might be embarrassing if you guess wrong. Besides, within ten minutes duplicate tapes will be in the mail for two people. One is a lawyer who already has a copy of the disk describing your organization's setup, goals, and timetables. He has a copy of Stretch's software to run the codes with. And, of course, he has a list of interesting phone numbers and names."

"Bullshit," said Eddie. "Besides, if you drop out of sight, how would he know what to do with it?"

"Everything but tonight's tape is in a safe deposit box. He has power of attorney to access the box and instructions to open it in the event of my death or disappearance for over twenty-four hours."

Eddie thought about it. "How will he know you've disappeared?" Hey, the guy was trying.

"I'm to call his office every morning and give him a code word, so he'll know it's me. If I don't, he'll retrieve the stuff from the box. There are instructions inside to give it to the press."

Eddie screwed up his mouth. This was getting complex. "Very clever. And who gets the second tape?"

"An AP reporter I know. I sent him the other stuff, too. He can use the information however he sees fit. Same restriction applies, he only opens it if I don't contact him every day. And I still use the code."

Dover let that part sink in, then continued, "I've told him if he tries to use the information without my approval, I'll deny it all, say it was just a hoax. I'm sure your boys will back that up."

Eddie, Deadeye, and Cardwell exchanged pointed looks.

"Don't think about trying to squeeze the code out of me. It changes every day, according to a formula based on daily newspapers. And we change which newspaper we use according to a format I gave them."

Eddie looked confused. "So what'll we do?" he asked Cardwell.

The Lou cracked his knuckles. "Hell, I don't know. Shit."

Deadeye had a granite expression. "I say let's chance it. We don't know if he's telling the truth about all these arrangements, and who'd believe those fucking contacts of his anyway? Let's just do him."

Cardwell's face had gone sallow in the outside lights. He needed to make a decision. And it was a doozy.

"Just one other thing," Dover said, interrupting Cardwell's concentration. "Actually, two. In case someone thought along the lines that Deadeye was just advocating, I took a couple of other precautions."

Cardwell's head slumped forward as though he'd been whacked on the back of the neck with a two-by-four.

Dover forged ahead. "Naturally, I have a duplicate set of all the disks squirreled away just in case someone bagged mine. There's a key. Someone knows where it's kept. And I gave another copy of the disks to a hacker buddy of mine. If he doesn't hear from me every Saturday, he uploads all the information onto the Internet. There are enough influential users on that network to twist anyone's arm, regardless of their political or legal power."

Cardwell peered at Dover through bushy eyebrows. His eyes were as glazed as Mr. Kim's, but with none of the Korean's stubborn determination. "Go on, Dover, get the fuck out of here."

Dover moved faster than the Brits in *Chariots of Fire* as

he grabbed his weapons, jumped in the Volvo, and wheeled away. As he turned the corner, he remembered that the jamokes had missed the razor in his shoe. Not that he'd have cut anyone's throat. Unless he'd had half a chance.

But despite the close call, he felt the ploy had worked well. At least he put a ding in their armor. The smug bastards learned they weren't, as per the country song, ten feet tall and bulletproof.

And he'd gotten a damn good tape. Real evidence from admitted players in the conspiracy. Being specific about their despicable goals.

At least he hoped he had.

He grabbed the walkie-talkie. "Biscuit to Bird." He waited, but got no response. Repeated the call. Nothing. The cheapo set wouldn't reach far; Falcon was out of range.

He wanted to hear the tape, to make sure it was audible. But it was more important that Falcon got out of there. He could listen to those slugs tomorrow.

Turning onto Santa Monica Boulevard, it struck him that they'd achieved some victories tonight. Maybe a small celebration was in order. Have a little fun before the sun comes up. He'd pick up some munchies to go with the six-pack he bought earlier. Been a long time since he'd chilled.

He spotted a convenience store and pulled over. A few brews and some crunchy snacks while watching a good late night flick should hit the spot. Besides, he wouldn't be able to sleep for hours. The adrenaline would have to disperse from his charged-up system.

As he pushed open the door, a sharp pain shot through his chest. Better get a tube of Ben Gay. He'd be sore in the morning.

He surveyed the aisles of junk food. Picked up a *TV Guide.* He'd watch a love story or a comedy rather than his usual thriller, action, or cop movie. He'd been living too much of it.

As he approached the sales clerk, he wondered if his life would ever get back to normal. Whatever normal was. Being a homicide dick was probably nowhere near it.

He tossed a five on the counter, for which he got pork rinds, some dried sausage, and the magazine. They didn't have Ben Gay. His change was paltry. Life could be as savory as a hearty Burgundy, if you were rich.

But then, happy was better than rich. He knew some ol' boys in Kansas who'd be as content as cows to plunk their boots on a porch rail, swig some cold suds, and take in a Chiefs game. While a lot of folks in L.A. would be depressed bedding in a Bel Air mansion, dining at Drai's, and flaunting Charlize Theron at the Oscars.

The simple life had many advantages. He couldn't stand this recent craziness with everything helter-skelter and nothing as it seemed. The horror of Stretch blown to pieces, Terri kidnapped, and Chuck gunned down. All too awful to comprehend. Even for someone as saturated in blood and mayhem and violence as he.

And his personal life had turned into vinegary drool. The wine cask of gusto drained. His Chevy blown to bits, his career kaput, his relationship with April uncertain. He knew everyone's life must change, but did his whole existence have to be trashed?

He pushed open the door and trudged out. Maybe the worst was behind him. Maybe now he could make a new—

Or maybe not.

Deadeye sat with one haunch on the hood of the Volvo. Eddie was parked in the adjacent spot and stood leaning his bulky arms over the top of his T-bird. Some pair to draw to.

"Fred and Barney. Thought I'd seen the last of you two

stone heads for one night. Stop for some Brontosaurus steaks?"

Deadeye glanced at Eddie. Not hard to read his so-called mind. More mayhem afoot.

Eddie said, "We decided to countermand the Lou's decision vis-a-vis your need to continue breathing."

Dover was shocked. Eddie had obviously been reading the vocabulary words in *Reader's Digest.* Large print edition, no doubt.

"The Lou'll fry your asses." Hit 'em on their own level.

Man of Few Words said, "What he don't know . . ." Augmented by an artful shrug. Too clever by half.

"Now you guys shouldn't get too far afield with new tricks like thinking for yourselves."

"What's in the bag?" Deadeye said. Not a graceful segue.

"No Preparation H, Deadeye. You'll have to soak in bath oil tonight."

"Empty it."

"Beg pardon?" This shorthand speech was catching.

"On the ground."

"Ah." Deadeye had added another meaningful gesture by reaching under his jacket. Not to scratch, either.

And all this melodrama not thirty feet from the front door of a busy store. Didn't cops patrol this area? He dumped the snacks by the Volvo's front tire. "Want the receipt?" he asked.

Eddie sounded weary of the witty repartee. Sort of like sex, no fun unless you're a participant. "Same play, second act," he said. "Put your hardware in the sack, and hand it to Deadeye. Be discreet."

Sure, and subtle—like Sly Stallone, Pamela Anderson, and these amateur hit men. He went through the routine.

Still kept his razor, though. Might have to give one of these dorks a close shave.

When he handed the bag full of goodies to Deadeye, the mope actually smiled. "Get in."

"Okay." He even unlocked the door for the taciturn turd. Shucks, he could be as cooperative as anyone. To a point.

"Drive." Now the pithy fellow had his pistol in his hand. Gave his words a lot more weight. Damn near Shakespearian.

Dover backed out of the parking spot. "Better buckle up," he told Deadeye. As expected, Mr. Macho ignored the safety tip.

"Turn east," Deadeye said. Not Dover's choice. He'd planned to travel west until he caught the PCH to his humble abode.

He whipped onto Santa Monica and checked his rearview mirror. Eddie was right behind. No legitimate cops in sight.

"Where to?" Best to keep Deadeye's brainpan stimulated so his trigger finger wouldn't activate from primal instinct.

"Go north on Beverly Glen."

"You guys brought your clubs?"

"No, dipshit, we're going to cruise Mulholland Drive."

"Should I watch for a romantic overlook?"

"No, just a dropoff."

On the way, Dover kept quiet. He had to risk Deadeye's atavistic urges with deadly weapons. He needed time to think.

He had two advantages over Deadeye, not counting the thirty IQ points. There was the razor. Effective at close range, but hard to reach, especially when driving. And there was the ex-Bruin's pistol under the front seat. Also tough to get at, but if he were to make a sudden stop . . .

"Let's go west," Deadeye said. Dover took the exit. Not that far to the 405; they'd be pulling over soon. He watched Eddie fall in behind him. Another car was farther back. Not much traffic up here this time of night, and what a gorgeous view. Lights stretching from here to eternity.

They wound along the sinuous canyon road. He checked his rearview mirror. Be nice if Eddie had a flat. He hadn't figured out how to handle him, even if he could take out Deadeye. And then he noticed.

"After this next curve there's a pullout," Deadeye said. "Take it."

They'd done reconnaissance. Impressive. He scratched his leg, then felt on the seat until he touched the walkie-talkie. Pressed the button. "Turn after the next curve, Deadeye?"

"Yeah, shit for brains. At the turnout." And he smiled.

He must've loved Biology the day they dissected the frog.

So Dover took the curve, spotted the turnout, and angled over. But just before the Volvo reached it, he hit the brakes and yanked the wheel to the left. Put the vehicle into a slide. Rear end hit a couple of boulders that ringed the turnout. Deadeye slid over and banged his head against the door. Dover went under the seat for the pistol, which had slid to the right and jammed under the seat spring, so he dipped into his shoe with his left hand and came out with the razor just as Deadeye turned and aimed his pistol at Dover's ear.

Hand with razor being quicker than hand holding heavy pistol, Dover whisked the business edge along the bottom of Deadeye's wrist, making him drop the gun, then came back across and sliced a gash in the prick's cheek.

Eddie scrunched to a stop close behind. Dover grabbed Deadeye's pistol, flung open the door, and rolled out onto the ground. Eddie had one leg out, his pistol at the ready. Dover squinted against the bright glare of the right headlight of the Mercury which roared up and rammed into the T-bird.

Seconds after the shock of the crash, Eddie appeared to be scrabbling on the floorboard to retrieve his weapon. So much for his iron grip.

Falcon jumped out of his car, Beretta in hand, but Dover ran up and waved him back. Reaching into the buckled T-bird, he grabbed Eddie by the collar, and yanked him across the seat. Eddie slid out sideways, but Dover could see he'd found his pistol, so he dumped him on the ground. When Eddie rolled over and came to his feet pointing his gun, Dover deflected it with his left arm and snapped a kick into the iron pumper's groin.

Even strong men cry sometimes. Eddie probably would now, but he still had his gun, and though hurting, he looked like he'd use it. So Dover did the only decent thing by cold-cocking the bastard with Deadeye's pistol. Eddie went down in a pile of limp muscles. Dover's chest flared in pain. The store should've carried Ben Gay. They could all use a squirt.

Deadeye came out of the car screeching about his scratched face, drenched in blood. Falcon told him to chill. It was hard dealing with sissies.

Later, Falcon told Dover he'd stashed the tape, as Dover asked, in a plastic bag beneath a bush on the UCLA campus. They could pick it up later.

Luckily, Falcon hadn't driven straight home after hiding the tape, per Dover's instructions, because leaving the big old tuna swimming in the pond with all those sharks made him uneasy. So he'd made a pass by Cardwell's house to see how the play was proceeding.

"That's when I spotted those two crackers tearing down the street."

"And you trailed them?" Dover said.

"Sure. I lived in Watts long enough to know the workings of the devious mind. They were lookin' to get it on."

"And they saw my Volvo . . . but, wait a minute. I called you on the walkie-talkie before I stopped at that store. You didn't answer."

"I heard you calling, same as I heard you hustling Deadeye before you went into that slide. But when I radioed back, the fuckin' button was stuck, and I couldn't transmit."

You get what you pay for.

"Sorry, man. My credit's anemic. Had to economize."

"You're starting to think like the brass. They'll be putting you up for a higher rank."

"No call to be a wiseass. At least you heard me."

"Yeah, I figured you had a handle on cooling Deadeye. But I suspected you could use an assist on layin' down brother Eddie."

"You got that straight. He's a real bonehead. Felt like I'd hit an anvil when I thumped the gat on that Neanderthal skull."

"Don't be talkin' smack about your ancestors. Besides, that bunch got tossed out of the family tree."

Dover shook his head. "Whatever, there's no way around it, brother, we all came from *The Planet of the Apes*."

They drove by the campus to pick up the tape. The audio was superlative. Murphy's Law is sometimes suspended.

Life could be as fine as wine. Stretch was right. Go figure.

Chapter 28

Dover called a meeting the next morning in the Lou's office, playing the tape for the Three Stooges as he and Falcon fought to keep from smiling. Cardwell, Eddie, and Deadeye sat rigid in their chairs, not commenting, except when the Lou nervously cracked his knuckles. When it was over, they held a brief discussion, with Dover doing most of the talking.

Back in the squad room with Falcon, whom the Lou had decided would make a good homicide dick after all, Dover gave Falcon a high five. He figured they had Cardwell and the group buffaloed to the point that they wouldn't be starting riots any time soon. Especially not tomorrow. But he'd still be watching.

Dover then brought up the ballistics results in the jewelry store and the fireman murders. He was excited, but Falcon looked sullen. No partners are a perfect match.

"Perfect match," Dover said. "The 9mm cartridge you found at Ryong's jewelry store and the casings we recovered where the fireman got aced were used in the same weapon. Extraction marks are identical."

Falcon whined, "Still don't prove Hammer did it."

"Just a theory. Based on his description and the fact he hung with Gorilla. And we know he wanted to be an Eight-Tray Crip."

"And all that. But we don't know he's got a nine. And anyway, how would we get us a warrant to grab it?"

Dover cocked a foot on the table. Stared at the clock on

the wall, thinking. Then he dropped his leg and sat up. "Time to check sources," he said. "Let's start with our spouting fountain, Bullet."

Falcon narrowed his eyes as Dover stood up. Then he shook his head and grinned. "You be right. He the man."

They found Bullet weasel-walking down the street alone and pulled up behind him slow and quiet. At the last moment, when he sensed their presence, he froze, then jerked his head back toward them. From the saucer size of his pupils, Dover saw the effects of Sherm and fear.

"Muthafucka!" he commented. Then he craned around to see if any of the homeboys were watching. "You done scared my ass off. I thought you was some Bloods fixin' to fade me."

"Keep walking, and turn left at the next corner," Falcon said to Bullet as Dover pulled away in his department Grand Prix. The motor coughed once before it powered up, but Dover ignored it.

Dover turned left, drove a block, then pulled to the curb. The engine sputtered, wheezed, and then died. He seriously considered doing Titus.

Soon Bullet came boogeying along. Falcon popped the lock on the back door, and Bullet slid into the seat. "What the fuck you want now? You dudes done rousted me once. Tha's all I gonna say. I sees you around."

Dover held up a piece of paper. "See this?"

Bullet paused, his hand on the door handle. "What's you got?"

"A felony warrant for your ass, in case you decided to jump salty."

"Shit." He slumped back against the seat. "I don't care, nohow. Take me on in. I ain't saying nothin' more."

"Works for me," Dover said, cranking up the Pontiac. It belched a small black cloud and lost the will to run. Second try it caught, and they drove in silence.

"Way I hear," Falcon said to whoever might be listening, "big old Gorilla be bending bars in county lockup." Falcon turned in his seat to stare at Bullet. "He's all mad dog. Thinks he got dimed. Purely set up."

"That don't bother me none." Hard, defiant look.

"We just need one thing. Could have come from any-where."

"Not from me." He crossed his arms and stared out the window.

"See what I told you?" Dover said to Falcon.

"I still don't think we should give up Bullet. We tell Go-rilla who played him, he'll be pissed big-time."

"Gorilla can pull Bullet's tongue through his asshole, for all I care."

"Shit, he'll ace him," Falcon said.

"Yo, what the fuck're you guys—"

"Gorilla's going away 'til he's old and bent," Dover added. "Another whacking means nothing to him."

Falcon nodded. "So be it."

"But I, but you . . . hey, man, you can't tell Gorilla that shit."

Dover turned onto a surface street that led to the freeway.

"Wait, I . . ." He sat there, his mouth open.

Falcon said, "All we need to know is if Hammer got a nine. Ever'body know if he do or not. We just need someone to say so."

"Tha's all? You not runnin' a drag on me?"

Dover pulled into traffic, the Pontiac hesitating. "It's up to you, Bullet. But I wouldn't want to take a shower or go to sleep when I knew Gorilla was waiting to do me."

Bullet licked his lips and his pupils got larger. "Hammer gots a nine, and tha's all I know. Now take me back."

Dover peered up ahead at the lanes choked with shiny metal cubicles. Los Angeles. What ambiance.

Falcon smiled at Bullet. "Tha's cool."

Bullet relaxed against the seat. "That next exit be fine."

Falcon kept his gaze on Bullet. "Where he keep it?"

Bullet went stiff. "You say one question. Tha's two."

"You got me there, bro. Where he keep it?"

"But you say, but I can't—"

"Don't do us no good if we don't know where it is."

"He's no fucking help," Dover said, accelerating. Not even a backfire. Damn, what a ride.

"Wait, you miss . . ." His head twisted to watch the exit slide past. Falcon shrugged and looked away. Bullet collapsed, shaking his head. "He keep it in his closet. Saw him get it out of a shoe box the other day."

Falcon turned back and said, "What day?"

"Oh, man. Muthafucka."

"What day?" Now Falcon wasn't smiling.

Bullet held his head in one hand, his eyes closed. "Two nights ago. Tha's when I seen it. 'Bout ten o'clock."

Falcon nodded. "Good. Thanks, Bullet."

Dover drove on.

"Wha's up, man?" Bullet said as they passed another exit.

Falcon said, "You needs to sign a paper 'bout what you just told us."

By the time Dover and Falcon finished chatting with Bullet, he'd told them he'd heard Hammer and Gorilla jacked the jewelry store the night Mr. Ryong got decapitated with a shotgun. Gorilla toted the gauge and Hammer carried a nine. And afterwards, they were showing off a sackful of candy.

"You mean jewelry," clarified Falcon.

"Tha's what I said," Bullet complained.

"I know. But this's for your statement for the honky court, y'know what I'm sayin'?"

"Yeah, yeah. Jewelry. Tha's what they had."

"Did they say anything about wasting Ryong?" Dover asked.

Bullet squinted at him. Stupid question.

But Bullet also admitted he was with Gorilla and Hammer and a bunch of 'bangers watching a blazing building the night a fireman got faded.

Dover leaned in close to Bullet's face and said, "Your gang was watching the fire and—"

"Not the whole gang. Just a few."

"Like who?" Falcon asked.

Bullet crossed his arms. "You asked 'bout Hammer, and I told you. Tha's all I gonna say."

"You see the fireman go down?" Dover said.

"I seen it, but I didn't have nothin' to do with it. I bounced right then. Tha's all I know."

"Bullet, you're facing some heavy charges—"

"I ain't gonna snitch out nobody 'cause of no muthafuckin' warrants. Fuck that shit."

"You better stall out until I finish," Dover said.

Bullet's face hardened. "Wha's that?" he said like a challenge.

"Let me run it down for you. You know Gorilla and Hammer robbed a store and aced the owner. You knew Hammer was going to cut down a fireman, and you saw it happen. That's misprision of a felony and accessory after the fact on two murders. That'd give you . . . how much time, Falcon?"

Bullet's gaze flicked to Falcon. Eyes now wide open.

Falcon calculated on a notepad. "I figure with his record and the pending charges we'd also make stick, the two aiding and abetting charges would tack on about twenty bullets to Archibald's sentence."

Bullet grimaced. Both at the thought of twenty-some years behind the wall and because he hated to be called by his real name. "You muthafuckas can't do that. I was helpin' you."

"That's right," Dover said. "We won't forget that. Might even talk to the D.A. for you. He likes cooperation."

"Maybe," Falcon said, "you gets immunity on the guilty knowledge shit."

"For sure?" Said with an undertone of pleading.

Dover patted him on the shoulder. "You work with us, and we'll help you out. Those guys are going down either way. You want to hold Gorilla's hand in the joint for the next twenty-five, that's your call."

Falcon laughed. "Gorilla going to want more action than that." Archibald stared at the floor. His shoulders looked thin and fragile, and he trembled. No more street attitude.

Archie, as they agreed to call him, gave them what they needed. He'd seen Jarroll Jefferson, aka Hammer, shoot the fireman with a 9mm pistol. Same one he took to jack the candy store. Same gun he knew Hammer to keep in the top of his closet.

Archie left by the rear exit, a broken man at seventeen. Elderly, by South Central standards. They would have kept him in protective custody, but they figured with Gorilla locked up and them going after Hammer in the next couple of hours, it'd be better not to finger Bullet as a snitch. They just hoped he could survive on the streets until he could testify.

They visited the D.A. and got their search warrant and arrest warrant for Hammer and his trusty pistol. Then they called the SWAT team leader, who was down for some action on the mean streets of South Central. By two o'clock, everyone was in position.

The SWAT team van parked two blocks down and around the corner from Hammer's bungalow. Two other detectives, Griggs and Renton, came along to help. Dover and Falcon explained the layout of the house.

Then Dover cranked up the Grand Prix and they made a pass through an intersection just down from Hammer's house. Spotted him on the front porch, drinking a beer and yakking. But no one was with him.

"I might take that up," Dover said, "boozing and talking to myself."

"You're sprung enough without that," Falcon said.

Dover raised an eyebrow. "And that from the Wizard of Watts."

"What's true is true, just like Forrest Gump said."

"That's not what he said. And leave your mentor out of this."

"You know," Falcon said with a wistful look in his eye that Dover knew meant trouble, "I bet I could walk up to Hammer, sit and chill a minute, then lead him through the search warrant and arrest by the numbers, no muss, no fuss."

"And I bet your momma dropped you on the soft spot on your head when you were in didies."

"No, on the real. Hammer and I got to respectin' each other. He's not jammed by me. And that way no one's illin'," no one pops a cap, and no one gets lit up. It's a safer gig for everyone."

Dover thought it over. It made some sense, which is why it scared the shit out of him. He pulled over to the curb behind the SWAT van.

"We'll try it. But watch him close and dive for cover if he makes a move. Griggs and I will cover the back. If we hear any commotion, we break in. Renton goes with you as cover. SWAT can stay here, but move in quick if we need 'em."

Minutes later, Falcon strolled down the sidewalk alone. Renton snuck along the back alley and slipped up by the side of Hammer's house where he crouched, ready to jump in if Falcon got into trouble.

Dover and Griggs worked their way up to the back of the house, trying to keep profiles no higher than a couple of dogs. Which Dover suddenly realized might be roving around back there. But they heard no barking as Falcon approached the house.

Falcon sauntered into the yard. Jarroll's face went stony when he saw him. Jarroll looked more than ever like a 'banger known as Hammer.

Hammer jumped up from a nylon web chair and reached down toward the floor of the porch. A low railing blocked Falcon's view, and he almost went for his piece, but he hesitated. "Hammer, stall it out. Chill, man. I just come to rap."

Now Hammer raised up, holding his small sister in his arms. He glared at Falcon. "Got nothin' to say." And he wheeled and barged into the house. Falcon stayed out front. He'd wait it out a few more seconds.

Hammer headed for the back bedroom. Once there, he put Alceeda into the closet. He pulled a blanket from the top shelf and said, "You stay here. Don't come out unless I call you. I gonna put this over your head so no one can hear you. Don't cry now."

Her eyes were huge and moist, but she nodded and held back the tears. Even when he lowered the blanket over her. He patted her on the head. "You my sweetie. Be quiet now. I'll be back."

He closed the closet door and turned to leave the room when he saw out the back window what looked like two large dogs in the back yard. But as he watched them a moment, he could see they moved like Five-O.

He hustled to his own room, grabbed the nine from the top shelf, racked the action, and jammed the weapon into his belt behind his back. With at least three cops coming after him, he'd need more juice. He yanked down a box from the back of the shelf. Something Skull had told him to hide.

He fumbled the top off the box and grabbed out another weapon, holding it in his right hand as he fed a long clip into the base of the handle. He took a deep breath and let it out. The Mac-10 made him feel like the Head Nigger in Charge, bad enough to do the job.

"Hammer, this's Falcon, come on out." He banged on the screen door. The inside door stood open, and Falcon had a good view of the front room. He still wanted to talk Hammer down.

Hammer came through a door into the living room. His right hand hung behind his leg.

"Hammer, be cool. Just rap with me, and everything'll be dope. Don't be showin' how hard you is."

"Wha's up, man?" He took a few more steps forward.

Falcon opened the screen door and eased inside. "I'll tell

you straight up. We got a search warrant. Need to look around, that's all. Then we bounce."

"You dissin' me, man. You know I down for mine. Get yo' face outta here, or I gonna break on your ass."

The light Falcon had seen in the boy's eyes had gone out. Only a flat black stare remained. Any hope there might have been for him was—

Hammer swung the Ten from behind his leg and leveled it at Falcon.

Falcon did a shoulder roll to his right, diving behind a recliner. "No, Jarroll!" he yelled as bullets zinged over his head. He yanked out his pistol.

Renton ran up to the front of the house, but bullets tore through the door and walls, and he hit the ground. He screamed into his handie talkie for SWAT to move in now.

Dover kicked in the back door, and Griggs covered the room with a shotgun, then Dover ran inside and slammed to a halt behind the stove, covering the doorway with his Beretta. There was a pause in the shooting from the front of the house. Griggs scuttled up to the side of the doorway, and he and Dover both listened for someone coming their way.

Falcon stayed down low behind the slumping chair.

Hammer looked but couldn't see him, so he took a couple of steps to the side, aimed at the bottom edge of the padded armrest, just above the seat cushion, and pulled the trigger.

Bullets flew in a burst and ripped through the ruined sponge rubber as though it were paper. Then from behind Hammer, a shrill scream pierced his brain. Cops in the back! he thought, and spun around.

Dover jumped through the kitchen doorway into the front room and did a forward tumble roll. Griggs ran in at an angle behind him, the shotgun at his shoulder, pointing dead ahead. The screaming continued.

Falcon lay on his stomach on the far side of the chair. The barrage of bullets had gone right by his shoulder. But he hadn't been hit.

From the hallway door, a figure burst into the room, a blue ghost giving a high-pitched wail.

Before he could stop, Hammer jerked the trigger on the swinging gun and sent a string of lead hornets across the doorway, cutting off the scream.

Now, peeking out, Falcon saw Hammer's burst rip through the blue blanket, saw the figure stop in its tracks, then slump to the floor. Hammer howled and ran toward the crumpled form. Falcon got to his knees and watched as Griggs aimed the shotgun at the boy.

"No!" Falcon yelled. "Don't shoot!" He jumped to his feet.

Hammer tore the blanket away and shook the tiny limp form. Red circles smeared her dress. He hugged her to his chest. A piercing keen like the wail of an ambulance rose from within him.

Then, with tears rolling down his cheeks, he lowered her to the floor. Leaning over her small face he moaned, "Alceeda. No, no. Please, no."

"I'm sorry, man," Falcon said. "Real sorry."

Hammer looked up, and Falcon saw the hate in his flinty eyes. But he thought he could talk him through it. Cool him off. Not lose him, too. "No reason to get down now, man. It's played out."

But Hammer grabbed up the Ten and fired a barrage. Lead flew in a hailstorm. Falcon had no chance to dive away.

Then Dover saw Hammer spin back toward him, saw the

Ten coming around. Dover aimed chest high and snapped the trigger three times. The slugs drilled Hammer's young body.

Griggs fired the twelve-gauge. The pellets ripped away the right side of Hammer's face and splattered it against the wall.

As Hammer collapsed, Dover ran toward Falcon. He dropped his pistol and went to his knees. Falcon lifted his head just off the stained carpet and stared with glassy eyes.

"Falcon, are you . . ." But the lights were going down, the curtain falling.

"I know, it needs work," Falcon rasped. "My timing was lousy. Maybe I need . . . need a new . . ." And his head plopped to the floor, blood oozing everywhere.

Friday came and went, and no riot started in South Central. The group's plans had been sidetracked for the present. Dover spent Friday and the next couple of days in a slow motion fall into a yawning black hole from which not even light escaped. He was terrified he'd be engulfed, and yet, he was also afraid he wouldn't be.

Falcon lay in the ICU at Centinela Hospital Medical Center. Trauma and loss of blood had left him in a coma. Monitors bleeped wary predictions as to whether this human appendage might cling to its precarious life force. Doctors didn't like the chances.

The three bullets that caught him in the torso hadn't been so kind as to zip on through, leaving a cinematic "flesh wound," where the hero is inconvenienced a few days wearing a sling. This was real life in the 'hood.

One slug had nicked the pulmonary artery, which nearly bled him dry before it could be repaired in surgery. Another hunk of lead bounced off a rib and punctured a lung. The third metal auger bored through his abdomen, stopping just short of his spine.

After losing Stretch, Dover felt unable to deal with this. He felt numb, his senses deadened as if drugged. Zombie-like, he went through the daily motions, all the while replaying the shooting scene in his mind like an endless horror flick.

He lost his car keys, misplaced his badge, couldn't remember people's names or telephone numbers. At any moment he'd start to shake. A vise grip headache tortured every waking moment for three interminable days.

Sometimes as he stared dead ahead at nothing in particular, the edges of objects blurred, as though he were peering at them through a narrow tunnel. He thought he was going blind. Or crazy.

Finally he talked with a department shrink, and the guy told him his reactions were normal. He was experiencing post-traumatic stress disorder syndrome. But somehow he didn't care.

In a couple of weeks, he went back to work. Still in the RHD, still working homicides. The Lou and Eddie and Deadeye hovered about like a bloodthirsty tribe of Indian warriors circling Custer's encampment. But he wasn't going to ask for a transfer. Not yet.

Every night after work, or sometimes during the day, he'd visit Falcon in the hospital. Watch the green pulse spikes on the SpaceLabs monitor. Stare at the red glow of the pulse oximeter on Falcon's finger. E.T. lives.

None of this did Falcon any good, he just lay there in whatever world he saw in his own mind. But it gave Dover a lifeline. A process for hanging on to Falcon. Not letting go. Not giving up.

April called a couple of times. They talked some. Even

went out for lasagna one night. But the magic wasn't there. No sparkle. No flavor. Good wine gone flat.

After she quit calling, and he spent untold nights sitting in his living room or bedroom or kitchen drinking beer and not watching television or not reading the book in his hand, he realized something. His pain came not only from the loss of Stretch and April and maybe Falcon. There was more.

As he sat in his recliner one night mulling it over, his gaze fell on the chessboard. Ice formed along his spine. Was this the answer?

"Stretch," he said in a low voice, "I always seem to come to you for solutions to my problems. And this one is a certified bastard. You know why, too. It's Terri." He worked his hands together.

"You know there was never anything before. But when she was kidnapped, I felt an empty place inside me I knew would never be filled if she didn't come back. In a way, it was like when you left."

He picked up the white castle and juggled it in his hand, then put it back on the board. "I hope you're not pissed, partner, but I care for her. What do you think I should do about it?"

He let his mind go blank, trying to be receptive.

No images appeared. No reels played in his mind. No maxims rolled through his inner ear. He took a swig of beer.

"Maybe some other—"

Then he felt the rocking. His head swayed back and forth as though he were palsied. A rumble shimmied through the floor, glasses tinkled in the cabinets, and pictures swung in tiny arcs on the walls.

He didn't care enough to be afraid. So he leaned back in his recliner, resigned to fate. In a minute the quake paused, as though it were over, then a strong tremor rippled through the middle of the room, jolting the chess stand and knocking the pieces to the floor.

Except for three pieces in the middle of the board. The white king and queen stood close together, and a black pawn lay on its side, several inches removed. A somber scene.

He stared at the board. Is that it? That's your answer?

He shook his head, bewildered. Am I that unworthy? He closed his eyes in pain.

Then they flicked open. He sat forward and swatted the board like King Kong swiping at the helicopters that buzzed about him. The board, the pieces, and the stand all tumbled to the floor.

He stood up. "Stretch, I have to thank you for being a great partner and friend. You were there when I needed you. But it's time to say goodbye. Time to run my own life, whether I know what I'm doing or not."

A rueful smile lifted one corner of his mouth. A patented Harrison Ford expression. Give him credit, the guy had his moments.

"Never thought I'd quote Ol' Blue Eyes, Stretch, but I'm going to do things my way." He raised his chin in defiance of fate like Charlie Chaplin in *The Tramp*, twirling his cane, hopeful to the end. Then he picked up the phone.

Chapter 29

Terri seemed surprised to hear from him. They hadn't spoken in several weeks. After some small talk, he asked if she'd like to go hiking at Century Lake on Saturday. She stammered, but let him down easy.

He flopped back into his recliner. She was always gracious, he'd give her that. Said it might not be a good idea right now, but she wanted to stay friends, and they could probably do something like that some other time. He wished he were up at the lake right now so he could jump off the cliff like Butch Cassidy and the Sundance Kid. But never come up.

He sat there thinking about life, love, and fate. Playing in his head was the country tune about wishing on someone else's star. A surefire path to doom.

And he remembered the ballad that says the best song always ends. But this one never struck the first note. Never uncorked the bottle.

He heaved himself out of his recliner and gathered up the chessboard and the scattered chessmen. Threw it all into a box which he shoved to the back of a shelf in the closet. The stand went into the dimmest reaches of the yawning chasm, next to his roller skates and an old bowling ball. Maybe he should pack up and drive back to Kansas where he might frequent the smoky hubbub of the lanes again. Never happen in California.

The phone rang; he didn't answer it. He had no energy to talk. The machine kicked on.

"Rick, it's Terri. If you're there, and you feel like it, would you pick up? There's something I want to tell you." She paused. He felt like a gravestone wedged into the floor. She'd already told him enough to put a crack in his heart.

"Then please call me later at home."

He lunged for the phone. "Terri?"

"Oh, I'm glad you're there. I said some things before that . . . well, I'm sure they stung. I thought about how you must feel, and I was imagining being at the lake with you, and I . . ."

"Terri, are you—"

She sniffed and said, "Sorry, I'm fine. Anyway, I recalled something Stretch used to say. And I thought, maybe he's right."

Stretch again. But he was stuck with it. "What's that?"

"He said, 'In matters of love, listen to your heart, not your head.' "

Probably not original, but a lot of Stretch's maxims weren't. "Yes, that sounds like Stretch. He was always the romantic."

"Don't think you're not a softie yourself, Bub."

What was that line from? Completely stumped him. So he countered with his best John Wayne impression. "Heck, Missy, I'm as tough as an old boot."

"More like a Ferragamo pump. But just let me finish, instead of hanging out on a limb."

"Roll on, sagebrush."

"My heart tells me I'd be an idiot not to go with you."

With the Three Stooges, the Marx Brothers, and the Keystone Kops, Dover figured Hollywood needed no more fools. Except maybe Jim Carrey.

"Are you there, Rick?"

"Sure, go ahead."

"So, if I'm still invited . . ."

"Pick you up at eight on Saturday."

Maybe he'd lost his mind after all. Total Animaniac. As Patsy Cline sang in the best country song ever, no doubt he was plumb *"Crazy."*

Come Saturday morning, they hiked and talked and stared in awe at the canyon vistas. California was still magnificent. In spite of man's onslaught.

Terri went in search of a restroom or a bush, and Dover sat on a boulder. He juggled a pebble in his hand, pondering the future. Wondering if it was time for him to move on.

Back to Kansas? He did miss the change of seasons. Maybe L.A.'s continuous cycles of smoggy mornings, sunny afternoons, and cool evenings had hypnotized him. Might even explain why its eccentric inhabitants were in constant search of the unusual, the stimulating, the bizarre.

To convince themselves they were living meaningful lives, not merely existing like plants in a hothouse. Needing assurance they'd found life's innermost secret, experienced the ultimate rush, thrill, buzz, trip, high, and thus understood what LIFE was all about.

He tossed the pebble away. The philosophy was bogus. No matter how rich and famous, talented and influential, or wise and beneficent, one person was only a speck on the continuum of the collective consciousness on this trivial planet.

"Beautiful view, isn't it?" Terri said behind him. Almost made him leap into the canyon.

"Magnificent." He gestured for her to sit. "Let's finish the wine."

She pulled the bottle of Merlot from his backpack and

poured the last of the ruby liquid in their plastic cups. Then she tipped her cup toward him, smiling, and said, "If it doesn't finish me first."

They sipped and stared at the lush green valley and the ridge of mountains darkly carved against the pottery blue sky, etched with wisps of white wool.

Terri sighed. "Could I ask you something?" Her face was serious.

"About the group?"

She nodded.

"Okay, Sharon, slap leather and fire away."

"Not her best film. Anyway, why didn't you expose them? Release the disks, the names, and your tape recording. Splash it all over the press, and get them jailed for killing Stretch."

He gazed into her tourmaline eyes, as pristine as polar ice, yet as warm as the Merlot charging through his veins. "Even with the recording, we're weak on evidence to prosecute them for murder." He quaffed the last ruby droplets.

"Still, I was going to blow the whistle on them," he continued, "but I realized that if I did, we'd never be safe. Holding the information over their heads is our best insurance."

Her gaze swept the valley. "I see."

"And they're prevented from carrying out their plot any further, because I can expose it at any stage. They might formulate another plan, but that could take years, and some members of the group will be voted out, retire, whatever. I'm hoping they'll never get it together again."

A videotape replayed in his head. The one Larry Brightonfeld made of the encounter with the Lou. Copies kept at the coroner's office beside the videotape of Stretch's autopsy and at Larry's house on a shelf stacked with tapes of Dr. Quincy. Some extra insurance, just in case.

"You don't think we can coexist? That we'll end as a Tower of Babel?"

He stood up, pulling her with him, then tugged her against his side. It felt comfortable as they stared into the canyon and the future together.

"I hope so, Terri. If we can't, we'll self-destruct. And that damn Charlie Manson will get the last laugh."

A cool breeze pushed across them, and she shuddered. He didn't know if it was the wind or his words that chilled her.

"Come on, let's head back into that gorgeous California sunset."

She looked at him. "You mean together? Us?"

"You see a horse?"

The ICU nurses let Dover sit in Falcon's room without regard to the strict rules usually applied. After all, he wasn't bothering the patient.

Dover wondered if anything would ever bother Falcon again. Would he ever join the ranks of the afflicted, the careworn, the impaired? That is, most of the people on the planet?

The guy had a long ways to go. The doctors had run tests for brain wave activity. He hadn't hit any monumental peaks.

And now, as for weeks, his blood pressure and pulse rate monitor showed monotonous tracings of shallow red and green troughs. Not even having sexy or scary dreams. He could stay like this for a long time. None of the doctors would say how long. The way it was looking—

But the pulsemeter just picked up.

He stared at the green spikes glowing against the black

background. Had he imagined the difference? No, the number was higher, too.

He raised up from his slouched position and stared at Falcon's inert form. The guy never moved except when a nurse adjusted him like a sack of wheat. He'd begun to wonder if his partner would want him to pull the plug when no one was watching. He knew his own preference would—

Falcon's eyes fluttered open, gazed without focusing, then closed.

Dover stood up. Should he call a nurse? He stepped over to the bed. Looked at the call button. Studied Falcon's smooth brow, the gentle rise and fall of his chest, his motionless eyelids.

He reached for the button, then stopped. What was there to say? The patient improved for a second, but then he slipped back into an irreversible coma? Oh, happy day.

Maybe he should let the nurse know, anyway. He glanced back at his partner's face. Falcon was staring at him.

"Where the hell am I?"

Dover closed his slack jaw, shrugged, and glanced at the surrounding apparatus. Tubes snaked into Falcon's every orifice. Glucose IV dripped in slow motion. Oxygen tent hovered at the ready.

"Hospital?" Falcon ventured.

"Damn. You're spotting clues already."

"How long?"

"Six weeks, give or take."

Falcon snuck a hand under the sheet to where the catheter invaded him. "Aw, shit."

"Welcome back to real life. Where you have to pee on your own."

"Thanks, I think. Hold on." He moved each of his legs,

his arms, then turned his head side-to-side. "Righteous. Glad to be back. At least if my Johnson's still in order after I rip out these tubes."

Dover held up his palms. "Let's leave that to the professionals."

Falcon grinned. Then his eyes narrowed, and his body tensed. "Hammer? What about—"

Dover shook his head. "He didn't make it. Neither did his little sister. I'm sorry."

Falcon slumped. All at once he looked skinnier and weaker. Great, hit him with crappy news right off the bat. Wonderful bedside manner.

"Just like the rap song tells it," Falcon said, "Trigga Gots No Heart."

Dover changed the subject. "Your mom and sister just left. I'll give them a call, and you can talk."

"What about my lady?"

"Shakira hates to see you this way. It scares her."

"Yeah, that's cool. Anyway, thanks for hangin' with me."

"Office pool. Had to keep it honest."

"You a lie. You wanted me to make it."

He held up a hand, fingers spread. "I already lost. Had five weeks."

"I mean, like that book said, the white man needs the nigger. Sort of like a lightning rod, I suppose."

"No, I just need . . ." He searched for the words.

"Someone to watch your back while you fight City Hall?"

Dover shook his head. "I need a friend, you asshole. And if you ever mention I said that, I'll catheterize you with a garden hose."

"Uhhh, a muthafuckin' hose? No way. Code of silence?"

"Straight up. Also, we're still partners on the squad. But since L.A. hasn't become Xanadu, you better keep a low profile."

"You sayin' everything's cool, long as I don't get jungle fever and my blues stay mo' better than yours?" He grimaced in disgust.

"More like, let's be good fellas and do the right thing."

"I'd rather be like Sweet Sweetback and blow a baadasssss song."

"Follow the rules, Jules, or you'll get beat to a pulp."

"Total fiction, Vinnie. Hey, don't sweat the briars."

Dover nodded. "And maybe life can transcend Dom Perignon."

"Sure, you bogard. You give it a name." Raising his hand for a high five, he winced and touched the bandages swaddling his torn chest. "Oh, man."

Dover buzzed the nurse and told her Falcon was awake, but he was hurting. Said to bring some painkiller. Quick.

"She'll be here in a minute," he said, squeezing Falcon's arm.

Falcon nodded, then murmured, "You a funky white boy, and all that. Gives me hope. You may even have some nigga in you."

"Way cool," Dover said.

"Past," Falcon added.

Dover smiled.

Falcon winked.

Stalemate.

About the Author

Mark Bouton majored in sociology at Oklahoma State University and earned a law degree at the Oklahoma University School of Law. He entered the FBI, and for 30 years worked cases in Mobile, Alabama; New York; Chicago; Puerto Rico; Brownsville, Texas; San Antonio; and Topeka, Kansas. During his career, he captured killers, kidnappers, con men, bank robbers, and terrorists. He worked many high profile cases, including playing a key role in solving the Oklahoma City bombing. Father of four sons, he lives in Kansas, where he writes novels, lifts weights and practices yoga, and often contemplates the universe. He's currently writing two mystery series. For more information, visit his Web site at http://www.markbouton.com